LINES THAT BIND

PART TWO

WITHIN THE WHISPERS

BY ANNA LAZARIDIS

LINES THAT BIND

PART TWO

WITHIN THE WHISPERS

ISBN 978 - 0692360460

Cover design by George D.K.
Cover Illustration by © olgaman/Shutterstock.com
Interior Illustrations by © Vasiliki Mitakou

www.linesthatbind.com

To Maria and Pete, with love – the best sister and brother a girl could ever hope for.

PREFACE

OTHER TIMES, the shadows seemed unreal as in every dream, having no verifying existence. A stretch of my hand would have caused them to dissolve like mist, but now they seemed solid, coinciding with reality, occurring in fact, not at all imaginary like other dreams. Even the surrounding area was nowhere I had ever been before, not even a trace of something familiar to calm my nerves of not knowing where it was that my mind had placed me in this particular dream.

The smell of damp was all around me. Cold stone walls towered around the dark tunnel-like structure, infiltrated by echoes of the dreariest type, harshly sinister, and horror inspiring.

I started wandering around the narrow passages at first, looking for anything to help me navigate out of the hellish surroundings, but there was absolutely nothing familiar – nothing that could help me lessen the stress of being stuck in the unknown.

Why there? Why did my demons feel the need to bring me to such a twisted and threatening place?

The poorly-lit, uneven cobbled path made it difficult to keep my balance. It was, however, the sense that something or someone was behind me that quickened my pace. The pace quickly turned into a full-blown sprint the minute I caught sight of the two fiends that shadowed me. Slipping and falling as I ran, did not thwart my need to distance myself, and escape the shadows that trailed behind me.

Running seemed like a good idea at first, but it was getting me nowhere. The creatures that were on my tail were not letting up. The faster I ran, the closer they came, and then that's when I stopped and cried aloud, *"Keep your distance!"* The two faceless beings came even closer. *"Stay away! Leave me alone!"*

They seemed intent on testing my limits once again, disobeying my demands, relentless in their pursuit, coming all the more closer. Even so, I stood my ground unwilling to give into fear.

"Leave me the hell alone! You need to stop this," I yelled even louder, breathing in raggedly. *"What do you want from me?"*

Formidably inhuman in form, they simply stood there giving no answer to my question. It was then that I noticed that they seemed as disoriented as I was.

In those few seconds between catching my breath, the creatures turned their heads quizzically to the height of the buildings that seemed to be closing in on us. They appeared to be confused and displaced, standing there like statues, vexed by each and every sinister sound that echoed off the dark, brick walls. They both whiffed the pungent air, filling their lungs with the sulfurous smell of hell itself.

Within seconds, I sensed the sting in my wrist fully ignite, warning me of a much bigger danger – even greater than the two shadows facing me. The creatures that haunted my dreams stood stock-still in a preparedness state waiting, listening intently for something.

Soon, a deafening rush of air filled with a shrill of a thousand cries came upon us. The two shadows quickly turned and faced the opposite direction putting themselves between me and what was to come.

One turned and looked my way. Its gaze quickly dropped to my wrist. There was something alien in the way it looked at my throbbing scar. To my surprise, the creature quickly shoved me – pushed me so hard that it put an abrupt end to the weird sequence of my dream.

I quickly snapped my eyes open. My mind was marked by the sharp transition from dream to reality which needed some getting used to. Distinguishing between the two was becoming harder with each occurrence. However, I felt more in control over both my actions, and above all, my emotions. My dream stalkers would need to try much harder if they intended on reaching me through such repulsive dreams.

The sight of my scarred wrist alarmed them to something, but what, I was not sure of. Justin had warned me against talking to them, but there seemed to be no other way. It was not fear I felt when confronting the two shadows, but raw strength and complete confidence that I could, somehow, defend myself against them, and whatever else my mind conjured up.

~~~

It was three o'clock in the morning now, but although my body gave itself up willingly, my mind refused to surrender itself to sleep. Instead, it raced on and on, alternately turning back to the beginning, and then racing forward into the dreadful uncertainties of my future.

Sitting there in stunned silence, with my head up against the headboard, I tallied up the information I had acquired about my past and my uncertain future, but came to no end. I toiled aimlessly at trying to find answers to things I clearly had no answers to give. However, the fact that it was not something I had done that forced the Ellri to send me away five years ago seemed to ease the stagnated feelings of betrayal.

There was none of the sense of stricken loss that I had felt years before when the Ellri forced me to leave Oaks. Today, there was an upsurge of relief knowing that I was rid of those deep seeded emotions.

I was thankful that the cause of such incessant strain was finally removed. Feeling that I could finally put that part of my past to rest gave me all the more confidence to move forward and face whatever I was born into.

Just then, in the darkness of my room a dark thought had clawed its way up. *Were the Korbs behind my parent's untimely death?*

Nobody had ever talked about their death, knowing full well I would not remember any of the circumstances behind their untimely end. I had been told on several occasions of how sick my mother was. "Her pregnancy," they said, "only worsened her condition."

I accepted this at face value, because I wanted to – not because I truly believed it. *Did the Korbs have a role to play in all this? Was my father's passing short after my mother's death a mere coincidence or was it all tied together?*

The questions kept looping in my mind, trying to find some sort of order when out of nowhere I heard, *"Can you please go back to sleep? You need to stop thinking so much about things like this. Just relax and get some rest."*

Justin's voice in my head took me by surprise.

"You're in my head, again?" I asked out loud.

"Yeap...," he answered whimsically, *"three in the morning isn't exactly the appropriate time to be thinking of the dead. Now go to sleep. You're keeping me awake."*

He sounded rather amused by our unconventional means of conversation. Though, the feeling of having his voice in my head was like taking a drill to my skull, I still welcomed it. I would have, however, preferred to be with him rather than just listen to his sweet voice.

In an urgent need to share my deepest desire, my eyes closed and my thoughts were of Justin's face, his lips, his eyes. For the first time, I felt a yearning unfettered by girly inadequacy and inhibition. This had quickly set my heart racing at the possibilities of what it would mean to have him there with me.

"You're torturing me, Caitlin," he complained.

"Serves you right, Justin. You know what they say – if you can't take the heat...."

"Oh, don't make me come over there and show you exactly how much heat I can take!"

I gasped in shock at his shameless threat, but was not the least waned from wanting to see him now, more than ever.

Excited by the prospect, I quickly sat Indian style on my bed not sure of how to go about doing what I was planning on doing. With my eyes closed, I concentrated on the image of Justin's face the whole time I slipped into my solace, and in the darkness of my mind, thinking nothing but him I said, "I need to see Justin."

The stinging sensation in my wrist was back, but not as intense as other times. Feeling more in control of its force, quickly and without warning the darkness in my solace turned to a fast moving blur, dispersing inches away, not touching me, but instead, wavering away on either side as if it were bending around me. I knew I was in no way moving physically, but the swooshing sound in my ears told me otherwise.

In that split second darkness reemerged. I was not where I started from. The place was infused by Justin's breathing – his heartbeat was crisp and audible to my ears. There was no mistake about it – I was surely in his room.

I stood up knowing all too well that I was not limited by my earthly body once again. It remained propped on my bed back in my own room where I started from. I felt as I did the night of my initiation – exhilarated, launching my senses into overdrive. There was, to be sure, a slight cloud of anxiety as I sensed Justin shifting in his bed.

The lights suddenly went on.

"What do you think, you're doing?" he said angrily jumping out of bed, looking right through me.

My breath caught in my mouth as he stood there half dressed. Although he was unable to see me, he apparently felt my presence. I approached, leaving no distance between us. Gazing into the depths of his beautiful eyes, I caressed his face and kissed him softly on the lips, wanting him to feel my touch, wanting to satisfy my own addiction.

"My very own Succubus," he smiled devilishly, lifting his fingers to his lips.

I kissed him again enjoying the effect I had on him. My hand trailed down his chest and then up to where the beating of his heart was most crisp. It thudded harder and faster with every caress. For some unexplained reason, I was mesmerized by the thudding under my palm. The rhythm was hypnotic – alluring.

"Caitlin, you need to stop. I can only take so much," he protested, in sweet misery.

Justin could not hear my thoughts – not in the state I was in. It must have been maddening for him to feel me physically, but not be able to read my intensions. I finally took a step back, and put some safe distance between us.

Frustrated, he fell back on his bed, holding his head. "You need to leave," he said, through closed eyes. "You don't know how your absence affects your body. Please, just go back."

I walked over to the bed for one last kiss. His soft moan under my touch was the gratification I was looking for – more so than any drug could offer.

Reluctant at first, I closed my eyes and concentrated on returning home. In seconds, the restraints of my physical body were evident enough of my return. I opened my eyes only to find myself alone and back in my own room.

"If you ever try that again – I swear...," He was in my head again – threatening me.

"I couldn't resist the temptation."

"Will you please let me get some sleep tonight?"

"Who's holding you back?" I smiled, knowing full well that I left him in no condition to sleep.

There was absolute silence once again, and the piercing in my head had finally subsided.

He stopped for now, I thought as I tucked myself under the covers, allowing myself to drift off to sleep smiling.

For now, I was happily satisfied and totally content of driving him a bit crazy.

Running From Shadow

Illustrated for Lines That Bind - Within The Whispers

ONE

BEST OF FRIENDS

T HE FIRST DAY of exams was endless. Calculus came first, followed by History. One exam after the other was not exactly my idea of fun. Even the agonizing fact of having two exams scheduled per day could not willfully erase the thought of Justin's reaction to my ghostly touches. I longed to see him all morning, wanting to see his response to last night's incident. But first, I had to finish with exams.

By the looks of things, I seemed to be well prepared for my first two tests as was Tyler who seemed to wiz through Calculus. Surprisingly, it was Megan who did not seem quite prepared. I could feel her eyes piercing my answer sheet. I did not mind that she was copying, but I was surely not going to make it easy for her. At that moment in time, I purposely moved the answer sheet, making sure that she still had access, but had to work twice as hard to get the information.

Just then, I heard a sigh of frustration coming from her direction and I smiled within, but minutes later I felt bad for her so I pushed the paper to the edge of my desk, offering the She-devil the chance to do well on her mid-term exam – a chance that she would have never extend to others.

"Pencils down!" Mr. Travis said, in a commanding voice only moments later. "Make sure your names are written in capital letters on your answer sheets. You have an hour and a half to relax before you head to your next exam. Use it wisely and good luck to all of you."

Tyler waited for me to collect my bag and coat. "Come on, let's get something to eat before we have to sit for History," he said impatiently.

We headed to the back of the school knowing all too well that most of our peers would be gathered at the steps near the school entrance, asking each other millions of questions about the exams. With my powers in full bloom, I was somehow immune to the nosey bodies trying to read my thoughts.

"I'm going to the cafeteria to get us something to eat – you want anything?" Tyler asked, plopping his belongings on the bench next to the entrance.

"Just juice," I said, smiling at him.

"Juice, it is," Tyler beamed, scurrying off.

I leafed through my notes one last time preparing for my next exam, pacing up and down reciting all the information I had crammed in my head the night before. It was then that I froze, feeling the burn deep in my bones. *What's he doing here*? I thought. *He isn't allowed on school grounds.*

"So, how was Calc?" Justin's voice trailed off. Not waiting for my response, his arms slipped around my waist lifting me inches off the ground, crushing his lips to mine, forcing my back against the wall. I was pinned between the cold brick wall and his warm hard body. Savory minutes later, Justin eased off a bit. "Good morning!" he said, letting go.

Not expecting him to be so positively ruthless, I simply smiled and asked, "How was your night?"

"My night was excellent. It was earlier this morning that was quite frustrating. For some reason I couldn't get you out of my head – out of my room for that matter."

I giggled – glad he was as happy as I was. I folded my hands around his neck and kissed him tenderly wanting to melt in his embrace.

"Don't ever start something you can't finish, Caitlin," he warned. His smile widened to a sly grin. "It took all my energy to keep myself from climbing through your window at four this morning."

"Now, why would you go and stop yourself from doing something so wild and exciting?"

"Very funny!" He kissed me again. "Next time you won't be so lucky."

The sheer force of his presence was mesmerizing. "Is that a promise?" I asked, staring up into his eyes, wanting him to know that I wanted him as much as he obviously wanted me.

Justin's whole manner had suddenly stiffened. He quickly took a few steps back. "Tyler is coming," he grimaced. "You should eat something before you sit your next exam."

"Fine!" Was all I said – annoyed at the way he responded to my best friend, "Now go! It's way, way too early in the morning for a testosterone show-down."

"Is that what you call Tyler's immature behavior?"

"I wasn't only referring to Tyler," I admitted, smiling.

"I see," Justin said, raising his eyebrow wickedly, giving me a quick kiss. "I'll pick you up in a couple of hours. Good luck on History." He headed off towards the parking lot.

My lips were still burning from his kiss. *Will my response to him ever change?* I wondered

"*Not if I can help it!*" Justin answered my thoughts by projecting his voice from wherever he was.

I simply smiled.

Tyler looked at my stupid expression, not needing to ask who I was thinking about. "So, what's going on with the two of you?"

"Apart from the permanent fear of killing him – I would say we're doing fine."

"All relationships have some obstacles to overcome. You'll figure it out," he chuckled. "Here, I got you juice and a sandwich. You should really get something in you before our next exam. You haven't eaten anything all day."

Tyler removed the plastic wrap from the turkey and cheese sandwich and handed it to me.

Before I had the chance to thank him, Megan Gordon along with Loraine and Kim came round the back, infiltrating our hiding place. "There you are, Caitlin," she said, sounding casual, without her usual obnoxious tone "Thanks for earlier. It means a lot."

Not expecting to see her face for another hour, I sat there speechless for what seemed a minute or two before I said, "Yeah, no problem – anytime,"

She remained silent up to the time that Kim gave her a nasty look. "Anyway," Megan finally said, "see you guys in History and good luck."

"Okay, yeah, we'll see you there," I answered, watching them turn on their designer shoes – leaving the way they came.

"What the hell was that all about?" Tyler asked, looking a bit confused. "Did Megan just thank you for something?"

I shrugged my shoulders. "Yeah, I guess she did."

I bit into my sandwich, ignoring his questioning stare.

After a while Tyler asked, "So, did you finally find out where it is that the Ellri are sending us for winter break?"

I swallowed hard, "You're coming too?" I should have

sounded more excited, but I was, in fact, surprised.

Tyler took a sip of his soda to wash down his last bite. "What, you really didn't think they were going to allow you to spend two weeks with Bradford without a chaperone, did you?"

"I – I haven't really thought about winter break – wait, you're going to be my chaperone? You can't be serious. You're not, are you?"

Tyler looked at my horrid expression and let out a loud laugh. "I'm kidding. Lighten up! I was just kidding," he said, wincing away from my impending slap on the arm. "Marc invited me along. I just have to find someone to bring – don't want to be a third wheel to anyone."

"You'll never be a third wheel," I assured him, finishing off my apple juice.

"I don't know who to invite. Do you have anyone in mind?"

"Tyler, any girl you ask will say yes. I mean, what girl would be crazy enough to turn you down?"

He smiled. Clearly wanting me to continue with the flattery he said, "Do go on, Caitlin. Why wouldn't any girl turn me down?"

"You're really going to make me do this?"

He nodded devilishly.

Rolling my eyes at his quirkiness I started to say, "Well, okay – let's see. You're quite handsome – if you like the tall, dark, handsome type. You're sort of intelligent." He nudged me in the ribs. "Okay, quite intelligent, and let's not forget you're super kind – too kind, for your own good. What else can a girl want?"

Tyler's mouth slightly turned to a crocked little smile "Sure Caitlin, now you think of me in those lines – now that Bradford has his claws so deep in that there is no way to pry him off.

Great friend you are," he jeered. "So, I'm too handsome for my own good, am I?"

"No! I said, too kind for your own good. Come on, you know that you're handsome."

He started to shove me playfully while I was trying to collect my things. "Say it – say that I'm handsome again. Go ahead, say it." he insisted.

I was now laughing and trying to duck his hand from tickling me. "Okay, okay. You're gorgeous – geez!"

He chuckled. "You mean my irresistible Italian charm, don't you?"

I nudged him in the ribs. "Yeah, that's what I mean. Just choose who you're going to bring wisely.

"Any girl will do," he said, picking up his book bag. "You're not going to be jealous, are you?"

I rolled my eyes again. "Of course, I am, Tyler. I'll be crying myself to sleep at the thought of you and – no-name." I pulled him by the arm. "Come on handsome, we should get going."

We headed back inside the building not looking forward to the History exam. Not that I wasn't ready, but that it usually required long written answers which I hated.

"So, it won't bother you – whoever I bring?" he asked fishing for some sort of response on my part.

"If you're happy, Tyler, I'm happy, but that doesn't mean I have to like it." I purposely used the same words he once used to describe how he felt about Justin and me.

"Who said I want you to like it, Caitlin? I'd prefer it if you had a multitude of sleepless nights being tortured by thoughts of having her instead of you in my arms. It would only be fair for you to feel as I've felt at the sight of you and Justin."

I stopped dead in my tracks as his comment threw me off. "You don't mean that, do you?" He simply stared. "I'm sorry if

I've hurt you in any way, Tyler." I dropped my gaze to the floor searching ways to explain, "What Justin and I have is…."

"Caitlin, I like that you're crazy about somebody and not sulking around. Justin is a great guy, and I'm not just saying that to make you feel better. I love the fact that he losses it around me. It only means that he's crazy about you. I'm jealous in a good way. He loves you and that's all that matters."

"I do love you Tyler and that will never, ever change. You're my lifejacket – the only reason I have been able to handle Oaks."

He put his arm around my shoulders and led me to our History mid-term. "I know – I know. I'm your tall, gorgeous, best friend who's too handsome for his own good," he said, beaming a smile.

"'Too kind for your own good,' Tyler – I never said 'too handsome for your own good.'"

"Same difference."

"Really?"

He smiled and nodded.

"You're a big buffoon, you know that don't you?"

"Yes, but a tall, gorgeous and too handsome for my own good, buffoon."

"Why do I bother?"

"Because you love me – remember?"

I nodded as I tried to get control of my giggles, but soon after they were cut abruptly short by my agonizing need to know who he was thinking of bringing. "So, who are you going to ask?"

"You'll just have to wait and see," he said pestering me.

"I don't care who she is – anybody, but Megan would do."

Tyler didn't say a word. Instead, he looked at me wide-eyed and in shock; the way one does when caught doing something they shouldn't have. He continued to stare.

"No you won't!" I yelled, keeping back the urge to smack him. "Why would you? I'm not going to spend two whole weeks with an ignorant, self-righteous, all-loathing, ill-mannered, obnoxious, snotty speaking, arrogant….."

I droned on and on, slapping him playfully on the arm. There were some other names I would have liked to call Megan, but her sincerity earlier had censored my wrath.

I cringed at the thought of the two of them together. The whole school was aware of the fact that Megan would have sold her only kidney to be with Tyler. Heck, most of the girls in school would have.

Tyler burst out laughing at my ranting, looking at me sheepishly, knowing he got the best of me.

"You're such an ass!" I yelled, "Seriously now – you're not going to invite her, are you?" I finally asked, punching him on the arm for provoking me.

No answer.

"Tyler, answer me! Are you going to invite the She-devil?"

"Okay, stop! No! I'm not going to ask her," he said, trying to duck my assault. "You had to see your face, though. It was priceless."

"Jackass," I said jokingly. "So, who's it going to be then?"

"Well, I've had this on and off thing with this girl, but now…," He was hesitant about telling me – worrying about how I would take the news, "Anyway, we'll see," he added. "I'm not sure what I should do."

"Why have you kept this from me? Do I know the poor soul?"

"Look," he said, holding the door to our History class, "we'll talk about this later. I promise to tell you everything."

"Okay, but I want to know every juicy detail."

"Take a seat you two," said Mr. Myers, sounding annoyed for keeping up his class. We both apologized for running late, and took our assigned seats.

~~~

The exam was as difficult as anticipated. I finished way before anybody – faster than Tyler, which was quite unusual, raising flags of alarm. I scanned over my paper once again, checking to see if I might have missed something. It all looked as it should.

Surprisingly, my focus was on the box labeled 'name'. I filled it in, like I always did 'Caitlin Cathcart', but for the first time in my life I contemplated over this erroneous issue.

Should I change it? Should I fill in my real name? I pondered.

I must have gone back and forth writing and erasing, writing and erasing until I finally filled in the box with 'Caitlin Eileen Korbs'. I didn't know how to feel about my choice, but it looked right – it was my real name, after all.

I looked around the class and noticed that everybody was absorbed in the exam – frantically answering the questions. My mind drifted thinking of the past and how my whole life was a hoax, veiled in secrets and conspiracy in order to protect me, but from what? It made no sense. Why would my relentless pursuers, the Korbs, risk so much to have me? They knew nothing about me.

The thought that the Ellri did not know their intentions was worrying. 'A custody battle' is what they called it. Was it all so simple? Would a family go to such lengths to regain what they felt was rightfully theirs? Was I just the object of their insane greed for power?

Deep down I would have liked to meet them, get to know my father's side of the family, but the hefty price that I would have to pay for such an introduction was what worried me most. I had seen my grandfather Clancy; he was no monster, by any measure. He might have been set in his ways, but he believed he acted in his son's best interest, no matter how twisted his demand.

My parent's story reminded me of my term paper on Romeo and Juliet, back in Stone Hurst. I titled it 'Wasted Youth'. It was how I saw it – a meaningless waste of life. I kept debating over the fact that if they both just listened to their parents, things could have worked out so differently. Every time we would discuss the play in class I would always maintain that they should have never defied their family. I was an expert after all, accepting my exile in sheer silence.

Could the Korbs be feeling the same about me? I quickly thought. *Might they, in some twisted way, believe that they are guarding me? We are kin, after all, and our powers do tie us in more ways than one.*

I shook my head, banishing each thought. How could I possibly excuse such cruel acts? My grandfather 'breeds', was the word Marlene used, the gifted. It is a monstrosity to think that some of the gifted were forced into the sanctity we all hold so sacred. Our union with our other half was based on free will and love. To defile so pure a sentiment was sadistic.

An atrocious thought suddenly crossed my mind. *Had they chosen somebody for me?* "Holly crap," I yelled, shocked at my revelation.

In seconds the whole class turned and stared.

"Sorry, question five is a real dinger," I lied.

They all started laughing. Tyler was not at all amused by my outburst. I was sure it broke his train of thought. I stuck my tongue out at him, laughingly and said, "Get over it." He rolled his eyes disapprovingly and returned his gaze to the test paper.

"Settle down," said Mr. Myers, banging his book on the desk. "Miss Cathcart, please refrain from any further outbursts. Now! All of you, back to your exam."

All heads dropped, not wanting to provoke Mr. Myers any more than necessary.

From the corner of my eye I caught a glimpse of Megan's eraser about to fall to the floor. "Back," I whispered, in an attempt to keep the eraser from falling. It was not supposed to work, but in that split second the object inched away from the edge, moving safely back on the desk.

"Five more minutes," exclaimed Mr. Myers, attracting everybody's attention, "you should be rechecking your answers if you haven't already. I don't want to hear excuses that you had no time to look the test over."

Shocked that I was able to use my powers, I looked around to see if there were any witnesses. Luckily, everyone was way too busy rushing to fill out any last detail to notice my insignificant accomplishment. I wanted to test myself once more to make sure I did not imagine it, so I looked over to Tyler. He was rechecking his answer sheet for the quadrillionth time. I focused on his pen and paper and willed them off the desk. To my horror they obeyed – flinging themselves to the floor.

"Damn it," Tyler said, collecting them.

"Caitlin," Mr. Myers' authoritative voice sliced through the air. He was staring right at me. He knew exactly what I had just done, because his expression said it all. It was split between surprise and fear. "Can you stay a minute after class? There's something I need to talk to you about."

"Yes sir, of course," I answered, sliding deeper in my seat – putting my pen and pencil away.

One by one, we piled our test papers on his desk, exiting the door. I stayed behind to be reprimanded.

Straightening out his striped tie, Mr. Myers turned to Tyler who was lingering in the doorway waiting for me and said dismissively, "You can wait for her outside, Tyler. She won't be long."

Alone with Mr. Myers was not the best way to end any day. I let him speak first not knowing what I was supposed to say.

"How long? How long have you known?" he simply asked. He was not mad, but concerned. "This is quite unprecedented."

"I wasn't aware of anything until a few minutes ago. I didn't know it was possible."

"It shouldn't be, Caitlin. None of us are able to use our gifts in this building."

"Is there something wrong with me?"

"Wrong with you?" he asked, smiling for the first time in months. He was actually handsome in an awkward kind of way. "I would say not! Your ability is remarkable and one of a kind. But….," I knew there was a 'but' somewhere in there – there was always a 'but' proceeding any worse case scenario. "But, it has no place in this school. Now, go home and don't mention anything to anyone. I'll talk to the Ellri and see what steps we need to take."

"I'm truly sorry Mr. Myers. I didn't mean to break any school rules. I was simply testing myself."

"I know. Don't worry," he said patting me on the back.

"I'm in trouble, aren't I?"

"Why would you be in trouble? You did what any young person would do in this situation. Now get going and don't worry. The Ellri will know why this is happening."

There I go again, I thought as I walked down the hall. Tyler was waiting at the foot of the stairs looking at me questionably. "What did you do?" he asked, concerned.

"Nothing," I lied. "Myers just wanted to ask about my ability to…," I stopped mid-sentence, not wanting to finish.

"Serves you right! You shouldn't have finished so fast. He

probably thinks you cheated somehow. Why would you rush on a midterm? "

I did not correct him on his wrong assumption because I was not lying exactly. I just let him believe a different version of the truth.

Before exiting the building I decided to hum my father's melody in my head to keep my mind busy so neither Tyler nor Justin could read my thoughts outside the Shield of Knowledge. Approaching the black Audi I could tell that Justin was not amused by my distracting humming.

"How was the exam?" Justin asked, grinning as though he were in on some joke.

"Not bad," Tyler answered, ignoring my silence.

I left them standing in front of the car while I headed for the passenger's seat.

"Mr. Myers held her after class," I heard Tyler explain. "Nothing serious, I don't know why she's acting so weird."

"Oh, I guess that must be it," Justin responded, turning to look at me, shaking his head. "Let me get her home then," Justin said and walked towards the car, sliding into the driver's seat without saying a word, smiling his all knowing smile.

As he turned on the engine he turned to face me. "You can hum till the cows come home. I can still read your mind," he finally said chuckling.

Irritated, I turned and said, "How can you possibly be able to do that? Tyler couldn't."

"Tyler is just getting the hang of his gift," Justin smiled. "Now stop that annoying sound and tell me what happened. Was today the first day you were able to use your gift in school?" I nodded my head like a two-year-old caught with my hand in the cookie jar. "I didn't mean to. Megan's eraser was about to fall and I pushed it back on her desk."

Justin laughed at my plea for innocence. "Relax, you didn't do anything wrong."

"Easy for you to say – you don't keep getting yourself into these predicaments. Am I in big trouble? Will I get detention or even worse, expelled?"

"Don't get ahead of yourself. You're not in any kind of trouble. The Shield of Knowledge should have blocked your gift. It's not your fault if there's a glitch." Justin closed his eyes momentarily and concentrated. "The Ellri already know." he said.

"Remind me why I'm happy to be back?"

He caressed my face tenderly. "You're here for me, silly. I wouldn't be able to live without you."

"You might have to, after the Ellri are finished with me."

TWO

THE ABYSS

S HANNON'S face was wrought with concern as she waited
for us at the door. "Everybody is in the sitting room," she
said in a hollowed-out voice.

As we entered the room, all eyes fell on me. "We're still
waiting for Nathan and Marlene. Both of you take a seat,"
William offered.

Sitting on the edge of the sofa, I pulled my scarf free and
asked, "So, what are you guys going to do with me?"

"That's what we're here to decide. We have some choices for
you." Uncle Abbot offered, winking at me.

This was a first. I was actually going to be given a choice in
the matter. Just then, Justin jumped to his feet and headed for
the door. I did not hear a knock, but he would not have to –
Nathan and Marlene had arrived.

"Well, well. It's nice to see all of you so soon," Marlene
declared smiling, looking around the room. "Young lady,
you're sure keeping us on our toes."

"I'm truly sorry for the inconvenience."

"Save it child. This is not your fault," Nathan said, sitting
next to me, patting me on the hand. "Your ability to transcend

is what has penetrated the Shield. It's beyond your control. What we need to figure out is what to do with your education."

"Not being in full control of your powers, we cannot allow you to attend school," Aunt Leslie went on to explain. "None of the other students will be able to defend themselves in case...."

Then my heart twisted as her words suddenly echoed in my mind. "In case – what?"

"In case something goes astray, Caitlin."

"What do you guys think I'm going to do?"

My aunt smiled compassionately and added, "We trust you completely, sweetie. But your gift is raw and quiet unstable."

"So, what are you saying? Where does that leave me?"

"That's what we're here to decide," she said, stroking my cheek. "We are going to let you choose between dropping out of school completely or be tutored at home."

The way my aunt looked at me I knew there was no choice in the matter. She was just being democratic about the whole issue. The decision was a no-brainer. "I'm going to miss hanging out with some of the students, but if I have to choose, I'd like to continue my education, of course. I'm not a drop out!"

"Good, that settles that," she said surprisingly fast, "now, to the matter at hand."

"If school isn't the reason we're here, then what is?" I asked, puzzled.

The Ellri looked first to Justin and then their gaze shifted to me – moving their heads back and forth not knowing how to start. "Not again!" Justin said aggravated for some reason. "This is ridiculous! You can't intervene. I won't allow it." He stood up and headed towards the door, preparing to leave.

"We can't allow this to go on, Justin. You should have put a stop to this behavior the moment it started. You are both putting yourselves in harm's way," William said, sounding quite enraged.

I stood up, feeling left out. "I'd hate to cut in," I interjected, looking at Justin's father, "being handicapped in mind reading, can someone please let me in on what we're fighting about?"

Marlene's hearty laughter sliced through the tension. "You might not be able to read minds young lady, but you sure know how to drive a young man crazy."

My mouth dropped to the floor. I looked toward Justin only to see his mortified expression. "What's Marlene talking about?" I asked him.

"They know about last night," he said, raising his hands in surrender. "They know about your little visit to my room. They know everything."

"Oh – Oooh!" I exclaimed wide eyed, but still, I was not going to let them ruin my memory of last night. "And the problem is – what exactly?" I finally said stiffening up, ready to defend my actions.

"First of all, we never use our powers for self-indulgence, Caitlin, and secondly we do not use them if we don't have full control of them." Shannon said curtly.

"I do have control, Shannon, and I'd never put Justin in harm's way. Besides, it was innocent fun."

At that moment, Shannon took my scarred wrist in her hand, placing her palm right on top of my scar, squeezing it tightly. "Tell me Caitlin, how much control have you now?" she demanded, squeezing my wrist even more.

"Mother, Stop!" Justin screamed angrily, from the other side of the room. William held him back, not allowing him to approach. "Don't do this! Not now! Not to her," Justin pleaded.

"Caitlin will be fine," William reassured him. "She just needs to learn a lesson or two – the way you all did."

What they meant was, as always, cryptic. But at that precise moment I had direr things to concern myself about. My thoughts became twisted, fraught with anger – my wrist ablaze under her touch only ignited my restrained need to take malicious pleasure in tearing her to pieces. The intensity was toxic – my mind was split in two. I could feel torrents of energy moving up my spine towards my arm and down to my fingers.

"Shannon, let go!" I pleaded, fighting against the venomous thoughts that were taking form inside my mind. "You have to let go!"

I tugged at my wrist in fear of hurting her. She remained firm, tightening her hold even more.

"Can you honestly tell me, Caitlin, that you can control this?" she asked outraged, lifting our clasped hands in the air, "Can you even feel the power you're exerting at the moment? If I were not Ellri you would have killed me by now."

Completely consumed with the darkest and deadliest of thoughts, I fought to break free fearing the worst, trying my hardest to exert some sort of control over the power in my hands and the poison that inundated my brain. "Shannon, please," I begged through the blur of emotion, falling to my knees in tears, "it's getting stronger. I can't restrain it for long. Please, let go!" Fear was driving me. "It's way stronger than you, I can feel it. Let me go!" I growled, in hopeless frustration – not recognizing my own voice.

"Look at her." I heard Shannon say in a breathy voice as she quickly stepped back. Her features had darkened with the imminent threat my gift was ready to bestow upon her.

My wrist was finally free from her tight grip, however, the force did not subside nor did the thirst to rip her heart out lessen – instead, it escalated even more, embedding itself in the core of me. Disheveled and tearful, I blinked and squinted in the sudden realization that I was powerless to control the sudden urge to strike at her – to finally quench my sordid thoughts. My heart contracted as a deluge of tears surged to my eyes in my effort to suppress my bodies need to deliver her a sharp blow. My thoughts were raw and sadistic, and the only thing that would have given me instant gratification was to attack Shannon.

I raised my gaze in pleading anguish, but all I saw was Marlene's adorable old face, with her all seeing grey eyes, showing concern as she watched me fight my inner demons. There was no holding on for much longer. But hurting anybody in that room was not something I was prepared to live with – no matter the satisfaction it would have brought my altered state of mind.

"No Caitlin – don't," was the last thing I heard, before placing both my palms flat against my chest as I let out all the energy from my hands into my own body and closed my eyes shut to the pain I was under, but it was the horror of my incapability to curb the rage and hunger that hurt me most.

Slipping into solace was not a serene ordeal, as other times. The darkness that enwrapped me was pungent in furry and madness. My feelings were as intense and as vile there as they were before transcending, but now there was also the physical torment that I exposed myself to. Fear quickly overpowered every other emotion, and harrowing pain tore right through me, as I crouched on the floor writhing in agony.

"You're not breathing, mortal," I heard a faint whisper say. "You must breathe deep and take control of your gift." The words were marked by utter benignity. "You must rein it in."

"Please make it stop!" I said through the tears.

"What you did is fatal, young mortal. Your body is now suffering from your own doing."

"There was no other way. It was either them or me."

"You – them, it makes no difference. You need to learn control. You are now slowly passing from the life you know – dying because of your foolish decisions, and for what?"

"Please, help me," I begged with each painful spasm.

"This time, and this time alone will we intervene."

In seconds the pain dispersed, but I was still left with the anger and hatred I felt for Shannon.

"Don't try to repress the rage you feel because it just feeds on your insecurities. Guide it – focus it elsewhere."

"How do I do that? I – I don't even know what I'm feeling."

I felt captive in my own body and mind. I had no way of escaping the evil that possessed me.

The source of the whisper was suddenly closer. I could feel its warmth on my face. "Concentrate! Close your eyes and relax," the whisper instructed. "Now think of one place that makes you happy and focus."

Unable to get control, my breathing turned erratic and my mind slipped even deeper into a whole new level of the hellish abyss created by my raging thoughts. It was then that a warm hand touched my cheek as a melody formed in my inner mind, but not by notes, but by words that reached deep into the core of the madness. "Let my voice guide you, Caitlin."

There was a change in pitch in the airy whisper that served to distinguish it from the other. Apparently, there were two beings in my refuge. The second sound was much softer than the first – an angelic melody to my ears.

"Who are you?" I asked, feeling exceptionally aware of its closeness.

"All in due time," the whisper said, caressing both my cheeks. "Breathe in and relax. Rise above these emotions."

The touch reached not only the surface of my skin, but

under it – around it. It was so gentle and tender that I felt tears running down my face. My heart was going to burst from the tide of affection this being was emanating, slowly bringing into balance the hatred and negativity that overwhelmed me.

"Who are you?" I cried, feeling the warmth weaving its way to the center of the mayhem that overcame me - erasing, bit by agonizing bit the dark emotions, causing my heart to flutter as I bathed in its warmth.

"Young mortal, you do not have time for questions," the impalpable sound said, fading away. "You forget that Justin is feeling the intensity of your emotions as well. You must rein in your demons, and captain your power; otherwise you will hurt him,"

"I can't! Can't you see that I have no power over this?"

"Close your eyes, child, and breathe deep."

I did as I was told and took several consecutive deep breaths, letting my mind flush all the negativity from my soul, concentrating primarily on the hymn-like sounds imbuing the depths of my mind, bringing things into focus.

It took a lot longer than usual to calm myself, but the warm touch of the surreal being was what helped me get control.

"Good girl," the wisplike whisper said. "Let this be a lesson to you, Caitlin. The Ellri were right. Your power is not a game and should not be taken at all lightly. Last night's escapade must not be repeated, no matter how good it might have felt. You need to be guided to use that part of your power. It is dangerous to leave your body. There is no knowing who can reach you in the field of transcendence."

I nodded in agreement not wanting to speak in fear of ruining the majestic sound I had in my ears. In seconds, the warmth on my face faded only to be replaced with the stone-cold darkness of my solace. Remaining there momentarily, I allowed myself the time to digest everything that was happening in my life, and the sheer silence was therapeutic on so many levels. After a while, however, I opened my eyes and slipped back into reality. I looked around the room to see if Justin was okay. His body lay a safe distance away, asleep on the floor while Shannon and William were there as well stretched out, sleeping on opposite sofas.

Though the worst of the storm had passed now, I was still weak and trembling trying hard to catch my breath. My eyes felt bloodshot and sore. My whole body was ravaged by exhaustion.

For many minutes I could not move, but as soon as I got some control of the shudders I pushed myself closer to Justin and snuggled in his embrace. Within seconds his sleep strained eyes instantly popped open in great surprise. "You're back," he whispered in my ear.

"It would seem so," I answered, feeling somewhat changed by the experience.

The echo of the soft whisper was still in my ears as my mind refused to let it go. Shannon and William both got to their feet.

"Good, your back," Shannon said, moving closer to me. "Sorry for putting you through all that. All of us had to face our limits at one point. Unfortunately, making you go through all that was the only way to make you see how serious having total control is."

"It's okay, Shannon. I'm fine. I know you all meant well."

I looked around the room confused and disoriented.

"Abbot and Leslie left an hour ago," William said, fixing his slept-in shirt. "We all took shifts."

"Really? Was I gone that long?"

For several minutes William seemed unable to speak, either from the intolerable fatigue due to waiting for my reemergence from my comatose state or to the difficulty of putting words to events so surreal and inexplicable. "My son here, stayed with you the whole time," William finally boasted without answering my question. He then took Shannon by the arm and headed to the door, but before exiting he turned to Justin and instructed him to take me upstairs to rest.

I tried standing, but thanks to my lack in energy I collapsed back on the floor with a thud. My legs felt like rubber. They were in no shape to support my weight. Justin swiftly cradled me in his arms and carried me up the stairs. My head felt heavy against his warm chest – I needed to sleep.

~~~

Resting on my side, I gazed around the room. It was too dark to tell where I was. My body was sore and I could hardly move a muscle. *What a day!* I hugged the pillow trying to take in a deep breath. My lungs reluctantly expanded to let in the air, hurting with each attempt.

"Go back to sleep your body needs to rest," he said, stretched out next to me.

Using all my strength to move my unwilling torso, I slowly turned to face in the direction of Justin's soft voice. "What time is it?" I asked, trying to take yet another agonizing breath.

"About three in the morning," he answered, kissing me on the forehead. "Now go back to sleep. You have been out for quite some time."

"My chest feels constricted. It really hurts to breathe."

"That's because you haven't been using much of your body for the past three days."

"Three days!" I cried out in utter shock. "Was I gone that long? I swear it only felt like a couple of minutes."

"You don't know how lucky you are to have the Nobe guiding you. Hardly any of us have ever come in contact with them, let alone, talk to them. Not the way they come to you."

"Why don't they just appear? I can't even make out a voice. It sounds like a tune, a whisper in my ear."

Justin fixed the covers around my body trying to make me more comfortable. "They would never appear to us, Caitlin. Only to the Ellri, and that's only if the need arises."

"Have you ever spoken to them?"

He nodded. "When the Ellri sent you away five years ago, I wasn't exactly the friendliest person to be around. Our separation was physically exhausting and painful, and I was slowly ascending, causing all kinds of fluctuations in my powers and bed-side manner." Justin explained. "The Nobe came to me on several occasions, but not as whispers, as you describe, but as commanding voices ordering me to get control of my emotions. When you disappeared that night my whole world went straight to hell. I didn't care about anything or anyone."

I nestled in his embrace, burying my head in the curve of his neck. "That's the past," I said, trying to catch my breath. "We're together now and that's all that matters."

He kissed me on the head, tightening his hold. "I'll never let you go, ever again," he declared.

I felt tears pricking at my eyes. Justin meant every word. I could hear it in the way his voice cracked at each syllable. I wanted to be happy in his arms, but the little voice inside my head kept nagging at me, reminding me of a choice I would have to make. He stroked my back tenderly soothing me back to sleep.

THREE

ILL AT EASE

REAKFAST at Justin's was a bit awkward. Even though
I knew William and Shannon my whole life, sleeping
over in their son's room, of all places, made me quite
self-conscious.

Not knowing what I would like to eat, Shannon prepared an
overly abundant breakfast – making one of everything. Even
William was surprised by the array of dishes on the breakfast
table. "How many people are we expecting over for breakfast,
love?" He had asked smiling, knowing full well that she had
gone to all that trouble just for me.

Justin started chuckling at his mother's expense. Her
grimace was priceless. I would have loved to be able to read her
mind. Poor William did, his expression said it all. He quietly sat
down at the head of the table, tail between his legs, and picked
up his cup of coffee, and asked, "How are you feeling this
morning, Caitlin?"

"A bit soar, but nothing I can't handle." I lied. I was in much
more pain than that, but I was not about to go into that over
breakfast, not with Justin's parents trying so hard to make me

feel at home and part of their family by showing their love.

"It'll take a couple more days. Your body needs to refuel its supply of energy. It's no easy feat."

Still cross with William, Shannon returned to serving breakfast. My throat was like sand paper. I could not swallow water let alone eat solid food. I did, however, let Shannon over indulge her need to satisfy my hunger.

Not wanting to hurt her feelings I took a quick sip of my orange juice to moisten the roughness in my throat and reluctantly took a bite of crispy bacon. I was having difficulty swallowing so I took another big gulp of juice to wash it all down. Justin and William both noticed my attempt at eating and realized that I was not about to let Shannon down by not finishing my rather large portion. I could tell that both men felt sorry for me.

Shannon no sooner turned her back to put something on the counter, when both William and Justin stealthily dug their forks into my plate helping me tackle my serving. I held back my giggle not wanting to attract Shannon's attention. William winked at me, grinned with satisfaction at being able to put one over on the love of his life.

Unaware of our scheme, Shannon refilled William's cup of coffee and then turned to Justin's cup. He waved her away, biting into his toast.

"Leslie wants to know when she should be expecting you," she said, turning to me.

"Oh, did she call? I would have liked to talk to her. She must be really worried."

All three looked at me questionably. "There is no need for her to call," Shannon answered. "I can't remember the last time the phone actually rang," she added, searching her mind.

"Sorry, I forgot that whole mind reading thing," I said,

slumping deeper into the chair in the hopes of disappearing. How could I have forgotten such a detail? "I guess you can let her know that I'll be home as soon as we finish breakfast."

"No you won't," exclaimed Justin, looking at me. "I'm not taking you home – not this soon," he added looking at his parents for confirmation.

I wanted nothing more than to stay there – anywhere for that matter, as long as it was with him, however, I did need to rest a little more. Justin was too great a distraction for me to relax.

Shannon reached across the table and placed her hand on top of Justin's. "Caitlin needs to freshen up, son. She needs time to collect herself. She's been through quite a lot," she said. "A nice hot bath would do her body a world of good."

He took a minute, "I see what you mean," he said, reluctantly, "after breakfast then."

William and Shannon smiled at each other, clearly touched by their son's need to be with me. I wondered on many occasions if they agreed of our relationship. If they thought I was worthy of their son. Now I was sure it would not have mattered who I was. I could have easily been any girl. As long as Justin was happy, they were happy.

"Shannon?" I said, causing her to shift her gaze to me. "Did I hurt you at all that night?"

"Nothing I couldn't handle, but you could have easily done much damage if you didn't exert yourself suppressing the full force. You exhibited tremendous control. You did quite well for your first test."

"Test? Is that what that was?"

"There will be more trials, more difficult each time. We need to make sure that each stage of your gift's development is under your control and not the other way around."

"I didn't have much control, did I? You said I could have killed you if you weren't Ellri. I didn't even realize I was doing anything to you. I felt the current in my hands much later."

"Unfortunately for you, your power doesn't wait for your permission. It caters only to your well-being," she explained, taking a sip of her coffee. "So you see, the moment I grabbed your wrist its defense mechanism kicked in, wanting me off. You didn't become aware of its reaction until the force was so strong that it was too late for your mind to react to your bodies need. That is why you need to be patient. You have to grow into your power. Once you have complete control you will be able to wield your gift on command. Until then, both of you need to be more responsible."

William scanned our faces knowing how hard this all was for both Justin and me.

"It's dangerous for you to leave your body. Your gift is completely raw and you don't know how it will react at any given time. If Justin was to do anything that might have triggered your gift while you were out of your body, both of you would have paid a heavy price – one that we are not willing to allow."

I put my hands over my face ashamed of putting Justin in danger. "I thought I did have complete control. It was all in good fun. I didn't mean to...."

"That's the whole problem," William said, cutting me off, "your gift is only in its infant stage. It can't read your emotions clearly, not yet anyway. It reacts purely on instinct, not knowing how to decipher your feelings. Whether you're excited or scared it can only pick up on the upsurge of adrenalin in your blood and it simply reacts to protect you. As embarrassing as this may be, you and Justin need to cool it off. We are all happy to see you guys together, but we are not prepared to risk either of you. Do you both understand?"

I nodded in complete understanding.

"Caitlin, you must not test your limits – not on each other, especially not now – not when you are so close to ascending."

"Enough!" Justin said raising his voice. "You have no idea how hard it is for us. The bond is getting much stronger, pulling us together. It's maddening trying to stay away. She can be in the next room and I'll be drawn to her like a magnet. Pain aside, it is exhausting fighting it. So don't sit there lecturing us about limits. We are both well aware of who we are and what we can do. You all need to back off and let us breathe."

Hearing him respond with such anger only alerted me on how serious this all was. It was obvious that I needed to grow up and take responsibility.

"Son, we are not trying to keep you apart. On the contrary, we all welcome the two of you together. But none of us are going to stand by and watch you die," William said, determined to get his point across. "You need to stop putting yourselves in danger."

William was trying to make him understand, but Justin wasn't having it. He was tired of the lectures, tired of being told what to do.

"Your father is absolutely right," I said, being aware of how many times I came close to hurting him.

Justin's expression was marked by betrayal. To him, I was siding with the enemy. "Caitlin," Justin said, shaking his head. "How can you say that? We haven't done anything wrong."

"Apparently we – I mean, I have. I can't control this, not now. I thought I could, but I can't. We need to be more careful. They're only looking out for both of us, and I refuse to be a threat to you. I won't put you in that position ever again." I pronounced shaking my head. "I'd rather feel the pain of being separated than put you in any sort of danger. I can't do this."

"What's that supposed to mean? What the hell are you saying?" he yelled, slamming his hand on the table angrily.

My body unexpectedly reacted to his mood – the tingling sensation was back, this time more acute due to my physical weakness.

"I can't handle this, not now. Look at my wrist, Justin," I sighed, completely drained by my body's reaction. I put my head in my hands trying to concentrate, but it was impossible. "Your anger is feeding it. I should have control, but I don't."

"Don't touch her," Shannon suddenly warned Justin. "Caitlin needs to rest. This is too much for her. You must calm down, Justin. You are transferring your emotions to her and she has no control. You can't allow this to happen, not now, not after what she's been through."

My head was going to explode by the tremendous force I was exerting to bring my stupid gift under control.

William stood up and came to my side. "Caitlin, I know this is too much for you right now. You won't be able to control it any longer without our help. We're going to have to displace the force."

I nodded not knowing what he meant. I simply wanted the feeling gone, no matter what.

"You might feel faint afterwards, so be prepared."

Both Shannon and William locked hands and closed their eyes. They turned their heads to the ceiling breathing in real deep. On their third deep breath they each placed their free hands on my shoulder and instantaneously the rigid burning in my wrist surged up to where they were touching me. I instantly felt cold, my head light as a feather and then everything went black.

"She'll be fine. Give her some time," I heard Shannon say.

Barely able to open my eyes, I made an unsuccessful attempt at speaking, but there was no sound coming out of my mouth. Panicked, I looked around only to notice that I was lying on an incredibly soft, spacious bed – no longer in the kitchen where I thought I would be.

"Caitlin, are you okay?" Justin asked, sounding worse than I was feeling – sitting at the farthest corner of the room.

I bobbed my head to reassure him. I wanted to get up, but once again, I had absolutely no control of my body – paralyzed from the neck down.

"I can't move," I whispered, looking at Shannon.

"The feeling will fade in a few hours, but you need to rest

sweetie. Your body can't take any more. So just relax, okay? Leslie and Abbot are on their way."

Justin's parents left the room, closing the door behind them, but Justin remained in his seat – unwilling to move any closer.

"Why are you sitting so far? Come closer," I told him, needing him next to me. He stood up visibly reluctant to move any closer than he had to. Hesitant, he sat at the foot of my bed, acting rather peculiar.

"Is everything okay?"

"Sure, just go to sleep," he said expressionless.

Silence hung over us like a shroud, broken only by my faint deep breathing. Great sadness seethed within my breast. I fought it down before Justin could see it. There was no sleep to be had – not when Justin was acting the way he was. He did not look at me; instead he picked up a random book from the table and started reading, doing anything to avoid eye contact.

His indifference and need for silence was what triggered the tears I tried to stifle – fighting them back before they could spring to my eyes, but to no avail. The tears came, but I cried into the pillow trying to keep my breathing as steady as possible not wanting to ruin the silence he so much cherished.

Justin did not budge from his seat, sat there like a statue scanning the pages of the book. Unexpectedly, he jumped to his feet and headed for the door. The sound of the knock came seconds later.

"Are you alright," asked my aunt, entering the room; approaching the bed.

To conceal my sadness, I swallowed back the tears and answered, "I'm just tired. I'll be fine."

"You did terrific," she boasted, kissing me on the forehead. "We have never pushed anybody so hard on their first test. You're quite gifted Caitlin, you should be proud."

Proud was far from what I felt. Justin's mood was all I was worried about. He never acted this cold, this distant.

"I'll bring something for her to drink," Justin finally said, standing with one foot out the door. "Leslie, would you like anything?"

"No. Nothing for me, thanks," she replied, not taking her gaze off of me.

Minutes later Shannon came in with a glass of juice. "Drink up, Caitlin, you need your energy," she said, holding the straw up to my mouth.

Justin was nowhere in sight.

Aunt Leslie kept me company, trying to distract me from my own thoughts by updating me on how I was going to have to make up my exams. Unfortunately for me, there was no way of escaping midterms. Even worse, was the fact that the principal himself, Mr. Patterson, would be the one administering them.

"You should be finished along with everybody else," she explained. "You might have to sit more than two at a time."

"Super!" I said sarcastically, "More than two exams in one day; that sounds like so much fun."

She pulled a face

"When do I start?"

"Well, as soon as you're up to it. We'll take you home tonight and take things from there. You can feel your legs now, can't you? Why don't you try walking around a bit, get your blood circulating."

I did as I was told and strolled around the room. *This must be the guest room*, I thought. It was too generic to be lived in. Everything was in perfect order.

"Anytime you're ready, Caitlin we can go home."

"I'm ready now," I replied. I wanted to stay longer in case Justin returned, but it would not happen today.

A week later and there was still no sign of Justin. I was back on my feet, feeling as good as new, apart from the ache of having him so far away. I did not mention how I felt to anybody. This, whatever it was, was purely between the two of us.

"You have exactly an hour and a half to complete your English Lit exam," said Mr. Patterson, making a mental note of the time – jotting down this and that on some official looking paper. I was happy to sit for the exams in my Uncle's study. His big leather chair was by far more comfortable than the hard, wooden seats we had in school.

"You can begin, Caitlin," he said, pressing down on his stop watch, "and good luck."

I knew I'd ace the exam, I had read most of the books way before they were assigned.

Piece of cake, I thought. It took me a whole forty-five minutes to finish. My Patterson seemed happy by my progress, probably because he would be able to leave a lot earlier than expected.

Foreign Languages was next. At Stone Hurst I had advanced French. In Oaks I decided to start German. Beginners German was not exactly nuclear science. I matched the pictures to the words, translated several short German sentences to English, did a reading comprehension exercise and that was that – done in less than an hour.

"You're flying through these, good job, Caitlin," said Mr. Patterson, opening the next folder labeled Chemistry. "Would you like a break – maybe get something to eat or drink"

"No, I'd rather get this over with," I told him. "I'm sure you have better things to do with your time Mr. Patterson. I'd hate to keep you away from your family on a Saturday – especially on a sunny one like today."

"That's thoughtful of you, Caitlin, but you don't need to rush on my account. You're one of the best student's in school. This is the least I can do."

"Hand it over," I said, reaching for my Chemistry exam. "How long do I have for this one?"

"Let me see," he said checking his notes, "Exactly an hour and a half."

"Brace yourself," I laughed, "I'm going to need the whole ninety minutes. Chemistry is not exactly my strong point."

"I'm sure you'll do fine. Now go ahead and begin."

He had more faith in me than he should. I struggled through some questions, but thought I did quite well considering the subject. Poor Tyler did his best to catch me up to speed those past two days, leaving his own studying aside to drill me on my exam. It was quite entertaining to see him act the tutor. He brought with him a whole assortment of tests and quizzes. The flash cards were my favorite. We bet that with each mistake I would have to do something stupid. Aunt Leslie's face was priceless when she walked into the room seeing me hop around like a kangaroo, squealing. "You both need to grow up," was the only thing she said, shaking her head in disapproval. Tyler and I had burst out laughing.

It was most helpful to have Tyler around – he kept my mind off Justin, who was nowhere to be seen.

"Time's up," said Mr. Patterson, collecting his belongings.

I put my pen down and handed him my answer sheet. "I did the best I could," I said standing up.

"That's all we ever ask of you," he answered walking towards the door. "I'll be back on Monday with Latin and Human Behavior."

"Can't wait" I said smiling, thanking him.

No sooner did I close the door behind Mr. Patterson when

Uncle Abbot came down the stairs looking at his watch. "You're done already?" he asked, surprised at how quick it all was.

"Yeah, I breezed through German and English Lit., but Chemistry was difficult."

"I'm sure you did well."

"Uncle Abbot? Did any of you say anything to Justin? I haven't seen him or spoken to him in over a week."

"No, not that I'm aware of. Did you two have a fight?"

"No, that's the problem. I don't know why he's acting the way he is."

"Give him time, Caitlin. Whatever it is, it'll blow over." I knew my uncle was well aware of what had happened, but he would never interfere on something so personal. "Emily wants to see you upstairs," he said, strategically changing the subject.

I excused myself and went to Emily's room. I had seen her in passing the last few weeks because her time had been completely absorbed by Marc. "You wanted to see me?" I asked, poking my head in the room.

"We have one week left before winter break and you're asking me if I need to see you?"

"Oh, with everything that has been going on I didn't realize that we'd be leaving in a week."

"Caitlin, we're leaving this coming weekend, how can you forget something like that?"

I shrugged my shoulders. "I've lost all sense of time, Em. Have the Ellri told you where they're sending us?"

"Not in so many words, but it's somewhere hot. I got that much. Anyway, we need to go shopping for the trip."

"Em, I can't. I still have exams to study for. I'm sure you can lend me some of your old clothes. Why in the world would I need to buy new things for a two-week vacation?"

"You're impossible! Why would you want Justin to see you in my old clothes?"

"I'm sure he won't notice," I muttered. "I don't even know if he's coming or where he is, for that matter."

She placed a consoling arm around my shoulders. "He's in Cambridge with Kyle. They went to clean out his dorm room. They'll be back soon enough."

"It's not that, Em. He's changed. It's not like him to disappear without saying a word."

"Oh, come on Caity! Don't be like that. You've been through too much since you got here. Maybe seeing you go through all these changes is getting to him."

"That still doesn't explain how he's acting. Something's up."

"Well, whatever it is the sun and surf will surely help," she said, beaming a great big smile. "Now, since you insist on studying and refuse to go shopping with me. I'm going to have to shop for the both of us. You probably would've slowed me down, anyway."

"You really don't have to do that. You have already bought me so much."

"Nonsense, I won't have my little sister prancing around the beach in my old clothes. It's settled."

I knew that no matter what I said, she would still do what she had in mind. It was useless arguing with her.

"Did you know Tyler was coming with us?" I asked.

"Yeah, of course I knew. Marc mentioned it a while back. He didn't think it was fair to leave him out of our plans. He is family, after all. I just hope that he and Justin will keep it cool and not ruin or vacation."

"Trust me – Justin is in no mood to argue with Tyler."

"I hope you're right. Now, go get something to eat before you hit the books again."

Solace

Illustrated for Lines That Bind - Within The Whispers

FOUR

CONFESSIONS

THE DAY WAS COLD, but unusually sunny for the end of December. I did not have the heart to stay inside and waste it on studying. I changed into my track suit, pulled my hair into a ridiculously high ponytail and made sure I waited for Emily to leave before I took a walk around Oaks. I did not want to hurt her feelings, but she knew I would rather be hung upside down and tortured than go shopping. Just the thought of being dragged from store to store was grueling enough.

No sooner had I put on my ear-phones and turned on my MP3 player as I headed out the door, when down the driveway Justin pulled up in his car. Refusing to stop, I walked right past him, showing no sign of nerves, pretending he did not exist. If he did not want to talk to me, I was in no way going to force him. I turned up the volume on my MP3, blasting the tunes in my ears.

He stopped the car a few feet away, but I continued walking without even looking back.

The sudden slam of the door was deafening. Justin was

unmistakably annoyed. *"What, not even a good morning?"* I heard his voice vibrating in my head, causing me to automatically close my eyes from the piercing pain.

I stopped in mid-stride. I contemplated walking away, but did not think it was the mature thing to do.

As soon as I turned to face him my heart started beating like crazy. I wanted nothing more than to run into his arms. His gaze was intentionally scanning me up and down making me feel warm all over.

Kyle stepped out of the passenger seat and came round to our side looking back and forth at us standing there. "Am I going to witness a show-down?" he asked, chuckling at our frozen stance. "Sorry man, my money's on her."

Justin did not look amused. He glared at Kyle, throwing him the keys to the car. "Please park it up front," he said through clenched teeth.

"And miss the bloodshed?" Kyle said, shaking his head vigorously, "No way!"

"Kyle! Stop being such an ass and take the damn car up to the house," Justin sneered contemptuously.

Kyle knew when to stop. He gave me a quick pat on the head, and said, "You can take him."

"Kyle!"

Justin's angry voice caused him to stop laughing and he finally slid into the driver's seat and pulled away.

"So, you're talking to me now?" I asked, agitated by his audacity to come and go as he pleased without any consideration for my feelings.

He hesitantly moved towards me. "It's not like that and you know it."

"It's exactly like that, Justin! You've been ignoring me, not talking to me." I said, focusing my gaze on him, sounding angrier with every word. "Do you think you can turn me on and off as you please? I don't work that way."

Justin was only inches away, too far for my liking. He looked at me in silence, not knowing how to answer.

I wanted to reach up and kiss him, take him in my arms, but I was too angry – too hurt to allow myself the satisfaction. Irritated by his silence, I turned on my heel to leave and said, "Well, I guess we're done here."

"Stop! Don't be a child!" he said, grabbing my arm.

"I'm the child?" I lashed out furiously, yanking my arm free. "You haven't spoken to me in a week and I'm acting childish?"

"You don't get it, Caitlin."

"What don't I get? Enlighten me, why don't you?"

He was rather upset. I could tell by the way he combed both hands through his hair, swearing under his breath. "You need to decide what you want, Caitlin," he finally blurted out, frustrated.

"Decide what I want? That's easy. I want you! That's what I want!" I confessed rather loudly. He stared in disbelief. "Are you seriously questioning my feelings?" I accused him.

He rolled his eyes irritated. "You sat there, in front of my parents denying what we have. Accepting that what we felt and did was wrong. How could you? You are everything to me. Why can't you just see that?"

I shook my head, shocked at what he was saying. "You misunderstood, Justin. It's just that I can't risk hurting you. I just won't," I yelled.

"So, what are you saying, Caitlin? We're back to that again. You're going to let them control your life? Where does that leave us then, exactly? How am I supposed to react to that? Tell me, damn you. What do you want me to do?"

"I don't know what you want me to say," I cried. "I love

you, lord knows how much. But if giving you up means keeping you safe, so be it." Tears rolled freely down my face, but I was too proud to wipe them away.

"Why are you doing this?" his frustration was etched on his face. "Why do you continue to fight what we have? Insisting on letting others control you. Wasn't five years apart enough?" he asked, coming even closer. "If you think you'll be better off without me – not worrying about hurting me, then I'll go. You won't have to see me ever again. But I'll stay away only because you want me to, not because they do."

My heart stopped. I was not sure if I had heard him correctly. "You're actually thinking about leaving?" I shuddered at the thought of another day without him.

"If you think it'd be easier if I went away, I'll go. But it has to be your decision, no one else's – yours and yours alone." he said, pushing back his hair even more annoyed. "Is this what you want? Will that make you happy?"

"How can your leaving possibly make me happy?" Tears continued to roll down my face. "Don't say things like that? Please, just stop."

"You allowed my father to make you question your own feelings, Caitlin. Why didn't you stand up for us? Tell him that you were in complete control. What are you really afraid of?"

"But I'm not in control," I finally snapped. "Can't you see that? I don't want to hurt you, Justin."

"How can loving you possibly hurt me?"

Unable to look into his eyes, I stared at his upper lip. "You know what kind of pain I'm talking about. I don't have complete control of my gift."

He leaned in and kissed me on the mouth. His lips were full of longing, warm to the touch. I welcomed his every caress, hating my body for responding so willingly to him. I wrapped my arms around his neck pushing myself closer. He backed off just enough to look at me. "There is nothing wrong with what you're feeling right now. There's nothing wrong with what we have. Don't ever question it again."

"You heard what they said. It's dangerous. I have no control," I repeated.

"Caitlin, we're going to set our own limits, nobody else. You've got to be with me on this."

"I am, but what if something goes wrong. What if one of us oversteps the line, then what? We both know how strong this pull is. How long do you think we can fight it?"

He tightened his hold on me, lifting me inches off the ground, "We won't let things get that far. You have to trust me."

"You? Who's worried about you? You, I trust. It's me I'm having problems with. I can't seem to get enough of you," I confessed totally reddened by my candor, hiding my head in the curve of his neck.

He started laughing – the kind of laugh that only comes from days of unexpressed emotion. "You forgive people way too easily."

"I'm still mad at you," I muttered, trailing butterfly kisses up and down his neck. "You stayed away for a week over this? Why didn't you simply say something – anything?"

He let go momentarily and dropped his gaze to the ground before speaking. "I almost killed you that morning in the kitchen. You were way too weak to handle all that."

"It wasn't that bad," I lied.

His eye brow arched up as he shook his head. "You're kidding me right? You don't even know how close to the edge I pushed you. There's just so much energy that the body can survive without. You were just coming out of a terrific trial and

I just gave you the last push right over the cliff. I could've killed you."

"Yeah, okay, but you didn't"

"Caitlin, you're not the only one who's having problems with their emotions, you know. I don't want to hurt you like that again. I feel useless seeing you struggle with all this. I feel like I'm adding to the pressure. Seeing what I can do to you – I thought – well I believed staying away would be best, but who was I kidding?"

"Enough!" I yelled, raising both hands in the air. "Just stop already. No more talk about what could've happened. Agreed?"

Justin simply nodded.

"Okay then." I exhaled rather loudly, letting all the tension drain away. "But now what?" I asked. "Are we really going to do this our way? Defying the Ellri?"

"It's our life and no one has any right to tell us how to live it. They warned us about the dangers. We're not stupid to risk our lives, and as long as you stop talking and thinking about sacrificing yourself on my behalf, we'll be fine."

I rolled my eyes at him aware that he knew more about me than he let on. "You really need to stop reading my thoughts, it's disturbing!"

"Your thoughts are what's disturbing, nothing else. Why do you keep thinking about making a choice? Do you really think, I'll allow you to choose my life over yours? Whatever is brewing on the other side of the Atlantic will be confronted when the time comes. There's no need for self-sacrifice, besides, what good is my life if you're not in it?"

"I'm not sure it's that simple, Justin. If it was, the Nobe wouldn't need so much time to deliberate."

"Why worry about that now? Nothing's certain. It keeps

changing every second we speak. You and me, here, now, is the only thing that should matter."

I nodded, not completely convinced at how easily they all had accepted a potentially bleak future.

"We saw Emily down the road heading to the stores," said Justin, changing the subject to lighten the moment. "She said you had studying to do."

"Yeah, well you caught me. I didn't want to go shopping with her. She would've dragged me to all the stores. You know how she is. What I did want to do is take a walk around the town or at least the grounds."

"You don't look too excited about our vacation. Aren't you looking forward to being away for two weeks?"

"I am, but with exams I really haven't had the chance to think about the trip. Where are we going anyway?"

"The Ellri haven't said a word. They're not thrilled about us going without one of them chaperoning."

"You must be joking! We're all adults. What do they think we'll do? They really need to loosen the leash a bit. I'm starting to feel it digging into my neck."

"We might be adults as far as age is concerned, but all our powers are quite young and not at all stable."

"Oh, great, I can see the headlines now: 'Seven super people who lose control and annihilate a whole town'."

"Really? Super people?" Justin suddenly looked at me questionably. "Wait! Who's the seventh?"

"Um..."

"You said seven."

I decided not to utter a sound and let him read my mind - willingly for once.

"Who invited Tyler?"

"Marc did and it's a good thing he did. He's part of our

family, Justin. We all grew up together. Besides, he's fun to be with."

"If you want him along I don't have a problem, but he'd better keep his hands to himself the whole time we're there."

"Don't worry his hands will be quite busy, for two weeks." I said smiling, thinking of Tyler with the mystery girl.

"Good going, Tyler!" Justin exclaimed, happily.

"Oh, sure, now you love the guy. Two seconds ago you wanted to kill him."

"Two seconds ago I thought he was going to be all over you. Now I'm happy that he's found another victim." Justin said smiling "Enough about Tyler. Would you like me to tag along on your walk or would you like some time alone?"

"Why would I want to be alone if I could be with you, but don't you have things to do with Kyle?"

"With Kyle? No, nothing. I came here for you, to apologize for being so callous and beg for your forgiveness."

I nudged him in the ribs and said smiling, "I haven't seen any begging."

Justin lifted me up unexpectedly and twirled me around in dizzying circles. "I told you – you're just too easy on me."

~~~

Justin suggested walking around the grounds rather than go into town where we were sure to bump into familiar faces. I agreed completely, satisfied with the idea of having him all to myself on such a beautiful day. We followed the stream away from the house, letting it lead us in any direction it snaked through the woods.

Walking alongside him, I suddenly had the urge to ask him the one question I was dying to know the answer to, "When did you know?" I finally got up the courage to ask. "I mean, when did you realize that, well you know? That you liked me?"

His mouth curved into a cute, crooked smile. "I've always liked you."

"You're not going to make this easy, are you?"

"Nope," he said grinning, satisfied at my awkwardness, "If you want to know, you have to learn to ask directly. I have nothing to hide from you."

"Fine! When did you realize that – well you know – that you loved me?"

He leaned into me, playfully, "See, that wasn't so hard, now was it?"

"Well?" I insisted.

"Pushy, aren't you," he chuckled. I smiled. "To tell you the truth, Caitlin, you always did intrigue me. Even when you were really small, you seemed to pick me out of the crowd, insisting I play with you." He grinned and squeezed my hand, noticing my discomfort. "Why the face? You're the one who asked. I'll stop if you want."

Though I was beet red, I wanted him to continue. There was an ease about him – a level of maturity that I could only aspire to reach. "It's nothing, I promise you," I finally said, looking him in the eyes. "Please, go on."

His eyebrow arched slightly as he looked at me, but then continued on to say, "I'm over three or so years older than you, but at that small age three years is a huge difference. Growing up I knew there was something between us. We both felt it, didn't we?"

I nodded.

"I was obsessed with you, Caitlin and not in a good way."

I smiled. "You were obsessed with me?"

"Oh yeah," he said, leaning into me. "The longer I stayed away the more I wanted to be with you." Justin slowed his pace to a full stop and turned to face me. "The physical attraction was always there, you know that. It was beyond our control. The older I got the stronger it became. But love, well that came much, much later. When you were at Stone Hurst, I missed you. The agony of the separation was horrific, but I wouldn't go as far as to classify it as love. It was more of a crazed, unhealthy and compulsive need to be around you, but far from love."

My gaze dropped to the ground. "When, Justin? When did you really know then?"

He laughed awkwardly, his face crinkled up with amusement as he stroked my cheek. "Well, the night you returned to Oaks the burn was intense. I knew you were back. I was at the movies with Kyle and Emily. For some reason they weren't aware of your arrival, so I didn't mention anything in fear of ruining some kind of surprise Leslie might have prepared. We came home that night way past midnight. Kyle insisted on showing me the gift he bought for Sandy so we headed up to his room. The second we crossed your bedroom door, we knew you were inside. Kyle was so excited, but I – I was terrified. He decided to sneak in and get a peek at you. That's when I knew, Caitlin. I fought the feeling for so long, but the moment I saw your face and heard your breathing, I knew that I was madly – deeply in love."

Feeling a surge of love that made my eyes water, I reached up and kissed him softly. Justin tightened his embrace and buried his face in my hair. "Lord knows that I wanted nothing more than to hate you, Caitlin. I went home angry that night, angry because I blamed you for the sweet torture I had to endure – blamed you for leaving me behind."

Leaning into him as he held me I waited for the sadness to pass before I looked at him again. Remembering the second most difficult day of my life was not easy.

"My first morning back in Oaks and I had to deal with you," I said. "You were so mean and spiteful. I thought you hated me."

He apologized and kissed me again.

"Your turn, Caitlin. When did you know that you were crazy in love with me?"

I giggled. "Great choice of words," I laughed as I tried to collect my thoughts. "I did, at some point, think I was crazy – If that's what you meant. There was no other way to explain how I felt about you. It was completely out of my control."

His brow arched inquisitively. "That's not an answer. When did you know?"

"It was different for me, Justin. You were older, gorgeous and unattainable. What more does any girl need to start obsessing over any boy?"

Justin's grin widened. "You thought you had a crush on me?"

"Call it what you like. You were the reason for many, many tear-filled nights. When I was twelve I even picked out my wedding gown." I giggled at the memory.

His face suddenly lit up with satisfaction.

"Feeding your ego, am I?"

He nodded, smiling.

"I was looking through a bridal magazine at the dentist's, of all places, and secretly tore out the one I liked, stuffing it in my pocket to glue it later in my diary."

"So, you dreamt about getting married like the non-gifted?"

His face was suddenly expressionless – lost in thought, as if he were contemplating something – something very serious.

"Justin, you need to understand that half the girls, if not all, dreamt about marrying you. I bet if we took a poll you would see that at least eighty percent, if not more, of the female residents in Oaks have a wedding dress picked out because of you. The other twenty percent dreamt about Kyle or Marc."

"Thanks for thinking so highly of me. Your exaggeration is really flattering, but I don't care about the other girls in town, I only care about one in particular, and for some reason she is evading my question."

"What question would that be?" I asked, smiling at his brilliant face.

"Did you really want to be married to me?"

"I was twelve and in love – of course I wanted to be married to you."

"How about now?" he asked. His whole manner was way too serious, without even the slightest hint of humor in his voice. My mind suddenly went blank as I looked at him, waiting for the punch line – but nothing. Justin was sincere in his question.

I took a deep breath, trying to collect any fraction of brain I had left. "Marriage? Me...," I swallowed, "and you?"

"Yes! Me and You!" he insisted, "Have you considered it? At least thought about it?"

"Isn't it a bit premature to be discussing something that serious?" My heart started pounding against my chest. "It's not as simple as the non-gifted." My breathing hastened as my mind was grabbing for logical reasoning. "We don't just show up in church and vow everlasting love. I'm only eighteen. Just came back to Oaks. I'm just frazzled by everything. I know that you know absolutely what you want. You've always been totally together about stuff. It's...," I shrugged. "There's just so much more...."

His unexpected kiss put an abrupt stop to my ramblings. It was rather unclear whether the culprit of my light-headedness was the topic of marriage, or the fact that his lips were so damn titillating. Either way, I felt faint and ready to collapse.

"Woo, there," he said, slipping his arm around my waist, keeping me from falling back. "I'm not proposing, Caitlin." He chuckled. "So you can breathe, now."

"Oh," I exhaled, regaining my composure, feeling stupid at how I jumped to the wrong assumption, and how I kept rambling on and on about things I can't even remember. *What in the world made me think that Justin was proposing? What an idiot I am!*

"I'm just curious if you've ever thought about it," he added, "and if you would be willing to take that step."

I slowly raised my gaze to meet his. "Willing to take that step?" I fell quiet again. "Yeah, I guess I have thought about it, but not – not seriously. I mean – not any time soon." I stopped and waited for his reaction, but nothing. He stood there looking at me calm and collective. "Justin, we are already bound to one another, how would taking the Oath of Unity change anything?"

"For our kind, it changes everything, Caitlin."

I did not want to continue a discussion that I was not mentally ready to dig deeper into, so I advanced our stroll, taking him by the hand and said, "So, I told you my fantasy as a child. How about you? Did you ever fantasize about me?" He paused for a moment before he spoke. "I've done nothing but fantasize about you, but don't expect me to divulge any secrets. A gentleman never tells," he said smirking.

We both laughed knowing full well what his hormone crazed mind fantasized about.

The topic of marriage well behind us, we continued walking around. He kept our physical contact limited to holding hands and the occasional kiss. Justin was well aware of the Ellri's warning, even if he pretended not to care.

While Emily was still out shopping, Kyle and Justin retreated into the den with uncle Abbot talking about sports. My aunt and I were in the kitchen preparing snacks for everybody.

"I'm happy to see you and Justin together again," she said, slicing tomatoes.

"It was all a big misunderstanding. I seem to say one thing, but mean something else."

"Here...,"she said, handing me a loaf of homemade bread. "Cut it into thin slices." I followed directions as she continued to say, "We all find ourselves in those situations. The mature thing to do is to face up to it, apologize and move on. It does no good dwelling on the past. It takes away too much of our present, which, if you ask me, is priceless."

I shifted my gaze to her momentarily. "Justin said the same thing earlier. He was however referring to the future, but the connotation was all the same."

Placing a fresh leaf of lettuce and two slices of tomatoes on each slice of bread, my aunt added, "He's a wonderful young man, sweetie. You're very lucky to have him. Now, let's make these three with turkey and these with ham. What do you think?"

Finishing with the sandwiches I helped her put everything away and cleaned the counter.

"Aunt Leslie, can I ask you about our vacation?"

"Sure sweetie what would you like to know?"

"I don't care about the location. I'm sure anywhere would be great. What I'm concerned with is my gift. What if something triggers it and it's beyond my control? What do I do?"

"There's nothing to worry about," she said, patting me on the hand, "You've proven your self-control days ago. Besides, you're going on vacation. It's going to be fun, I promise. If anything does arise, Marc, Kyle and Justin are quite capable of getting any sort of situation under control."

"Okay, but don't blame me if something goes disastrously wrong. I have this knack for getting myself into exceptionally bad situations."

"I promise," she said smiling, "you'll be perfectly fine." She picked up the tray with the sandwiches and headed to the den, "I think it's time I told you guys where you'll be spending your two weeks – no reason to keep it from you any longer."

We both turned round as Emily barged into the foyer holding a couple of bags in her hands and another in her mouth, "Kyle! Justin! Get your butts out here and help," she yelled through clenched teeth, winking at me.

Kyle emerged followed by Justin. "What the hell is all the yelling about?" Kyle asked looking at her.

She lifted her bag laden hands, "There's more in the car! Why are you still standing around? Go and bring the rest from the car and carry it upstairs."

Kyle would have reacted differently to her domineering command, but lucky for her, she was already half-way up the staircase.

"Emily, before you start going through your purchases I'd like to see you all in the den in about fifteen minutes," said Aunt Leslie, rolling her eyes at her daughter's voracious need for material things. "Kyle, Justin, go get the rest of the things out of the car. I need to talk to all of you about your vacation. Marc and Tyler will be here momentarily – get going."

"What about Sandy" Kyle asked.

"She's not at home. She's out shopping with her sister," Aunt Leslie replied, knowing full well that Sandy was very important to her son and that she would never be left out of any family discussion from now on. "You can convey the news to her later. Now, please go and help your sister with the bags."

We all gathered in the den, much later than Aunt Leslie would have liked. Emily took forever to change into something more casual. We all scattered around the room.

Emily finally sat snuggled up against Marc in one of the leather sofas. Tyler came and sat next to me, so Justin had to sit across from us, next to Kyle.

"I'm sure you're all wondering where we have decided to send you for your winter break. You're all going to love the destination."

"You guys are going to have so much fun," Uncle Abbot added, unable to control his enthusiasm at our pending surprise.

"C'mon, tell us. Where is this place?" Emily asked impatiently.

Aunt Leslie took a look around at all our faces, prolonging the anticipation we all felt. "It's an island – a few hundred miles south of the Spanish Canary Islands," she blurted out waiting for our response.

"No, way! Are you serious? You guys are actually letting us go that far?" Kyle was apparently surprised by their decision, "What's the catch?" he asked suspiciously.

"There's no catch," answered Uncle Abbot, annoyed at his son's insinuation. "It's off the western coast of Africa. Undoubtedly, it's one of the world's most exclusive and completely private islands."

"How did all the Ellri come to find this Island?" Justin asked, as suspicious as Kyle.

"We just can't win with you kids, can we?" Uncle Abbot said, raising his hands in the air completely agitated by the boy's condescending response. "I expected you to be jumping up and down, happy to be going. Instead you're all looking at us skeptical. What's wrong with you guys? I thought this is what you wanted."

"Oh, sit down Abbot," Aunt Leslie muttered. "They have every reason to feel guarded," She sat down in the armchair next to my fuming uncle and started to explain, "The Isle of Indigo is privately owned by all our families for many generations now. Marc and Justin have already been there in the past, but they were too young to remember."

"The Isle of Indigo?" Marc asked. "I remember my parents talking about their adventures there.

I could not help but wonder, when she said the island was owned by all the families, did that include the Korbs as well.

"Yes, Caitlin, the Korbs are also part owners," Uncle Abbot said, answering my thoughts. "You needn't worry. The Korbs aren't expected on the island this time of year. Besides, this will give you all a chance to meet a few of your cousins."

They must be joking, I thought. *How could they possibly risk my running into a Korbs?* I looked over to Justin seeking his understanding. He was disturbingly silent, lost in thought, contemplating something. He raised his lowered gaze and looked at me

"Caitlin, if you don't feel comfortable about going we don't have to. I wouldn't want you to worry the whole time we're there," he said.

"Nonsense," said Aunt Leslie. "You're all going together, and that's that. We would never put her in harm's way, Justin. You should know that. What's more, not all the Korbs share her grandfather's ideals."

Uncle Abbot stood up and faced Justin, "Apart from the staff, the seven of you and a few others – twelve at the most, will be vacationing there. I give you my word, Justin. Caitlin will not be in any danger." Justin nodded in agreement. Uncle

Abbot never gave his word if he was not one-hundred percent sure. I took a deep breath and slumped back into the seat satisfied by his answer. "You should all know that it's unusually warm there this time of year, so pack light. You'll be having summer holidays in December."

All at once Emily stood up, beaming with happiness, hugging anyone she saw in front of her. Marc, of course, took advantage of the opportunity. It was not every day that he could exhibit so much affection in uncle Abbot's presence.

"Come on sweet-heart let the kids have their fun," said uncle Abbot, taking Leslie by the hand. He quietly led her outside the room closing the door behind them.

Justin hoisted me out of the sofa wrapping his arms around me. "You don't look too happy."

"I'm fine."

"You know, we don't have to go. It's our decision," he said, kissing me on the nose.

"No, I want to go. We're going to have fun. I can feel it," I smiled, trying to sound all positive and eager.

Emily placed her hand on Justin's arm and said, beaming a bright, beautiful smile, "Justin, you're going to die when you see what I've picked out for Caitlin to wear on our trip. I went all out this time."

Justin turned his attention to my cousin, "Caitlin, doesn't need your designer labels to look exceptional, Em. She's perfect in anything she wears."

I was blushing, turning all shades of red. Tyler rolled his eyes at me, feeling a bit uncomfortable by Justin's remark.

"You say that now, Justin, but wait till we get there."

Intrigued, Justin raised an eyebrow. "Well then, I'll just have to wait and see," he said smiling.

FIVE

HAPPILY SILENCED

THE LAST WEEK before winter break was unbelievably listless. Looking forward to our departure made each passing day seem endless. With one exam left I didn't have the luxury to accept Emily's invitation for dinner. She and Marc along with Kyle and Sandy went to a nice restaurant to celebrate our upcoming holiday. Justin stayed behind and helped me on Biology. He was quite meticulous at asking just the right questions without even opening my text book.

"Caitlin…" Justin said, pushing aside all the books, "your powers are blocking me from reading your thoughts from time to time? It's really irritating. The Ellri are having the same problem."

I looked at him smiling, happy beyond belief. "Are you sure? You discussed this with the Ellri?"

"I thought there was something wrong with me. I'm not used to silence when probing a mind"

"Finally…!" I exhaled smiling at him, "there's something I like about my gift."

Justin didn't look amused.

"So, what did the Ellri have to say?"

"They're not worried. They said it's just a phase your gift is going through. What they did want me to warn you about was that when you block us out we have no connection to you. We don't know where you are so keep close and don't wonder off."

"Why do I need to be so careful?" I asked confused. "Normal people all around the world live their lives without this connection, and they seem to be surviving just fine."

"We rely on this particular power, Caitlin. It keeps us all connected. You'll understand what I mean as soon as your ability to read surfaces, but until then – keep close."

I took advantage of his last words and crawled on all fours in his direction, like a tigress ready to pounce on her prey. "How close do you want me?" I asked, in a seductive voice, inches away from his luscious lips.

"Not this close if you know what's good for you," he said critically, pushing me back, not enjoying my joke.

Disappointed, I sat back on my feet and stared at him. He hadn't touched me in over two weeks, just the occasional kiss and the holding of hands. Justin went out of his way to avoid any physical contact.

"So is this how it's going to be between us? Distant?" I asked, standing up infuriated at his casualness.

Needing to vent my frustration I concentrated my powers on moving the books off the floor, slicing them through the air and piling them neatly on my desk. I walked around aimlessly tidying up, not wanting to deal with Justin just yet. I knew he was aware of how hurt I felt; still he sat there, on the floor following me with his gaze.

"Caitlin, stop!" He started to say. "This is ridiculous. I'm simply not in a playful mood," he added standing up. "It has nothing to do with you."

"I don't believe you," I replied accusingly. "This has

everything to do with me – with us, for that matter."

"This is insane. I refuse to get caught up in this. I'm just tired that's all."

Justin wasn't in any mood to argue and neither was I. Pressing the topic would have incited a meaningless argument. We had two days until our departure and I wasn't about to ruin it by fighting with him.

"Okay, fine, you're right. I'm making a big deal out of nothing. Let's just get something to eat, shall we?" I said conceding defeat, temporarily.

~~~

Bright and early the next morning Mr. Patterson was as happy to be administering my last exam as I was to be sitting it. It only took an hour and fifteen minutes for me to fill out the answer sheet. I noticed that the questions on the exam were exactly the same as the ones Justin drilled me on the night before.

"Caitlin…," Mr. Patterson said, looking over my answer sheet to make sure I didn't forget to answer any questions, "everything is as should be," he added stuffing all his belongings in his briefcase, looking around to see if he had left anything behind. "Enjoy your two weeks off. I guess we'll talk after you get back about your schedule and tutoring."

"Of course, Mr. Patterson, I hope you have a nice holiday as well," I said, leading him to the door. Closing the door behind him I felt relieved to have finished with my exams. "Free at last," I said out loud running to my room overjoyed.

I wanted to call Tyler to see how he did on Biology, but I knew he was still in school. He wouldn't have finished yet. It was way too early in the morning. Calling Justin would have been my other choice, but the way he left last night kept me from ringing him up. Even though we talked all through dinner he seemed distant, somehow.

Ever since that morning, at his house, he hadn't been himself. Although we talked about it, supposedly resolved our differences, even agreed to do things our way, he still seemed reserved. I decided to brush those feelings aside and look forward to our trip. I had a ton of things to do. I hadn't even packed.

I stopped in on Emily to see what she was doing. Two suitcases lay on the bed, heaped in clothes. "You're not taking all that are you?" I asked, entering her room.

"It's not all for me. This one," she said, pointing to one of the two suitcases, "is yours. I wasn't going to have you stuff these beautiful garments in your duffle bag."

"All this is new? You bought all this for me?"

"Yes I did. Now go and get all your personal things together and bring them here so I can close this thing up."

"Em, what did you buy me?" I said, wanting to look through the suitcase.

She suddenly smacked my outstretched hand "Oh, no you don't. I'm not going to allow you to see anything. You'll just start complaining and ruin this for me."

"Just a peek? Please Em?"

"No! Absolutely not! Now go do what I said!"

The seven of us had planned a lunch date in town to iron out the details of our departure. Seven in the morning a car was scheduled to pick us up at Tyler's house and drive us to the airport. Emily wasn't exactly thrilled about waking up so early, but she knew she had no choice in the matter. Justin, on the other hand, sat at the table hardly participating in the conversation. He just observed and moved his head in agreement now and then. He was reasonably distracted by his thoughts, not really paying much attention to any of us. On several occasions he unexpectedly kissed me not saying a word.

I wanted to know why he was acting the way he was, but I had decided to let things be and wait till whatever he was going through to blow over. I was certain that our trip would improve his otherwise dark mood.

Leaving Justin to his thoughts I concentrated on my conversation with Tyler, and compared notes on our exams. He obviously did quite well. Justin listened in on our conversation expressionless.

During the whole ride home Justin didn't say a word; he simply turned on the radio and ignored me the entire distance.

"Did I do something wrong?" I finally asked, severing the earsplitting silence. "Why are you like this?"

"I'm fine," he answered, looking straight ahead, avoiding eye contact.

I breathed deep, shaking my head at his reluctance to speak. "If I did something wrong I need to know," I told him, grabbing at straws trying to figure out why the change in mood.

Surprisingly, he pulled over to the side of the road and turned off the engine. We were only minutes from the house so his maneuver disturbed me. Justin sat back combing his fingers tensely through his hair.

"Caitlin, you did nothing wrong. Why would you even think that?" he finally said turning to look at me.

"When's the last time you talked to me? I mean, really talked to me Justin? Or the last time you touched me, and I don't mean the friendly kisses or the hand holding."

He just stared into nothingness. Even now, only inches away he was able to shut me out.

"You know what, Justin? Just take me home," I finally said, hating him for making me feel so insignificant.

He reached for my hand. "Please, don't be like that."

I quickly pulled away. "Are you going to tell me what's wrong?"

"You need to give me some time. It has nothing to do with how I feel about you – you must know that."

"Your actions speak otherwise," I said curtly. "What am I supposed to think?"

He pushed his head back against the head rest. "Nothing's changed between us, Caitlin. I'm just having a few bad days – that's all. Don't make more out of it than it is."

"It's more than that and you know it. You promised that you won't keep secrets from me!" I yelled.

Justin's ability to keep his composer irritated me. I was beside myself and he simply sat there calm and unfazed by the whole conversation.

"Please, just take me home," I repeated, desperately wanting to get home before I started crying in front of him again.

For a space of time we sat in silence, before he spoke again. "A few days ago I had a vision of you leaving," he blurted out, shutting his eyes. "It was too real, Caitlin – too damn real."

"What do you mean – I left?" I asked with unrestrained terror, fearing that what he saw was the choice I would be forced to make. I started to smile as my eyes filled with tears. "That's just silly, Justin. Why would I ever leave you?"

"I don't know." His voice was shredded and frail. "You simply disappeared without a trace."

"That's what this is all about? You had a dream that I left you and that's why you've been shutting me out? You've been acting like this over a stupid dream?"

"It wasn't a dream, Caitlin. Somebody showed me versions of the future. It wasn't my mind that conjured up the images. Somebody more powerful was reaching out, trying to tell me something."

"You said versions of the future – plural. What else did you see?"

"I saw that you were happy somewhere far from Oaks, away from me. The vision was too real. You were smiling and laughing, dancing, playing around. You looked so beautiful and calm, away from all this craziness." Justin swallowed hard, rubbing his forehead in an attempt to erase the image from his mind. "Seeing you enjoy your life without me has been tearing me to pieces, Caitlin. I should be happy with this version of your future, but instead it's killing me. I know I'm selfish wanting you here with me, but there's nothing I can do. I can't stand the thought of you leaving again."

I stroked the side of his face with my fingers, pulling him towards me. I didn't make any promises I couldn't keep, nor did I try to conceal my own fears. Craving his touch, I kissed him on the lips. He responded willingly to my assault pushing me against the soft leather seat, kissing me fervently. He let out a little groan of satisfaction and just as quickly backed away, banging his fist against the steering wheel.

I needed for him to know that I wasn't going anywhere anytime soon so I said, "Aren't you the one who explained the ripple effect? No one knows the future and whoever is projecting these images obviously doesn't know either. It sounds to me like they're calculatingly selecting versions of the future aimed to hurt you."

Seeming to let it go for the moment, he said, "You might be right."

"You tell whoever it is that's messing with your head to come and visit me in my dreams," I said, recalling how spooked my shadows looked when they saw my scar. "I'll give him a taste of my own version of the future."

Justin's sad expression was suddenly gone – he started

laughing and said, "Easy killer, does nothing ever faze you?"

"Justin, the only thing I'm one-hundred percent sure of is that neither my faceless shadows nor your mystery demon have any idea about our bond."

Even though Justin didn't speak at that moment, I saw the flicker of recognition in his eyes. He seemed to realize that what I said was true – that somehow all this was connected.

"You have a point," he said, beaming with satisfaction. "They can't possibly know of our bond because if they did they'd know how dangerous it would be for us to be apart." For the first time in more than a week I saw him genuinely smile. "Caitlin, if the Korbs – or anybody for that matter, wants you that bad that they would go to so much trouble to mess with our heads...," he inhaled deeply, punching the steering wheel, "They'll take you over my dead body."

Unexpectedly, my scar started throbbing again. He looked at my horrified expression and followed my gaze to my wrist.

"Did I provoke that?" he asked concerned.

"I don't think so. It's different this time. It's like my power is in a state to protect you – feel...," I said, stretching out my wrist. "I won't hurt you. I'm sure of it. It's not like the other times, Justin."

He was hesitant at first. "I don't care what happens to me, Caitlin, it's you I'm worried about. My power is as potent as yours in defending me. "

"I know, but I promise, it's different. There's not an ounce of negativity flowing in my veins, Justin. It's triggered to protect somebody other than me." I reached for his hand. "Do you trust me?"

"This is too dangerous, Caitlin, I won't risk hurting you."

"You won't. I'm telling you it's different." I instantly grabbed his hand not giving him time to think.

My whole body reacted as soon as my skin touched his; a tingling sensation ran down my arm and to my fingers.

"I can feel it," Justin said, surprised. "It's quite powerful, it's amazing. Wow! I can feel it going up my spine. It's weird, but in a good way. I feel stronger."

"See, I told you it's different."

"How...? Why...?" he asked sounding lost in a drug-induced haze.

"I have absolutely no control of what it's doing. The only thing I do know is that I have this irrepressible need to protect you."

Justin suddenly closed his eyes and relaxed his body against the seat. "I can read your thoughts again," he said, smiling, "Your gift is quite remarkable. You're transferring your power to me, not all – just enough to boost my own."

"Um, Justin...," I said, feeling light-headed, instantly letting go of his hand. The throbbing subsided. "I....."

"Are you okay?"

Summoning a wavering smile, I said, "Yeah, a bit drained, but nothing serious. Are you okay?"

"Okay...? I'm more than okay, I'm great! The second you let go it was like you turned off the switch. Now I know why the Ellri have us on a short leash. Your gift is raw. I take everything I said back. We do need to be careful. It reacts purely to your emotions."

I leaned my head back. "Oh, great! You're never going to touch me again."

He grinned and said devilishly, "I wouldn't put my money on that if I were you."

Between us

Illustrated for Lines That Bind - Within The Whispers

SIX

THE ISLE

I T WAS NOT UNTIL we arrived at the airport that I became fully aware of how skillfully controlled our whole trip would be. We did not follow suit with the hundreds of other, soon-to-be passengers, but were instead led down a long corridor which was strictly reserved for airport personnel.

In a cloud of excitement and anticipation we followed Mike, the airport attendant, through the tightly secured area. "This is as far as I go," he said, beaming a generic smile. "Becky will guide you the rest of the way."

The attendant swiped his security pass through the slot and instantly the double doors separating us from the tarmac slowly opened. "Have a great trip," he told us emphatically and pointed us in the right direction.

Not more than a few yards away, we caught sight of the aircraft assigned to take us to the Isle. Emily let out a squeal of excitement. I would have done the same, but was far too flabbergasted at the sight of the slick, private Jet being prepped to take us to our destination.

The flight was surprisingly relaxing, considering it was my

first time on an airplane. It did, however, take me quite some time to get over my nerves and adapt to our luxurious surroundings.

Kyle, of course, was our inflight entertainment, keeping the long flight upbeat. For most of the trip he narrated accounts of hilarious situations where Marc and Justin were the key figures. Having grown up together, the three best friends had quite an array of comical situations, most of which Kyle was the root of all their mischief. He recalled several occasions when uncle Abbot had reprimanded him on 'inappropriate' behavior. That of course, didn't thwart him one bit.

Several hours later and what little sleep I did get, we landed on safe ground. The landing was smooth, but that didn't keep me from clutching onto my seat for dear life, never happier to touch down on land.

A gentleman, roughly in his fifties, met us at the entrance. "Welcome, to Grand Canary," he said, in a deep Spanish accent. He was standing there, in the middle of the bustling airport, barefoot without a care in the world. His linen trousers were folded up to mid-calf, looking all the more out of place.

"I'm Alejandro, Alexander or Alex, whichever you prefer." He beamed a welcoming smile. "I'm the grounds keeper of your island," he continued to say with his pleasant smile. "It's nice to see the next generation come to visit."

In awkward silence, we all stood there as he scratched the top of his messy grey hair for some sort of clarity. His gaze kept moving from Marc to Justin and then back again.

"Is something wrong?" Justin asked, drawing Alexander's full attention.

"Wrong? No, nothing's wrong," he said, momentarily looking in my direction for the very first time, but quickly circled his head back to Marc and Justin. "I know your faces," he said, looking first at Marc. "Your Claudius' boy – no?"

Marc nodded.

"The resemblance is truly remarkable. I remember you this small," he said, stretching out his hand to only a few feet off the ground, "and you – you must be William's son, Justin. I can't believe how much you both have grown."

Alexander seemed to know our families quiet well. *But how well*, I wondered.

"I'm sure you're all really tired, but unfortunately, you have a few more hours to go before we reach the island," he said, surveying our luggage. "Let's take care of your bags first, shall we?"

He stopped, looked back over his shoulder and waved his hand to the three young men standing a few feet away, bellowing out orders in Spanish. They quickly bounced into action and collected all our things, piling them one on top of the other in a jeep parked right up front.

"This way," Alexander said, leading us a few yards farther. He suddenly stopped and slapped his forehead in forgetfulness. "One of you needs to ride with the luggage," he said, "I can only take six."

"I'll go," volunteered Tyler not wanting to split up any of the couples. He dashed off talking in Spanish to the young men; assisting them with the bags.

"He's a Falcone – no?" Alexander asked, turning to Marc.

"Yes, we're first cousins."

"Whose is he? Dominick's, Marcellus'?"

"Marcellus'"

"Ah, that would explain the good looks. That Aurelia is some woman," Alexander said, attributing Tyler's handsome features to his mother's beauty. I personally thought he took after his father's rugged Italian good looks.

"Come on, get in, we need to leave for the port," he called out, holding open the car door.

Tyler was already at the pier, waiting for us. Apparently his new found Spanish speaking friends were quite fond of the gas pedal as was he. Just then, I noticed that they were loading our cargo onto a racy, streamline motor-yacht. I turned to the boys only to see their expressionless faces, staring at the sea bearing beauty. Alexander held the car door open as we exited the vehicle, smiling at our astonished expressions. "She's a beauty – no?"

We all bobbed our heads with our mouths gaping.

He chuckled. "The Korbs decided to upgrade our transport a couple of years ago. I was sad to see the old one go." Alexander continued to say, leading us up the pier. "But this...," he said, pointing to the epicurean, three-decker yacht, "I fell in love with The Eileen at first sight – all fifty-five meters of her."

My breath caught in my throat at the sound of the name. *Did he say Eileen?* I impulsively turned and stared at Justin. I couldn't get my mind around the name. I hoped it was all just a coincidence, but deep down I knew otherwise. They all turned and stared at me not knowing how to react to my expression. Justin squeezed my hand, aware of how I felt.

"It's only a boat," he whispered in my ear, giving me a quick peck on the head. "You'll be fine."

I nodded unsure of how fine I really was. A stream of icy water seemed to be running through me tightening up my throat and heart. Emily let go of Marc's hand and encircled her arm around my shoulder. "It means absolutely nothing, Caitlin. Justin's right – you'll be fine."

But the pleasure of being there was suddenly mixed with fear because, although I wanted to believe Justin and Emily, everything I had ever learned about the Korbs told me that they should be feared and hated. The fact that I had to board the vessel sat like a stone in my gut.

"Alexander?" I said, turning to our guide.

At first I wasn't sure he heard me, but the second he finished giving orders to his crew he shifted his gaze to me – his face lit up. "Call me Alex," he said smiling.

"Okay, Alex. I'm Caitlin by the way,"

"A beautiful name for a beautiful girl," he said winking at me.

My eyes cast down with girlish modesty. He was a charmer this one. I smiled awkwardly and asked, "Who owns this vessel?"

"That would be the High Ellri, Clancy Korbs. He bought it for his beautiful wife, Ms. Eileen on their last visit here – a few years before their passing," he answered, leading us on deck. "Do you know them?"

Emily's hold tightened around my shoulders knowing full well how awkward I felt at the sound of my grandparent's names. "Only by name," I didn't lie. "I've never actually had the chance to meet them."

"Oh, that's too bad," he said, beaming a genuinely bright smile, showing us on board. "You would've liked them. Ms. Eileen was truly one of a kind. And Clancy, well, let's just say he was some character." Alex turned to the crew once again and gave them further instructions. "You'll have to excuse me, we really need to get going," he said, heading for the helm.

Kyle and Tyler, visibly smitten with the vessel, followed Alexander to the upper deck. The others, needing to change into something more comfortable, followed the three young deck hands to the staterooms of the lower deck. "Aren't you coming?" Justin asked, seeing that I lagged behind.

"No, I think I'll stay up here for now."

He took my backpack from my shoulder. "Are you sure?"

"I'm sure – now go."

Justin reluctantly went below, giving me time to get my emotions in check. I headed to the second set of steps which led to the sun deck on the roof of the upper deck. Alone and exhausted from the trip, I sat on the smooth teak deck, hugging my knees, taking in the rays, enjoying the refreshing ocean air against my tired face.

The stillness was short lived as the sound of a flurry of activity from the lower deck became rather distracting. Then I felt and heard the roar of the engines catch the yacht, felt it slip away from the dock. Minutes later we were off, on our way at last. The vessel rhythmically undulated across the surface of the brilliant blue waters, lifting my spirit.

So this is how the other half lived? I thought. I knew the families were well off, but I just came to realize how well off they really were.

"Aren't you going to change into your bathing suit?" Sandy asked, spreading her towel next to me. She had already changed into a bikini, ready to soak up the sun.

"I'm fine. I'll just wait to get to the island."

"Alex said it'll take a while. You should change."

Picking up her sunscreen, I dabbed a little on my face and arms. "I'll be fine, really."

Emily appeared a few minutes later sporting a gold, miniscule bikini. "Why aren't you in your suit?" she asked as she spread her towel beside me.

I didn't answer. I simply turned my head to the sun and let the rays do their job on my pale white skin.

An hour into our trip I felt awkward sitting between Emily and Sandy. Being stuck between two bikini clad women who could easily pose for magazine covers was rather intimidating.

I spared myself the comparison and headed towards the stern.

Leaning against the rail, I looked down into the blue water rushing past, watched the wake of the water trail behind us, clearly marking our passing. No matter how hard I tried to hide it, the nagging sensation that something terrible would happen lingered deep down. I couldn't seem to brush it off and being on this side of the Atlantic was feeding my anxiety.

A cloud of hair spilled over my shoulder as I bowed my head in sudden thought. *I'm on my grandfather's yacht.*

A hand touched my elbow. I jumped, surprised, and turned to see Justin standing right behind me. I was so lost in my thoughts that I didn't feel him approaching. *That's a first,* I thought, turning to face him.

He had changed into something lighter. The soft hue of his linen shirt accentuated his features even more. *How does he get better looking every time I see him?* I wondered, pushing my windswept hair behind my ear and continued to stare. *Would he ever have been interested in me if we weren't connected by the bond?* I suddenly thought.

He suddenly appeared troubled – seemed even more worried than I was. "What are you doing standing out here alone?" he asked, joining me on the rail.

My hair blew in the wind; I pushed it back when it fell in my face. "Emily and Sandy are sunbathing up front," I said smiling. "I just needed some time alone."

Justin took me by the waist and pulled me close. "Do you still want to be alone?" he kissed me lightly on the lips, teasing me.

The warmth of his lips was soothing. "I still can't believe that a few hours ago we were in Oaks and now...."

Justin's gaze narrowed, his beautiful blue eyes looked intently into mine. "Caitlin, I don't want you to worry about anything. This whole Korbs situation has really messed with your head."

"I'm not worried," I reassured him. "Just the sound of my grandparent's name threw me off a little. I'll be fine, trust me." I gave him a quick peck on the lips. "We're on vacation together, that's all that matters – the present remember?"

Justin raised his brow questionably. Ignoring his doubtful expression, I leaned against the railing, and looked into the bright sky. For once, the fog that swept across my mind dissipated. The slap of waves against the hull filled the air around me. Justin must have sensed my mood, for he said nothing, just watched the deep blue water as the yacht knifed through it.

"If you had accepted my proposal, this could've easily been our honeymoon," Justin told me, long moments later.

"First of all, it wasn't a proposal, remember?" I said, leaning playfully into him. "And secondly…." I laughed as he tickled my side. "Secondly…," I repeated, turning to face him, "great honeymoon we would have. No touching. No kissing. No – well you know," I said giggling.

His husky laugh filled my mind with joy. "I see your point. Somebody up there must really have it in for us," he added, kissing me. At that moment, Alexander approached and leaned against the rail eating sunflower seeds. "You want some?" he offered, opening his full hand.

I took a small step back to distance myself from Justin. "No thanks," I said, shaking my head. "If you're here Alex. Who's steering this thing?"

"Kyle is."

"Kyle? Oh great, we're dead," I muttered.

Both men started laughing. "Don't worry, Kyle is quite skilled. We couldn't be in better hands," reassured Justin.

Our host nodded his head in utter agreement. There was something about Alexander, something deviating from the usual. Alexander stood there, with his long sleeve linen shirt roughly folded up his arm, smiling at the both of us visibly enjoying our company. He turned and leaned against the rail, eating his sunflower seeds. "You both seem to like each other," he said, spitting out the husk.

"You can say that," Justin answered, kissing me on the head.

Alexander straightened out his posture "You're both good kids, I can tell." He took a step closer and patted my cheek and smiled. It wasn't a happy smile, but one that concealed his true emotions. "You'll make this work," he added, dropping his hand to his side. His whole manner shifted, somehow. "It was a good match, I must say," he muttered to himself as he casually headed back to take the wheel.

I turned to look at Justin, shrugging my shoulders, unsure what that was all about.

"He's a good man," Justin said. "I really like him."

"Yeah me too, but there's something about him."

"Whatever it is, it's all good," Justin reassured me.

We hung out for a while, enjoying the view from that side of the yacht. Everybody else was on the sun deck sunbathing when, without warning a thick fog descended upon us, a chilling quiet encircled us and had stayed with us for quite some time.

No matter what the Ellri said about there being no magic, this thick mist had the feel of unearthly influences about it.

Justin's arms clasped tight around my waist reassuring me that everything was going to be all right. Then all thoughts of mist and the supernatural were driven from my mind as Justin looked back over his shoulder. "What is it?" I asked.

"Kyle wants us."

I turned to look over his shoulder, but was barely able to make Kyle out through the fog. He was saying something over the thrashing of the jets, motioning for us to join him.

The roar of the engines suddenly softened and I could finally hear what Kyle was saying. "Justin, Caitlin, get your butts up here. You've got to see this," he yelled.

We quickly joined the rest of the group. As I looked, the mist parted, and we all stood in awe at what we saw looming in the distance. It was then that I realized where the island got its name.

The crystal clear, blue-violet waters were enticing enough to drink with a straw. It was an unspoiled castaway island with bone-white beaches that stretched as far as the eye could see, lush in vegetation and a seemingly brilliant rough terrain. Even at this depth the ocean floor was visible to the nagged eye.

"Here we are, home away from home," Alexander yelled, over the roar of the engines, maneuvering the vessel to dock. "Welcome, to the Isle of Indigo," he added. "Follow the boys to the main house. I'll be with you in a minute."

We were led up a winding footpath through a small forest to

a large complex, situated on top of a hill. The wide open French doors which lined the side of the building caused the light material of the draping curtains to flap in the light breeze.

The inside was tastefully decorated where the warm colors and the variety of woods set the atmosphere. The main feature was the seating area around the circular fireplace – where every angle of the lounge had a breathtaking, ocean view. It was hard to believe that anybody was lucky enough to actually live like this all year round. It did, however, explain Alexander's vivacious personality. Who wouldn't be happy living here?

"Life is not all sand and surf, Caitlin!"

The familiar voice pierced my thoughts. I quickly circled my head to the sound of her voice. I hadn't expected to ever see her again, to thank her for everything she had done, for being there when I had no one in my life.

"Ms. Leedey!" I screamed, excitedly running into her out-stretched arms, "What in the world are you doing here?"

"I was on the Ivory Coast and heard you were going to be here. I just couldn't stay away and please, Caity, call me Ava. Now, let me look at you," she said, pulling back to check me up and down

"It's only been two months, nothing's changed," I said, teary eyed, ecstatic to see her.

Her gaze fell on Justin. "I'll say something's changed," she scoffed, winking at me.

Justin's grin widened satisfied with Ava's statement.

"Great Auntie Ava," Kyle and Emily said in unison, walking over to greet her.

"We didn't know you were going to be here?" Emily said, hugging her.

"I only got here yesterday, but don't worry, you won't even know I'm here," she said, turning to the rest of the group and introduced herself as our great-aunt. "Their grandfather, Cecil, is my brother," she told them, clearing up our family tree.

Silence hung after the round of quick introductions.

"Well, I hope you all enjoy your stay on our island. It's been a home to all our families throughout the ages," Ava said, trying to break the ice. "Even though most of the islands around here have been pillaged by pirates not once has anyone set foot on this land that wasn't welcomed?"

Alexander came in moments later, lugging some of our belongings. "Ava, you've met the kids," he told her, allowing Justin to help him with some of our bags.

Ava placed her hands on my shoulders. "Alex, this is Caitlin," she told him, "Carolyn and Winston's daughter."

The lines on his face quickly softened. "So you're the young Eileen?"

I didn't answer. How could I? I didn't quite come to terms with my full name just yet.

"Yes she is, Alex, but we call her Caitlin."

"Oh, does the name mean anything in your tongue, Ava?"

Her eyebrow rose questionably. "Yes, it actually does. It's derived from the Celts meaning 'pure' or 'purity'."

He turned and faced me. "Great name," he said smiling.

Moments of awkward silence were quickly severed by Ava's orders. "Alex, show the kids where they'll be staying. They must be exhausted.

He nodded dutifully and headed to the open door. "This way," he said.

I didn't want to let go of Ava just yet. I felt much safer that she was there with me. "How long are you staying?" I asked her.

"As long as you want me to," she winked, realizing how I felt.

"Good," I sighed in relief.

Everybody was already standing by the door, waiting for Justin and me to join them.

Ava turned to Alexander and said, "I'll show Justin and Caitlin where they'll be staying. You take the others to their rooms."

Tyler rolled his eyes at me, but being the good sport; he kept quiet and followed the peculiar man down the footpath which led to the private bungalows.

"Now, you two will be staying here, in the main house. I'm not one to keep young love apart, but knowing your history it'd be best if you didn't share a suite."

I hadn't even thought about our sleeping arrangements up until then. Justin didn't say a word, he just nodded in agreement. I wasn't sure if that's what he had in mind when we started out on this trip. Did he even think about how we would spend our nights?

"The main house is as secluded as the bungalows, so you'll still have your privacy." she smiled, stroking my cheek. "There's plenty more things to do here, for both of you to occupy your time. The bungalows aim to cater to couples if you catch my drift," she said smiling, "Nobody will bother you here, I promise. It's just more open space. It'll give you more room to breathe. Look, you can even play Ping-Pong."

Ava was obviously aware of our situation, of course she would be, she was an Ellri, after all.

"Where will you be staying?" Justin asked not wanting to impose.

"My cottage is on the other side of the island. A twenty-minute walk through the forest. Each family has their own accommodations. We added the bungalows about twenty years ago to accommodate the younger generation who wanted to vacation separately from their family. This building, the main house, belongs to the Korbs. It was the first structure to be built on the island, centuries ago." She stopped, her eyes widened with thought. "What was I thinking?" she said, putting her hand to her head. "Justin, if you'd prefer to stay at the Bradford cottage on the southern point of the island, I could ask Alex to get it ready for you. It's been closed up for a few years because mostly everybody prefers this part of the island, so when your relatives do come here they stay in one of the other homes."

"Ava, thanks, but there's really no need. We'll be perfectly fine here."

"Well, then…," she said, giving me one last hug. "Let me get out of your way. And you young man, take good care of her."

"I'll do my best," Justin beamed.

Ava left soon after, leaving us in the spacious house all alone. Seeing her disappear from view incited a barrage of questions.

"Do you think it's a coincidence that she's here?" I asked Justin.

He picked up my backpack and threw it over his shoulder. "I was asking myself the same question. An Ellri just happens to be island hopping on our two weeks here? Coincidence, I think not!"

"I don't know what it is, but this feeling I have doesn't seem to fade."

His expression darkened "Nothing's going to happen! I won't let anything happen to you. Get that through your head. Now let's go upstairs and get settled in."

We opened the first double doors that we came across. "This looks perfect," he said, standing in front of the twelve foot high bay window that covered half of the room. It was like being in a glass cage with a magnificent, eagles-eye, ocean view.

"So, where are you going to sleep?" I asked taking dibs on the room.

"Right next to you."

"You haven't even seen the room next door. How are you so positive that you'll like it?"

"I didn't mean next door to you. I meant next to you – on the bed"

My cheeks flushed with embarrassment. I didn't know why. It wasn't the first time we shared a bed. "Oh, what about what Ava said?"

"Caitlin, do you really think keeping us in separate rooms will make me want you less. Or do you think Ping-Pong would distract me from desiring your touch or the feel of your skin?"

My face couldn't get any redder. "We'll play it by ear," I answered, smiling at his crocked little smile. "If at any point we get out of hand you're going next door!"

Justin traversed the length of the room to a door on the right-hand corner. It connected to the next room. "You see, easy access," he said laughing. "Do you want to take a stroll down the beach before dinner?"

"Yeah, that sounds great. Let me wash up first and see what Emily has packed for me."

"You mean you don't know what she bought you?"

"I haven't the foggiest. She refused to let me see."

Justin placed my suitcase on the bed opening it to reveal the colorful assortment of fabrics. He pulled out the bag with all my essentials and pushed me towards the bathroom. "You wash up and I'll unpack," he said, devilishly smiling, wanting to see what the fuss was all about with these clothes.

I needed to freshen up badly, so I didn't complain. Having somebody unpack for me was perfectly fine.

Cut Too Deep

Illustrated for Lines That Bind - Within The Whispers

SEVEN

GLASS CAGE

FTER LUXURIATING under the warm shower, I wrapped the towel tightly around my body, hating myself for not taking a change of clothes in the bathroom with me. I cracked the door open to see if the coast was clear. Thankfully, Justin was nowhere in sight.

He apparently had hand-picked some clothes for me to wear. I instantly blushed at his choices. I picked up the light beige tunic. It wasn't exactly sheer, but you could easily make out what someone wore underneath. A chocolate-brown bikini was the other piece spread across the cotton bedding. I started giggling at the thought of him picking this out from the suitcase. Even though I was rather self-conscious about wearing a bathing suit around Justin, I knew he was testing to see if I would wear something so revealing.

Two can play at this game, I thought.

I tore off the towel and slipped into the two-piece. I refused to look in the mirror in fear of chickening out. It left absolutely nothing to the imagination. I pulled the tunic over my head, feeling partially covered up.

The material came up mid-thigh, covering much less than I would have liked.

We're at the beach! I kept telling myself. I breathed in deep, combed my hair hastily, pinned it up again with my butterfly hairpin and let it dry naturally.

As I headed downstairs, I heard Tyler and Justin talking about cars. One last deep breath to gather my wits and I headed to the lounge. Both men stopped dead as soon as I entered the room. I could tell Tyler was happy with what he saw. He was always easy to read, but Justin – he was another story.

"Let me look at you," Tyler said, grabbing my hand and turning me around in circles "Damn, you're perfect!" he exclaimed. "You know what, Caitlin? I don't want to be friends anymore, not if you're going to look like that."

"Shut up!" I said, smacking his arm. "Do I look okay?" I whispered, knowing he'd never lie to me.

"Do you look okay? Are you blind woman? I can't even think straight having you stand there looking like that."

I shifted my gaze towards Justin; his eyes were fixed on me. I didn't expect him to be so serious. I honestly thought that he would laugh at my discomfort.

"Justin and I are going for a walk, what are you doing?" I asked Tyler, purposely not inviting him along.

He smiled knowing full well what I meant. "We're all going to be at the pool, so after your walk just meet us there."

"Sure, that sounds great," I said, watching him head for the door.

Tyler momentarily stopped and patted Justin on the shoulder. "What I wouldn't give to be in your shoes, man."

As soon as my best friend left I turned to Justin. "Are you ready?"

He swallowed hard. "Ping-Pong sounds really good right

now," he confessed, making me laugh at his funny remark, remembering his earlier comment.

I took his hand and lead us down the same path we came. The sand was amazingly soft; the warm air soothed my nerves.

"Is there any other place in the world this beautiful?" I asked, stopping Justin in mid-stride. He was too thoughtful for my liking. "What's the problem? Do you want to go back inside?"

His hand went around my back and pulled me impatiently into his arms. Not saying a word, he kissed me softly.

Hungry for his touch, I pushed myself on tip toe to reach him easily, stretching my arms around his neck. Justin tightening his hold, lifting me against his toned body, trailing kisses down my neck. He groaned softly and slowly let go, backing inches away. "You're going to be the end of me," he said smiling, kissing me again on the lips, leaving one hand on the small of my back.

"Not if I can help it," I responded, pulling him closer, needing him.

He closed his eyes and touched his forehead to mine. "Caitlin, this is the worst kind of torture. We're here in paradise and you're my forbidden fruit."

I laughed. "From what I know of that story...," I giggled, "Adam survived well into old age."

"The proverbial apple was surely not as mouth-watering and beautiful as you."

I gave him a quick kiss and said, "Justin, my wrist didn't respond just now, not at all. Other times, as soon as you touch me, I feel the surge growing, but just now – nothing."

"You're simply getting stronger, gaining more control. Don't think I'm going to test your limits, if that's what your diabolical mind is considering. Not that I wouldn't want to," he said, looking me up and down. "You're making it very hard to focus on anything else."

I took his face in my hands and guided his gaze back to eye level. "Listen to me – and will you please stop gawking at me like that."

"How do you want me to look at you," his voice exultant, and leaned down to kiss me. "I'm trying real hard here, Caitlin. It's a good thing you can't read my thoughts. You'd be shocked at the things I'm thinking."

I tried to swallow the lump in my throat "Is that what you're thinking about? About us being together – together" I asked.

"Every minute of every day and seeing you like this...." Justin shook his head vigorously. "Even poor Tyler is having a hard time getting you out of his mind. Although I must say he is quite the gentleman. His thoughts were nowhere as foul as mine are. It was the only thing that kept me from hurting him back at the house."

"You're impossible," I laughed

He pulled me back into his embrace, running possessive hands down my body. "And you're simply perfect."

"Yeah, okay. Now, please, concentrate!" I said, pushing him away, smiling at his pleading expression. "Please, listen. I think that the reason my power hasn't reacted has something to do with the other day in the car."

I finally had his undivided attention. "What are you saying? What about the other day in the car?"

"What if...," I continued to explain, "When I passed my power to you it neutralized it?"

Justin looked at me and said, "There's only one way to test your hypothesis."

I knew I wanted him for so long, but I never thought my being with Justin would be the result of an experiment.

"Now? You want to test it now?" I asked, completely mortified at the thought of Justin and me together, together.

"Get your mind out of the gutter, young lady," he told me, sounding annoyed at my presumption. "Do you really think I meant that?"

"Then, what?"

"This," he said. With one swift move, Justin shoved me hard, causing me to lose my balance and fall hard against the sand. Instantly, my gift ignited, inciting an onslaught of rage. My scar started to throb against my pale skin, clearly threatened by his action. Unable to control the raw force, I instinctively turned my back to Justin, keeping him out of harm's way.

"Would you like to prove your theory now?" he asked taunting me, trying to make his point.

"Stay away," I screamed.

"Don't ever underestimate your power, ever again," he yelled. "You have absolutely no control over your emotions."

"Shut up!" I pleaded, "Stop!"

"If I had pushed anyone else, their primary response wouldn't be to kill me, yours unfortunately is. So, get a grip!"

"Justin, I'm having a hard time controlling this."

"Well, get control. It's about time you took the bull by the horns. We all had to do it. You must learn to harness the energy. Wield it to do your bidding."

With a wave of his hand, Justin shoved me further back.

"What the hell are you doing?" I screamed, stunned at his persistence. "Stop it!"

Again he pushed.

My insides wanted to tear him apart. The taste for his life was on my lips, dark thoughts of how to kill him surfaced each and every time he pushed me. What I felt was evil at its purest form and the force in my arms was escalating alarmingly.

"How dare you!" I screamed through the mangled thoughts that rang in my brain. "Who the hell do you think you are?" I heard myself say getting to my feet.

The sound of the words were surely coming out of my mouth, but the voice was not my own, but a hollow version – a horrific sound from the depths of my soul.

"Damn it, Caitlin, get control."

"What control?" I finally said, swallowing back all the vile thoughts and deadly impulses I suddenly acquired.

"Work through the emotions. Sort them out. You don't really want to hurt me, do you?"

I raised my head to face him. "Hurt you?" I was confused and fell back to my knees. I found myself questioning the fact. "Do I want to hurt you?" I asked again, not sure of the answer.

"Caitlin! Snap out of it and get control."

My gift was intense and fighting it was impossible. I had to do something to defuse it.

Without thinking, I placed both my palms against the sand and relaxed my arms, allowing the energy to drain into the ground. In seconds the ground shook under my touch. It wasn't at all violent, but the tremors did cause the otherwise still waters to become choppy.

"Caitlin, stop!" I heard Justin scream. "Think of the consequences! Stop messing around." His voice was severe and quite harsh.

I kept my back turned to him and lifted my arms off the sand. "What am I supposed to do?" I cried. "I can't control this."

"Damn it, Caitlin!" He sounded mad. "Get a grip. Relax, and everything will come naturally."

Closing my eyes, I hugged my knees and retreated into the

place in my mind where nothing touched me. I took a deep breath and relaxed my whole body, trying to get some control. I felt much better having released most of the force into the sand.

"Welcome home child." The sharp male voice penetrated the fog that clouded my mind after each of these panics. *"We can feel how close you are. How powerful you've become. There's no need to fear us, Caitlin Eileen."*

Strangled screams caught in my throat, threatening to choke me as I snapped my eyes open, forcing myself out of my solace, unwilling to listen to the intruder. Whoever he was, I wanted nothing to do with him.

"Justin," I wailed, "they know I'm here," I yelled terrified, turning to face him. "He talked to me – in my head – he talked to me!" I repeated not making any sense

Justin came and sat about a foot away, keeping a safe distance. A worried frown creased his brow as he looked at me. "Of course they know you're here, Caitlin. The closer we are to our relatives the easier they can sense us."

"I don't want them talking to me. I'm not ready for this," I cried, scared out of my mind.

"Caitlin, look at me," he said, raising his voice to get my full attention. "Nothing can happen to you here or anywhere else for that matter. The Nobe won't allow them to touch a hair on your head and neither will I."

He was promising the impossible.

"We are here to enjoy our vacation. If they feel that they want to communicate, tell them to go to hell," he said angrily, punching his fist in the sand. "If you can scare them in your dreams you surely can do much worse when awake."

I bobbed my head in understanding, still shaken by the stranger's voice in my head. "You're right. I'm stupid to worry," I finally said closing my eyes momentarily to collect my thoughts. I rubbed my forehead wanting to erase the harrowing effect the voice had on me. They were all going to drive me into screaming fits, that, I was sure of.

The soft sound of Justin inhaling and exhaling rhythmically alongside mine was surprisingly calming. My wrist was, at last, back to normal. Knowing it was safe Justin pulled me in his arms and cradled me. "I'm sorry for pushing you. I just needed you to see that we need to be careful.

"I'm losing it, Justin. I'm completely losing it."

"We all went through the Exorcist moments."

"Exorcist?" I looked at him puzzled.

"That's what Kyle calls those moments you feel completely and totally evil."

"Where do those feelings come from? I would never hurt you, but just then I wanted nothing more."

"It would seem that you're close to ascending. That's when we all experience the darker side of our character. You merely need to choose which way you want to go. Which will give you greater satisfaction," Justin said smiling.

"Who would ever choose those disgusting horrid thoughts?"

"For some it's more difficult than for others. You felt how addictive those hellish thoughts and emotions are. It's a choice one needs to make. I'm happy you keep making the right one"

I rested my head on his shoulder trying to dispel all the rotten things the experience left behind.

"This will all pass, you'll see. I want nothing more than to be with you – you must know that. Even die in your arms, but just not yet, Caitlin. I'd prefer to enjoy our life together, into old, old age first."

"I know," I said burrowing my head deeper against his neck. "I'm just so…."

I closed my eyes and allowed myself to be pulled closer. His face bent so it was inches away from mine. "You know I love you." he declared, kissing me softly on the lips.

I nodded and fell silent again.

Exhaustion battled with fear as I slit open an eye to the sound of Justin's faint voice. "Caitlin, I'd hate to bring this up now, but what you did before is forbidden. We can't afford to be reckless with our powers. The tremor you caused might seem insignificant, but you really can't tell how it will affect the delicate balance we live in. You must exercise better judgment."

I was than aware of having broken the first cardinal rule as far as the gifted were concerned. We were never to mess with the natural order of things.

Realizing how bad I felt, Justin didn't press the issue. Instead, he allowed me the pleasure of resting against his shoulder. Silence hung over us like a shroud, broken only by my faint deep breathing. He stroked my hair and back, easing my state of mind. It was peaceful. With each stroke of his hand, I could feel the stress of the last few days draining out of my body.

∽∽∽

We finally reached the back of the house where everyone was playing volleyball in the pool. Kyle and Emily were on one team while Marc and Tyler were on the other. Sandy was keeping score.

"Two points for my man," called Sandy, proud of Kyle's spike. The brother-sister team had an unfair advantage over the boy's team. Kyle was captain of his water-polo team while Emily played varsity volleyball.

"Oh, good," yelled Marc as soon as he saw us approaching. "Justin, you need to get in and help out the team, they're slaughtering us."

"Give me a minute to change and I'll be right in to help,"

Justin said, disappearing inside the main house to change.

"Marc, I bet that the girls can kick your ass," challenged Kyle, climbing out of the pool. "What do you say, Caitlin? Are you in? The three of you, against the three of them?"

Emily was begging me and so was Sandy. Both girls were athletic and I was the opposite of athletic.

"C'mon Caity, the team needs you."

Reluctant at first, I shook my head, but seeing my cousin's pleading pout, I gave in. "Fine! But I'm warning you, Stone Hurst wasn't big on water sports."

No sooner had I taken off my tunic when Justin came running to the boy's side of the pool and cannon-balled himself in. He resurfaced, pushing his hair back, glaring at Tyler angrily. "Falcone, you keep thinking that way and I'll drown you," he warned, following Tyler's gaze to me.

Tyler ignored his threat and said amusingly, "Because I can't touch, doesn't mean I can't look. Nice suit, Caity," he yelled purposely yanking Justin's chain, and everybody started laughing at how annoyed Justin was.

"Somebody drown Tyler already. It'll save me the trouble," I yelled, over the laughter, before diving into the pool.

The second I broke the surface of the water, Emily was by my side. "Do you like your clothes?" she asked.

"This is the only piece I've seen. Justin insisted on putting the clothes away while I freshened up."

Emily started giggling at the thought. "Hey, Justin," she yelled across the pool, "Which one's your favorite?"

"The black lacey one," he answered, laughing at their private joke.

"You're trying to kill us aren't you, Em?" I whispered.

"What Tyler said – Justin might not be able to touch, but at least he can get a good look."

"Thanks Emily, it's nice to know you care," said Justin. "Are we playing or what?" I wasn't much help to the team. Emily and Sandy amiably held their ground. It proved that technique was above brute strength, but we lost nonetheless. I had stopped counting after the guy's quadrillionth spike.

After an hour or so in the pool, I turned to the sound of Alexander's voice. "Dinner is being served on the roof terrace," he said, "You best get something to eat. All this exercise has surely made you hungry."

"I'm famished," said Kyle as he climbed out of the pool. "What's for dinner?"

"You won't be disappointed, young man. I promise that everything will be to your liking."

Satisfied with Alexander's response, Kyle and the rest of the group went indoors to change. Being the last out of the pool, I quickly toweled off and slipped back into my tunic and turned to our host. "Alex, will Ava be joining us?"

"I'm not really sure," he smiled. "Would you like me to summon her?"

"Could you please? I'd hate for her to dine alone. She should sit with us. Don't you agree, Alex?"

"Yes, of course. If that's what you wish. I'll see what I can do."

"You're going to join us as well, aren't you Alex?" I asked, knowing he deserved this meal more than any of us. Managing the island was no small feat.

"I usually don't..."

"Nonsense," said Justin. "We have tons of questions about the island. Who better to answer them than you?"

He looked to the ground momentarily for his answer, and then said, "Certainly, it would be my pleasure."

Tremors

Illustrated for Lines That Bind - Within The Whispers

EIGHT

NEW VISITOR

INNER THAT EVENING was a rowdy affair as we all got caught up in the excitement of our holidays. The meal was a rich assortment of seafood and exotic salads. Ava sat at the head of the table while Alexander sat on the other end. He seemed uncomfortable at first being seated there, but we wouldn't have it any other way.

"You should know…," Alexander said, taking a sip of his Sangria. "Tomorrow we're expecting more visitors – the three McDevitt sisters and two Falcones. They're flying straight from Palermo."

"Don't tell me it's Dmitri and Paolo?" Marc asked excitedly.

"Yes, I think it is. You know them?"

"I stayed with them last summer," Marc informed us, and then turned to Tyler. "They're our second cousins. I've told you about them, remember? God they're a handful."

"Yeah, I remember you talking about them," Tyler said casually, "Now, about the sisters?"

Everybody started laughing at his heightened interest in the girls rather than his own blood relatives.

"What?" he asked at our amused expressions.

Ava turned to Tyler and smiled at his innocent face. "My nieces are lovely Tyler. Laura is the oldest. She's twenty-four. Dawn is about your age, maybe a year older and then there's Karen." Her face suddenly lit up. It was all too clear which of the three she held a soft spot for. "Karen must be seventeen now, if I'm not mistaken."

"Uncle Richard's girls?" asked Emily excited.

"Yes," answered Ava. "They heard you guys were here so they decided to change their plans and come here for their holidays.

Apart from Emily and Kyle, I knew practically nothing about my other cousins from my mother's side of the family. I never had the chance to meet them before, but knew them only from pictures my aunt had left lying around. Richard was my mother's and Leslie's brother. He never came to visit us in Oaks. He remained with the rest of the McDevitt bloodline somewhere in Europe.

"This vacation is just getting better and better," Emily said enthusiastically.

Alexander was rather quiet the whole evening, preferring to watch rather than participate in most of the conversation. "It's the eastern-most edge of the island that you need to be most careful," he said at one point, informing us about the dangers we could expect. "It's full of dangerous crevices and drops, and you should stay away, or at least be extra vigilant when venturing out to that particular part of the isle, and always stay together.

"Awesome!" blurted Kyle, excited by the prospect of getting into more trouble than usual.

"It was meant as a warning, son. You need to keep close to each other and try not to lose your way if you plan on exploring the area." Alexander looked to each of us before adding, "The cave is a complex maze of tunnels within other tunnels. With the gifts you all possess, you should have no problem finding your way. But, you really need to keep an eye on each other so none of you get separated." He turned and met my gaze. "Especially you, young lady; no one can sense your whereabouts, so be extra careful."

"I will be, I promise." I felt as though I was ten again, but what else was there to say to Alexander's kind smile?

Later on that night, while everyone else retired to their rooms, Ava and I decided to take a stroll down to the beach to catch up on old times.

Arm in arm we talked about the past five years. She felt she had to apologize about all the secrecy. I insisted that she did it for my own good, but she was still rather sorry. She retold me the story of my parent's struggle with the Korbs not mentioning anything new. I must have thanked her over twenty times for her part in the scheme to keep me safe.

"There is one thing that still bugs me, Ava," I finally asked. "Why was my mother so sick?"

She wore serenity like a mantle. It surrounded her, kept her emotion from betraying her deeper thoughts. "I'm not sure sweetie," she answered, "I wasn't around to know all the details. When my brother – your grandfather Cecil summoned me to help, I was in Brazil at the time."

I knew she wasn't telling the whole truth. The Ellri were connected to one another. Distance was never a problem to get their thoughts across.

"One other thing then," I started to say, wanting her to know that I wasn't going to just drop this topic. "Why do the Korbs really want me? I don't buy that whole custody story the Ellri told me. I know it's a lot more than that."

"Is that what's going on in your head? You've been blocking

the Ellri out for about a week now. It's maddening not knowing."

"I guess you all finally know how I feel for once," I said, aware of her sidestepping the question "About the Korbs?"

"Caitlin, I'm not sure, none of us are. The Korbs have blocked out the bloodlines for many centuries, keeping their secrets well locked. Don't get me wrong – some of them are great people, but they hold their immediate bloodline in a cloud of mystery to the rest of us."

"Okay, last question. But this one you have to answer," I said, looking at her intently. "If there is nothing for me to worry about then why are you here? The truth – please."

"I've already told you, Caitlin. I simply wanted to see you."

"The truth," I insisted, raising my voice.

She looked at me trying to read my expression and then turned and looked out to the ocean, contemplating her next words. Ava seemed to be struggling with her thoughts – unable to word the things she was thinking – weighing the most appropriate way to put things.

"Caitlin, you shouldn't worry about these matters. You have absolutely nothing to worry about. We just thought that by having me here you'd feel a lot safer and could finally relax. We're all aware of how difficult your return to Oaks is." She wasn't going to answer me, evading questions was an art and she was quite masterful at it. "It's getting late and I'm an old woman in need of my beauty sleep."

"If you don't mind, Ava, I'd rather stay a couple more minutes. Besides the main house is only up there," I said, pointing to the hill where the structure was perched.

"Caitlin, isn't that Justin?" Ava asked, looking up at the building.

I glanced over to where I pointed, and tendrils of excitement wrapped themselves around me as I caught sight of Justin's figure silhouetted against the large window which framed the entire wall on the second floor where our room was.

I stood there staring.

Ava laughed a fresh, good-natured laugh and said, "Okay, sweetheart – well, have a nice night."

I didn't answer. Not that I didn't want to. I just couldn't get my brain to work. My eyes remained glued to where Justin stood, looking like an angel perched so high, clad in only the bottom half of his attire.

"*Come inside, Caitlin,*" he said, in my thoughts.

As the sweet tone of his voice unbent my puzzled mind, I dashed across the beach and headed to the main house taking the stairs two at a time. I slowed my pace only to contain the pull our bond was exerting on me.

"*Get in here, already,*" he said in my head.

My smile reached from ear to ear as I entered the room.

"It's about time," Justin said, taking a few steps to lessen the distance between us.

Unable to contain my teenage urges, I flung myself into his arms, wrapping my legs around his waist, showering him with kisses. My action was met with unbridled excitement. Justin whirled us around enjoying my mood, responding as intensely to my kisses, letting his hands roam up the sheer material that barely covered my body, pinning me up against the wall.

With his lips trailing their way down my neck, he muttered something inaudible.

"Justin…," I breathed deep.

At the sound of my words he instantly went cold and lifted me back to my feet. "I don't care how much I want this, we're not testing any of your theories," he said, turning his back.

Agitated, he turned to the glass wall and looked out into the darkness. I took two steps closer and placed my cheek on his bare back, hugging him tightly. He took both of my hands and held them up to his chest. I trailed little kisses up and down the contours of his muscular, bare back.

"You're killing me. You know this, don't you?" he said, turning around in my embrace, pulling my butterfly hairpin loose, allowing my hair to cascade down my back. He carefully placed the heirloom on the coffee table next to him, not wanting to damage it in any way. I leaned my head against his chest taking in his freshly bathed scent. He felt solid and strong, toned every which way. Justin was chiseled to perfection.

"I love you," I confessed, burying my head against his hard body.

He brushed my hair aside and kissed me on the shoulder, "I love you more, but we need to be adults about this."

"It's not fair," I pouted, giving him another taste of my lips.

"You're telling me!" he exclaimed, pushing me away playfully. "Now change for bed. I'm going to take a quick shower."

I looked at him puzzled, "But didn't you already take one?"

"From the looks of it, Caitlin, I'll be taking quite a few cold showers in the next few days," he said kissing me, laughing as he walked away.

With Justin in the bathroom, I had plenty of time to look through the clothes Emily bought me. "Dear lord," I exclaimed, scanning each piece. You wouldn't even call them clothes. They didn't have enough material to fall under such a category. The dresses were exceptionally short and the shorts were sinfully revealing. "Poor Justin!"

Glad to have sneaked some of my own clothes in my back pack; I pulled a cotton tank top out along with its matching cotton shorts. I refused to wear any of the provocative, lacy pieces Emily packed – even if the black one was his favorite.

Ready for bed, I tucked myself under the cotton sheets and stared out the window. A little while later, Justin lay down next to me and whispered in my ear, "I'll stay until you fall asleep."

I was about to complain, but then I realized how difficult this whole ordeal was for him, so I just kissed him good night and closed my eyes.

~~~

The next few days were exhilarating with our new visitors. There was so much to talk about. The girls were a riot. Tyler seemed to like Karen, the youngest of the three and I could see why. Her deep auburn hair only emphasized her sparkling amber eyes and bubbly Scottish personality. She was only a few months younger than me and enjoyed reading as much as I did. I found comfort in our endless conversations over common interests. Her older sister, on the other hand, was rubbing me the wrong way. I was used to seeing girls falling madly for Justin, but Laura was flaunting it, doing anything to get his attention.

Emily kept reminding me that Justin had eyes only for me, but Laura's persistence set off my powers on several occasions. I could feel my wrist burning at the sight of her touching him or simply playing with him in the water. Even her Scottish accent was getting on my nerves, and to think I loved that accent. But hearing it coming out of her mouth only made my hair stand on end. And here I thought only Megan could make me react that way. I said nothing to Justin, about how I felt.

The brothers on the other hand were a handful. Dmitri and Paolo were about twenty years old and dangerously crazy. Kyle loved them, he would; they were a mirror image of him. From the moment they arrived Paolo seemed to take an instant liking to my cousin Dawn. We all felt the sparks between them.

Our days were split between meals, the beach and the variety of water sports. Justin and I, however, were playing it rather safe, holding hands and the occasional kiss now and then.

We both fought the unfathomable need to be with each other each minute of every day, but it was hard to stay apart for more than a few hours. We were instinctively pulled back together after some time apart like synchronized magnets, colliding from different directions.

NINE

THE COVE

E VERY MORNING at around five, when everybody slept, I sneaked down to the beach for a swim. I loved needing only a few hours rest. This was the best part of the day and they were all missing it.

Several footpaths on the island snaked through lush, green vegetation. While roaming the island the previous mornings, I came across my private little cove about half a mile down the beach.

On that particular morning, I noticed a beautiful sail boat anchored not too far out. *Were we expecting more visitors?* I thought as I spread my towel in my usual place and prepared for my morning swim. Just as I was about to head in the water, I froze, surprised that I wasn't the only one around.

"Didn't mean to scare you," he said slowly wading through the water. "I just arrived and couldn't resist a dip. It's beautiful this time of day, isn't it?" The stranger asked, looking rather godly like as the early morning rays bounced off the water running down his torso.

"I have never seen you on the island before," he continued

to say; pushing his wet, dirty blond hair from his face "I'm Gabriel by the way."

"Hi – I'm Caitlin," I answered, awkwardly, "It's my first time on the island. Is that your sail boat?" I turned my gaze towards the vessel.

"You could say that. It's my families, really. I've recently graduated and I'm taking a break. I've been sailing around the coast for about a month."

"For a month? Wow! That sounds like fun."

Smiling, he casually stretched out on the sand, blocking out the sun with his arm over his forehead and said, "So, how do you like our island?"

I noticed that he said 'our island'. That would make him a member of one of the families - but which one? He was too fair to be a Falcone, and way too blond to be a Bradford – that left another three – but which one?

Gazing into the gentle depths of the secluded cove I turned to him and said, "I love everything about this place." I toyed with the sand for a couple of seconds before I spoke again. "I still can't believe that there's something this beautiful on our planet and I'm just discovering it."

He turned on his side to face me. His honey-hued gaze bore into mine. "I know what you mean," he said, gazing at me, letting his eyes roam up and down my body. "Everything here is beautiful."

Gabriel's stare should have made me uncomfortable, but it didn't. There was something about him. His gaze stopped at my scarred wrist and instantly looked away.

"How many days are you here for, Caitlin?"

"For another week or so," I sighed. "Not enough if you ask me."

"This place would do that to you. It's a trap. It doesn't want to let anybody go. I could easily live here forever and ever."

"How about you, Gabriel?" I asked, "How long are you here for?"

"That all depends on the company." he answered, flirtatiously.

Under normal circumstances I would have gotten up to leave. There was something that intrigued me. He was quite aware of his physical appeal – knew how to work his charm. I wasn't impressed by either attribute. There was, however, a connection – a familiarity that I felt towards him. It didn't feel forced by any means. His voice was alluring – seductive in many ways, keeping me interested.

"So, where have you sailed to?" I asked, changing the subject

"Mostly around the African coast. It's my favorite," he said. "It blends many cultures together. Nothing like it in the world"

"Have you ever been to America?"

"South America, Brazil, Argentina, I've been all over, but not North America. I haven't gotten round to that part yet."

"I can see why you prefer this side of the Atlantic. From what little I've seen, it's stunning and steeped in history."

We continued our friendly conversation, talking about his travels and interests. Gabriel seemed to feel comfortable. He was a bit full of himself – too self-confident, if there is even such a thing. The thing that alarmed me was the fact that he didn't ask about me, not one piece of information. Not that anything in my life would remotely compare to the worldly things he experienced.

From the things he said it seemed that we liked similar things; books, movies, but still I couldn't help but feel that something was off; his need to impress alarmed me.

It might have been the fact that deep down he was nervous.

That would have explained why he was trying so hard to make such a good impression.

"You're only twenty-four and you've seen so much," I told him, impressed by his extensive travels. "This is my first trip abroad."

I came to realize that the families in Europe were more lenient with their young members, allowing them the freedom to travel the world and experience new things. In Oaks young people were under stringent rules, traveling only with the Ellri.

"Do they have you locked up somewhere?" he asked, whimsically.

I smiled. "You can say that. I'm still in high school."

"Ouch," he exclaimed, chuckling. "That's brutal."

"You're telling me! A few days ago I was sitting for exams and today I'm somewhere in the Atlantic soaking up the sun!"

"That's life for you – full of surprises." Gabriel turned his head back to the sky "Just this morning I was on my boat all alone with nobody to talk to and look at me now – sitting here with a water nymph."

I colored slightly and looked out to sea. "I wouldn't go as far as to call me that. You haven't seen me swim."

"That bad?"

"Ten times worse than anything you can possibly imagine." I giggled.

"I'm quite good at swimming. If you'd like, I can teach you."

"Um, thanks, but I'm kinda used to my handicap. Wouldn't want to spoil something I worked so hard to master – would you now?" I teased.

Gabriel started laughing. "I see your point – wouldn't want to ruin your drowning technique in any way."

I smiled, collecting my towel. "Well, I should be heading back. Wouldn't want them sending out a search party."

"Why would they do that? Where could you possibly go?" he asked, questionably "Unless you've been thinking of running away. I'm sure I can sneak you out. How about it Caitlin? Sail away together into the unknown," he said, cunningly charming.

My body suddenly tensed up. I didn't feel at ease with Gabriel any more. "For now, I'm perfectly content where I am, but I'll keep you posted on any sudden need to make a break for it," I jested, trying to sound as comfortable as possible.

I wasn't at all used to having men flirt with me. I didn't know how to respond. My initial thought was of Justin, but I knew talking to Gabriel was harmless. He was quite fun to be with and very polite.

"Do you really need to go?" he asked pouting. "Come on! I just found you. Stay a while longer."

I was in two minds about staying. His stories fascinated me, but the nagging in my gut was all too real, impelling me to leave. "I really need to go, Gabriel. This was fun," I said, attempting to be cordial. "You should come and meet the rest of the group. I'm sure you'll love them."

"Caitlin!" I quickly turned my head to the sound of Ava's distinctive voice calling me. "What are you doing here, alone?" she asked, completely ignoring Gabriel's existence.

Gabriel stood up instantly. "Ava! What a nice surprise. What in the world brings you to this neck of the woods?"

Apparently they knew each other, but even so, she didn't look too thrilled to see him – more bothered than anything else. It was unlike Ava to be impolite. I had seen her react on many occasions over our five-year period together at Stone Hurst, but never had she been this discourteous.

"I could ask you the same question, Gabriel?" she answered rather curtly. "When did you blow in?"

"A few hours ago – I hope that's not a problem. I know I should have announced my arrival, but it was last minute."

"I'm sure it was," she said surly. "Are you coming up to the house or are you staying on the boat?"

Having never heard her speak to somebody so brusque, I was taken aback by her manner. I didn't understand why she was snippy with him. He was quite cordial after all.

"I was going to stay on the boat, Ava but...," he stopped in mid-sentence and turned to look at me, "but seeing that the island got much prettier from the last time I was here, I think I'll stay up at the house if that's okay with you?"

I went slightly red. He was deliberately making his interest in me known to Ava – flirting openly. I wanted the ground to open up and swallow me whole. How could he presume to think that I was in the least bit interested – in that sense anyway?

"Do what you like Gabriel," she said, wrapping her arm around my shoulders. "Come on Caitlin, let's go."

"Nice meeting you, Caitlin!" he yelled behind us.

I turned to look at him, but he was already in the water enjoying the dive.

~~~

For some reason Justin was waiting for me – silhouetted against the door frame, looking a bit glum. "Are you okay?" he asked, taking me in his arms.

"Why wouldn't I be? I always go for a swim this time of day. Apart from the occasional crab, there's no real threat to worry about."

He looked at Ava and then back to me.

"I'll leave you guys alone," she said "and don't wonder off. Not until your gift allows us to read you again."

"Is that what this is all about? I'm always down at the cove this time of day. You know that." I said, turning to Justin. "Why didn't you come down to get me? Why did you send Ava? It's so out of her way."

"Justin didn't send me," Ava said, "I woke rather early this morning and decided to take a stroll around the island. Haven't done that for quite some time, and there you were. Anyway, let me get back home. I have a few things to take care of. See you both later," she said, walking away.

They were both acting weird. Justin kept his hold on me tight, not letting go. "What's the matter?" I asked, worried that something was wrong.

He brushed his lips against mine, "Now that you're back, absolutely nothing. I know this is too much for me to ask, but I don't want you wondering off alone for the next few days."

"Justin, this isn't the first time I went down to the cove. Why are you acting like this?"

"It's just that I hate not being able to read you. Our bond allows me to know how close you are, but that's just not enough, Caitlin. Please, do this one thing for me?" he sighed kissing me on the forehead.

Justin was visibly upset about this. I didn't know why, but seeing him in that state of mind was disturbing.

"I promise," I said, taking his face in my hands. "I promise never to wonder off – ever again. You don't need to worry. Besides, what could possibly happen to me on this island?"

Before he could speak Kyle and Sandy came up the path hand in hand. "Are you guys coming for breakfast? Alexander has set up at the south terrace overlooking the pool," said Sandy, flashing a sparkly smile.

"Yeah, of course we're coming" Justin answered, dropping the subject.

We all sat around munching away. Paolo and Dawn were

nowhere to be seen. *Young love*, I thought. I would have wanted my two weeks with Justin to have been that way. Nestled in bed all day enjoying each other's company – instead, he was keeping himself busy; snorkeling, jet skiing anything to keep his mind off the obvious.

It was funny really – even Kyle had picked up on his avid interest in water sports. "Didn't know you were going out for the Olympics," he commented one day after Justin had swum a million laps in the pool. Marc was more understanding by suggesting different sports for them to do, spending endless hours with his best friend in order to keep him busy.

Emily and I caught up on old times while the guys ran amuck around the island. She was head over heels in love with Marc. I was so happy to see the two of them together. Though I loved her dearly, she was a handful. Marc, however, was up for the challenge.

Tyler and Karen were also hitting it off rather well. Sitting across from me, I could see it in the way she looked at him. One night I saw them holding hands walking down the beach. I was happy for my best friend, but wondered how hurt he'd be when we'd have to leave. I could tell he was quite taken by her. He didn't mention her to me at all and that's how I was sure it was something serious. Otherwise, he'd have spilled the beans on the first day.

Finishing their breakfast, Dmitri, Tyler, Kyle and Sandy took a dip in the pool, fussing around the water. The rest of us sat it out, enjoying the conversation and the morning sun. Laura sat beside me, gazing across the table towards Justin, stirring her cold tropical concoction with a straw. Her flirtatious manner should have bothered me, but after a few days I got used to it. It helped that Justin was indifferent to her charm.

"Justin…?" she purred, placing her hand on top of his.

"What do we have planned for today?"

He looked up at her questionably, gently pulling his hand free. "I don't know. Do you have something to suggest?"

"Why don't we visit the west coast of the island? You haven't seen the caves yet, have you?"

Justin's eyes flickered enthusiastically as he said, "Alexander mentioned something about caves," he turned his attention to the rest of us. "How about it guys? Do you want to see the caves?"

We all seemed to agree that it would be a great idea. Though, Laura looked a tad bit disappointed as she hadn't planned for a group trip. She sported a smile, nonetheless, taking a real deep sip through the straw.

"The caves were used as storage for pirate treasures centuries before the Korbs decided to settle here," she started explaining a few minutes later. "Some even believe that there are underground caverns that connect this island to the others some miles away."

"Really? That sounds exciting," Marc said, wide eyed.

"You'll love it!" she said, looking around the table stopping at Justin's gaze. "It's really romantic on that part of the island."

Should I smack her and get it over with? Would that make her stop looking at him like that?

I looked over to Justin to see his reaction. He simply took a sip of his coffee, indifferent to her words. *Was he not aware of how she felt?* I knew that was impossible since he could read her mind and I'm sure she was quite adamant about her true feelings.

It must have been rather frustrating to be Laura. She was used to getting what she wanted, looking the way she did. She probably never had problems attracting men. Justin, thankfully, was unsusceptible to her lure, but that surely didn't stop her.

Someone should tell her of our bond, I thought. She'd feel much better knowing that Justin had no choice but to feel attracted to me.

"We'll have to do some trekking through the rough terrain or we could simply take the boat out," said Laura.

"It's more fun to walk," Marc responded, kissing Emily's hand. "Plus, it would give us the opportunity to explore more of the island.

We all agreed with him. The island was big enough to offer adventure, but small enough to get around on foot.

"It'll take us about two hours to reach that part of the coast," Laura said, "but it'd be well worth the....."

For some reason she stopped. I waited for her to continue, but she didn't. Being so absorbed by Laura's elaborate plan to get to the other side of the island I didn't get whiff of the charged atmosphere around me. Just then, I turned and saw how Justin stiffened in his seat grabbing the table with both hands. Marc unexpectedly stood up and moved next to him placing his arm on Justin's shoulder in an attempt to calm him. Both man stared in the same direction. Kyle, Tyler and Dmitri all climbed out of the pool and stood next to Justin as well.

"Hi, beautiful," I heard the familiar voice say. "So, this is where they've been hiding you?"

I turned my head and saw the reason for Justin's altered state. Gabriel was merely a few feet away smiling at me, ignoring everybody else.

"So how was your breakfast, Caitlin?" he asked, gazing down at me.

"Great!" I smiled.

I turned to look at Justin. He was staring at Gabriel menacingly as though he was ready to attack.

"Have you eaten?" I asked, turning my attention Gabriel.

"Yes, back at the boat. I wanted to come up and see you. You've made a lasting impression on me," he said, smiling boyishly.

"You haven't met the rest of the group," I told him, ignoring his last comment. "These are my first cousins. This is Emily, Karen, Laura and that's Kyle over there. Then there is the Falcones, Marc, Tyler and Dmitri. That's Justin." I said, introducing everyone. "Oh, and that's Sandy in the pool. Sorry Sandy!"

My wrist started burning for no apparent reason. I looked over to Justin and realized that he was the source of my pain. He was angry, real angry, but I didn't know why.

"Guys, this is Gabriel, he sailed in this morning," I said, looking at all their blank expressions. "I ran into him down at the cove."

Not a word. They all seemed to know something I didn't. My hand continued to burn, nothing I couldn't control, but it was uncomfortable all the same. I kept my eyes on Justin hoping that he might give me a clue to what all the fuss was about.

"Good morning everybody," Ava said, louder than was necessary. She came up to Justin and placed her hands on his shoulders causing Marc to pull away. "Well, I see you all met Gabriel. Doesn't the lad have an amazing effect on people?" she asked, sarcastically.

"Very funny Ava," said Gabriel, visibly annoyed. "Is that any way to treat a member of the family?"

"You're right, young man – where are my manners?" she said condescendingly. She turned her gaze to me and smiled. "Caitlin, I forgot to introduce you to our visitor this morning."

What in the world was she talking about? She knew full well that I was well aware of who he was.

"This," she said, gesturing to our guest, "is Gabriel Korbs, your distant relative."

I wasn't sure if I had heard correctly. I stood from my seat instantly and backed a few feet away from him.

"Did she say Korbs?" I gasped, looking at him in utter shock.

"Yes, Korbs," he answered, staring at me. "Is that a problem?"

My darkest fear had finally surfaced. How could I have been so gullible? Gabriel must have known who I was from the second he saw me. That would explain his lack of personal questions. He knew all there was to know about me.

Fear instantly turned to panic causing my power to escalate. My wrist was throbbing, but not in response to my own feelings. Justin seemed to be the cause of the intensity in my veins. *Was he in any danger?* I questioned my body's response. *Could Gabriel be the threat my power was protecting Justin from?*

"You knew who I was all along, didn't you?" I snapped at Gabriel, angry at myself for being so stupid as to trust him.

"It wasn't hard to guess, Caitlin. You felt the connection as I did. We are related after all - distant relatives, but family all the same."

"You lied to me!" I accused him vehemently.

"Come on Caitlin, don't be like that," he said, reaching out to touch me.

Jumping to his feet Justin snarled, "You stay the hell away from her!"

Kyle and Marc instantly grabbed him by the shoulders, not letting him go.

Within seconds, Gabriel grabbed his head with both hands looking like he was in some sort of pain, and said through clenched teeth, "Is that all you got, Justin?"

To my surprise Emily walked in front of Justin taking his face in her hands. "Don't, you'll hurt him," she whispered. "Everything will be fine, trust me."

Justin simply stared at her, and nodded. I positioned myself a few feet in front of Emily, wanting to shield all of them from any kind of danger.

Gabriel on the other hand ignored Justin's threat and shook his head momentarily before taking another step closer.

I was furious at his persistence. "Go ahead – touch me. I dare you!" I sneered, taking one step forward to lessen the distance between us – overwhelmed with the need to protect the others, knowing I could hurt him with a mere flick of my hand.

I wasn't frightened any more. My touch would be lethal. I could feel it deep in my bones. For the first time ever I felt in complete control over the force. Another step forward was all I needed to send him back to his creator.

Gabriel instinctively looked down at my throbbing wrist and took a step back. His otherwise calm expression suddenly mirrored his alarm. I could tell he feared what I could do to him. Like my faceless shadows in my nightmares, he collected his tail between his legs and stared at me in horror.

"Caitlin, why are you acting like this? I'm not here to cause problems," he finally found the courage to say.

"I hope not!" Ava said. "You should've been honest with her from the start, Gabriel."

"Yes, I guess you're right. I didn't expect to see her at the beach, Ava. Caitlin took me by surprise. I was never told how beautiful she is," he said, looking right at me purposely provoking Justin.

From the corner of my eye I could see Justin struggling against his better judgment. Emily and I remained a barrier between him and Gabriel. Marc and Kyle wouldn't have it. They held him back with all their strength wanting to avoid any bloodshed.

Ava took a quick look at Justin and casually walked over to me and stood between the devil and myself. She was rather calm considering how deathly charged the atmosphere was.

"What's your reason for being here?" she asked austerely, turning her gaze to our visitor.

"I don't need a reason to come to this island."

Ava took a step closer to him. I could tell she was tired of his games. "Don't be coy with me boy. I can snap you in two with a blink of an eye," she warned, causing him to withdraw a couple of steps back in agonizing pain, clutching his waist.

It was the first time I heard an Ellri threaten another human. I shuddered at the thought. *Is this what it would be like if there was a clash between the bloodlines?* I shook my head to suppress the shudder – banishing the frightful pictures I was conjuring up. I couldn't allow this to happen – not over me.

"Caitlin, I meant no harm," Gabriel repeated, looking over Ava's shoulder. "I was just curious to see you. I'm not going to apologize for anything, especially my feelings."

His words meant absolutely nothing to me, but just then I realized that he would be the only person who could answer some of my questions – shed some light on the mystery.

I knew that playing with fire was dangerous, but I was getting nowhere with everybody else. In seconds I was calm. My wrist returned to normal, responding to my ultimate decision.

"Gabriel, you're right. I'm sorry. I overreacted," I said, taking a step to the side to get a better look at him. "I was just surprised by the name. You should've said something earlier. It's not every day I run into a Korbs."

My voice was composed, and unusually relaxed. I wanted to sound sincere, wanted him to believe my every word.

"I'm really sorry, Caitlin. I had hoped we could be friends," he said, taking the bait.

I displayed the warmest smile I could conjure up considering how vile I really felt about the person. "Well, this morning was great, Gabriel. Seeing we have so much in common I don't see why we can't be friends," I smiled even more. "Look, nobody means any harm, really. Everybody here is great. They just tend to be a bit over protective, that's all."

Ava was reluctant to step aside. Unable to read my thoughts she had no way of knowing what I was truly thinking.

"Ava, he's a Korbs and belongs on the island as much as any of us, doesn't he?" I asked, touching her arm. It was more of a squeeze than a touch. She instantly got that I hadn't somehow lost my mind.

"Of course, sweetie, if you don't have a problem with this, Gabriel is more than welcomed," she said, moving out of the way and took a seat next to Justin in an attempt to neutralize the situation. She poured herself a cup of coffee as if nothing had happened. "Justin would you like a refill?" she asked, holding up the pot.

Relaxing his posture Justin shrugged off Marc and Kyle. He knew I was up to no good. He was the only one who could read my expressions and sense my real emotions.

"I'm fine," he told his best friends who were awaiting the littlest reaction. "Sure Ava, I could use another cup," he answered, holding up his empty mug.

"Have a seat Gabriel," Emily offered smiling, taking a seat herself. Marc joined her.

Unsure if he should at first, Gabriel finally accepted and joined the group, avoiding eye contact with Justin. Everybody seemed relaxed on the surface. "I should've announced my visit," he repeated. "I'm truly sorry to have caused all this," Gabriel said, looking around to everybody.

The atmosphere was, for the time being, defused. In the guise of a misunderstanding everybody sat around acting normal, feigning comfort in Gabriel's presence. On the surface I was acting the gracious host. On the inside I was a volcano ready to erupt. I hated being taken for a fool.

"Oh please, don't worry about that now," I said, continuing to stand. "You sit here and enjoy your morning. The yacht can't be that comfortable."

"Aren't you going to join us?" Gabriel asked, in his alluring voice, seeing that I was the only one still standing.

Justin stared at me, waiting for my response.

"There's nothing I'd like more," I answered, placing both hands on his shoulders. "I have thousands of questions about our family."

"Then come and sit," he insisted, offering the seat next to him.

"I'd really love to, but unfortunately I didn't get a chance to wash off the sand from earlier."

"Caitlin, that can wait – come sit."

"I'll be down later. I promise." I said, as I walked away, leaving them all behind.

TEN

CUT TOO DEEP

I PACED BACK AND FORTH like a caged lion. A tangled ball of emotions bubbled through the back of my mind. "Damn, that bastard." I swore, long and hard – hating myself for being so stupid.

Anything that wasn't bolted to the floor swirled around my head suspended in mid-air. It was my way of keeping my mind busy, keeping me from going downstairs and showing Gabriel what I really thought of him. Others would twiddle their thumbs, play with their hair or even bite their nails. I moved anything that could be moved.

Justin burst in, slamming the door behind him, shocked at the sight of the room, "What the hell was that all about?" he yelled. "And for heaven's sake put the furniture back down!"

"I don't know what you mean?" I answered, returning everything to its rightful place.

"Caitlin, I came close to killing somebody today don't patronize me. You can fool the others, but whatever you're plotting you need to drop it. This is too dangerous."

"Justin, that half-witted jackass has my answers. That

bastard knows things," I cursed, annoyed at letting Gabriel take me for a fool. "I swear, Justin, it's times like these I wish you could read my mind. The man is a self-centered, self-righteous ass. You should've heard him earlier, going on and on about his life, as if I gave a damn."

Justin stood there quietly. It took him a few seconds before he uttered another sound. "I could've sworn you were interested this morning, Gabriel sure was."

"You were listening in on our conversation?"

"Actually, I couldn't read your thoughts, but his mind was crystal clear," Justin said, detesting Gabriel.

"So he likes me, does he?" I grimaced at the thought.

"Like, is not a strong enough word for what Gabriel feels," Justin said, wrapping his arms around me. "He was rather stunned to see you looking the way you do. For some reason he hadn't imagined you so exquisite."

"That's just it." I started pacing. "Why would he be imagining me at all? He's not part of the immediate Korbs family. How does he even know so much about me?"

"Good question. All the more reason to stay away," said Justin holding my upper arms in a tight grip. "Promise me you're not going to do anything stupid. Promise me!" He demanded, seeing how hesitant I was. "He's quite powerful, Caitlin. Don't let him fool you into thinking he's scared of you. He's testing you to see how far he can push you. He was intrigued by your gift – not afraid. He's toying with you."

"That was pure fear, Justin. I have seen that look before. Gabriel knows not to push me. I felt his limit. It's you he was testing. He wasn't at all a threat to me. My wrist responded to protect you," I said, shocking him.

Justin dropped his hands to the side and just stared at me in disbelief. "I didn't feel threatened by him the least. It took all my strength to keep from tearing him to pieces. Caitlin, he was deliberately thinking of you – projecting vile images. He must have felt the connection between us, testing to see how I'd react. It's a good thing Emily was there otherwise…," He fumbled with his hair. "I don't even want to think what could've happened"

"I noticed that. What did Emily do exactly?" I asked, interested in knowing how Justin's mood had changed so fast.

"She's taken after Abbot. Her touch drains any ill feeling anyone might have, inciting an instant feeling of calm and compassion."

"Really? I thought she was only able to read minds."

"She can only hear people's thoughts as Kyle can, but her powers are growing every day. She also has an acute intuition – able to guess the outcome minutes before the actual event. She's great to watch football matches with," he said, on a lighter note.

"Can you all sense each other's powers? I mean do you know what Gabrielle can do?"

Shaking his head, he said, "It doesn't work like that, but from the way your gift reacts, you seem to be able to somehow detect somebody's potency."

"That would explain the fluctuations in the surge of my gift. I had a hard time keeping it together downstairs. It reached extreme proportions," I admitted, snuggling in his embrace. "My power seemed to think you were in grave danger or at least that's how I interpreted it."

Justin hugged me tight. "You know better than any of us how powerful your admirer is. Your gift let you know," he said, kissing me. "I'm going to have to destroy that bastard if he even thinks of touching you." Leaning his forehead to mine, he said, "There is something about him Caitlin, I don't like it."

"Gabriel is rubbing you the wrong way, I can see that. He's

intentionally using me as the lure. I should've paid more attention to my instincts. At the cove earlier today, my gut knew that something was off. I should've listened to that little voice inside my head and stayed away. Justin, can't you dig a little to see what he's doing here or at least learn what he knows?"

Pushing my loose strands of hair behind my ear Justin leaned down and kissed me lightly on the lips. "Don't you think I already tried? He's being blocked from a higher source, way too strong for me. I can only read his trivial thoughts. That's why it's imperative that you don't do anything stupid. You have to promise me, Caitlin."

"I just want to know the truth!" I said, scanning his beautiful face. "I can't just sit around and wait. Something is up and I need to know what. You saw Ava's response. When was the last time you heard an Ellri talk like that?"

Justin perched himself on the bed absently pushing his hair back with both hands. "She meant every word. I read her resolve. The Ellri are aware that something is up, but they don't know exactly what it is. The McDevitts have called a meeting at the end of the week."

"The McDevitts? My mother's bloodline?" My eyes widened in terror, "I thought they were all going to wait for the Nobe to decide?"

"I'm not really sure what it's all about. The Ellri keep blocking me out. Letting me in on things they want me to know."

The mere thought of my mother's family calling a meeting on my account was a cause for alarm. Nothing seemed to add up. I had to get to the bottom of this and Gabriel was my window of opportunity – making him my new best friend.

Justin was not going to like this, but I saw no other way. I wasn't going to sit back and allow the people I loved to sacrifice even a hair off their head.

Seeing how close they all came today, willing to risk everything to protect me was an indication of what loomed ahead. I wasn't going to stand for it.

"Why did all of you respond so strongly to Gabriel? It couldn't only be the images he was projecting. You all looked real pissed off."

Justin strolled across the room and stood with one hand leaning against the window, looking out towards the ocean, absorbed in his thoughts.

"Gabriel was masterfully attempting to read us, searching our minds for something in particular."

"The whole time he was talking to me he was in your head, searching?"

"Marc, Kyle and I blocked him out from the rest of the group. The reason we were mad was because he didn't back off until Ava showed up and blocked him out completely. The bastard is persistent and quite resilient."

"So we know he can read minds. Can he manipulate them as you can?" I asked, making a mental note of Gabriel's abilities.

"No he can't. I got that much out of him. But I'm sure he can do much worse. It was effortless for him to try and read all of us simultaneously. It was rather amazing."

Leave it to Justin to admire his adversary's gift – he was honest in that way, knowing when to criticize, but also when to praise. It was amiable of him to distinguish between the two – always judging fairly each situation.

"You're as powerful as he is," I said, knowing that both men incited the same degree of intensity in my own gift.

"I'm aware of that, Caitlin. I felt the strength of his power. It's just that he's more in control of his ability. It would seem that the Korbs ascend much younger than we do, giving them more time to grow into their heightened abilities."

"Gabriel isn't aware of our bond, is he?"

"I don't think so because if he was, he wouldn't be trying so hard to win you over. The only thing he is aware of is my feelings towards you."

I turned red with embarrassment. "Why in God's name would he be trying to win me over? He's here for other reasons. He's just trying to get on my good side, nothing more," I said, rationalizing Gabriel's flirtatious character.

Justin turned his back to the window and stared at me stone cold. "The guy's crazy about you, Caitlin. He's not going to back down that easy. Let's just say he's made his intentions known."

I shook my head vigorously refusing to accept what he was saying. "You're being ridiculous. He's just met me a few hours ago. How could he possibly be feeling that?"

I felt rather uncomfortable talking to Justin about this. I knew this couldn't be easy for him. It was imprinted on his foul expression.

"Trust me," he said, turning back to look at the magnificent view outside the window. "When you both were at the cove this morning, his guard was down making him rather easy to read. He's known you for quite some time."

"How is that even possible?"

Justin shrugged his shoulders. "Gabriel wasn't lying when he said you surprised him. He wasn't expecting to be physically attracted to you. It wasn't his initial plan."

"His initial plan was what then?"

Justin realized that I was side stepping part of his comment. I should have refuted the physical attraction bit, but I didn't. I would have been lying.

"I wasn't able to probe any deeper, he blocked me out the second he sensed me." His posture was rather stiff, and his voice quite stern. "Caitlin, you can't deny being attracted to him. I felt how strong you responded to him the moment you saw him."

Mortified, my mouth dropped open in shock. "How can you possibly think that I could be remotely interested in anybody else?" In seconds, I crossed the room and wrapped my arms around him, and placed a kiss on the curve of his back. "I was intrigued," I admitted, "but that's as far as it went. I didn't know why Gabriel felt so familiar to me. How could you even think it was anything more?"

Justin didn't move, didn't even turn to face me.

"You know how much I love you," I told him "Why are you even thinking these things?"

Justin finally turned to face me. He spoke his next words with dour determination. "I don't want you to be alone with him ever again! Who you choose to be with is your choice. I'd never stand in your way – but just not him," he added taking a few steps away.

I took offense to his words – would have rather been kicked in the gut than have Justin say those things to me. Irritated that he would even consider such a thing, I grabbed him by the arm and forced him to look at me. "What the hell are you saying? Our bond is for life," I cried at the top of my voice. "How can you say something like that to me? What do you mean, 'whoever I choose to be with'? How dare you question my loyalty?"

Not wanting Justin to see how much he really hurt me, I turned my back to him and walked to the other side of the room. My tears didn't take long to surface. "You'd give me up that easily? How can you be so heartless?"

"If being with someone else makes you happier I'm not going to stand in your way," he said, meaning every word. "This bond should not define who you're with, Caitlin. The Nobe will know how to sever the bond if you want."

"Why?" I cried, refusing to face him with tears in my eyes. "Why are you doing this – now? If this has anything to do with Gabriel you're insane! How could you have such a low opinion of me?" I was finding it hard to breathe. My chest constricted even more with every word I said. "Are you seriously telling me that you would give me up that easily?"

Justin didn't respond for a few minutes, and then he said, "I just want you to be happy, Caitlin."

I circled my head in order for him to see the extent of what his words were doing to me "Am I happy now, Justin?" I yelled "Answer me – damn you! Am I happy now? Do you even know how deep you've cut me?" I heard myself say through the tears.

Offended by his words, I sat down on the bed confused and broken. Evidently, he had not been paying much attention to how much he meant to me – how much I was willing to sacrifice to have him in my life. How could he believe that there could ever be someone else, someone other than him?

My gift instantly responded to my whirl of emotions. My hands throbbed by the raw power of it all. I sat back, wounded deeper than I thought possible. I swallowed back the tears feeling completely numb inside, devoid of any sort of feelings.

That moment, Justin came and kneeled in front of me wanting to say something, but he knew there was absolutely nothing left to say. My blank stare was an indicant of the damage he had caused. Justin quickly stood up and left the room without uttering a sound.

I closed my eyes and quickly regained my composure,

putting an end to the lethal surge that coursed through my arms. I was left behind feeling hollowed-out and achy. My head throbbed like an open wound and my stomach was a mass of cramps.

Several hours passed and I didn't want to get out of bed. I simply stared out the window not caring for the view. *How could he believe that about me? How could he?* I kept repeating in my head.

The sudden knock on my door shredded the silence. I didn't care for visitors, so I didn't answer hoping whoever it was would simply go away.

"Caitlin, you've been up here all day," Alexander said, poking his head in the door. "Dinner is being served. Your friends are all downstairs waiting."

I turned my back not meaning to be rude. I simply didn't want him to see the mess I was in. "I'm not hungry, Alex."

"I see," he said lingering for a few minutes before closing the door behind him.

Darkness descended and I was still in bed. With every passing hour my need to see him grew. The bond was forcing us back together. I fought it for five long years and I knew I could fight it again. Back then we didn't have the connection we had now. Painful as the separation was, I had no other choice but to endure it. This time it was my pride that was at stake. He mentioned having our bond severed, which meant that he had seriously considered it in the past.

Halfheartedly, I dragged my numb legs out of bed and walked to the window. The view from my second floor vista was mesmerizing. The whole island was illuminated by a healthy dose of exotic eclecticism. Hundreds of soft lights accentuated the lush landscape creating an angelic atmosphere.

There, in the distance a single silhouette walked the length of the beach against the breathtaking backdrop. "Jackass," I muttered, the second I realized who the person was. Gabriel was heading towards the dock to spend the night on his boat. As I looked on, I noticed that he half turned. From where I stood, it seemed that he had stopped and looked in my direction, but it was too dark to be sure.

Either way, it made no difference to me. I cared nothing for the man. Apathetic as I was towards Gabriel, I turned my back to the window and made my way to bed, crawled under the cozy sheets and closed my eyes to the outside world.

~~~

Having absolutely nowhere to run, I turned down a long passageway where the air reeked of decay. I was suddenly trapped like an animal, nowhere to turn. The sinister, faceless shadows that haunted my dreams had backed me into a corner against a cold stone wall. They didn't advance, but simply stood there staring with their piercing dark eyes.

I made no move. Their immediate proximity should have triggered my powers, but my mind was marked with disinterest, refusing to fight them off.

At first they seemed a bit confused at my unwillingness to stand my ground, turning to each other fraught with uncertainty

They moved in closer, only a foot or two away. I should have been afraid, but now I was cursedly tired – tired of running, tired of absolutely everything.

"Eileen…," One of the shadows finally spoke, "There's no need to fear us."

I wasn't afraid. Even there, in the depths of my mind, I felt nothing – a vast emptiness. I looked at my intruders and simply shook my head.

"Enough," I sighed. *"I had enough."*

I didn't care to listen to anybody. I knew there and then that my dream needed to come to an end, and so I simply opened my eyes weeding out any connection my shadows had to my subconscious.

Once awake my thoughts returned to Justin. "Damn you," I said, into my pillow even more frustrated.

My nightmares ceased to scare me. There was nothing anyone could do to make me feel any worse than I already felt. The strange thing was that with each dream the intensity escalated which made the images seem all the more real. That night was no different

It was about two in the morning and the moonlight outside was beckoning me. I decided to take a stroll to clear my mind knowing full well that I would be alone. There was no chance of running into Gabriel. I knew, for a fact that he was on the yacht – a safe distance away.

Slipping into a short, white Boho dress, I decided not to head down my usual path but follow another, instead. It was impossible to get lost on the island, but with such poor visibility the terrain was quite dangerous. Though there was an inexplicable aura in the air, I continued on the path knowing that my gift would alert me of any danger. However, the sensation that usually preceded the onset of something foul was definitely surrounding me.

A drop of moisture against the back of my neck was enough to make me jump out of my skin. Looking around, however, I noticed nothing out of the ordinary so I continued to hike up the lush, green slope, hoping that the view from up top was worth all the work. Then, as I pulled and pushed my way through the undergrowth, a thought ghosted across my mind – *I'm not alone.*

I stopped climbing and stood my ground, turning in a circle to survey the area, but still, I saw absolutely nothing. But no sooner did I take my next step when I felt a soft brush across the face. It was as soft and subtle as a feather but worrying enough that it ignited my wrist.

"Who's there?" I asked looking around.

Eerie in its silence – the sound of the forest was smothered by the loud beating of my heart in my ears.

"Get a grip!" I told myself, shrugging the fear off and decided that I was too far into the hike to turn back, so I continued to the highest point of the island.

Once at the top, I sat a safe distance from the edge of the cliff, inviting the fresh breeze to wash over me. I attempted to take a deep breath, but the knot in my throat made it impossible. Over and over again I tried to inhale, and finally after the fiftieth or so attempt, I was finally able to breathe in deep. Then, as I sat there more confused than ever before, I concentrated on the sound of the crashing waves against the rocks. The rhythmic sound was soothing and rather relaxing. It was the crisp clear early hours of the day that showed the moon and the stars in all their clarity. The moon seemed close enough to reach, its brilliance mirrored on the ocean below casting a soft light on the crest of the waves.

Emptied and exhausted, I felt numb. Even the dream that was meant to scare me did not rattle me one bit. I looked towards the edge of the behemoth, fifty-foot drop, fascinated by the sheer distance. Something in my mind suddenly altered, thinking how easy it would be to end it all.

Nearly sick with fear, I felt the same soft brush against my cheek. *You would be saving the families from any imminent danger.* I heard my mind say in a whirlwind of dark thoughts. *They wouldn't need to worry about putting themselves in harm's way once you are gone for good. You can do this, Caitlin. Take the leap.*

The sound of my own voice in my ears was terrifying. It alternated from a whisper to a crisp sound and then to a whisper again. This insanity continued on and off for what seemed forever. I tried to shake the vulgar thoughts completely out of my head, but something was tearing my inner mind to pieces.

Come on, jump Caitlin – just jump and you'll be free.

Though the voice inside was my own, I had no control of it. In one quick thought it triggered a horrific pull – a pull towards the edge. *It's easy Caity. Come – jump. They'll all be safer.*

I struggled against it, tried my hardest to keep my body from moving forward, but the force driving me to the edge was much stronger than my own need to stay put. My wrist suddenly started to throb in reaction to the rabid need to jump. Whoever or whatever was causing this was seriously messing with my head. I willed one thing while my dark thoughts willed another. *Come – one more step, and you'll be free. They will all be safe.*

"Stop!" I finally found the voice to scream, shaking my head – trying desperately to banish the vile thoughts from my mind. My legs however were defying me – moving dangerously close to the edge.

Come Caity. You know its best you jump. One more step - come on, you can do it.

Within those fierce moments, the narrow line between sanity and insanity was obscured by my own putrid thoughts and inability to control my own mind.

"Come – that's it – one more step. Come on - jump. You know it will feel good. Do it Caitlin."

I had both hands on my head squeezing it hard – hoping that it would somehow force the voice to stop, but it was useless. *"Don't fight it. You don't need to feel sad anymore. One more step and you'll be free – free of everything – free of everyone."*

"Enough!" I yelled through clenched teeth, holding back the intolerable pounding in my skull. "Whoever you are, get the hell out of my head!" I said, stumping my foot on the ground, stopping my body in mid-stride. "Stop – damn it! Get the hell out of my head and show yourself!" I was furious and quite ready to defend myself.

Minutes later the satiated need to harm myself had vanished as quickly as it appeared, leaving me with the full brunt of my own gift.

Breathless, fearful and in utter shock, I sat on the nearest protruding rock realizing how close I came to ending it all.

"Caitlin, good morning. What are you doing here?" The sound of Alexander's voice made me turn.

He appeared out of nowhere holding some fishing gear in hand. His sudden presence did not even startle me. I could not think of anything to say. My mind was now a mush of emotions and thoughts – all jumbled in one great big ball of nothing.

Alexander propped his pack and gear against some rocks and sat beside me unaware of my throbbing wrist and said, "You look a bit pale. Are you okay?"

I didn't have an answer to give, so I remained silent.

He sat quite close – to close for someone who was not immune to my gift. Instinctively, I shifted inches away not wanting to hurt him accidentally. He smiled at me for some reason, questioning my impulse to secure a safe distance.

"Don't worry about me, Caitlin. There's not much your power can do. Not in the state you're in," he said, looking concerned.

I sat there in stunned silence.

"Emily wanted to come up and see you last night, but I told her you needed your rest. I hope I did the right thing."

I looked towards the sheer drop again and shook the whole ordeal off. "No," I finally said, coughing back the word, finding it hard to speak, "I didn't want to see anyone."

An uncomfortable silence once again descended in those tranquil surroundings. Neither of us spoke.

"These small hours are what I live for," he started to say. "I have been coming to this spot forever and this is the first time I have been blessed with good company."

Just then, I realized I was intruding on his private time. Running around all day meeting our needs, Alexander needed his peace more than anyone.

"I'm sorry. I didn't mean to intrude. I'll be on my way," I said, preparing to stand. "I really don't want to ruin this for you. You need this time more than anyone. We've been driving you crazy, I'm sure."

His smile broadened. "Even in your state of mind you put others before your own needs. That's a remarkable trait to have."

"Yeah, well, I should still get going." I wasn't sure how to respond to his compliment.

He instantly took hold of my throbbing wrist, "Sit down, Caitlin!" he ordered, beaming a genuine smile. "You needn't go anywhere. There's enough room for both of us. Besides, I'd love some company." He reached out and took my hand. "Please!"

"Alex, you shouldn't – you'll –," My voice tapered off as I looked down at his hand on my wrist. He didn't even flinch from the force my gift exerted to his touch.

"Child, just sit down," he repeated, letting go of my hand, and patted the rock next to him. "Come and sit – it's beautiful up here."

I sat back down astounded by his insusceptibility to my power. "How did you do that?" I asked in disbelief. "How did you…."

"We all have our little secrets, Caitlin. What I did or can do is not important," he said, grabbing for his thermos.

"Some secrets are not so little, Alex. I'm tired of all the secrets – tired of everyone and absolutely everything."

"Now, that sort of attitude gets you nowhere. How can you be in such a foul mood on such a magnificent time of day? You should be here with Justin. Instead you're here contemplating the worst."

I looked at him shocked once again. "You can read my thoughts, can't you?" I asked knowing that no one else could – not even the Ellri. "Can you tell me who that was – in my head, I mean? Who wanted me to take a dive off this cliff?"

Alexander did not answer. Instead he handed me two cups – pretending not to hear my question.

"Help me will you?" he asked, twisting open the thermos only to unleash the invigorating smell of freshly brewed coffee. "Hold steady," he said, smiling, "wouldn't want to burn you."

Once he filled each cup with the mouthwatering contents he tucked the thermos back in his sack, and turned to take one of the cups from my hand. He lifted it up to his mouth, sipped the warm liquid, and closed his eyes to relish in the moment.

"It's amazing how clear things seem after a good cup of coffee," he said, motioning me to drink up. "For someone so young…," He took another sip, "You have great control of your mind. It's truly amazing how you cast out all those morbid thoughts – quite a feat."

"It was one of those stupid tests, wasn't it? I should've known."

His calm expression altered for a slight second – just long enough for me to notice his concern. With his lips to the cup he said, "No. That was most certainly not a test."

My fear was quickly shadowed by shock. I did not respond immediately – just sat there drinking the coffee that he offered.

"If it wasn't a test, then the only other logical explanation is that someone out there wants me dead – right?" I finally asked, and let the sound of the words take their course to settle in my mind because even though I said them I did not want to believe them. "Someone, wants me dead," I repeated softly.

Neither of us spoke for quite some time. Alexander simply sat next to me motionless, allowing the silence to hold the answer to my comment.

It took a full cup of coffee to wash down the underlying meaning of his refusal to speak further on the topic. However, when he did finally speak again he said, "Caitlin, a great man once said that the best relationship is one which your love for each other exceeds your need for each other." He took another sip and half turned to look at me. "Justin seems to put you above all else. Why is that so bad?"

Far from anything I had expected to hear, a treacherous tear, nonetheless, betrayed the calm façade I was displaying. "Where did that come from, Alex?"

"Well, Caitlin – am I wrong?"

"You fight for what you love, Alex. You don't simply let it

go or worse yet, accept a life without it."

"You're absolutely right, Caitlin. I couldn't agree with you more. But would you fight to keep someone knowing they'd be happy elsewhere? Correct me if I'm wrong, but wouldn't that be selfish?"

"Selfish or not, you keep the people you love close. You don't push them away. You don't accept a possible life without them."

Alexander smiled. "You're so, so young, Caitlin – so very young. Don't allow your ego to construe Justin's feelings. You know the boy loves you more than life itself. Sacrificing this in the hope of seeing you happy is commendable. Not many would be so generous with their affection."

I knew what Alexander was saying was right, but I was still not ready to accept the truth. "I was offended. I'm sorry, but I can't see past that," I confessed, raising my eyes to his, only to be met with green pools of compassion. "I'm willing to sacrifice everything for him, and he...," I turned my gaze out to sea, swallowing back the pain.

"The only thing you can't see past, Caitlin is your own selfish pain – the part of you that relishes in Justin's devotion and commitment. Would you not want to see him happy? Haven't you, on many occasions, thought of leaving him to keep him safe? How is that any different?"

I half-turned and looked at him. "How could he possibly think I could want anybody else, Alex? We were born for each other. Our bond reminds us every day. How could he think that I would throw that away – and for what? For the likes of Gabriel? Give me some credit."

Alexander simply shook his head, "Why can't you see the obvious? He's a young man, Caitlin. He felt threatened by your new admirer. Gabriel simply triggered his insecurities. Don't blame him for being a bit jealous. Don't you think you have more important things to worry about?"

His profound understanding of my problems raised a flag of concern.

"Alex, who are you? You seem to know an awful lot about me?"

He stood up and started collecting his things. "I'm just the grounds keeper," he said, winking at me, taking the empty coffee cup from my hands. "Life is way too short to be wasting it on self-pity, Caitlin. Find the strength to forgive and take great caution on your quest for answers. This path you're on is full of peril and turmoil. Be sure you have weighed your adversary rightly," he said, picking up the last of his stuff. "Keep your wits about you. You need to be focused and your mind must be clear of all negativity."

I remained seated as he prepared to leave. "There's just so much one person can take, Alex. I'm tired of running into walls."

"Aren't we all, child? Aren't we all?"

"What am I supposed to do, Alex?"

"The only thing you can do."

"And what's that exactly?"

"Simply plant your feet firm on the ground and wait out the storm."

"You make it sound so easy, but it's not, Alex."

"Who said it was going to be easy? You were born to go down the road less travelled. Don't look for shortcuts."

I raised my hands in frustration. "What shortcuts? I haven't noticed any shortcuts. Some road signs would have been nice."

He chuckled. "I'll see you around, Caitlin, and think about what I said."

Pushed To The Edge

Illustrated for Lines That Bind - Within The Whispers

ELEVEN

GROWING UP

TWO DAYS AND JUSTIN was nowhere in sight. I did my best to act normal in front of everyone, but most of the time I returned to the seclusion of my room where I hid under the white cotton sheets with a good book.

Emily looked concerned, but at no time did she bring up the topic. Kyle, on the other hand, commented on our 'lover's quarrel' as he put it on several occasions making light note of it. Tyler seemed to be unaware of my problem. His attention was otherwise occupied. Karen seemed to be all he could think about.

It was then that I noticed that everybody around me was in a little love cloud of their own. Emily was sitting in Marc's lap on the far-east corner of the terrace while Sandy and Kyle were splashing away in the pool. Even Laura had found a formidable chess partner in Dmitri now that Justin was nowhere to be seen.

Surprisingly, Gabriel fit in quite well with the group, staying by my side on the occasions when I did leave my room.

"I've missed not seeing you around," he said, over breakfast that morning. "You seem very sad. What's wrong?"

"Nothing, I'm fine," I lied, smiling at him. "I just didn't get a good night's sleep, that's all."

"Oh, and here I thought I was to blame."

I turned sharply to face him, putting my plan in motion. "Why would you think something like that?"

"I just don't want to be the reason for you and Justin to be arguing."

I hated the sound of Justin's name coming out of his slithery mouth. He had no right to even think about him. I pushed the hair back from my face and shook my head. "You're not, and you really don't need to be concerned about Justin."

"I'm not," he answered curtly. "It's you I'm worried about."

"Don't be. I'm perfectly fine. How could anybody be miserable in paradise," I lied, stretching out my hands wide open, motioning to our splendid surroundings. "Gabriel, why don't you tell me a little about the Korbs? Nobody speaks of them back in Oaks."

"What would you like to know?" he asked, taking a bite of his croissant.

I ground my teeth behind my soft smile. "Anything really – I know so little."

"Well, let me think. You know about your grandparents, don't you?"

"Apart from their names – nothing," I lied.

"Your grandfather Clancy and your grandmother Eileen had four children. Your father was the eldest, as you well know – then came Caradon who has twin sons Clancy Jr. and Albion who are about...," he rubbed his forehead. "They should be twelve, if I'm not mistaken. Then there's your uncle Brett, who has three kids." Gabriel took a quick sip of coffee before saying, "and your aunt Rebecca's the youngest. I'm not sure how many children she has – two I'm sure of."

"That's quite a family."

"That's nothing. Your grandfather is the eldest of eight siblings so you can imagine how big your extended family is. Somewhere in some book the family tree has been kept quite up to date. There are multitudes of branches. The family's legacy spans for many centuries, eons even."

"Which branch do you fall under?" I asked, looking intrigued.

"You could say we're cousins of sorts – fifth – sixth," he smiled, taking another sip. "I'm not clear on the details. Your great-grandfather and my great-grandfather were either first cousins or second. I'm not sure."

"Interesting! Do you guys all live in the same community as we do?"

"More or less, it's just that our family is so big that there are several smaller communities spread out in Europe. Your great-great-grandfather had a passion for wine. Not drinking it but making it," he said smiling. "He had moved our particular community – the biggest and purest in blood to northern Italy about a century or so ago. The town is called Velius. It's one of a kind, magical in more ways than one."

"It must be beautiful out there." I said thinking about my little trip to the past.

"You have no idea. You're going to love it, Caitlin. You'll never want to leave. There's so much to do."

"You sound like you miss it?"

Gabriel exhibited the warmest of smiles. "I do – I really do. I haven't been back for quite some time."

There was a tinge of pain underlining his every word.

"So, what's been keeping you away? Don't you have a girl pining for you back home?"

Gabriel sat like a stone, his face impassive, but reluctance to speak writ large in his eyes. "Not that I know of," he said, after a short pause, "At least none that I'm attracted to."

"You want me to believe that you don't have someone waiting for you? I mean – look at you. Are the girls in your community blind or something? How can they have left such a catch go?" I giggled.

"Is that how you see me?" he asked, visibly satisfied by my words. "Well – things are different in Velius, Caitlin. It isn't that simple."

"What isn't? How hard can it be? Boy meets girl, girl likes boy, they get together and the rest is history."

"It's a bit more complicated than that as far as the Korbs are concerned. We are matched to our other half. You can call it an arranged marriage."

I bit my lip. "You can't be serious! That's so cruel. What if you love someone else?"

"Caitlin, don't look so shocked. It's not as bad as it sounds. Traditions are there to protect us – to keep our kind from disappearing. Before suggesting a possible mate, our Ellri see to it that our powers are matched in strength."

The period of worry came from the knowledge that my theory didn't seem so juvenile after all. *Did the Korbs find a suitable match for me?*

"Wow, Gabriel that sounds too intense. What if someone was born for another?"

"What do you mean – born for one another?"

"Well, I've heard that the none-gifted have soul mates. Some people are supposedly bound to someone from the moment they're born. What if that occurs – what then? What would your Ellri do?"

"You're not seriously suggesting the Life-bond, are you?" he said chuckling. "The chances of something so patently absurd actually existing are billions to one. The whole notion of a Life-bond is ludicrous."

"Oh c'mon, Gabriel, don't make fun of me. I told you I don't know anything." I smiled girlishly. "What if it did occur? What then?"

He placed his hand on my shoulder and smiled. "You really don't know anything, do you?" he said, teasing a lock of my hair free so that he could run it through his fingers.

I forced myself not to wince as he touched me.

"I'm not sure what to tell you, Caitlin," he continued to say. "The Ellri would know, but it's highly unlikely that anything of the sort exists. Besides, bonds between our kind are only a myth – love stories that were passed down from generation to generation. Nonsense, if you ask me."

It was rather hard to keep myself from smiling at the thought of how rare Justin and I were. We were an exception to the natural order of things – one in a billion is how Gabriel put it. I was stupid – real stupid! How could I be so dense? Justin would forfeit his own life, his own feelings to see me happy. Determined to atone for my muddled interpretation of his sincerity I wanted nothing more than to locate Justin, but first I needed to finish up with Gabriel. He was open and willing to answer my questions. It would have been a mistake to get up and leave, just yet.

I took a long relaxing sip of ice-cold lemonade and turned to look at him. "Well? What are you waiting for?" His brow lifted in uncertainty. "Tell me one of the stories you know about this Life-bond. This is the first time I hear of it."

"You know, Caitlin, it's one of those sappy love stories set thousands of years ago."

"Tell me!" I insisted "I want to know."

"What is it with girls and stories of hopeless love?"

"Humor me!" I said smiling.

"Fine!" he finally conceded. "The legend takes place thousands of years ago before the Korbs family even existed. It talks about a young girl who was born into one of the former gifted tribes, long gone now. Hassimin was considered gifted, like no other. You see, she was able to control the elements with precision. Such great gifts weren't heard of in those days. It was said that for some unexplained reason she suffered greatly."

"What kind of suffering?" I asked, wide eyed.

"She was in great pain – complained that her blood was on fire. At first, nobody knew why this was, but soon after they concluded that the pain resonated from the overwhelming energy she used to control her gift." Gabriel stopped momentarily and chuckled at how intense I was looking at him. "You really like this kind of stuff, don't you?"

I smacked his hand playfully and said, "What can I say? I'm a hopeless romantic. Now go on!"

He chuckled again and continued, "Hassimin was betrothed at the age of fifteen to a much older man named Tibbs, against her will. Loyal as she was, she didn't make a fuss when her family sent her away to live with her husband's family. Unfortunately for her, the moment she reached this new land she felt an immense elation. The burn she felt in her veins had completely vanished the second she was introduced to eighteen-year-old Biden – her husband's youngest brother. Both Biden and Hassimin didn't know what to make of their attraction."

Completely rapt in the story I said, "That's not good."

"It wasn't." Gabriel answered and continued with the legend. "You see, it was excruciatingly painful each time they were apart. They both felt torn the second they separated. They longed for the opportunity to exchange but a single word."

"How unfair," I sighed.

Gabriel grinned. "It's only a story." I pulled a nasty face. Smiling, he continued on with the tale, "One morning they were no longer able to suppress their desire – a force much greater than any element on earth was pulling them together. A meeting point and time was then established. This was near a tomb outside the small village where the young couple would meet for the first time. Hassimin waited eagerly for the last rays of sunlight so that she could finally make her way under the cloud of darkness. Never had her young heart beaten with such fervor."

"Weren't the others in the village gifted? Couldn't they read her thoughts? Wasn't it dangerous to sneak off like that? What about her husband, Tibbs? Wasn't there anyone to stop her? "

Gabriel simply stared and rolled his eyes. "Are you finished?"

I nodded, acknowledging how stupid I sounded.

"Good," he said, beaming a wide smile. After another sip of coffee he continued the tale from where he had left off. "Torn between his love for Hassimin and his devotion to his family, the younger brother had decided to confess his love for the young Hassimin to his brother, Tibbs. Surprisingly enough, Tibbs didn't show any sign of jealousy. In the guise of understanding, the betrayed older brother allowed Biden to go freely, secretly following him to the meeting place. Once there he confronted his young wife. At first he tortured her and then, when he had his fill of vengeance, he cut her open with the intention of tearing out her heart, but stopped the moment Biden reached the horrific scene." I gasped in horror.

"With wails of grief, young Biden called for the young woman, holding her hand and caressing her face in her struggle to stay alive."

"What happened? Did she survive?"

Gabriel shook his head. "No she didn't. What's most interesting about the legend is that Biden also died the moment Hassimin drew her last breath."

Gabriel picked up his cup of coffee and put it to his lips, abruptly ending the story. "And that's how the story goes. The Life-bond supposedly tied them in life as it did in death. Not one could live without the other."

"That's so sad. Do you think it could be real?" I asked all the more intrigued by the sheer power of the bond.

"We're talking about thousands of years ago, Caitlin. I'm sure it didn't pan out exactly in that way. I personally don't believe in the so called, 'bond'. It's never been documented nor has any other story surfaced since then. I don't see how that particular tale can be true. The whole scene might have been exaggerated."

I took a few minutes to absorb the impact the tale had on me. I couldn't help but think if that could possibly be a reflection of what was to come. I shook it off ignoring the intense sadness I felt for Hassimin and Biden's demise.

"Gabriel? Have you been matched to somebody?" I asked, purposely shifting from the story.

He instantly swallowed hard, in reaction to my question. "Sort of," he said, visibly uncomfortable. "She merely needs to accept. Nobody is ever forced into anything," he said, looking down at his cup, deliberately not making eye contact.

I slurped up the last of my lemonade through the straw, trying to think of a way around his discomfort. "Do you even have a say in the matter? What if you don't like her?"

"Caitlin, you grow to love the person. Don't they teach you anything in Oaks about our kind? After the Oath is taken the couple becomes one, sharing their powers as well as their thoughts and emotions. The oath binds you to the other."

I pretended to act surprised. I didn't want him to suspect me in any way. Gabriel needed to believe that I was left in the dark about everything. At the time, it seemed to be the only way to underhandedly elicit information.

"So, tell me about her. Is she at least pretty?" I asked elbowing teasingly.

"She's distractingly beautiful," he said, gazing into my eyes, smiling wickedly.

"That's great. You're one of the lucky ones, I guess. You really like her, don't you?"

"Let's just say, I was hooked the moment I saw her."

I patted him on the shoulder like I would my best friend, "Wow! That's something. Has she seen you? Does she know who you are?"

His grin widened, showing off his perfectly white teeth. "Yes she's seen me, and yes she finally knows who I am."

"Lucky girl," I exclaimed, stroking his ego.

He refilled my glass, finding it hard to hide his satisfaction. "I'm glad you think so, Caitlin."

"So what are you two waiting for? Why haven't you taken the plunge," I giggled.

"Well, there are still some loose ends to tie up, and as I said before, she simply needs to accept."

"Oh, right, I forgot. So what do you do till then? Do you guys go out to get to know each other better?"

"Caitlin? Why the sudden interest in my personal life?" he asked, intentionally cutting me off.

"It's just so interesting. Not that I would ever allow anybody to arrange my own relationship, but seeing that you're happy about their choice sounds fantastic. I'm sure she's a wonderful girl."

I knew it wasn't that simple. He talked about choices – once the match was made neither partner had a choice in the matter. My father and mother were testament to that. The fury my grandfather displayed at my father's defiance; choosing my mother above the rest, was not, in any way, congruent to the belief of free will. Gabriel was obviously sugar coating the breeding process in the hopes of conveying how civilized their traditions were.

Ava, just then, came up to us all bright eyed. "You guys seem to be hitting it off."

"Ava...," I exclaimed excitedly, "Gabriel's been telling me about the Korbs and the story of Hassimin and Biden."

I knew she was questioning my mood. She didn't appear to doubt me – on the surface anyway.

"Really, Gabriel?" she said scowling. "Have you told her the one about Winston and Carolyn – her parents? I'm sure you'll have her rolling on the ground laughing – am I wrong?"

I looked at him doe eyed, pretending not to know what she meant. But Gabriel didn't seem to find her words, at all, amusing. He quickly stood up, visibly annoyed at Ava. "I need to get some things off the boat," he said, attempting a smile. "Caitlin, hope we get a chance to talk later."

"Do you really need to go?" I asked sulking. "I'd love to hear the story about my parents. I know so little about them." I swallowed back the vile in my mouth.

"Next time, I promise," he said, stroking my hair tenderly.

I nodded in agreement and watched him casually walk away. Seeing him leave was a relief because I was tired of playing stupid. I missed Justin, and not knowing where he was worried me.

"Caitlin, you don't have to do this. Gabriel is much smarter than you give him credit. He'll eventually see through your charade." Ava warned, taking the seat across from me.

I put my head down on the table exhausted. Acting the gullible teenager was not as easy as I thought. Half the time I wanted to leap out of my skin.

"Can you think of a better way to discover what the Korbs are after?" I asked, slightly raising my voice.

She laid her hand on mine. "I see your point. Just be careful. You're treading on real thin ice as far as Gabriel is concerned. Don't let his angelic looks deceive you."

"Why are the McDevitts holding a meeting?" I asked out of the blue, taking her by surprise.

"Ah, I see Justin's been doing some digging!"

"Don't hold it against him, Ava. He's just as keen on figuring this thing out as I am."

"No, it's fine. I know he means well. That boy always does."

I caught the double meaning of her words. She obviously blamed me for the argument I had with Justin. It was in the way she said it. I knew her all too well to be mistaken.

"We're meeting to discuss probable outcomes," she added.

My eyes widened as I said, "What outcomes are you anticipating?"

"Caitlin, there is no reason to be scared. When you decide to stand up for the things you believe in, you always take some kind of risk. We're meeting to see what the impending risks might be."

I stood up and rapped my hand flat upon the table attracting everybody's attention. I was infuriated by how casual she was about the bleak future.

"I won't allow any of you to risk anything for me," I yelled, looking around to all my family and friends. "Do we have an understanding? Nobody needs to do anything for my sake – I mean it."

Hand in hand, Emily and Marc made their way to where Ava and I were seated. Then Kyle came followed by Tyler.

"What's the problem?" Kyle asked, looking worried.

"I won't have any of you..," I took a deep breath. "Anybody for that matter risk their life for me. Do I make myself clear?"

"That's not a choice for you to make, little sis," Kyle said, putting his arm around my shoulder "Wouldn't you risk everything for one of us?"

"You know I would!"

"Then, there's your answer. Why would it be okay for you to risk your life for us, but not the other way round?" Kyle was once again the older, wiser brother. "Whether you like it or not we are all family. We laugh together and cry together. Get that through your thick skull."

"Yeah, Caity," Emily added. "Did you really think that we would simply sit back and allow anybody to lay a finger on you? I mean, really. The only reason we haven't tore Gabriel to shreds is because you want him here. Until you say otherwise we'll be on our best behavior."

"You guys mean everything to me and none of us know how this will turn out. What if the Korbs refute the Council's decision – what then?"

Tyler took a step closer and said, "Why do you always think of the worst case scenario? We all know what risk this whole situation has. Just because we don't sit around talking about it doesn't mean we're not aware. There's no point in worrying. We all know where we stand on the issue. You are part of our family and we'll be damned if we let anybody say otherwise."

I hugged him – held him quite tight not wanting to let go. Tyler responded by tightening his hold.

"Caitlin," Marc said, drawing my attention, "I'm not one to intervene or even pretend to know the reason behind what you're doing. It's just that Gabriel is not a toy you can play with. He is lethal and quite capable of doing much harm. Take Justin's advice and stay away from him. I beg you."

"He can give us insight on what the Korbs are after. That's the only reason I'm keeping him close," I explained. "You have to trust me on this. He means absolutely nothing to me."

Out of nowhere Emily let go of Marc's hand and lessened the distance between us, looking rather angry. "Since everything is out on the table," she said, raising her voice. "Gabriel aside, Caity. What the hell is wrong with you?" she screamed infuriated. "Can you please finally open your eyes and see how much Justin cares about you? Why do you insist on making your life miserable? I mean for heaven's sake, enough is enough, grow up already!"

They were all bobbing their heads in agreement.

"She's right," Tyler said, squeezing me a bit tighter. "He's going crazy – aimlessly wondering the island. You really need to put an end to this."

The connection they shared kept them abreast of each other's thoughts. Apparently, Justin wasn't blocking them out, knowing they would be too persistent in their quest to know what was wrong.

"How in the world did we go from discussing the possibility of losing our lives to the topic of Justin and me?"

Kyle chuckled under his breath. "You and Justin are the present. Whether we live or die – tomorrow even, is not for us to say. Why worry about it?"

"Kyle is right Caitlin!" Ava said, adamantly. "We only need to worry about the things we are handed to solve one day at a time. The future is not in our hands to guide. That's the beauty of life. We never know what tomorrow holds. The only factor we need to worry about is whether we have done the best with the things we are dealt with each and every day, and that's all."

I felt as though I was in one of those clichéd after-school specials, where the wise teacher takes the troubled student aside to give her a lesson in life. However, apart from the banal lecture, Ava's words were unsurprisingly, spot on. Why worry about something I had no control over?

"Fine, you all win. Now go. Leave me alone!" I said smiling, waving them away. They didn't budge. "Seriously, go," I repeated, taking a seat.

They all returned to what they were doing. Tyler took Karen by the hand and led her down to the beach. Marc and Emily joined Kyle and Sandy in the pool.

"They're amazing, aren't they?" I said looking at Ava.

"You all are!"

I put my head down on the table. "What am I going to do?" I asked, overcome with the need to see Justin. The pull was much stronger with each passing hour.

"You know what you need to do. Justin meant well. You can't blame somebody for loving you so much," she said, patting me on the shoulder. "I'll be at my cottage if you need me."

TWELVE

FORGIVENESS

THE HOURS THAT FOLLOWED were, for me, a time of inner change, a time for the glum insecurities that made me question Justin's pure intentions to be put permanently aside.

Suddenly, as though summoned up by my own inner, deepest thoughts I stood up and headed to the main house. Once inside, the air was charged. It caught in my lungs like some giant hand pressing against my chest. I shivered back in awareness, knowing it was the intensity of the bond that caused my body to react so.

Justin must be upstairs, I thought, as I hesitantly made my way to our room. Whether caused by the anxiety of seeing him or by the unremitting pull of our unique connection, I stood there, on the other side of the door, breathing in short and unsteady breaths. *I need to be mature about this*, I thought.

I didn't know how to go about apologizing for my innate ability to misconstrue everything.

I'll grovel. That's it – I'll just kneel in front of him and beg for forgiveness.

Pausing only long enough to catch my breath, I reached for the handle and opened the door. He was in the midst of packing. In disbelief I stood there watching Justin collect his belongings, deliberately ignoring me.

"Are you going somewhere?" I asked, getting up enough courage to speak.

He continued to fold his clothes and stuff them in his suitcase. "I thought you might need your space," he replied, avoiding eye contact.

As soon as he turned to retrieve more articles of clothing from the drawer, I quickly positioned myself between him and his suitcase, blocking his path. As Justin turned to pack, he nearly ran into me, not expecting to find me only inches from his face.

"What makes you think I need space?" I asked, intentionally meeting his gaze.

I sensed his awkwardness – Justin wasn't at all ready to face me. He took a step back.

Although he stood there, inches away, his face was slightly turned to the side – eyes to the floor, biting his lower lip.

"Shouldn't you be heading back downstairs? Gabriel shouldn't be left waiting," he finally said, with distaste in his mouth.

I didn't respond. I just stared at the perfect creature in front of me. *Alexander was so right*, I thought, *Justin is jealous. Why didn't I see that earlier?*

"Gabriel? Gabriel who?" I asked.

He shifted his uneasy posture and finally looked at me. "The guy you're hanging around with - the one who can't seem to get his mind out of the gutter. The one who keeps touching you every opportunity he gets. The one you seem to be so interested in knowing."

I shook my head vigorously, "Nope, I don't know anyone like that," I said smiling "But if you mean the tall blond guy who I'm pretending to like to get my answers, then yes, I think I know who you're referring to."

Justin raised his eyebrow, not one bit amused. "Will you move? I'd like to get this done."

"Nope," I took one step closer to him, leaving absolutely no space between us.

He turned his head even further to the side. "I need to get this done, please."

Acting against his wishes I reached up and kissed the curve of his neck, giving him no time to react. His whole body responded to my lips. "Don't!" he exclaimed, fighting back the need to touch me.

I ignored his plea and trailed kisses all the way up the side of his neck and stopped at the lobe of his ear. There was no way he could resist the pull we both felt. It was undeniably strong, intensified by the days we were apart.

Poor Justin took a step back shaking his head, looking lost; contemplating his next words. "You need time to think, time to make the choice you've always wanted to make."

"And what choice would that be?" I said, moving forward.

I took his face in my hands and kissed him on the mouth. He didn't back away; not that he could. Slowly, I moved my arms around his neck pushing myself up against his body. His mouth responded painstakingly to mine, arousing every living cell in my body. Everything he was holding instantly fell to the floor. I continued to kiss him. Wanting nothing more than to make him understand how much I missed him, how much I needed him in my life. Justin put one hand on my back bringing me even closer towards him. I tightened my hold burying my head against his neck.

"Caitlin...," he whispered against my skin, holding me closer, brushing my shoulder with his sultry lips, caressing my back. "Damn it Caitlin, I can't stay away from you."

"Why would you want to?" I said between kisses.

"You're going to drive me crazy." Justin said, letting out the stress that burdened him.

"We established that already," I said, giddily; completely intoxicated by his closeness. "It's the when we're trying to figure out."

He pushed me slightly away with both hands. "Why the sudden change? Why forgive me for the rotten things I said? It wasn't my intention to offend you. It just came out all wrong. I can't bear to think of you with him," he admitted.

"Stop talking." I kissed him. "Why in the world would I ever be in another man's arms?" I asked. "Enough with the apologies already. That's all we seem to be doing, and as far as my choices are concerned," I stopped and took his face in my hands. "You are it. You've been it from the second I was born. You're stuck with me, whether you like it or not?"

He smiled, leaning his forehead to mine. "I love you," he whispered softly, and then kissed me tenderly.

"You'd better," I giggled, kissing him back.

"I hated being away from you, I really did. I was going mad."

I took his hand in mine and smiled. "No, I was stupid for – for everything. This is all new to me. I've never been in a serious relationship before – any kind of relationship for that matter. You'll have to be patient with me. I'm a walking disaster."

He chuckled. "You're perfect!"

"Yeah, Yeah – you have to say that."

I was about to let go of his hand and head for the bed to sit, when he pulled me back in his direction. "Caitlin, there's one more thing," he said, sounding all too serious for my liking.

"What is it? You're scaring me."

"I don't want you to ever wonder off to that part of the island again, especially at that time of day. Those cliffs are dangerous enough in the day time. You could've gotten hurt."

"How did you know where I was?"

"Alexander kept me informed of your whereabouts." He walked to the window with both hands combing through his tussled hair. "I hate that I can't read you," he said, turning to face me. "You have no idea how infuriating it is."

I didn't know what he expected me to say. I kind of liked the idea of finally having my thoughts to myself. Being unable to block any of them out all those weeks was frustrating. Some things were meant to be personal – meant to be kept only for me.

"Is this going to be a permanent thing?" I asked, hoping that it would be.

"Only time will tell. But from now on you stay close, no wondering off without letting me know first. Okay?"

"Sure, yeah, no problem," I didn't sound too convincing, but Justin made no fuss about it. Instead he gave me a quick kiss. "Justin? What do you know about Alex? He seems to know an awful lot about us."

"What's there to know? He's the grounds keeper. He's gifted, but apart from that, I know nothing about the man."

Something seemed to be preoccupying Justin. He didn't seem all too interested in talking about Alexander.

"There's something you want to say to me, isn't there?" I asked, seeing that his discomfort was getting the best of him.

"I don't want to reopen this topic in fear of getting into another argument."

I took his hand in mine. "What is it? Talk to me."

He was hesitant at first. "You need to stop whatever you're doing with Gabriel," he finally said ardently. "The guy thinks you're really interested in him. He's not playing."

"That's the whole point, isn't it? I didn't spend all morning with him because I couldn't stay away. He knows so much about the Korbs, and I plan on learning every last bit of information."

Justin wasn't at all thrilled at my response. He let go of my hand and traversed the length of the room, running his fingers through his hair. But this time it looked like he wanted to pull it out rather than just comb through it. Aggravated, he turned and said, "Where does that leave me? Am I supposed to stand back and watch you flirt? Can you honestly see me doing that without killing someone?"

My initial response was to laugh at his inability to hold back his adorable temper, but I controlled my urge and simply smiled. "I know this is going to be difficult for you, but I need to find out what they're up to, for all our sakes. You'll just have to grit and bear it, I do!"

"Caitlin, this isn't going to work. The guy knows exactly how I feel about you. Hell, he doesn't need any gift to see that. How are you planning to pull this off?"

"He might know how you feel, but he's in the dark as far as I'm concerned. Our supposed break up warmed him up to me. He answered every question I asked. We are family after all, shouldn't I know about my relatives?"

"If he...," Justin shook his head vehemently, "if he as even lifts a finger to touch you in any way, I swear I'll kill him."

I kissed him wanting him to stop his meaningless threats. He responded by hoisting me up against his warm body. "Promise that you'll stay away from him – promise me."

I combed my fingers through his tussled hair and kissed him feverishly and said, "I don't make promises I can't keep."

Justin's breathing deepened. He wanted me as much as I yearned for him. Just that second our eyes met. His hesitation to continue was clearly visible in his eyes. "Damn it! Catlin, we can't," he sighed, leaning his head to mine, wishing things were different.

"You really know how to kill the mood," I said, smiling. "You know, it might not hurt to try?"

He caressed my cheek and took a small step back. "You see, that's where you're wrong. It won't merely hurt; it will surely kill us both."

"You're being too dramatic!"

"I'm being real, Caitlin. Not until you ascend!"

I plopped myself on the bed face down, smothering my frustration with the pillow. "How can you stand it? How can you be so mature about this?" I asked, keeping my head buried in the pillow.

Justin came and sat himself on the edge of the bed. "Don't lie to yourself, Caitlin. You know you're still not ready, even without all the obstacles. The other day at the beach you were practically hyperventilating at the mere thought of you and me – you know." I raised my head just enough to look at him from the corner of my eye, "You picked up on that, did you?" I said, mortified. "Can I please die now?" I screamed into the pillow, red as a beetroot.

Justin shoved me to the center of the bed, making himself comfortable. "It's natural to be nervous. You don't have to feel weird about that. Powers aside, you don't have to do anything that you're not ready for. We'll wait until you're good and ready."

"Can you please stop? Please, just stop! Do you know how

humiliating it is talking to you about this? It's just not right."

"Fine, if you're going to act all weird – I'll stop. I just don't want you to feel pressured into doing anything."

I shyly sat up, straightening out my clothes, dodging his gaze. "I don't feel pressured into doing anything."

"Then what is it?"

"It's just that…," I couldn't finish the sentence. I put my face in my hands shaking my head in utter humiliation.

Justin gently lifted my face to eye level. "What is it?" He repeated. His smile was now erased from his face.

"You're older than me, and more experienced in this. What if…," I swallowed hard not knowing how to continue. "I've never – well – you know. What if I'm not – and you've been so patient – and – oh, forget it!" I hugged my knees and refused to look up.

I knew I wasn't making any sense. He just sat there quietly trying really hard not to laugh.

"What?" I yelled, frustrated, at his amusement.

He leaned over and effortlessly pulled me into his lap. I wanted to struggle free, totally annoyed that he considered my awkwardness amusing. I was crimson with shame and he thought it was funny.

His innocent chuckle turned into a full blown laugh. "You'll never cease to amaze me, Caitlin," he said, fiddling with my hair, "Of all the stupid things to worry about."

"Easy for you to say," I muttered, leaning my head against his shoulder. "You're experienced in this field. I'm not."

Justin didn't want to press the topic any further. He simply kissed me and held me tight, cradling me in his embrace. "I love you," he whispered in my ear before kissing me again.

"I love you more," I muttered, into the curve of his neck.

"Humanly impossible," Justin answered closing his eyes

momentarily, turning his head to the ceiling.

"What is it?" I asked.

"Emily wants me to tell you that she's happy we're working things out and she wants to know if we're up to going to the caves"

I was horrified. "Please tell me you're at least censoring what they can read?" I asked, worried that our friends knew the reason behind my reddened face.

"They only know what I want them to know. It saves a lot of time and questions," he answered.

"Good," I exhaled, a sigh of relief.

"Will I ever be able to do that?" I asked, whining. "Be able to communicate the way you all do?"

"Sure, in time. Emily can't project her thoughts to me. She simply concentrates on me, calling me in her mind. Then I simply read her thoughts. Now, what should I tell her?"

"I thought they would've gone to the caves by now. They were planning it two days ago."

"You didn't think they were going to leave you out of the adventure, did you? Now what should I tell her? She's really annoying. My head is starting to hurt from her nagging."

I laughed at how Emily could get under his skin. "Yeah, of course, I'd love to go."

~~~

Laura led the expedition along with Dmitri and Paolo, guiding us carefully through the rough terrain and thick vegetation. The further we walked, the darker the scenery became – thanks to the towering trees along with the hanging vines which blocked any beam of light from penetrating the thick canopy from all directions.

"This can't be right," said Laura stopping to get a sip of

water, "We must've taken a wrong turn somewhere. How is this even possible? I never got lost before."

The day was hot and muggy. Our clothes were wet – stuck uncomfortably against our skin.

"How lost can we possibly be? I can hear the ocean," said Emily, agitated by the sweat trickling down her porcelain features.

With a graceful wave of his hand, Paolo cleared away some of the ferny undergrowth that obstructed our hike. The vegetation simply collapsed forward with each movement of his hand, creating a passage for us to cross. "We're fine," he reassured us, continuing to move ahead, opening a path for us to walk. "It can't be too far. We're on an Island. How can we possibly be lost? We'll get there soon. Just stay close."

As I followed the group, a strange sensation crept up on the back of my neck. It felt like the brush of a feather across my damp skin. I was sure it was some sort of insect so I continued walking without giving itsy-bitsy spider the satisfaction of sending me into a girly screaming fit over an insect against my skin. And again, the feathery feeling was back. I stopped and wiped the back of my neck with a towel. Everyone else continued a few yards up ahead.

"Is pretty, Caitlin afraid of the big bad wolf?"

I looked around wondering where the sound came from. This time it wasn't in my head. It reverberated off the trees, the ground, everywhere all at once. Instantly the group back stepped and gathered around me. By the shocked expression on everyone's face, I wasn't the only one hearing voices.

"What the hell was that?" Kyle said, approaching me.

"Young mortals out on a walk with pretty, pretty Caitlin...."

There it was again.

"What would you sacrifice to keep her safe?"

"Caitlin, don't you dare move." I heard Justin say.

Without uttering another sound, my cousin Laura quickly pushed and pulled Tyler, Sandy, Emily and me behind her. "Stay put. Don't any of you move a muscle," she ordered, "Oh, and close your ears. This is going to be painful."

The rest of our group stood shoulder to shoulder, forming a tight circle around the four of us.

"These damn caves better be worth it," I heard Karen say through clenched teeth as she positioned herself next to her older sister, Dawn.

Tyler turned to me and looked concerned. "Don't worry," he mouthed. He grabbed my hand and held it tight.

In the next few seconds the eight Ascended members of our group all clasped hands and turned their heads up to the ski. With perfect synchronization they started to verbalize some sort of chant, and then out of nowhere Dmitri broke formation and bellowed out an order in his rich Italian accent, "Mostrati Spirito!" The sound of his voice was piercing, forcing Tyler, Sandy, Emily and I to cover our ears. "Show yourself!" he yelled again.

I raised my eyes only to see that a film of translucent light encompassed all of us – that was Kyle's doing, I was sure. But then Dmitri spoke again and with each syllable the forest growth yielded, flattened around us as if a sonic blast pancaked everything to the ground – undergrowth, trees, the lot.

"He's coming," I heard Kyle say, "Prepare!"

Before the order was complete, an earsplitting shrill cut through the forest approaching us in deathly precision. In seconds a fog so thick and pungent encircled us, filling my lungs with a vile, putrid aftertaste. It moved and circled around us like a snake around its prey.

"How tragically, sweet," said the hollow voice emanating within the decay. *You all choose to die for her?"*

Nobody answered. Instead, the monotonous low dull sound of their chanting turned into a spine-chilling, unchanging intonation – a droning of intelligible words. My attention shifted to Sandy. For some reason she looked stone-cold, in a trance like state. She was completely unresponsive to what was happening. Unlike Emily, Tyler and me, who were on the ground with our hands over our ears, Sandy was standing motionless – untouched by the way things were unfolding in front of our eyes.

"Can little Caitlin come out and play?"

Again, there was no response from the group. They started whispering some old text over and over again, until the strangest thing happened. All their voices fused into one soft, continuous whisper of chants.

The monster's laugh was bone shattering. *"To be young and stupid,"* it said laughing. *"Do you really think you can protect her?"* The dark serpentine cloud that encircled us started to shift and morph into a bodily form. *"Well, well – a group of brave young mortals – stupid, but brave,"* the creature said.

Its form was not made of substance, but an airy dark-grey element. Its face, on the other hand, was well concealed behind a veil of darkness. It was the absence of morality that frightened me most. The creature was pure evil. I could taste the wickedness – feel the vileness on my skin. My senses were heightened and I felt drawn to its every word and movement.

"Don't fight it, Caitlin. You know you feel it."

Too frightened to speak, I closed my eyes and turned my head to the ground.

"Don't fight your own instinct, mortal. You can taste it in your mouth. It appeals to you. The darkness comforts you. Why fight it?"

I refused to speak – scared of what the repercussions would be if I did, and then came light – the purest and most blinding light. We all looked away, unable to gaze in its direction.

Too shocked to speak, I turned momentarily and saw a being draped in beams of light as bright as the sun. Standing there motionless, like a luminous pillar, it spoke not a word. It was the dark human form, however, that turned quickly and faced the brilliant being.

Slowly the source of the brilliance started shifting into something that resembled a human form, but it was way too airy and bright to see who or what it was. In the seconds that followed, a bone rattling high-pitched noise resembling a human cry brought my hands to my ears again. This time it was the radiant being that let out the deafening sound. At once, the dark figure bowed its head in submission followed by silence – a deathly, ominous, silence and then – nothing.

The sinister presence and the ethereal being both dispersed within a wink of an eye.

"Are you guys okay?" asked Justin taking me by the hand. "The sound must've been painful without being able to block it out."

"What the hell was that?" asked Tyler dusting off his knees.

Justin let go of my hand and answered, "I'm not sure. But whatever it was, it's gone now."

Laura went over to where Sandy was standing motionless. "This was hardest for her." I heard my cousin say while placing both hands on Sandy's head. Sandy was still motionless. "That should do it."

Whatever Laura did, it snapped Sandy out of her trance. At that moment I saw Sandy wipe the side of her face. Her left ear had traces of blood. "What happened?" she asked confused. "Did I faint? Everything went black so quickly."

Kyle quickly went to her side barking out orders for Tyler to help her. In one swift move Tyler placed his palms on either side of her face, "This might sting a little," he told her.

The poor girl nodded. Her face mirrored her terror. Sandy clutched onto Kyle clearly scared out of her mind.

"Okay, back to normal," said Tyler taking a step back. "How do you feel?"

Justin was right. Tyler was a healer, after all. Sandy's intense features softened. "Much better, thanks," she said and walked into Kyle's open arms.

"Are you sure you're okay?" Kyle asked. "We can go back if you're not up to it."

She shook her head. "No – I'm fine. I just feel weird, that's all. I don't remember fainting."

"It's okay. Don't worry about it. It's probably the heat and humidity. Come on, let's walk it off." Kyle wrapped his arm around her shoulder and walked on ahead, leaving us to talk freely. For the time being Sandy seemed content with Kyle's explanation.

"Okay then," Emily said once the coast was clear, "Which way to the caves?"

"You're kidding," was what Dawn said, "After all that you still want to go?"

"Why the hell not? Whatever that thing was is long gone. I

don't see why we need to cut this trip short."

Justin took a step forward.

"No Justin, I don't want to hear it," Emily said, with a stretched out arm to stop Justin dead in his tracks. "Whatever just happened was a test and you know it. You handled yourselves amazingly. We deserve to see these caves, now more than ever."

"Test...?" I looked around to all their faces. "You're telling me this was a test? It sure as hell didn't feel like a test."

Justin and the rest of them didn't say a thing – bound by secrecy the Ascended were not allowed to divulge anything they might have known about what just transpired.

"Justin, that thing wanted to kill me."

"Nonsense," said Paolo, "You heard Emily. It was one of those tests to keep us on our feet. Don't worry about it. It's over with."

Justin remained quiet. He didn't want to lie to me more than was necessary especially since everyone else seemed to be doing a great job on their own.

"This way," is what Laura said, continuing down the path that Paolo cleared. "No need to worry about things we have no control over. That's what the Nobe are for."

"Is that what that was?" asked Tyler in utter amazement.

Dmitri nodded and smiled, "They're beautiful aren't they?"

"What was that other thing? That monster?"

"Enough!" Justin snapped, "It's over. No need to dwell on it. It's over." Without even waiting for me, he followed Laura down the path.

"C'mon, sis," Kyle said, leading Sandy and me to the caves.

Nobody talked about the experience again – not to me anyway.

Light To Darkness

Illustrated for Lines That Bind - Within The Whispers

THIRTEEN

DEEP IN BLUE

ENTURIES OF WAVE action had sculptured shorelines throughout the Isle of Indigo. Paolo had explained earlier that the caves revealed themselves along the water's edge, promising us an unforgettable adventure.

He was so right. As we took a steep descent into the well-concealed entrance my gaze strayed above my head noticing that the walls and ceiling of the mouth of the cave formed a massive vaulted chamber with delicate arches which only added to its mystery.

In the huge cavern, conversation trickled away into a silence that grew gradually more complete. At last Paolo spoke into the stillness that was fused with an overwhelming feeling of wonder. "There are several hidden passageways," he said, pointing to the multiple connected arches in the rock formation. "It's important we all stay together. Some of those passages can lead you deep underground where you can get lost or trapped, and other paths can even lead to the neighboring islands."

His voice reverberated against the variegated sandstone causing an eerie effect. The large waves, on the northern side, generated plumes of spray and thunderous explosions against the exterior walls of the cave. Each violent thrash, caused me to jump out of my skin.

"Don't be scared, Caitlin," said Dmitri, patting me on the back. "We're quite safe in here. The hollowness of the cavern only intensifies the sound. It's nothing to worry about. You'll get used to it soon enough."

"Thanks," I said, still shaken by each lash of wave.

After pausing at the entrance we proceeded into the depths of Indigo caverns. My eyes wide with fascination at the natural rock sculptures abounding within. Eerie lights spilled over huge boulders and structures intensifying the unearthly feel of our new surroundings.

"Damn it!" Paolo yelled, a few meters up ahead. "The main cavern is blocked off. There must've been an earthquake or something."

Justin's slate-blue eyes fixed on me as if they bore through to my soul. "I know, I'm sorry," I mouthed, so nobody else could hear.

I walked up to where Paolo and the other guys were standing, to get a better view. Three to four yards further down the passage a large heap of rocks obstructed our progress

"What now?" I asked, feeling rather guilty. I wasn't sure if I was the one to blame for the setback. *Did my powers really let out that much force into the sand a couple of days ago? Did I really do that?* I wondered, looking at the end result

"What's the holdup?" Emily asked impatiently.

Laura pointed to the pile of debris, "How do you expect us to get through this?"

Frustrated, Emily raised her hands in the air and said, "Geez, people! Twelve gifted individuals – three of which can move things with their mind, and you're all standing there wondering what can be done to remedy this situation." Emily looked around to our astounded faces. "What good is having your powers if you're not going to use them?" She huffed in annoyance. "Justin, why don't you just clear away enough of the debris so we can get through? What's the big deal?"

"I'll tell you what the big deal is," Dmitri said, facing her, "We don't know the extent of the damage. What if it continues for the whole length of the cave? What if the fallen rock is actually supporting the rest of the ceiling? If it collapses we will have the Atlantic Ocean crushing down on us, and we are way too deep into the cave to survive. Kyle won't be able to sustain a shield against tons, upon tons of ocean."

I looked over to Kyle. He didn't seem too happy with what Dmitri had to say.

"I'll check," exclaimed Sandy, letting go of Kyle's arm. "Just give me a minute and I'll tell you what's waiting on the other side," she added, approaching the largest of the fallen rocks.

"You've been through enough today," said Kyle, stroking her back. "We can come back tomorrow."

"No!" Sandy shrugged him off. "I'm fine. I can do this. I want to do this."

I felt as though she was trying to prove herself – prove to us that she belonged among members of the five families.

With her palms flat up against the debris, Sandy closed her eyes to concentrate.

"What's she doing?" I whispered to Emily.

"Her gift allows her to see through objects, projecting visual images to her mind of what's hiding behind the wall of rocks."

"Wow, I didn't know that was even possible!"

"Yeah, it's pretty awesome. Her mind works the same way as a CAT scan. It tires her out quite a bit, though. Her gift doesn't come as natural to her as it does to us. She's going to have to exert a lot of energy to accomplish it."

I looked over to Kyle and noticed he looked rather worried. His eyes were glued on Sandy; probably listening to her every thought. Mere moments later, he placed his hand on her shoulder, featherlike, "Sandy, that's enough. Your body can't handle anymore. You must stop," he pronounced, prying her hands off the rock.

"I'll be fine," she complained, pushing him away. "Stop pestering me. I'm finished anyway."

Her nose was bleeding. Tyler was the first to notice. "Are you okay? If you're in any pain I can help."

Sandy sat herself down on the damp cold floor, breathing rather heavily. "Just give me a minute to collect myself," she said, scanning all our faces. Her deep breathing echoed in the large chamber. "The coast is clear," she started to say, between breaths. "There's no more than two yards of rock." She shifted her gaze to Paolo. "Why didn't you tell us anything about the pools on the far end of the cavern?"

He looked at her in amazement. "It was going to be a surprise," he said in his deep Italian accent, "It's remarkable that you saw it. It must be more than a quarter mile away."

"Less than that," she responded. "Now go on, clear the path. I didn't do all that for nothing."

Justin was clearly in two minds about the whole ordeal. "There must be some other way around," he said, apprehensively. "Moving even one of those rocks might cause a chain reaction. We don't know if they're supporting the ceiling overhead."

"They're not," reassured Sandy as she stood with Kyle's support, "It only seems that way. None of the rocks are actually touching the ceiling. I'm sure of it, Justin. I wouldn't put our lives at risk. I know what I'm talking about."

But although I tried to accept Sandy's assurance, I found

myself thinking more and more often of the dark, narrow crevices and the caverns where the slightest vibration might bring tons of rock crashing down from the ceiling dome. Paolo, however, didn't require much convincing. He quickly got to work, removing the rocks effortlessly with a simple wave of the hand. One by one, he stacked them alongside the wall. Justin stood close enough to give a helping hand if the need arose.

"Um, we have a problem," said Paolo after having hauled most of the debris to the side.

"What's it now?" asked Laura troubled. She wanted nothing more than to continue with the exploration.

"This one is way too big. I can't move it," Paolo said, pointing to the wall of rock that came unglued from the ceiling, "And it's too tight a squeeze to try and go around it. None of us fit, it's way too narrow. It's hopeless."

"That thing is probably supporting this whole ceiling," Justin said, trying to put an end to our cave exploration.

"It's not. I promise," pronounced Sandy, "I wouldn't say something if I wasn't absolutely sure, Justin."

Justin looked at the towering obstacle that obstructed our path. "Anyway, let's just head back and go to the beach for a swim," he said, refusing to help.

"Move it already!" Emily yelled at him. "We all know you're the only one who can. We won't tell the Ellri – promise."

"Like that will keep them from finding out," he answered "It's just that...."

I was cursedly tired of waiting. There was simply too much whining and nagging for my taste. And after what we had been through I wanted to see those pools now more than ever.

"There!" I commanded under my breath, pointing to one of the vast corners of the large chamber, compelling the rock to move in that direction.

As soon as the word left my mouth the massive stone vibrated, attracting everyone's attention. No one spoke. The rock moved forward a few inches, but then ground to a halt. For some reason I could feel resistance, like it was being pushed back by some invisible force. It was the first time I actually tried moving anything so colossal.

Certainly not ready to accept defeat so easily, I raised my voice and pointed, "I said – there!"

In no time, it loosened completely from the rubble and swooshed by so fast that, to the naked eye, it seemed to simply disappear and reappear again in its new location.

They all looked at each other confused. Justin was the only one smiling. "I knew you could do it," he said, sounding proud.

"How the hell did you do that?" Kyle asked in utter disbelief. "I didn't even see it move."

I was determined to move this expedition forward. "You didn't expect us to wait all day, did you? You heard what Sandy said. There are pools waiting on the other side. We didn't wear these ridiculously small bikinis to sit around and deliberate now, did we?"

"You can say that again, sister," Emily squealed, advancing down the opened passage. "Come on, what's wrong with all of you? So she moved a rock? What's the big deal?" She winked at me smiling.

Without further ado, we all filed behind her. Justin and I were trailing a few yards behind in complete silence.

"You were pushing against it, weren't you?" I accused him.

He beamed with pleasure, "I wanted to see if you could do it. You're not mad are you?"

"Why would I be mad? For you, I'll move this whole island if you ask me to." I said, stopping to kiss him.

"Oh, please, don't start that," Kyle yelled from up ahead. "I feel nauseous as it is. C'mon, keep up you two,"

Justin gave Kyle a nasty stare. I didn't need to be telepathic to know his thoughts.

"Don't take your sexual frustrations out on me, Bradford!" Kyle teased. Everyone joined in Kyle's amused laughter.

"You're an ass," yelled Justin.

Kyle's laugh was uplifting. "You love me Bradford and you know it."

"I do love ya man, but you're still an ass. Now, shut up and keep walking."

~~~

Trailing behind, Justin and I were able to exchange some sweet kisses now and then without having Kyle's smart remarks ruin the moment. After a few yards, I spotted a strange colorful lizard crawling up the damp cave wall. Curious to see the little critter from up close, I momentarily released my hold on Justin's hand. It was within that mere second that I felt a sudden pull at the waist, as though somebody snatched me away. To my horror, I suddenly found myself in a whole new tunnel – all alone. It forked in several different directions and the stench of damp was everywhere.

Disoriented at first, I did not know what to do. I called out for Justin, then Kyle, Emily, but as soon as my voice left my mouth, the sound returned right back in my ear. I called out again only now the sound of my voice came seconds later. The way it would in dubbed movies where there is no synchronization between the movement of the actor's mouth and the soundtrack. After several attempts at calling out for help, I heard a laugh. Soft at first, but then it grew louder, bouncing off the stone walls.

"No one can hear you," a male voice said.

Frightened that it was the same scary being that we encountered in the forest, I started running – running in no particular direction. It made no difference which way I went because any which-way I turned, I found myself right back where I started and to make matters even worse, the monsters laugh was a constant reminder of how powerless I was against it. Exhausted and completely out of breath, I finally stopped.

"Give up already, young mortal?"

"Who are you?" I asked, looking around – aware of the grave danger I was in. "What do you want?" I yelled. "You got me here for some reason. What is it?"

I felt a warm breath against my forehead, but there was still no one in sight, and then I heard the monster say against my skin, "Is the little mortal girl afraid of the big, bad monster?"

From the fear that overtook me, I had no voice to answer. The monster that held me captive continued to laugh sinisterly as I remained motionless, trapped against the cold stone wall.

The laughter ceased abruptly, and in no time at all I was back to facing the colorful lizard once again – the very same creature that got me into this mess.

"Are you okay?"

Justin's voice made me turn to face him. "Okay? Am I okay?"

He looked at me confused. "Don't be frightened. It's only a lizard – an ugly one at that. But we really need to get going. Everyone is waiting for us."

"Yeah, okay – let's go." Whoever or whatever the monster was, it was powerful enough to keep a person like Justin in the dark. Overwhelmed with fear and the sense of being way too vulnerable, I allowed Justin to take my hand, but kept the whole incident to myself. There was no need to worry him. This was my problem.

Indigo Caverns

Illustrated for Lines That Bind - Within The Whispers

Stalactites pointed down from above and equally imposing stalagmites on the caverns floor. Paolo had mentioned that the cave had been open to visitors for less than half a century.

The paths were cleared away of any obstacles making our crossing effortless. Just up ahead the otherwise dimly lit cavern was suddenly infused with light from above. The rays from the vast opening in the ceiling reflected on the numerous, small sapphire pools which created a series of falls. Each pool was one level lower than the next, creating a stair-like structure.

We worked our way down to the bottom, ending in, what seemed like a twenty-foot-deep pool. The limpid pool mirrored the open sky from above.

Kyle whipped ahead to one of the pools and took a dive in. His body broke the surface of the water into a million ripples of light.

The colossal chamber must have been more than seventy feet high and its massive columns created a mesmerizing, natural cathedral.

"You see, Justin," said Emily, "you were going to miss all this if we'd turned back. Aren't you glad we didn't?"

"It's like nothing I've ever seen before." he gasped at the sight, bringing his head round to survey the intricately structured natural wonder, "It's – it's simply amazing."

After the initial shock of our mind-boggling surroundings wore off, we all splashed about in the crystal clear waters, but not one word was said about the sinister fiend who wanted me dead in the forest – not one single word.

A few, carefree hours later, as we were all sitting on different levels of the pools, we noticed something moving in the depths. Out of nowhere, Gabriel emerged from under the water and we all froze, not knowing what to say, shocked to see him surface.

He pushed back his wet hair and looked around at our surprised expressions. "Didn't mean to frighten you," he said smiling. "The pool connects to a small underground waterway that leads to the beach. There...," Gabriel explained, pointing to the farthest wall, "you see that dark spot at the bottom of the pool? It leads straight out to the beach."

Expressionless, everybody continued to stare at him.

"Alexander told me you'd be here. I anchored just on the other side of this wall. Thought I'd come and join you. It's not a problem is it?" he asked looking in my direction.

"Why would it be a problem?" I answered, distancing away from Justin. I held onto the side of the wall not being too fond of the depth of the pool.

Gabriel chuckled, innocently enough, at my undeniable fear of drowning. "You're not scared, are you?" he asked, smiling at my discernible discomfort. "I think it's time for your first swimming lesson. I can't have you drowning on me – not now that I've found you."

"I'm fine for now, thanks. Maybe some other time," I told him, smiling gratefully.

"Oh, c'mon," he said, pulling me into his arms for support. "It's now or never!" His tight hold caused me to gasp. He was purposely holding me up against his body trying to infuriate Justin. I wanted nothing more than to drawn him for being so insufferably bold.

"Let her go," Justin said, sounding rather calm. "Can't you see she doesn't want to? Didn't the Korbs teach you any manners? That's no way to treat a young lady."

"If Caitlin doesn't want to swim, she doesn't have to," added Kyle furiously. "If you know what's good for you, you'll let her go."

Kyle was clear on how he felt, but Justin seemed rather calm on the surface. His anger might have been brewing in my veins, but to all appearances he seemed in complete control, concentrating his attention primarily on Laura, and she relished in the moment, enjoying the closeness she was sharing with Justin.

My emotions now under ironclad control, I gracefully turned to Kyle. "You guys are being rude," I said, defending the monster. "Gabriel didn't mean to be so forward, right Gabriel?"

"No I didn't, but the guys are right," he said letting me go. "I shouldn't have acted without your consent. I'm really sorry Caitlin."

"Don't be silly. There's nothing to be sorry about," I muttered pulling back to the pool's edge. "I simply don't feel like swimming, that's all. I don't understand what all the fuss is about."

"Did you guys know that Caitlin's grandfather proposed to her grandmother in this chamber?" Gabriel asked, drawing everybody's attention once again. "Eileen was only sixteen or seventeen at the time. They didn't even wait to announce it to their family. They took their vows right here, choosing to share an eternity together." Gabriel's eyes met mine. "Your grandfather was crazy about her. They were a perfect match," he added. His eyes bore into mine full of meaning.

"I didn't know that. Why were they in such a rush?" I asked.

"It was different back then," answered Gabriel, moving intimately close. "Couples were fixed up at a very young age. Your grandfather probably wanted to avert any unwanted suitors from her side of the family. He wanted to be with her and nothing would stop him."

"I thought you said that the Korbs were adamant about the whole arranged marriage thing. Wasn't my grandfather one of those who supported this particular tradition?"

"You could call him the head of the movement. He knew Eileen was his match. It was her family who didn't want her to marry a Korbs. They didn't agree with our ideals."

"Oh, I see. You're lucky you're not going to have that kind of problem."

Unexpectedly he leaned in rather close, his mouth only inches away from my ear. "I, too, know what I want, Caitlin. Nothing or no one will stand in my way of having it," he said real softly, against my cheek.

I forced a smile knowing all too well that his words were a clear threat. As soon as he dove into the water, I looked over to Justin and met his gaze. His features were carved in anger, fuming with distaste. Even though my insides were turning in response to Justin's fury I knew I had to figure things out. Find out more about the Korbs.

Gabriel surfaced on the other side of the pool, giving me ample space to feel comfortable and think. *Was he referring to me?* I wondered. That's when the nagging notion of the Korbs finding me a suitor re-emerged. *Am I the girl Gabriel is waiting for? Is that why he is so persistent?* I looked across the pool and noticed Gabriel looking right at me, relaxed in knowing contentedness. I knew right there and then that my nightmare was staring me right in the face.

With unease I looked away, trying desperately to hide my new found understanding. I needed to get away, and fast.

I was just about to climb out of the large pool feeling noticeably uncomfortable with Gabriel's stare when shrieks of unwariness escaped me as a shockingly quick tug around my waist pulled me right back in, sending my forehead against the cold hard rock that lined the pool.

The sound of everyone's anguished screams quickly faded

in my ear, replaced by a sharp acute pain stabbing my forehead as the hold around my midriff tightened, dragging me even deeper into the vast depth.

Fighting hard against the deathly grip, I found myself defenseless against an invisible enemy. Quickly, I was tugged harder back and instantaneously found myself falling from an inexplicable height onto a heap of something so horrific that my mind refused to accept it as real. The stench of decomposing bodies everywhere around me was vomitus. Terror rose in me as I knew this was no nightmare.

In seconds, a shrill, as acute as the pungent odor of death, escalated to brain shattering decibels when out of nowhere a dark sinister mist approached – swirling around me like a purified and potent form of everything dark and evil.

The swirl stopped and soon it materialized in a pseudo-human form. The creature's true character was concealed with a cloak of darkness with the intent of hiding his real identity.

"Little Caitlin is all mine." Its hissing was ear-deep, "No one can help you now – not here."

My mind scrambled for coherency – fought to remain calm and find some way out, and finally said through deep breaths. "Why are you doing this? Who are you? What do you want from me?"

"Who I am, you will soon find out, but wish you never had," he answered circling around me. The frightful creature quickly stopped, took a whiff of the air around him. "They are keeping quite a close eye on you, mortal. Do they really think they have any control of this – of me?"

"Where am I? What do you want?" I cried.

Agitated, the creature once again sniffed the air. "Damn them," it swore. "This will have to wait – now back in the water with you."

Without any sort of warning, I was once again fighting for breath as I heard the monster in my mind say, *"End it now. Don't fight this."*

Trying to break free was impossible, the more I fought the tighter the hold became, until I let out the last bit of air I had in my lungs. *"That's my girl."*

The last thing I remember of the ordeal was the darkness that came once I let out my last breath.

Fighting For Air
Illustrated for Lines That Bind - Within The Whispers

"Caitlin?" It was Tyler's voice that summoned me. "I know you can hear me."

I wanted to speak but coughed up water instead.

"Good girl," Tyler said, "now stay still, I need to do something."

I instantly felt a cold hand on my burning forehead. Just as I was about to say something, my wrist ignited. Afraid that I would injure my best friend, I pushed myself back, away from his touch. "Don't touch me," I said, coughing even more. "What was that?"

"Caitlin, you hit your head. I can help."

I put my hand to my forehead and saw traces of blood. "I'll be fine," I said, wanting Tyler nowhere near me – not when my own power reacted so.

"I feel fine, Tyler thanks. I'll be fine. I turned my head around and noticed that they were all staring. "What happened? What was that?" I asked again.

"You slipped and hit your head," said Kyle smiling a weak smile.

I sat there for a few minutes with my head in my hands, "I didn't slip! It was that monster again."

"Sweetie, it's okay now," Emily reassured me, kneeling next to me "We all saw what happened. You lost your footing and hit your head. You'll be okay, don't worry."

"I didn't slip," I looked at Justin only to find him worry stricken. "Justin there was...,"

"Your power is so raw," said Gabriel starring at my throbbing wrist, "So pure...." His admiration was ill timed and annoying.

I looked back to Justin, "I didn't slip!"

He said nothing.

They all gave me some breathing room and time to collect

myself. I was not one to scare easily, but now fear was gravitating to the surface – stomach churning, nail biting fear. Someone very powerful and dreadfully calculating wanted me dead.

"I didn't slip," I heard myself say one last time in my hands, "I swear I didn't. It was...."

"We should be heading home," Justin quickly said dismissing any sort of explanation on my part. "Caitlin, if you're up to it, we need to go."

Having my wrist back to normal, I looked around at all their blank stares. "I'm a little banged up, but perfectly fine," I finally admitted knowing that they were not going to shed any light on what had just happened.

"Okay then," Justin said, "we have a long hike ahead of us."

"That won't be necessary," Gabriel intervened, relaxing against the beautifully draped limestone. "We'll all go back together in the yacht. No need to trek all the way back."

Scared, I looked to the bottom of the pool. "No way am I diving into that hole down there," I muttered, looking at Gabriel. "I can't swim that good, let alone hold my breath for that long. And there is no way in hell I'm getting back in that water again."

"You'll be fine," Gabriel promised. "There's nothing scary down there. No monsters to worry about."

He was baiting me, but I was in no mood to play games. "I don't think so. I'd rather walk, but thanks for the vote of confidence." I said, with a smile laced in irony.

"The rest of you will go with our friend Gabriel and I'll head back on foot with Caitlin," Justin said firmly. "Come on, let's go," he ordered, pulling me by the hand, not giving anybody else the chance to say differently.

"That's ridiculous," complained Gabriel, "she can easily

make the dive. Why would you walk all the way back?"

I happily followed Justin up to the last pool, ignoring Gabriel.

"I said, she can make the dive," Gabriel sneered, appearing in front of us out of nowhere.

Justin pushed me behind him, shielding me from Gabriel. "Step aside," Justin said through grit teeth, "if you know what's good for you."

"Is that a threat, Bradford? Do you really think you can take me?"

"Just move to the side so Justin can take Caitlin home," Kyle said. "She almost drowned. What makes you think she wants to dive in again? Let them pass."

Kyle seemed calm, but his words were as sharp as a knife.

"You heard him, Korbs. Now move." Justin spat out.

Gabriel stood there for a few seconds measuring himself against Justin. Then he turned to me and said, "Till next time, then."

Justin was quiet, didn't say a word until we exited the large chamber and entered the dimly lit tunnel. As soon as we were all alone, he stopped to examine my forehead. He looked preoccupied. "Does it hurt?" he asked giving it a sweet little kiss.

"No, I'm fine. But I didn't slip. There was...."

Justin unexpectedly grabbed me by the waist and pushed me up against the wall. "If he ever – ever lays a finger on you again...." There, against the cold cave wall, Justin leaned in and kissed me possessively, eagerly taking his time to satisfy his hunger. Long minutes later, he finally backed a few inches away. "I'm not pretending any longer," he finally said, catching his breath. "Find another way to learn what you need."

FOURTEEN

UNLEASHED RAGE

W ITH ONLY three days remaining on the secluded, picturesque island, I took full advantage of those last hours talking to Ava, knowing that once we return to Oaks, I would not have the opportunity to see her again. Indulging my own selfish need to be around her, I deliberately spent endless hours basking in conversation while Justin was away with the guys on yet another water-sport adventure.

Ava seemed to be the only repellent for Gabriel's persistent charm. He did try on two occasions to get me alone, but his plans were thwarted by Kyle and Marc who, coincidentally, just happened to be walking by.

Gabriel was extra careful around me. He wanted me to like him, wanted to make a good impression. His flawless manner was what, on many occasions, made me question the viability of my suspicions. It seemed highly unlikely that he would want anything bad to happen to me. On the contrary, I was somehow sure he would risk everything to keep me safe.

"Caitlin, we're going down to the beach are you coming?"

asked Sandy, holding her towel and water bottle in hand.

"No, you guys go ahead. I was down there earlier this morning with Justin. I'll just sit it out and catch up on some reading," I said, waving my book in the air. "You guys, have fun."

Sandy shook her head regarding my choice of pastime as a meaningless waste of time. "Okay, but if you ask me it's a real shame to spend your last days on the island with your head in a book."

"You guys go ahead," I smiled at her warmly.

"Okay, but if you get bored you'll know where we'll be," Sandy said walking away, leaving me to enjoy 'The Divine Comedy'.

A few minutes later, lugging a bunch of towels in hand, Alexander came up the path heading towards the main house.

"Why are you sitting all alone?" he asked, squinting at my book, trying to make out the title. He carefully placed the tall stack of towels on the table and leaned one hand against them and said, "That's quite a book." He sounded surprised at my choice of reading material.

"My favorite," I replied.

"It's an odd book to read in these surroundings, wouldn't you say? You are reading about hell in paradise. A bit strange, don't you think?"

"Actually, with what I've been through, and with what I've seen, I think it's most appropriate." I closed the book and pushed it to the side giving Alexander my undivided attention. "It keeps me on my toes. On the straight and narrow, if you know what I mean," I smiled.

"Ah, yes, I see your point. Do you really believe that people should be punished so harshly for their sins?"

I straightened up in my seat always ready to debate the

virtues of this particular book. "I personally don't believe that hell exists – not the way described in the book. But now that think of it, some current events have proved me wrong."

Alexander, visibly uninterested in my last comment, pushed aside the towels and sat on the edge of the table and said," This I have to hear – explain, please."

"What I mean is that I don't actually think that our creator would punish us so harshly."

Alexander raised an eyebrow questionably. "Why in the world, not?"

"Well, the creator knows that life isn't fair, right? He knows that we all try to do what we can to survive. But, everyone is not born on an even playing field. Most people have to fight their own personal demons to survive each and every day while others, me included, glide through life without a care in the world."

"You don't seem to be gliding."

"Compared to others – I am. I have absolutely everything I need – some hitches here and there, but nothing I can't handle. It just doesn't seem fair, Alex, that everyone will be judged on the same scale. Some have an easier time choosing right from wrong while others have to literally go through tremendous tests of will to reach the right decision."

"That's an interesting perspective," he said.

"That's just my personal opinion," I told him, shrugging my shoulders.

He straightened up collecting the towels. "So, why aren't you down at the beach with your cousins?" Alexander asked, changing the subject.

"I'm not up to it," I replied, getting to my feet. "Do you need any help with those?" I asked seeing that he was struggling to keep the pile from tumbling over.

"No, I can manage," he answered smiling. "Instead of sitting here all alone with your nose in purgatory, why don't you go for a walk down to the dock? It will get your nose out of that book."

"The dock?"

"Yes, you can spot dolphins this time of day."

"Seriously – dolphins? Wow! Thanks Alex. I'll do that."

"Good, good. Now, let me get back to work."

Watching Alexander walk away made me realize that on my two week stay on the island I hardly got to see him, apart from a couple occasions when he accidentally ran into me. Even so, I had grown quite fond of him. He always knew exactly what to say to make me feel better.

"I'm really going to miss you Alex," I called out to him.

He instantly stopped and turned to look at me. "I'm going to miss you too, Caitlin. But you'll be amazed at how small this world really is. Before you can even miss somebody – Poof, there they are, right in front of you."

"I hope you're right, Alex. I'd like to believe that our paths will cross again."

He beamed a great big smile. "I surely hope so, Caitlin. Whenever you need me, all you need to do is call." he winked and gave a schemers smile.

His capricious manner incited a faint giggle. "You're the best grounds-keeper ever," I said amusingly.

Alexander started chuckling, "Yes, I aim to please," he muttered. "Don't you worry about anything. You're blessed with people who love you. There's no gift greater than that."

Without a second thought I walked up to him and gave him a great big hug, almost causing him to drop the towels.

"Whoa, there," he said happily surprised. Alexander encircled his laden arms around me. "This is turning out to be the best day ever," he whispered into my hair and kissed the top of my head.

The second I touched him an overwhelming feeling of unparalleled love flooded over me, there was nothing like it in the world. I felt tears spring to my eyes unable to control the surge of emotions. "Thank you for always being there," I said, swallowing back the tears.

He gently patted me on the back with his free hand and said, "Haven't heard a heartfelt thank you in quite some time, Caitlin. It means a lot."

I took a small step back and raised my gaze to meet his. "For what it's worth, Alex, I'm never going to forget you."

"Neither am I," he said stroking my cheek. "Neither am I."

As he was about to leave he turned to face me one last time. "Oh, one more thing before I get back to work, Caitlin. Choices needn't be so difficult. Allow your heart to tell you what is right and your mind to guide you in the right direction. Don't ever forgo your virtues and beliefs, no matter the sacrifice."

He didn't give me any time to respond, he simply walked away.

~~~

Heading down to the dock I came to realize that it was not dolphins I was there to see. The dreadful sight before me brought me to a stunned halt. Gabriel was sitting on the edge of the dock dangling his legs in the water, kicking up plumes of water with his feet. He seemed to be deep in thought.

Instinctively, I wanted to turn and run, but soon realized that there must have been a real good reason why Alexander led me there. With a great deep breath, I apprehensively approached Gabriel.

"Hi," I swallowed hard. "What are you doing here all alone?" I asked, trying my best to sound sincere.

"Caitlin! Hi! Here, sit." Gabriel moved to the side to make some room. "You're probably the only person that can sneak up on me. It's really strange not being able to sense your presence," he confessed half smiling. "Why aren't you at the beach with the others?"

"I came here to see some dolphins," I told him, sitting right next to him.

"Just missed a group – look, over there," he pointed to a few yards away.

Alexander wasn't lying about the beautiful animals after all, I thought.

There, several yards away, between the dock and Gabriel's sail boat, a few dolphins bobbed up and down in the water. They were magnificent. Their sleek lines glistened in the morning sun adding to their mystery. They took a dive into the deep waters and just as fast disappeared into the vast unknown, leaving only ripples in the otherwise still waters.

"You haven't answered my question, Gabriel," I finally said, shifting my gaze back to him. "Why are you sitting here all alone?"

He turned his whole torso to face me, "Just needed some time to think."

"How can you possibly think of anything in these surroundings?" I asked, looking around, trying desperately to avoid eye contact.

"It's you I'm thinking about, Caitlin," he said, looking down into the transparent water.

For some reason he sounded hurt, not overly confident like other times. I wasn't aware that he even had that side to him. I nudged him with my elbow trying to make light of the situation. "I'm sure you can find more interesting things to think about. I'm rather dull."

"There is absolutely nothing dull about you," he smiled.

There was something different in his voice. He didn't seem to be the Gabriel I had kept my distance from. I needed to know what he wanted from me. At least that much the Korbs owed me.

"What am I to you, Gabriel? What's all this really about?"

His eyes looked distant, deep in contemplation. "You're everything to me," he finally said softly.

I didn't expect him to sound so sincere

"You can't mean that. You've only just met me. How is that even possible?" I asked standing up, not feeling comfortable sitting that close to him anymore.

"Caitlin, please don't leave." Gabriel's sullen expression quickly shifted to one of calculating treachery. "You haven't got all your answers yet, have you?"

"So you knew?" I snapped, quickly taking a further step to distance myself from his conniving face. "This whole time, you knew what I was doing? Knew that I was pretending? Why didn't you say anything?"

He suddenly exhibited the most scheming of smiles and said, "It was adorable seeing how you work your charm to get what you want – quite the little vixen." He stood up and took a step closer. "You only had to ask, Caitlin. I'd do anything for you."

Step by careful step I eased back, hardly daring to breathe. "What's your real reason for being here then?"

He seemed to find my apprehensive state of mind amusing.

"I came for you. I came to take you home."

"My home is in Oaks," I answered, surprisingly calm.

"Caitlin, you know that's not true." His voice was now much harsher. "You belong with your true family. You belong with me," he insisted, taking a few steps closer. "You can't deny who you are. You can't deny your true family."

"I know who I am," I said, taking another step away. "I also know that you are gravely mistaken to believe we belong together. It's ridiculous!" I shouted, turning to walk away.

He quickly grabbed my arm, forcing me to stop. "You don't know what you're talking about, Caitlin. You and I are meant to be together."

I glanced down to where his large hand encircled my arm and just as quickly turned and glared at him. "Look at me Gabriel. I mean really look at me. Do you really think I want anything to do with you?"

His hold suddenly tightened around my arm, pulling me closer towards him. I tried to break free, but he was way too strong. I just stared at him in disbelief, only inches from his face. To my astonishment my power didn't react instantly.

"You need to decide what is more important to you, Caitlin." His words slithered, inches from my mouth. "If you come with me this whole thing ends here, now. Nobody would ever need to get hurt. It's your decision to make," he said, determined to sway me to his own logic. "I'm not a monster, Caitlin."

"Says who?" I pronounced, trying to break free. "If you cared so much about me you wouldn't be putting me in the position to choose."

Gabriel pulled me up against his body with brute force. "I don't simply care about you."

He kissed me against my will, forcing his lips on mine. I struggled to break free, and as soon as he released his hold the force in my hands had escalated to an alarming charge.

Marked by complete madness, I wiped my mouth, and quite impetuously struck him a powerful back-handed blow across the face, nearly felling him. But Gabriel kept to his feet. He said nothing, merely stared at me – grinning full of satisfaction. Blood from a split lower lip trickled down his chin.

In one swift motion he grabbed me again.

"You bastard, let go!" I screamed, reaching boiling point.

Gabriel was pushing my buttons, testing my resolve, tightening his hold around my waist.

"You don't know what you're doing," I yelled.

He refused to listen to my plea, but my gift once again did not respond.

Taking liberty, he forced his mouth on mine again, but this time I bit hard – bit his lip deep. He quickly let go reaching for his bloody mouth and took a step back. As soon as he did, my gift was merciless.

His willful stupidity made me absolutely irate and utterly unforgiving. I pushed against him with both hands exerting the purest force, hoping to fatally harm the animal that was taunting me.

The instant my hands touched him he was catapulted a few yards back and with a spine chilling thud, he landed on his back against the hard wooden platform. But again he managed to regain his footing and stood up weak and bleeding.

"How dare you," I screamed, wiping my mouth and spitting out the taste of his blood on my lips, trying to somehow erase any trace of his touch.

Now I was angry – mad as hell and he was on the receiving end of a well-deserved beating. The rage inside me surged, breaking the flood gates of the fury I had so long suppressed.

"You stupid, stupid, little man," I yelled.

With every syllable I uttered, the waters around him rose, ready to swallow him alive. Everything around me went dark.

The wall of ocean roared and hissed as it grew even higher. I felt energized, ready to strike him down.

"Don't you ever touch me again – or else...!"

It was fear that stopped me – fear of what I could do – fear of my own gift. The unleashed rage that caused me to lose control was fueling my every decision.

I quickly stepped back in horror, and took a real deep breath realizing that I allowed myself to get completely carried away. This was not who I wanted to be. It was a conscious decision to back down.

Suddenly the ocean wall was in a slack and fell back – the waters were still again.

Gabriel was visibly shaken not expecting anything like it. It took him a few minutes to catch his breath.

"You're much stronger than I expected," he finally said, between gasps of air, staring at my throbbing wrist.

Dusting himself off, he slowly got to his feet bringing his fingers to his lips. He smiled contently, seeing the smear of blood on his fingers. "I must say it was well worth it," he added with a snigger.

The mere thought of wanting to pound him to the ground quickly materialized the second it crossed my mind. Gabriel was fiercely suspended in air and quickly hammered onto the deck with a loud thump – my gift was catering to my every whim.

He didn't look at all bit amused, but he didn't look that much in pain either.

Gabriel cocked up his head and smiled, coughing up a bit of blood and said, "You can do much better than that," love," annoying me even more. He paused again for some reason and looked over my shoulder. "She's much sweeter than I thought, Justin," he said, dryly, "Now I can see why you're not giving her up so easily. Too bad you'll lose her in the end."

"Why don't you come closer and I'll show you sweet," I

screamed enraged. "You want me don't you? Well, come and get me!"

"He doesn't have to do that," Justin snarled only a few feet away.

I turned my head only to see everybody standing behind me. I was so lost in my anger that I hadn't noticed they were all there.

"It's me he wants," Justin barked. "Isn't that right, Gabriel?"

"I'm here only for, Caitlin. If I have to go through you to get her – well, let's just say that'll be my pleasure."

Justin's expression was impassive, but his eyes were full of fuming anger.

"She's not going anywhere against her will," he barked, sauntering the few steps to stand next to me.

I looked at Justin and then circled to the rest of the group. Kyle, Marc and Dmitri were standing only a few feet behind Justin while the rest were further behind, standing side by side creating half a circle.

Did Gabriel really think he had any chance with all of them there? His open threat to Justin only ignited my gift even more. Never before had I felt it so lethal. It coursed through my veins, burning as it flowed to my hands. The need to protect them was overpowering.

"Did he hurt you?" Justin asked caringly.

"Are you serious?" I scuffed. "It's him you should be worried about."

"This is not your fight, Caitlin," Justin said, attempting a smile. "Gabriel is one of your shadows. He's been the one picking your brain night after night. Isn't that right Gabriel?" he asked, turning to his adversary. "Our friend is here for me. To get rid of me, because he feels I'm a threat to your future together."

"You must be joking," I gasped in disbelief, turning my gaze to Gabriel, angrier than ever.

I knew he disliked Justin, but to want to cause him harm was not something I was going to stand by and let happen.

"On your damn knees," I ordered, and Gabriel fell to the sand obeying my command – not that he had a choice in the matter. My gift forced his knees to buckle under him.

Gabriel remained kneeling, and said, "Caitlin, you need to come with me. None of them matter to me. It's you I want."

I took a few steps forward only inches from him and said, "The only thing I need to do is this...," and without any warning – with my wrist lethally charged, I slapped him across the face so hard that Gabriel fell forward, rubbing his burning cheek. "Don't you dare ever lay a hand on me again – ever! And stay the hell out of my head."

Astonishingly, unscathed by my lashing, Gabriel effortlessly got up smiling and reached out to grab me, but lucky for me Justin's reflexes were much faster. He reached out and took my hand and thankfully pulled me away, putting some distance between Gabriel and me. The weird thing was that my gift did not react to Justin's touch – not one bit.

"Come now Caitlin, you know you liked it."

Lividly aroused for a fight, I was ready to pounce down on him when Justin's glare stopped me in mid stride.

"Don't," Justin said abruptly. Just stay put, will you? Can't you see that he's just playing with you?"

I eased up, allowing Justin to get control of the situation.

Back on his feet Gabriel started laughing, "That was fun, Caitlin. If you come with me you will fine tune your craft, and finally learn what it means to be a Korbs."

"You purposely let me do this to you? Are you mad!"

"Don't look so disappointed. You were great – weak, but

great. This is how we learn. This is why the Korbs are superior. But next time, I promise to fight back. Caitlin, if you come with me your problems end here and now," he said with a smug smile.

His words rendered me speechless. This was the second time he took me for a fool. I promised myself that there wouldn't be a third.

"Hold on one second," Justin said, "If Caitlin does go with you, what then?"

"This feud would cease to exist," Gabriel told him, wiping away what little trace of blood was left on his lip. "Our families would return to how they were in the past."

"Oh, I see. And if – let's say Caitlin decides to stay with us – then what?"

"You know exactly what will happen, Justin. You know my mind – know how far I'm willing to take this."

"You see, Gabriel, that's where you confuse me." His posture of total annoyance flailed with each breath. "Do the Korbs really think that I, that we would just sit back and allow Caitlin to make such a sacrifice?"

Justin clenched his teeth in anger as he continued to say, "It's not a feud that you should be worried about, but a war! Our four families will not take a back seat to this. You of all people know this. The reason you're still standing is because we respect Caitlin's wishes. If it were up to me you'd be meeting your creator – pitchfork and all."

"If your families stand in our way, a war is what they'll have. Caitlin belongs with us. We are her true family. Her blood is our blood. None of you matter to me. Caitlin belongs with her own kind. She isn't anything like any of you, and you refuse to see it. Refuse her true calling."

"Caitlin is free to choose what she wants, nobody has the

right to force her into anything," Justin replied, with icy contempt.

"You mean to tell me that you won't fight to keep her?" Gabriel asked, taunting him "What kind of twisted love is that?" He took a step closer. "Oh, and don't worry Justin, now that I've tasted her sweet lips there's no turning back. She'll come to her senses. There's no other way to end this."

Enraged, Justin wasn't going to stand around talking any longer. He was about to take an offensive step forward to close the distance between them when out of nowhere we heard Laura scream, "Something's coming!"

Despite her warning, both Gabriel and Justin didn't seem to be wavering in their course of action, but to our great surprise, the ground started to tremble with violent force, causing both men to step back to keep their balance.

As the earth continued to shake violently, thunderous tremors tore open the ground we stood on. Our fear-driven yells and screams were muffled by the deafening roar of nature.

At first, nothing happened. But with panic came one last, unrestrained blood chilling vibration, followed by a thunderous clap, tearing the earth's surface in two.

Nearly losing my balance, I fell back a few steps finally finding my equilibrium. I heard the sickening thump as Laura hit the ground, heard Emily frantically calling for Marc, and then I heard a piercing, angry wave of a shrill cry that drowned all other noises – a periling tone that slammed into me as it blasted and echoed in my ears.

I put my hands over my ears fearing that my head would burst from the pressure. And then quiet – total silence – the kind that makes death seem animated.

Slightly disoriented, I crawled backward, touching my forehead to the ground now and again until I was able to lift myself off the earth. Too startled and surprised to respond, I gazed over to where Gabriel stood motionless.

There was a long, shockingly painful silence – a silence that pulsated with dread and suffering. Surprisingly, he was standing on the opposite side of a large crevice, looking as I was; stunned and confused.

My distressed gaze quickly moved to the others, wanting to make sure that no one was hurt. But what I saw was surreal. No words could possibly explain what my eyes bore witness to.

It was only the faintest and most uncertain of feelings, but I recognized the answering tremor in my own mind as one of fear. Every last one of them stood frozen in time. Nature stood inanimate.

How can this be? I wondered. *How could anyone be powerful enough to do all this?*

I advanced with each uncertain step, literally slicing through the suspended air particles that varied greatly in size. Fascinated by the circumstances I found myself in, I made my way around to everyone.

Justin along with the rest of the group stood there like statues. Stony silence filled the air. Even the ocean stood deathly still. Not even a rustle of leaves from the forest floor – the air completely static.

I felt as though I was standing in the middle of some sort of time warp – trapped, hypnotized by the whole setting.

I stared at all their blank expressions, waving my hands in front of their faces to see a hint of life, but there was none. There was nothing there but, empty vessels. "What the hell is going on?" I asked as I moved from one person to the other, hoping that at some point, at least one of them would snap out of the trance they seemed to be in, but still nothing. They remained motionless.

Uncontrolled Anger

Illustrated for Lines That Bind - Within The Whispers

FIFTEEN

UNNATURALLY STILL

A SOUND FROM the distance caught my attention. I turned and saw Alexander approaching. He was plodding through the golden sand with his trousers folded up, barefoot as always. He walked towards me without even stopping at the gapping crevice in the ground. I gasped, unable to call out, fearing that he'd fall in. He didn't even bother to look down. Alexander simply walked over the six-foot chasm, suspended in air.

"I'm too old for this, Caitlin," he grumbled.

Shocked, I just stared at him. "Alex?" I whispered, repressing my initial need to scream.

"Caitlin, I shouldn't intervene, but you must make a choice. You cannot allow this to happen. It's not time yet."

"How? How did you pull this off?"

"Look at me child," he said, ignoring my shocked expression. "The Council of Nobe hasn't come to a decision yet. What Gabriel and Justin have in mind goes against our laws. They are violating the code of ethics as far as our kind is concerned. If they even lift a finger to hurt each other, before the Council's ultimate decision, they will be faced with dire consequences. Your Dante's Inferno will seem like a walk in the park compared to what they'll have to endure."

I breathed deep in horror. "How am I supposed to stop this? Either way...," I took a deep breath, "the outcome seems to be the same," I cried. "Alex, if anything happens to Justin...."

"Nothing needs to happen to anybody. Do what your heart tells you and let the chips fall. The only thing you need to do right now is get them to back off. You don't want the Nobe to intervene – not now!"

I nervously pushed back my hair with both hands not knowing what to do. "Look at them, Alex! They're ready to kill each other. How am I supposed to defuse this? I can't even control my own anger," I confessed, raising my wrist for him to see the way my scar was throbbing.

"Come here. Give me your hand," he said reaching for me. Alexander took both of my hands in his. "You can do real damage with this power young lady. Our little earthquake the other day was just a hint of the destruction you can cause. You need more time to learn how to harness all this power. Tidal waves, earthquakes are all a no-no."

His touch was soothing against my skin. I could feel the power drain from my hands into his. "You know about that, do you?" I said embarrassed, remembering Justin's warning about using our gifts against nature. "What you did is much, much worse," I reminded him, scanning the area.

His eyebrow lifted distinctively. "Just be more careful next time. Don't use your power on a whim."

"Justin told me the same thing," I muttered feeling stupid, having done something so irresponsible. I pointed to the deep gap in the middle of the beach. "So Alex, what do you call that?"

"Precautionary," he exclaimed. "It kept them from killing each other, didn't it?"

I started to hyperventilate, from all the stress and tension. "First that monster in the forest and the pool and now this – I can't take it anymore. Somebody needs to explain. I can't handle anymore."

"Look at me," he said, "you need to learn how to handle things, young lady. This is what you were born into. Life is full of ups and downs. You must handle both with equal zeal."

"I can't! I'm tired of all this. I would've preferred not knowing any of this."

"Caitlin, look around you. This is so much bigger than your wants and needs. All these people that you say you love are ready to lay their life down for you, and instead of standing strong you're ready to throw in the towel?"

"Damn it, I'll fight. But I don't know what I'm fighting against."

Alexander raised my chin to eye level. His eyes reflected a calm and inner peace I only wished I had. "You don't need to fight, Caitlin. You need to decide."

I took a step back unwilling to discuss any sort of decision.

"Alex? What are they feeling now that they're frozen like that?"

"They're not frozen, Caitlin. Nobody can stop time."

"Then how is this all possible?"

"You have more important things to think about. None of this matters. They don't realize this is happening, so don't worry. When this is all over they won't have missed a second of their life."

My eyes widened in astonishment. "For a grounds keeper you're really powerful!"

"You have no idea what it takes to keep all this in motion," he said, raising his hands in the air, looking around.

I looked at him suspiciously "You mean the island, don't you?"

"Of course, what else could I possibly mean?" he chuckled. He took my hand in his and lifted my wrist to get a better look at my scar. "Once you ascend you'll be able to redistribute your power and have complete control."

I continued to stare at him wondering what kind of creature he was. He obviously didn't belong to any of our families, but yet he was more gifted than anyone I knew.

"Your accent keeps changing, Alex. I've meant to ask you. I haven't been able to figure out where you're from," I said, wanting to know more about this amazing person. "At the airport it was Spanish, then later in the week French, then Italian and now clearly American. How do you do that?"

He smiled. "You're quite perceptive for a girl who has so much on her plate. What you should do is focus on more important things," he said, preparing to leave.

"I know – I know. But since we're here can I ask you one last thing? I wanted to ask you this earlier while we were having our little discussion on my reading choices."

"Caitlin, you're trying to delay the inevitable, but go ahead, ask away."

"At Stone Hurst we had to do a project and choose one person who we wanted to interview and then make a list of questions that we would've liked to ask."

"That's not a question, Caitlin, but I'll bite. Who did you choose?"

"The creator," I said.

"You did say the interview had to be with a person. I wouldn't go as far as to call our creator a person. He's a supreme being and lives within all living creatures," Alexander said, gazing at me. "Anyway, what did you want to ask him or her?" he smiled.

"Actually, I had hundreds of questions, but only one stood out in my mind. How could such a powerful being just sit back and allow such atrocities to happen to small children? To be honest, I was thinking of my own misery at the time, being trapped in a school I didn't much like, but I really meant the children who were abused, molested even killed. I don't understand why. Why would anyone with all that power allow this to go on?"

"Um, that's very insightful, but the creator could just as easily ask you the same exact question, Caitlin."

"What do you mean? What question?"

"Where were you when all this was happening? It does take a village to raise a child. You of all people should know that. The creator has left this planet to seven billion people. That's seven billion pair of eyes to watch over each other. You'd think that'd be enough, wouldn't you."

"The pebble effect," I said smiling.

"Yes," he answered in full knowledge of Justin's theory. "Good deeds work the same way. If each person didn't turn their back on their fellow men this planet would be paradise on earth. It would seem that it's much easier to turn a blind eye to a person in need. What humans do not seem to comprehend is that by pretending that a problem does not exist only perpetuates it. For some reason people prefer to live in a virtual reality, acting surprised when bad things happen – shocked when they see the violent aftermath of their own doing."

I stood there reflecting on what he said. It all made complete sense to me – simple and absolutely true. "Too bad I'd never get the chance to have such an interview. You know Alex, for a grounds keeper you're wiser than anyone I know."

"Nature and fresh air will do that to you," he said, huskily laughing. "Don't think I don't know what you're doing."

I smiled.

"Now, enough procrastinating and do what you have to do to calm the boys down."

"I'm not going with the Korbs. You can tell the Nobe that I belong with Justin and that's my final decision."

"Well then, you see that wasn't that hard. Now all you have to do is convince Gabriel." Alexander looked to the sky and raised both hands in the air. Without an inkling of effort, the gaping chasm instantly disappeared, returning the terrain to its original form. There was absolutely nothing dividing Gabriel and Justin anymore.

"Thanks again, Alex," I yelled behind him, "till next time I screw up."

His laughter was carried in the wind.

Having to put a stop to everything, I quickly traversed the distance between Gabriel and Justin and stood between the two enraged men, blocking either of them from attacking one another. Everything and everyone was slowly returning to normal, moving in natural time. They all looked surprised at how I ended up so close to Gabriel, ignoring the fact that the surface of the beach was, once again, normal.

Surprisingly enough, I had never been so calm in my life – sure of what I had to do. Justin looked infuriated as did Gabriel.

"Get away from him," Justin said irritably.

I decided to take action and resolve this, there and then. I smiled hoping he'd understand, and defied his wishes by walking up to Gabriel.

"We need to talk," I told him.

Gabriel couldn't hide his surprised expression. As he was about to say something, I turned and faced the rest of the group and said, "Justin, I need a few minutes with Gabriel. He won't hurt me. I'm sure of it."

"Of course I won't," Gabriel responded, sounding offended.

"No way!" yelled Kyle. "We're not moving an inch."

"Justin, please!" I begged, walking up to him and taking his hand in mine. "This doesn't need to happen this way. I can't risk losing any of you. Please! Five minutes is all I ask."

"Why? Why do this? Why do you feel you need to be the one to protect us?" He was beside himself. "We're all in this together. You don't need to talk to that bastard."

I took his face in my hands and kissed him on the lips. "Five minutes is all I ask. Please, do this for me. It's the only way to keep us all safe. Trust me. I know what I'm doing."

He shook his head refusing to give me what I wanted. For a few minutes he just stood there staring at me, unwilling to listen. But then he kissed me one last time before turning to the others. "Let's go, they need to talk." He hated going against his better judgment, but I knew he'd never deny me anything.

Kyle didn't seem happy with Justin's final decision, but he didn't question it. "We won't be far, Caity," he said, clearly hesitant about leaving me with Gabriel.

"I'll be fine Kyle, just go. I'll be okay."

Reluctant at first, they finally all walked up the pathway to the main house. Justin lingered behind not wanting to leave.

"I'll be fine," I repeated, reassuring him.

"If you even think of touching her," he yelled out, pointing threateningly to Gabriel.

"Justin, I'll be fine," I repeated, cutting his threat short.

"I don't like this, Caitlin."

"Please, just go!"

He kicked the sand annoyed at having agreed to do this. Shaking his head, cursing under his breath, he finally yielded and reluctantly made his way up to the house, leaving me behind.

It was funny how they were all worried about me. I knew I could handle Gabriel. He was absolutely no match for my gift. I took a much needed deep breath and turned around to face my nemesis.

"What do the Korbs really want with me?" I asked brusquely.

"We don't want anything from you. We simply want you to be where you belong. We are your family – not them."

"For heaven's sake, I'm eighteen years old. I don't have to be with anyone. I can choose to live anywhere."

"You know better than that. To us you're considered an adult only when your gift has matured not your age. Years are insignificant...."

"Yeah, yeah, I know. They're insignificant. I'm an infant. Don't worry, I've been told a million times before. But we both know there is something you're not telling me, Gabriel. Why all this fuss over me? What makes me so special that the Korbs will risk everything to have me?"

"You're a direct descendant of our blood line, the purest of our kind. It only makes sense that you be with your true family. We can guide your gift. Make you reach your full potential."

"That's bull, and you know it. Why won't you tell me? What are you all keeping from me?" I pressed.

He looked annoyed once again.

"Caitlin, as I see it you only have one choice here. It's me or Justin. You'll have to choose between your desire for him and your destiny with me. Either way destiny always wins in the end. Justin's seen your future. You don't belong to him."

"So it was you all along, wasn't it? Projecting images of a future without me – playing with his mind."

He didn't answer. He didn't need to.

"But you couldn't have done it alone. You're not powerful enough to break through Justin's barrier. So who, Gabriel? Who is it that is playing these tricks?"

"Your future is set. Like the sand in the hourglass, your time with Justin is coming to an end, Caitlin. You belong with us, and we won't stop until you join your rightful place among us."

"I don't belong to anyone," I enunciated. "I choose to be with him and leave the future out of this, Gabriel. Seeing that you're refusing to answer honestly there is only one thing left for me to say."

"Caitlin…"

"I'm not going anywhere with you – ever! For some reason you don't seem to want to understand. I'll wait and see what the Nobe decides. Until then, I plan on returning to Oaks – to the people who've been there for me all along.

"You belong with me. You belong with you true family."

"You're deluding yourself if you really believe we can have any sort of future together. It won't happen, any which way you look at it. You don't even know anything about me. Some information, maybe, but that's all – nothing substantial."

"We're you're family. We would've been there if they had allowed us."

"I accept the Korbs as my family, but for now that's all I'm willing to do," I answered honestly. "You tell my uncles that I hope that one day I'll get to meet them under no duress, but that day will have to wait until the Council delivers their verdict, and if you meant what you said about only wanting me back in the family with no strings attached, than I don't see what the problem is in waiting."

Gabriel looked lost for words. All five families were bound

by some sort of secret code. None were willing to tell me the whole truth.

"Caitlin, the Council of Nobe will be on our side. Sooner or later you will be with us – with me," Gabriel finally declared, giving absolutely no weight to the words I said.

"We'll have to wait and see, won't we? Either way, I'll never be with you. I might end up living with the Korbs, but never with you."

"You'll change your mind soon enough," he said, exceptionally sure about the future. "I don't want to leave without you. This could be much easier, for all of us, if you simply come home with me, willingly."

"You flatter me, you really do," I smiled at him for trying so hard to talk me into the impossible. "If I leave with you, Gabriel, I'll be leaving my heart and soul behind. What good would I be to any of you? I belong where my heart wants to be. Nobody can tell me differently. I know what I'm feeling."

"Is that your final say in the matter?" he asked, knowing full well that it was.

"I'm afraid so."

"Then, there is nothing left for me to say. We'll just have to wait till the Council's decision," he said. "But before I leave, you need to promise me one thing, Caitlin."

My senses were suddenly heightened. "What would that be?"

"Once the decision is made, don't fight it. Save the families from impending doom. Promise that you will come to us willingly."

"If the Council believes that my rightful place is with the Korbs I will come willingly, that much I can certainly promise."

He closed his eyes momentarily and turned his head to the sky.

"They will honor your decision," Gabriel said grinning broadly, eyes shining with satisfaction.

"Good," I said relieved that it all ended the way it did.

"I'll be waiting with open arms, Caitlin. But before I go, can I have one last hug before I sail off?"

"Don't push it. The fact that I spared your life earlier should suffice."

"You and me Caitlin, we're meant to be," he said, heading for the dock.

"Gabriel!" I called, making him turn. "Thank you!"

He snapped his head back, surprised. "You're thanking me – for what, exactly? Why would you thank me?"

"For rising above all this – for not forcing my hand, for walking away peacefully."

"I told you before, Caitlin. I'm not a monster. You'll see, you'll grow to love me soon enough," he said winking at me.

"How about being friends? Isn't that enough?"

He smiled warmly, surprised at my comment. "What you offer is amiable, but I'd be lying if I accept. What I want from you is much bigger than friendship, Caitlin. But until then, you'll just have to exist in my dreams and I in yours. I'll be seeing you soon," he said and headed towards the dock.

For some reason I stood there waiting for him to sail off. I couldn't hate him, not now that he showed so much understanding. It also helped to see his face all bruised and bloody.

Ava emerged from the forest and stood next to me waving goodbye to Gabriel. "Good riddance," she yelled, smiling.

"Ava! You take care of her. I want her coming to me unscathed," Gabriel answered, smiling cunningly.

Even now, after all this, he was still being snide with Ava, knowing all too well her feelings on the matter.

She deliberately turned her back to the ocean. "You handled that quite well."

"Yes, I think you're right. The decision is still pending, but till then we'll all be fine."

"Of course, sweetie," she said, placing her arm around my shoulder. "Love what you did to his face, by the way."

I smiled in satisfaction. "Is what he said true? Is my future to be with him?"

"Nobody can know that. Gabriel chooses to believe in his own version of the future."

"He sounded absolutely sure that the Council will side with them. I promised if that were the case, I wouldn't fight it."

"You did what you thought was right. Nobody knows the Council's wishes, not even the Korbs," Ava answered. "Come on, you only have two days left on the Island no use spending them here. Everyone is waiting for you back at the house."

Unable to keep my excitement bottled up, I kissed her quickly on the cheek and picked up my pace leaving Ava behind, all too eager to see their faces.

<center>~~~</center>

"He's gone!" I squealed excitedly, causing everyone to turn around surprised. "He sailed off only minutes ago"

"To bad it's not hurricane season," Kyle said smirking.

"Be nice! He is my blood relative," I laughed.

I looked around the room and noticed Justin wasn't anywhere in sight.

"He's upstairs with Marc," said Tyler. "We needed to restrain him."

"Restrain him?" I was confused.

"He wanted to come back down to the beach so we locked him in your room."

"You didn't!" I exclaimed laughing.

"Heck, yeah we did!" Kyle chuckled. "It was actually entertaining to see him and Marc go mental on each other."

"Mental? What do you mean?"

Emily took my arm and led me up the stairs. "Ignore Kyle. He's an idiot. Justin is fine. They just went upstairs to have a better view of the beach from your window," she said. "So is Gabriel really gone?"

"You know he is Emily. You probably foresaw all this before it even happened."

"I sort of did, but the possibilities were endless. I couldn't be a hundred percent sure. Things change in an instant."

"Well, he won't be bothering us anytime soon. I assure you."

We reached the room and knocked on the door. Marc answered smiling. "Got rid of him, did you?"

"Not soon enough, if you ask me," I answered, giving him a hug. Justin kept his distance for some reason, looking lost in his thoughts.

"Okay well, let's get out of your hair," Marc said, noticing the strange atmosphere between Justin and me. "We'll be at the pool if you guys feel up to it." He took Emily's hand and closed the door behind them.

I headed towards the window and looked out into the ocean. Gabriel was already far out to sea.

"You're not angry with him, are you?" Justin asked, severing the silence.

"I think I exhausted my anger on his face."

Justin laughed a hardy laugh.

After some time he spoke again, "Our paths will cross again," he said, with his hands up against the window. "And it won't end well."

"It's over for now," I sighed. "He's gone. He won't be bothering us, not until the Nobe come to a decision."

Justin turned to face me, noticeably worried. "And then what? You promised to go to them without a fight. Why would you do that? Why would you promise something so stupid? We're never going to allow you to leave, whatever the Nobe decide."

I took his hand in mine interlacing our fingers.

"Aren't you the one who's always telling me not to worry about the future? Well, for the first time in my life I'm not. You and me, right now is all that matters."

Justin wrapped his strong arms around me, holding me tight in his embrace.

"The Korbs will never have you. I'm never going to let you go, Caitlin. I don't care how selfish that may sound."

"Where would I go without my heart?" I asked, folding my arms around his neck "I…"

I laughed breathlessly when his urgent kiss interrupted my train of thought.

Willingly, I surrendered myself to him, responding just as passionately to his every caress. Justin's breathing deepened, allowing small moans of satisfaction.

My heart raced with excitement at his response.

"I want you so bad," he whispered, trailing kisses down the side of my neck. "Damn it! Will you ascend already! The anticipation is killing me," he growled, kissing me hungrily.

I started laughing uncontrollably at his eagerness. I felt the same way, needing him all the time.

Hearing Justin say it out loud after all we had been through was hysterical.

"I believe this is a far worse punishment than anything the Korbs can do to me," he added, chuckling at our pathetic state; taking a few steps back.

"We can try," I said, seductively taking a step closer, slowly unbuttoning his linen shirt, one button at a time, exposing his perfectly toned chest.

"Oh, no you don't," he flinched back, slapping my hand off whimsically. "Not until you ascend," he added, walking away.

"Where are you going?" I complained, already missing his touch.

"To take a long cold shower – the quadrillionth I might add, no thanks to you," he murmured, scanning me up and down, "and then I'm going downstairs to play Ping-Pong."

With one quick unexpected swoop he lifted me up and kissed me one last time.

I was giddy with excitement.

He shook his head and took a really deep breath. "Somebody up-there has a really sick and twisted sense of humor – must love to see me suffer," he said looking down into my eyes.

Relieved To See Him Leave

Illustrated for Lines That Bind - Within The Whispers

SIXTEEN

UNWRITTEN

COLD WEATHER in mid-march and Old Betty was giving me a hard time. My once slick cherry-red beauty which, sadly so, was now just a patchwork of rust and duct tape, had been acting up.

I had bought her from my school's custodian, Mr. George. The pious man did have a last name, but it was simply way too long and Greek for any of us to pronounce. The sheer size of this large brawny man with a masterfully twirled mustache which, when in deep thought would whisk his hand over the raven black curls and twirl the longer bits between his fingers, came in direct contrast to his sweet and quiet nature.

As luck would have it, I had overheard him talking to Ava about needing to clean out his garage, needing more space for his whatnots. He asked if she knew anyone who needed a car. That's when I, excited, probably for the very first time back then, and happy about the prospect of owning my own car, bolted into their conversation, wanting first dibs, saying that I would be interested without even being asked for my opinion.

Mr. George did his twirling bit for a couple of minutes

before offering me a look. Later, back at his garage he was hesitant at first. "Do you know anything about cars?" he asked while clearing Old Betty of all the junk he had stacked her with.

"No, nothing," was my answer, helping him with the smaller, less heavy objects.

"She needs a lot of work."

I heaved the last carton out of the driver's seat. "Don't we all?" I answered, wiping my hands on my worn Levi's.

Mr. George twirled his mustache again as I scanned Old Betty. "I'll gladly take it off your hands," I told him, believing she was a great investment, hoping to get around to restoring her to her former glory. Regrettably, I didn't have the means to do it. All my savings, which was not much, went to purchasing the old clunker.

Now on this particularly cold day, it became apparently clear why I had bought her at such a great deal. It would seem that every week something new would break down. This week it was the heater. Normally, a couple of forceful punches to the dashboard seemed to work, but today, for some reason, it refused to cooperate. Uncle Abbot had even offered to buy me a 'real' car, one that was more reliable. I, of course, refused. Old Betty was, as Kyle put it, "Rough around the edges but strong to the core."

Days like this, cold as it was, I longed for the idle days we had on the Isle of Indigo. I came to realize that I had left behind two of the most influential people I'd ever come across. I found it nearly impossible to say goodbye to Ava on the day of our departure, even harder to Alexander. They had both made such a tremendous impact on my life. If it weren't for their presence, my existence would surely not be as it is, safe and at home where I belonged.

Wrapping my coat tighter, I put the car in gear and headed

off to school on my second, first day this year. The Ellri had finally decided that after three months of being tutored at home, it was safe to return to school. It would seem I wasn't at all a threat to the student populous and agreed to allow me to return to Oaks High. I had control of my powers – not complete control, but on the whole I was able to restrain my gift.

"Here we go again," I exhaled anxiously, as I pulled into the parking lot.

Pulling into the high school parking lot was more like pulling into an auto-showroom. Affluent in every way, the residence of Oaks loved their cars. Parking Old Betty between a Porsche and a BMW was rather humbling, but once restored, I was sure that my sad looking car would surpass both imports.

Old Betty had character – fifty-eight years under her hood was no small feat. *I'd like to see those two foreigners last that long,* I thought.

Reluctantly, I got out of my car and tried pushing against the door, but it didn't close. The corroded metal along with the low temperatures made it impossible to shut.

"We need to do something with your ride. This is ridiculous!" Tyler said, coming up from behind and forcing the rusty door to close with a loud bang. "I'm surprised Justin hasn't thrown it off a cliff yet," he added, shaking his head in disbelief, "not that he doesn't want to, I'm sure."

"Justin has cursed the day I bought Old Betty, doesn't really find it amusing that she's left me on the side of the rode a couple of times."

"Can you blame the guy – now c'mon we're going to be late," Tyler said, grabbing my school bag. "You're so slow, let's go!" he demanded.

I noticed a drastic change in Tyler since our return form the Island. I was quite worried about him. He and my cousin Karen had grown rather fond of each other on our two-week holiday. It was heartrending to see them in each other's arms during our last two days there, knowing that their separation was forthcoming.

As a typical guy he rarely expressed his true feelings on the matter, always seeming cool on the surface. Karen, on the other hand, was having a reasonably difficult time coming to terms with their imminent goodbye. Her eyes were constantly red from the tears.

There was no talking to Tyler now. He didn't allow any of us to discuss the topic openly. Friendship aside, he was being an ass about it. He took all his frustrations out on me, being fairly cruel at times. I knew he needed to vent his emotions so I really didn't mind being on the receiving end. In actuality, it took my mind off my own problems.

"Are you okay?" I asked Tyler, noticing his foul mood.

"You keep asking me that. I'm fine!"

"You need to talk to somebody about it. I know you miss her. Stop pretending that you don't," I said, needing to finally get this whole topic out in the open. I was tired of walking on eggs shells around him.

"I said I was fine," Tyler repeated. "Why are you making such a big deal out of it?"

"I hate seeing you like this, Tyler. I miss my best friend," I nudged him in the ribs playfully. "I miss your smile."

"I could say the same about you. When's the last time you were happy, Caitlin?"

His remark took me by surprise. "What are you talking about? I'm fine!"

"Well, there you have it then. We're both fine," Tyler said, heading for class.

He wasn't fine. Who was he kidding? The mere mention of

Karen's name caused him to jump out of his seat screaming "where – where?" Kyle, annoying as he was, had a lot of fun with that. He teased Tyler every chance he got, taking advantage of his vulnerable state.

The seven of us were much tighter than before. The experiences we shared on our vacation had forged a much deeper friendship. Even so, none of them ever mentioned Gabriel. I wasn't sure if they did it on my account or simply because they believed the whole incident was over with, a thing of the past.

"Why are you walking so slowly?" Tyler asked, pulling me by the arm.

I stopped abruptly, pulling free from his vise. "You're a jackass!" I screamed, attracting several prying eyes. "I've had it up to here with you." I shoved him to the side. "I understand you not wanting to talk about things, but how you feel doesn't give you the right to treat me like dirt."

"Caitlin! I didn't mean to...."

"I don't want to hear another excuse," I exclaimed, cutting him off in mid apology. "Don't you dare talk to me again – not until you're ready to discuss what's bothering you – understand?"

I didn't give him a chance to respond. I simply pulled my school bag off his shoulder and headed to first period Calculus.

I took the farthest seat away from his, not wanting to even look at him. Megan, of course, had noticed our seating arrangement. It wouldn't have taken her long to meddle in my business, I was certain of that. I kept my distance all through the day refusing to even sit with him at lunch. Instead, I headed over to Gina and Lisa's table.

"Do you guys mind if I sit with you?" I asked, standing like an idiot in front of them with my tray in hand.

"Sure, yeah – have a seat," Gina said, smiling. "You and Tyler having a fight?" she asked, knowing that there wouldn't be any other logical reason for my being there.

"Yeah – you can say that. He's being a real pain lately. You're sure you don't mind?" I asked again, not wanting to impose.

"Just sit down, Caitlin," said Lisa. "We can actually use another opinion."

"On what, exactly?" I wondered, opening my carton of apple juice.

"About senior prom, of course!" Lisa squealed, looking at me as if I came from another planet. "What else is there to talk about this time of year?"

She stared at me, probably wondering how I could be so blasé about such a momentous event. Having direr things to worry about, school events weren't exactly on top of my list, especially senior prom.

"Give her a break, Lisa! It's Caitlin's first day back – again," Gina said, defending me.

"Oh, right. I'm sorry Caitlin, I wasn't thinking."

"Don't worry about it. I just haven't thought about Prom, that's all."

"Being tutored must've been murder," commented Gina.

"It was. I missed having classes with you guys. It was excruciating. I hated every minute."

Lisa took a sip of her juice and said, "Well, you're back now."

"Yeah, until I mess up again." Both girls laughed. "So, tell me, who are you guys going with? Did you pick out your dresses?"

I wasn't particularly interested in such details, but both girls were always so nice to me – accepted me for who I was.

"I'm going with Brian Harper," Gina said, with a great big smile.

"The one from English Lit?"

"Yeah, that's him. Isn't he cute?"

I nodded in agreement. Brian was easy on the eyes, if you liked tall, red headed comedian types. He was a pretty decent guy who had even saved me from a lot of embarrassing moments in gym. His corky laugh was to die for. I could see why Gina would choose to go with him.

"How about you, Lisa – who are you going with?" I asked.

All normal seniors, all over the country, were looking forward to, if not their senior prom, at least their graduation, making plans for their future. I was indifferent to both. I was too busy worrying about the freakish monster that wanted me dead.

I looked over my shoulder to where Tyler was sitting. Of course he wasn't alone. It took Megan and her team of Barbies all of ten seconds to take advantage of the fact that I wasn't sitting with him. He turned and looked my way. I instantly sat upright and turned my back to him.

Tyler had a point. I wasn't happy. Even though I looked and sounded content on the surface deep down I couldn't shake the sound of the monster's voice. It reeled around and around in my mind, reliving that insane incident on the island.

Incapable of reading my thoughts, nobody could possibly know what I was thinking. I kept upbeat for Justin's sake. He didn't need to know about the numerous sleepless nights I spent crying and fearing the worst.

"Peter Egan," said Lisa, blushing.

"Peter – really? Hasn't he graduated already?" I asked.

"Yep, last year but we've been dating on and off for a couple of years now."

"Wow, I didn't know that."

Lisa looked at me curiously, "You've been gone for five years, and it's only natural for you not to know."

"No, that's not an excuse Lisa. I'm here now, how come I didn't know who you're dating."

"Don't worry about it. You seem to have a lot on your plate."

"Yeah, still."

I was aware that both girls looked at me inquiringly, wanting to ask me something personal – something about my past. Most students in this school were intrigued. It would seem I had become a legend over my five year absence. Living among the non-gifted for so many years along with the Korbs' last name seemed to have gained me notoriety. Unfortunately for Lisa and Gina, I refused to go into such a personal discussion with anyone.

I innocently stood up and collected my things, feigning the need to use the bathroom before our next class.

"See you in Biology, and thanks for letting me sit with you guys."

"Sure Caitlin, anytime," said Gina, with a genuine smile. "See you in a few."

Gina and Lisa were two of the nicest girls in school. They were both heavily involved in extra-curricular activities making them quite popular among the student body. It just happened that Lisa was also class president. I would have loved to hang out with both of them, but it made absolutely no sense to open myself up to more pain. If Gabriel was right - if I would have to go live with the Korbs, there was no point in making things harder than they had to be. A clean break would be for the best. Making friends now would be meaningless.

From the corner of my eye I spotted Tyler following me

down the hall. "This is childish," he yelled, causing me to stop in mid-stride.

"Are you going to talk to me about it?" I said, turning to face him.

"There's nothing to talk about, Caitlin. Why can't you just drop this?"

"Fine! Find another friend. I refuse to stand by and watch you beat yourself up."

I turned on my heel and headed to my next class, ignoring him the rest of the day. Being so infuriated with him, I hadn't noticed how fast my first day back was. The last period bell rang causing students to flock to their lockers. Once outside, the crisp cold air was rather welcoming. With my earphones in place, I headed to my car to get as far away from there as possible.

"Caitlin, welcome back!" Megan Gordon said, from a few feet back.

I turned my head and looked at her. Of course, she wasn't without her accessories. Kim and Loraine stood on either side completing the ensemble.

"Thanks! I'm glad to be back," I answered, continuing to walk towards my car, not wanting to stop for a chat, fiddling with my MP3 player.

"You're still driving that?" she asked distastefully, pointing to Old Betty.

With my earphones on, I deliberately turned up the volume bobbing my head up and down to the beat, pretending not to hear her rude remark. I didn't want to get upset, didn't want to ignite my powers over such a trivial matter. The sheer knowledge that I could cause her real harm without even lifting a finger was quite satisfying – enough to make me walk away peacefully.

I pulled the door open with all my might and slid in, flinging my school bag in the back seat, refusing to look at Megan and her cohorts. They stood there watching me struggle to get the door shut.

"Damn it Caitlin!" said Tyler, pushing against the door with all his might. "We need to talk!"

"There's nothing left to say." I put the key in the ignition and circled my head to face him. "When you start treating me the way I treat you, then we'll talk. I'm not your damn punching bag. Now get the heck out of my way – wouldn't want to run you over."

"I already apologized about this morning. What else do you want me to say?"

"I don't want you to ap...,"

Megan took a few steps forward snickering, "Are you guys having a lovers' quarrel?"

Tyler snapped. "Go home Megan!" He barked, causing the poor girl to take a step back. "This is none of your damn business."

Megan wasn't expecting such a response. Her shocked expression was verification that Tyler's uncouth retort slightly wounded her. I knew she had a crush on Tyler as far back as grade school. His tone was uncalled for. She was, after all, just being herself. What was his excuse?

I drove off wanting nothing to do with him, not if he was going to act so rude. I could see Tyler from my rear view mirror raising his hands to his head in frustration. I was being difficult, but there was no way I was going to face up to it.

No more than a mile from home, Old Betty decided to call it quits for the third time that month.

"Damn it!" I screamed, slamming my hands on the steering wheel, cursing the day I bought her. "I can't win." I added, collecting my things from the back seat. I headed up the road towards Uncle Abbots.

At that moment, Tyler pulled up to the side of the road in his sporty two-seater. "Get in," he said, swinging the passenger door open. "You'll freeze."

"No thanks, I'll walk," I answered, picking up my pace.

The violent slam of the car door was deafening. Tyler's footsteps quickened, catching up to me in seconds.

"What the hell is your problem?" he asked, pulling my arm and swinging me around to face him.

"You're hurting me, let go!" I said, angrily.

Standing on the side of the rode in the middle of nowhere Tyler and I just stared at each other waiting for the other to talk.

"Can't I just keep whatever I'm going through to myself?" he finally asked.

"No! Not when it affects our friendship. You've been cross with me ever since we returned from the break."

"That's ridiculous!"

"Missing Karen isn't something to be ashamed of. It's natural to feel sad."

"Caitlin, just stop. You have no idea what you're talking about."

"Why are you denying it? It's not like you to be this distant. Why have you shut me out?"

"Damn it Caitlin, are you blind? This has absolutely nothing to do with Karen. Sure we had fun, but do you really think I could fall for someone in two weeks?" Tyler kicked the dirt in one swift move. "Karen and I both knew it wasn't going to last."

"Then what the heck is your problem? Why are you acting so strange?"

He was annoyed with my persistence. He grabbed both of

my arms forcefully. "You need to drop this," he said, through clenched teeth.

"No! Not until you tell me. If this change in mood is not over Karen then why are you acting like this?"

"You're impossible!" he yelled, letting go of my arms "It's you, okay! I'm like this because of you," he snapped.

My expression must have said it all. That whole time, I thought he was acting weird because he was missing Karen, but in actuality I had hurt him somehow. *Did I say or do something that offended him?* I racked my brain to think of anything I did, but came up blank.

"What did I do?" I finally asked, completely in the dark.

"I'm not getting into this – not here – not now – not ever."

"Tyler, if I did something, I need to know."

He looked at me shaking his head – refusing to divulge his thoughts. "Let's just drop it. There's nothing that can be done anyway."

"How do you know? C'mon, this is killing me. Just tell me already."

Tyler took two steps forward, only inches away, towering over me. "I'm in love with you," he said, in a soft voice, "So go ahead and tell me, Caitlin, what can you do about that?" he added, shaking me lightly.

"You can't be – I mean – why would you be?"

"Don't you think I know that? Don't you think I feel horrible every time I look Justin in the eyes? We can't help who we love, Caitlin. You of all people should know that."

"Damn it Tyler! I swear I want to slap the shit out of you so bad right now!" I confessed, raising my voice.

"Why the hell would you want to do that?"

"So you can snap the hell out of this delusion."

Tyler grabbed my arms again, even tighter this time. "I

know what I feel, Caitlin," he said sounding determined to make me understand. "The guilt for feeling this way is driving me mad. There's nothing anyone can do."

"Tyler you can't be...,"

"Let her go, Tyler," I suddenly heard Justin speak softly. Utterly shocked by Tyler's confession I hadn't noticed Justin's presence. "C'mon man, just let her go."

Tyler dropped his head defeated.

"This is why I didn't want to tell you." he said, and simply headed to his car without even meeting Justin's gaze.

I was still in shock by his admission. Seeing him drive away feeling the way he did made me hate myself.

"Are you okay?" Justin asked, hugging me.

"I'm fine it's Tyler I'm worried about."

"I've told you before how Tyler feels. Why are you so surprised?"

"But he knows – knows what you mean to me. Why would he put himself through all this?"

"He'll be fine. You should talk to him though. Show some understanding."

"Why would he possibly love me?"

Justin's whole expression changed, amused at my question. "You're irresistible, Caitlin. You're sweet, cute, and stunningly beautiful. What more can one want?"

"Sweet and cute I can handle. Why did you go and ruin it by adding the stunningly beautiful bit?" I said smiling at him. "You really need your eyes checked Justin. I think the pressure from our bond has caused some vessels to pop."

"My vision is perfect and so are you," he said, leaning in to kiss me softly on the lips, taking his time, arousing every living cell in my body.

No matter how many times this man kissed me, it always

felt as if it were our first. I wrapped my hands around his neck intensifying Justin's response.

Just then Kyle pulled up beeping his horn, "Get a room you two," he yelled out the window, laughing. "Oh, I forgot. What good would that do in your circumstance?"

Justin glared at him, warning him to stop.

"What happened to Old Betty?" Kyle asked, changing the subject.

"She's thrown in the towel – given up," I said, smiling.

"We'll take care of her, isn't that right Justin?" Kyle said, winking at his best friend.

I was afraid to ask what they were planning for poor Old Betty. "Don't do anything stupid. Just take her to the mechanic and I'll pick her up later."

"Leave her to me," said Kyle, driving away.

Justin turned back to face me smiling cunningly. "Now, where were we?" he beamed, kissing me again.

~~~

Kissing and the occasional caress was the extent of our physical contact. It was however enough to drive us both crazy.

It became second nature to back off just before my powers kicked in. There were, however, numerous instances where we came quite close to crossing the line. My gift was unforgiving on two separate occasions, both times causing Justin great pain.

The Ellri kept a close watch, warning us on several occasions. They even threatened to keep us apart if we continued to push the limit. We, of course, agreed with everything they said, but unfortunately our physical attraction was stronger than our resolve. It was agonizing fighting something so natural.

"I meant to ask you," Justin said, driving me home. "Did

you get round to reading your grandmother's letters to your parents?"

My eyes widened. It had completely slipped my mind. "I forgot! How could I forget something so important?" I exclaimed, turning in the seat to face him. "Wait, I don't even remember where I stashed them?"

"You don't remember because I'm the one who hid them in your room. It was the night Marlene was getting you drunk on wine, remember?"

"Yeah, now I remember. You took them upstairs." I let out a deep sigh of relief. "How could something so important simply slip my mind? They might have the answers we're looking for."

"You can't blame yourself for forgetting. I'm sure your mind has enough things to worry about," he pointed to my head, "Especially with all those crazy things you have jammed in there."

Could I be any more transparent? This blank spot in my past was a hole in my life that I both feared and kept coming back to because I couldn't quite fill it. My need to find out the whole truth, to fill this void was a way to paste together the pieces of my existence. I felt incomplete not knowing the reason behind everything.

We pulled up to the house in complete silence. I didn't know what Justin expected me to say. He was more aware of my feelings than I gave him credit for. Once in my room he plopped down in the armchair looking at me, displeased with my unwillingness to talk about what's been bothering me.

"You're not going to let me in, are you?" Justin said, shaking his head in disappointment. "I would've thought that after all we've been through you'd feel comfortable sharing your thoughts with me."

"I could say the same about you," I replied.

"That's different. There's a code I have to follow. But you, Caitlin – you are purposely acting calm, covering your true feelings."

"I tell you everything."

"It's really frustrating the way you shut me out. Why do you feel that you're the only one worried about the Council's impending decision?"

"Okay, I'm worried," I finally conceded, sitting in his lap.

Justin, of course, accommodated me by pulling me swiftly in his embrace, rousing a shriek of excitement. For the last five months I had spent infinite hours studying his face, wondering how exceptionally happy the creator must have been when he created Justin. He was a true masterpiece, perfect in every way.

"Whatever the outcome, we're in this together," he said, pushing my hair behind my ear.

"Gabriel was rather sure that the Nobe will side with them. What if he's right? What then?"

"Have you forgotten that your little admirer doesn't know

about our connection? The Nobe, however, know everything. Why would they separate us? They know better."

Gazing into his brilliant blues was all I needed to get my hopes up. There was absolutely no false hope in his words. Taking his face in my hand I slowly leaned in and kissed his sumptuous lips. Justin's face was as happy as it was handsome, glowing with pleasure at my touch.

"I love you," he said, pushing me slightly back to get a better look at me. "I won't let anyone take you form me, you must know that."

"I know," I nodded, trying not to dwell on the fact that the decision wasn't ours to make. "Where did you stash the letters?" I asked, strategically changing the topic.

"Hold on one second," he said, pushing me to my feet, "they're right here."

Justin headed towards the foot of my bed and lifted the mattress, "Here they are!" He exclaimed, pulling out the neatly tied pack.

Sitting on the bed I took the pack of the twenty or so letters and tried to sort them according to postal date. Seeing that there were so many, I simply closed my eyes and threw the envelopes in the air while whispering, "By date," It took a mere second and then the letters, one by one, quickly stacked themselves in front of me according to the day they were posted.

"That's one way of doing it," Justin laughed, amused at my need to use my powers for such a trivial task.

"Everybody else gets to use theirs out in the open, why not me? I want something done, and it's done. I'm my own personal genie," I smiled.

"Just don't overdo it."

"The first one is dated months before I was born," I said,

ignoring his last comment. "Why would she start writing only then? My parents had moved to Oaks way before that."

I let the detail bob around in my head, trying to make sense of why my grandmother would wait seven years to write to my parents, and only a few months before my birth.

"It might simply be a coincidence," Justin said, not believing his own words. "There's only one way to find out." He picked up the first envelope. "Let's see what this sucker says." He held the first envelope in his hands not opening the contents, simply stared at it for a minute.

"What are you waiting for?" I asked, impatiently.

"Shhh, I'm reading. You're not the only one with awesome supernatural powers," he said smirking. "Besides, I don't want to rip the envelope open. It'd be nice to keep them in tack, they're old."

Happily surprised by his ability, I threw myself at him, kissing him maniacally, causing Justin to fall back on the bed. He started laughing at my response and put his hands around my back squeezing me against his chest.

"If I'd known my powers turned you on, I'd have used them more often," he said, chuckling at my eagerness.

"It's not your powers that turn me on. It's you – just you!" I said, kissing him vehemently.

"Oh, I see," he said, rolling me on my back, pinning me to the bed. "Now this is more like it," he smiled, looking hungrily into my eyes.

It was truly amazing how one minute my sharpest fears were engulfing my every pore, surrounding me by darkness and just as soon as Justin touched me, every last insecurity was instantaneously erased.

"This would be much more fun if you had ascended," he said, pulling himself up.

"I wouldn't know," I responded.

"Ascend first, and then I'll be glad to tutor you," he chuckled, kissing me lightly on the lips. "Now let me get back to my reading."

My cheeks were crimson at the thought of Justin and me actually consummating our relationship. I wasn't sure if I was nervous due to my lack of prior experience on the subject or the thought of being so close to him that caused my insides to go completely berserk. Maybe Justin was right, maybe I wasn't ready for the two of us to go down that path just yet.

All the same, his patience was commendable. It proved how devoted he was to what we had.

"Eileen was really worried about your well-being," Justin started to say, holding the envelope between his palms. Like a fortune teller, he was talking with his eyes closed. "She warned your father on your uncle's plans to come to Oaks, urging him to seek Abbot's help. Eileen didn't mention anything about your mother's illness. She seemed more worried about your birth. Apparently, she was expecting some sort of complication. That's about all this says," Justin said, picking up the next envelope.

"Why wouldn't my grandma mention my mom's health? From what I know my mom was quite sick even before her pregnancy."

Justin shrugged his shoulders not knowing what to say. "This one is mostly about your uncle Caradon's union to Holly and how happy she was that he'd finally settled down into a serious relationship."

Justin seemed preoccupied with something.

"What is it?" I asked worriedly.

"I'm not sure. There seems to be something more to these letters – something she hasn't actually written." He shook it off.

"I'm probably making a bigger deal of it than it is."

Not being interested in anything apart from the obvious, Justin quickly scanned through all the letters giving me a quick run-through of their contents, stopping only on the few that had anything of interest.

My grandma had kept my father up to date on the running of their estate. It would seem that he had a love for horses and of Ancient Greek history. She had mentioned his horses by name in several of her letters. They each bore ancient Greek names like: Dionysius, Victor, Achilles and so on.

She also mentioned the family. This wasn't the first time I had heard of my father's siblings. Gabriel had told me about my father's big family, revealing things about his two brothers Caradon and Brett. He had also brought up my father's youngest sibling; my aunt Rebecca who was, according to my grandma, happily united with a John McDevitt, living somewhere near Scotland away from the Korbs.

Apart from a couple of precautionary words, the letters weren't of any help, at least as far as what we were looking for. The only thing that did stand out was the fact that she hadn't mentioned my mother's ailing health which was strange for a person who caught glimpses of the future. She would have known the possibility of her demise. *Why didn't she bring it up?* I wondered.

"I think you should read this one on your own," Justin said, handing me the last letter after carefully opening the flap.

Intrigued, I unfolded the letter carefully not wanting to crease it any more than was humanly possible.

The opening was addressed to my mother, congratulating her on my birth and wishing her well. My grandma was visibly sad at knowing that she'd never get to meet me up close. The letter was typical, like the rest, warning my parents to be careful and then there it was. Eileen had closed the letter with one bold line, making sure it stood out from the rest.

Good luck on your long journey, and know that I love you both.

Till we meet again

I gasped, dropping my hands in my lap. "They knew! They both knew they were going to die, didn't they?" I asked, looking down at the letter I was holding. "That's why she never mentioned her health."

"I don't know, but there's something with these letters that I can't put my finger on," said Justin, looking at them. "Help me open the envelops, I want to see something.

"What is it?" I asked, helping him with the task.

"I'm not sure, but there is something here, more than the written word."

With all the letters opened and spread out on the bed, Justin scanned them over. "I don't see anything, do you?"

I shook my head. "Wait. Let's put them chronological order."

Still nothing.

With his hand hovering over the letters he said, "There is definitely something hidden here. I have an idea. You did say that your grandma had the same scar as you."

"Yeah, so?"

Justin turned to me looking deep in thought, "This might work."

"What are you talking about?"

He placed the letters one right next to the other, five across and five down and then turned towards me. "I want you to put your hands on top of them and ignite your wrist."

"What? Why?"

"Just do it, will you?"

I followed his orders and as soon as my hands were fully charged I felt my wrist start to throb. But it wasn't' the only thing in transition. The papers too, were changing – fusing one with the other to form one large sheet.

"Give it more juice," Justin said, making me turn to look at him. He cracked a smile, "You know what I mean."

I shook my head and forced more power to the tips of my fingers, and just like magic a bright line started forming on the large sheet. It circled around turning and twisting as if a ghost was drawing something. "That's so cool," I exclaimed, feeling a bit weak. I had to stop otherwise I was sure to faint.

"You did well," Justin beamed, sitting next to me. In sobering silence we both looked on as the line continued to form, and only when it stopped did Justin and I stand again.

"It looks like a drawing of a barn," he said, sounding quite disappointed.

"What does it mean?"

Justin shrugged his shoulder. "Caitlin, your grandma was much more powerful than you. I think you need to exert a bit more force. It doesn't seem finished."

I breathed in deep. "Okay, I'll try, but be ready to catch me if I faint."

"Just concentrate," he said, smiling.

I repeated my actions, this time concentrating even more, forcing as much power as possible to my wrist. That's when it happened. The drawing came to life. It didn't last long, but it was wildly exciting to see it in action. It was a confrontation between two beings, two very powerful creatures. They were not human in form, but blurs. The scene ended with one of them falling, and in seconds the letters returned to their normal state.

"Who were they?" I asked, looking confused. "What does it mean?"

"I have absolutely no idea."

Justin collected the letters and stuffed them back in the envelopes, placing them carefully in a pile. Without uttering a sound he tied the letters with the ribbon and placed them back in their hiding place, under my mattress. "When you get your strength back, we'll try again," he said, "There must be more to it than that."

I nodded knowing that I was in no position to test my limit just then. "Come on, let's get something to eat," Justin offered.

"What does it all mean?" I asked again, shaking my head confused.

"I'm not sure. But sitting up here on an empty stomach won't get us any closer to what we're looking for. C'mon, Leslie has summoned us downstairs. She's prepared something for us to eat."

Aunt Leslie was very happy to have us back in Oaks. Even though she didn't express her feelings or even mention our two-week vacation to the Isle of Indigo, her actions spoke louder than any words could. She compensated for the two weeks of our absence with ample amount of food and endless hugging.

"Sit down, the food's getting cold," Aunt Leslie said, kissing me on the head for the millionth time. "How was your first day back?" she added, serving us chicken with potatoes.

"Not as bad as I imagined it would be," I lied, digging my fork into the tender meat thinking of how it ended with Tyler. "I'll need a ride to Tyler's," I said, turning to Justin.

"Of course, as soon as we finish," Justin replied smiling, understanding the urgency in my voice.

Secrets Beneath The Floor

Illustrated for Lines That Bind · Within The Whispers

SEVENTEEN

DEEP IN SECRETS

TYLER WASN'T TOO happy to see me. His expression was as hard and grim as a stone wall, and his eyes held no welcome, only a cold indifference. I smiled, but nothing seemed to ease his discomfort. Of course he felt awkward. It's not every day you tell your best friend of eighteen years that you're in love with her.

"So now you're not going to talk to me? Is that how this is going to pan out?" I asked taking a seat next to him in the family room.

Tyler shook his head and saw the puzzlement rise in my face. "What do you want me to say, Caitlin?" His voice was soft, but cold as a blade. "Do you want me to tell you that I don't feel what I feel? That I didn't spend two weeks of my vacation driving Karen crazy, talking about you? Is that what you want to hear? The poor girl can write your autobiography."

"I really thought you guys hit it off. It seemed that way from where I was standing."

"I told you before, she's great, but she's not you," Tyler said, standing up. He crossed the room and looked out the window, deep in thought. "She was amazing, she really was, but for some reason it actually felt like I was cheating on you."

"You're kidding me, right?"

"You and Justin I can handle. I came to terms with your bond a long time ago," Tyler continued to explain. "Gabriel on the other hand," he stopped and turned to look at me, "Let's just say that it took all my self-control from taking his life. Justin is the bigger man. I can't understand how he could just sit back and watch that bastard touch you."

"As far as Gabriel was concerned, Justin was aware of my intentions."

"Still, if it wasn't for Marc, I would've taken Gabriel's life with a mere touch."

"You can do that?"

Tyler came and sat across from me on the sofa, dropping his gaze to the floor, he said, "My gift has evolved over the months." He took a deep breath. "Justin says I'm close to ascending."

"I'm glad one of us is."

Tyler smiled, a bare twist of the lips, and his voice went up an octave. "You and Justin…," He raised his eyes to meet mine, "You two haven't yet, have you?"

"That's personal!" I snapped, being in no mood to discuss the subject with him, not after his confession.

"So you haven't," he beamed, overly excited "Good!"

"I thought you wanted to see me and Justin happy."

"Happy yeah, but not…," Tyler was rather frustrated, putting his face in his hands, sweeping back his hair. Governed by his emotions he stood up again and paced around the room, turning to me suddenly. "I hate this – hate feeling like this. Why did you come back anyway? I was finally getting over the idea of you. I've had a crush on you ever since fifth grade. Do you know how hard that is to get over? Do you?"

I couldn't believe my ears. Tyler felt that way about me for all those years? I always considered him part of my family the way I view Kyle, in a sense. Justin was right. I had to be extra careful with what I came to say.

I got to my feet and stood right in front of him, taking his hand into mine. "Look at me," I told him, forcing his gaze on me.

Hesitantly, he turned to me clearly uncomfortable with my hand in his. "You are my best friend, the one person I can rely on and feel completely at ease with. I love you Tyler. What we have is important to me. I don't want to lose you from my life, but if you'd feel better not hanging out with me anymore, I'll understand. I'll hate it, but I'll understand," I finally said wrapping my arms around his waist and leaned my head against his chest.

He kissed the top of my head and tightened his hold. We stood there in absolute silence for a few minutes. "I'll work through this, I promise," he sighed. "I need you in my life. I love you."

I took a step back and smiled. "Yeah, I love you too," I said, knowing full well that what he felt was much deeper than what I could possibly offer. "So what are you watching," I asked, realizing that I had interrupted his program.

"Nothing special, anything to get my mind off – well you know."

Just then Aurelia walked in carrying two glasses of refreshments. *Perfect timing*, I thought.

"Thought you guys would like something to drink," she said in her distinct Italian accent. "So, did you two talk things through? Did you solve your problems?"

"Mom, stay out of it!" Tyler gasped, rolling his eyes.

"So, you love the girl, what's there to be embarrassed about?" she spat out, leaving Tyler pale faced. "We all love, Caitlin."

"We're fine Aurelia, nothing we can't handle. Isn't that right Tyler?" I asked nudging him in the ribs.

He just nodded his head, still shocked by his mother's lack of discretion.

Smiling, Aurelia straightened out the cushions on the sofa. "Caitlin, I'll need you to come round again. Tomorrow after school, if that's alright?"

"Sure! No problem." I held her gaze. "Is there something wrong? Something I should know about?" I looked at Tyler for a minute, as though seeking the truth in his eyes.

"Don't look so panic-stricken," Aurelia told me. "We decided that tomorrow is a good time as any for you to start learning how to command your power."

"Seriously?" I squealed, sounding overly excited. "You can teach me that?"

"Of course we can, Caitlin and I don't mean your power to move things either. I mean your real power," she smiled, pointing to my wrist.

"Really? You're going to allow me to use my gift?"

"I didn't say that exactly," said Aurelia smiling. "We'll guide you in controlling your powers. Nobody is allowed to use their gifts without proper guidance."

"Who am I going to use my powers on?" I asked looking to Tyler, confused on how this whole lesson would pan out.

"Don't look at me!" Tyler exclaimed, chuckling. "I'm not going to be your guinea pig."

"My brave son," she said sarcastically. "No, Caitlin, this one...," Aurelia added, pointing to Tyler, "hasn't ascended yet. Justin, Kyle and Marc will bear the brunt of your force."

"No! Absolutely not! I refuse to hurt them."

"Oh sure," Tyler said, poking me playfully in the ribs, "It was okay when you thought I'd be on the receiving end, but god forbid anything should happen to anyone else."

I laughed at his quirkiness. "Knock it off," I giggled, swatting his hand away. "You know what I meant. I don't want to hurt anyone, including you."

Aurelia fluffed up the last of the pillows and headed for the door, ignoring our immature behavior. "Who said anything about hurting anyone? They have all been through the stages, so they'll be able to help you. Tomorrow then," she said, closing the door behind her.

"Tyler? Did you go through anything like this?"

"My gift is nothing like yours, Caitlin. I can't actually test it on anybody – not if I want them to live after the experiment."

"What can you do exactly? You said something about taking someone's life. You were kidding, right?"

"I'd rather not discuss it."

"Oh, c'mon! You know everything about mine. What can you do?"

"I'll tell you if you promise to be cool about it – no freaking out."

"I promise," I insisted. "Now tell me."

"It would seem that I have the ability to drain the life force from any living organism with a mere touch." He made a grimace, distasting his own gift. Tyler waited a few seconds for my response, but I was way too shocked to say anything. "I can heal as well."

I must have looked really stupid, just staring at him the way I was.

"You promised not to freak out!" He walked to the opposite side of the room despondently and pulled the lush fabric that draped down the whole length of the window, hiding behind it like he did when we were little. "It's horrific isn't it?"

I walked the length of the room and stood in front of him. "What you can do is miraculous. Who wouldn't want your power?"

He pulled the fabric to the side, "I'm a monster!"

"What are you talking about? You can heal people! You're amazing!"

"Didn't you hear what I said, Caitlin? I can also take a life just as easy."

I pulled back the curtain even further. "I heard you, but I know you'd never choose to take a life. Now healing – that's who you are."

"You make the choice sound so simple. It wasn't that way on the Isle of Indigo. I felt how easy it was for me to lose control – to thirst for someone's life. My dad told me that the energy I drain from another human can become quite addictive. I need to have complete control."

"How about healing? Justin once mentioned that there had to be some kind of balance?"

Tyler took a few steps away from the window with his eyebrow arched as high as humanly possible. "So," he said, bright eyed and bushy tailed, "you talk about me with Justin, do you?"

"Of course I do. You're my best friend, stupid. If I'm not worried about you who else would I be worried about?"

Tyler cracked a sincere smile, pleased with my answer and said, "I don't have to take a life to give a life if that's what you mean. I'm not like other healers. For me the two gifts are completely separate. I can heal someone without needing to transfer the ailment. It just takes all my energy to do it. Dad says the bigger the ailment or wound the more painful it would be for me, and the person I help. Dad said that I shouldn't take my gift lightly."

"Join the club." I plopped down on the sofa. "At least you know exactly what you can do. I, on the other hand, haven't got a clue. The only thing I know is that I can do damage. Apart from that – nothing. Would you like to switch gifts?" I offered amusingly.

"Hell yeah! I'd love to be able to travel in the Inner Realm, leaving the limits of this world behind."

I drew a sharp breath. "What's the Inner Realm?"

"It's the space between time, a dimension where only the truly gifted can reach – the ones who can transcend."

I thought about the times I had my outer body experiences. On both occasions I didn't feel anything special. I was still on the same plane as the rest of them.

"Tyler? What can somebody do in this place? I haven't noticed anything special?"

"You haven't noticed anything because you aren't aware of your full potential yet. Once you start having complete control of your powers you will be able to take advantage of your time there. I hear it's really awesome, Caitlin. It's a place that transcends the laws of nature. Once mastered, you would be able to defy gravity, space as well as time." He shrugged his shoulders. "Well, that's all I know. You should ask the Ellri. They can give you more details about it. Anyway, all I know is that your gift is way cooler than any of ours."

"I'd still prefer to heal people, no matter the personal pain or sacrifice you said it entails. What you can do is miraculous."

"You would, wouldn't you?" Tyler said raising his voice. I wasn't sure why he suddenly got upset. "You might fool the others Caitlin, but you sure as hell don't full me."

"What in the world are you talking about?" I asked.

"This self-sacrificing binge that you're on, needs to stop. I meant what I said this morning – you're – you're not happy and you know it."

"I...,"

He waved away my objections. "No – you're going to listen to me, and listen good!" His expression was severely intense. "On the surface you exude this confidence when we both know how scared you are deep down. You can't even admit how terrified you were of Gabriel."

I was about to say something, but Tyler continued to speak. "Yeah, I know your powers were enough to protect you, but it's in here that I'm worried about," said Tyler pointing to my heart. "He shook you up real good - made you question many things. Bottling all this up is eating you inside out, Caitlin."

Silence greeted his every word. I felt the panic beneath it, knowing he spoke the truth. With tear filled eyes I slumped down along the wall. Tyler had guessed my inner struggle – he couldn't have been any closer to the truth. I moaned and buried my face in my hands.

"You need to let us in. We are all here to help you. The Korbs will have to wait till hell freezes over before we allow you to go to them – no matter the decision. Justin was right, it's a war they want and it's a war they're going to get."

"No! I won't allow it," I yelled, through the tears. "I'm not worth it."

"Let us be the judge of that," he said kneeling so that our eyes were level. I looked at Tyler's determined expression. My heart sank within me.

"None of you will be hurt – not on my account," I said, raising my voice, swallowing back the knot in my throat as I stood. "If the Nobe Council decides that it'd be best for me to go to the Korbs – then so be it. I won't fight their decision."

"You're crazy!" he yelled. "I won't allow it. We won't allow it. Did you even think about Justin? Think about me – about the others? How can you say things like that?"

While my heart thudded in my ears, my emotions warred within me. "The Nobe will know what's best for everyone."

"The separation will kill you both. Justin won't stand for it. Besides, he's determined not to let you go. We all are."

I looked at Tyler questionably while drying away my tears. "You've discussed this with him?" I asked, wondering how he was so sure of Justin's feelings on the matter.

"Of course we've all talked about it – weighed different outcomes. Did you really think that we'd just sit back and allow things to unfold the way the Korbs want things to? Give us some credit!"

Here I was holding back my true feelings in fear of making them all worry about the future, and there they were formulating strategies about impending outcomes.

"Why didn't anyone tell me anything?"

"We just thought you had enough on your plate. We didn't want to upset you more than we had too."

"Oh, I see," I sat down on the arm of the antique sofa, "So what are you planning to do, exactly?"

"Caitlin, don't look so glum. We're not planning on doing anything until the decision is final. Until then, we can only bounce ideas back and forth. Anyway, that's not important now."

"Not important? How can you even say that to me? This is my problem – not yours. The Korbs, like it or not, are my family – my responsibility."

Tyler vigorously shook his head back and forth refusing to accept what I was saying.

"We are your family, not them. If the rest of the Korbs are

anything like Gabriel, you have absolutely no business with those people."

"Like it or not Tyler they are my family. The Korbs are my blood relatives. Whatever they want, they want it from me. None of you have any say in the matter." I was deliberately trying to make it sound final. I was not going to risk any of them. "If any of you even consider putting yourselves in jeopardy...," I stood to make my threat sound more foreboding, "I swear, Tyler. I'll get up and leave tomorrow if I have to."

No sooner did I finish my sentence when the door swung open. Marcellus simply stood there staring at us. "This is not a topic for either of you to be discussing," he finally said, in a commanding voice. "And you young lady, the only place you're going is home to finish your homework. Only Ellri get to discuss such matters not you – not any of you have that right," he continued to say, turning to his son. "Don't think because we haven't said anything that we don't know what is going through your minds. You all need to put this topic to rest and enjoy your youth. Thinking about the indefinite future is a waste of your time. You will do as we say, nothing more, nothing less."

"I can't have anyone risk their life for me," I said drawing Marcellus' gaze away from my best friend.

"The only thing you need to worry about is getting control of your gift and doing well in school – nothing else. Do you understand? How do you expect to face the Korbs when you can't even control your emotions? You all need to trust that we know what's best for all of you," he said, looking back and forth to Tyler and me. "This topic is off limits. Do I make myself clear?"

Hesitantly we both agreed, nodding our heads in unison. Knowing that the Ellri were aware of my feelings somehow soothed my anxiety. It suddenly felt much easier to breathe.

Those past few months I had been fighting my own demons. The fear and uncertainty I felt were getting the best of me. I cried myself to sleep more nights than I'd like to remember. Even the energy to appear cheerful for everyone drained me emotionally. Surprisingly, it was good to have everything out in the open.

Marcellus headed for the door, fuming in anger. "Now you both have homework to do, so get to it!"

"I should be getting home," I responded, turning to Tyler. "Can you give me a lift home? Justin can't make it for some reason."

"Sure grab your coat," Tyler said all too happy to leave the house. Marcellus rarely got cross with anyone, but when he did it was best to distance yourself. His Italian temper was no laughing matter.

"Do you know where Justin is?" I asked, Tyler the second we got in the car

"No, he's been blocking us out lately. Justin has a lot on his mind Caitlin. I'm sure my actions today didn't help."

"He's fine. He's been aware of your feelings towards me all along. It would seem I was the only one in the dark."

Tyler turned his gaze to me and smiled. "I'll work through this, I promise," he exhaled. "I don't want our relationship to change. Besides, Justin's friendship means a lot to me."

I was touched that he put Justin above his own feelings. I took his hand in mine and squeezed it tight. "You're amazing, you know that? I couldn't have wished for a better friend."

"I know," he said chuckling. A few, quiet minutes later he spoke again. "What were you and the girls talking about in the cafeteria? You all looked so absorbed in the conversation."

"The prom, of course. What else is there this time of year?" I exclaimed, mimicking Lisa's response to the same question.

"I haven't thought about the prom," Tyler said, smiling cunningly. "Would I be pushing it if I asked you to go with me?"

"What do you think?" I responded poking him in the ribs. "Do the girls at school a favor and take one of them. I'm sure they're all waiting to see who you'll pick."

"What are you talking about?" he said, turning into the driveway.

"Don't tell me you haven't noticed how all the girls act around you?" I asked in disbelief. "How can you not know? They practically fall at your feet every time you pass by."

"I was concentrating on one girl in particular all this time," he confessed, looking at me with a side glance. "I guess I have to ask one of them to the prom – any suggestions?"

"Oh, no you don't," I laughed, opening the door to let myself out. "I'm not getting caught up in this prom thing. You pick whoever you want and have fun. I don't want anything to do with it."

Tyler got out and stretched his arms on the roof of his sporty car. "Caitlin, you can't be serious – we're both going. You're not going to miss out on your prom. Isn't that right Justin?" he asked looking over my shoulder.

I turned around and Justin's presence by the entrance caused my heart to accelerate by the mere sight of him. He casually walked over to where we were standing. He didn't want to exhibit any more affection in front of Tyler knowing full well how my friend felt.

"Don't you want to go to prom?" Justin asked concerned."

"Do we need to talk about this now – here?"

I turned to Tyler visibly upset for involving Justin in our juvenile conversation. "You find a date first and then we'll talk," I told him. "Oh, and by the way, you should apologize to Megan."

"Why the hell would I do that?" he asked, surprised that I'd even mention it.

"You were rather rude to her."

"Since when do you care about Megan's feelings? She was prying in our business – being annoying as always?"

"Megan was simply trying to get your attention."

"Why would she want my attention?"

"You're not that smart after all, are you Tyler?" I commented. "Megan has had a thing for you as far back as I can remember," I finally admitted, hating myself for bringing up the subject. I wouldn't have mentioned anything if I wasn't sure it was the truth. "She just doesn't know how to act around you, that's all."

"Oh, and being obnoxious is her way of showing how much she cares?" he exclaimed. "We're going to the prom Caitlin, and whether Megan likes me or not is a whole different matter."

"I don't know. We'll see," I answered. "Just apologize to Megan."

"Fine, I give up. Maybe you can talk some sense into her," he said looking towards Justin, slipping back into the driver's seat.

"I'll see what I can do," Justin answered amused.

Tyler stretched over the passenger's side and called out, "You need a ride to school in the morning?"

"Yeah, sure – thanks."

"Okay then, see you in the morning," he said and sped off.

In no time, Justin had his arms around my waist, pulling me close. "I guess your talk went well?" he asked, kissing me on the lips.

Justin's lips were intoxicating; his touch prevented any

coherent thought. I folded my arms around his neck bringing him in closer. In no mood to talk, I melted into his embrace allowing my senses to take over.

He pushed me slightly back smiling. "I missed you too," he said holding me tighter. "Now what's this about not wanting to go to your prom?"

"You're both crazy," I said, slipping out of his embrace and headed towards the door.

Once inside I shrugged out of my coat and headed towards my room. Justin followed without saying a word. Closing my bedroom door behind him, he sat in the armchair deep in thought. I walked to my dresser and picked out something more comfortable to wear. I disappeared into the bathroom without uttering a sound.

"Why don't you want to go?" he asked, as soon as I emerged from the bathroom wearing my comfy sweats.

"I'm not sure. My heart is just not into it."

Justin swiftly pulled me into his lap, causing me to giggle with excitement. "You can't miss your prom. It's an important event. Besides, if you don't go you'll regret it later."

At that moment my heart sank. I realized that he must have gone to his own prom, but with whom? I wondered.

"Who would I ask?" I said smiling, trying to smother my insecurity.

"Um, I see your dilemma," he responded. "I guess I'll have to take you if, of course, that's all right with you?"

"Why would you want to go to prom? Haven't you gone to yours?" I asked fishing for details.

"If you want to ask me something just come right out and ask," Justin spoke with certain wariness, with a hint of suspicion in his voice, "Don't tiptoe around the topic."

"Okay, okay. So, who did you take to your prom?" I finally

asked, dying to know everything, but fearing the truth.

"I went with Nicole," he answered nonchalantly.

Her name on his lips was like a cold knife through my heart. "Wait, you went with Nicole Cathcart – Marlene's daughter?" I asked rather surprised. "Isn't she older than you?"

"Only by a year. What does that matter anyway?" he grimaced, shrugging his shoulders.

I was suddenly besieged with jealousy. Nicole was Emily and Kyle's first cousin from uncle Abbot's side of the family. Her father Nathan was uncle Abbot's older brother.

Feeling uncomfortable talking about her, I got to my feet and fondled through my school bag looking for nothing in particular. *I can't believe he went with Nicole.*

Growing up I hated the fact that she was older than me and able to hang out with Justin and the guys. Images of the two of them together swirled in my mind causing my power to surface. My wrist started burning, causing me to wince in pain.

"Caitlin, are you alright?" Justin asked sounding worried.

Taking a deep breath to sooth my nerves, I continued to look through my things. "I'm fine," I finally said.

He wasn't buying it. He quickly stood up and walked over to me. He was about to take a hold of my arm when I instinctively backed away not wanting to hurt him.

"What's wrong?" he demanded, looking confused unaware of my condition.

"You shouldn't touch me right now."

He instantly dropped his hand to his side understanding exactly what I meant. "Why are you acting like this?"

"It's nothing. My gift seems to have a life of its own," I lied, turning back to my school bag.

"Look at me, Caitlin," he demanded. "Don't lie to me. Why are you so angry? What the hell is going on in that head of yours, and don't you dare lie to me. Tell me the truth?"

"I'm not angry," I turned to look at him, getting control of my emotions once again. "It's just that – forget it – it's real stupid. I'm fine now," I said, looking down at my wrist which was finally back to normal.

Justin lifted my chin up to face him. "Tell me," he insisted, in a hard tone. "I want to know what you're thinking. Even if what you're thinking is insane?

"Why didn't you ever mention Nicole?"

"What? Why would I have to?" he asked puzzled.

Annoyed that Justin wasn't willing to answer my question, I pushed passed him and walked over to the window, turning my back to him, overcome with jealousy.

"How long did you and Nicole date?" I finally asked, embarrassed to face him.

"Date?" he chuckled. "Is that what all this is about? You think that Nicole – that Nicole and I dated?" Justin asked, wrapping his arms around my waist, forcing my back against his chest.

"Well, didn't you?"

"She did Kyle a favor going with me to the prom."

I turned around to face him. It was hard for me to believe that any girl would need to be forced to go out with Justin.

"You're just saying that to make me feel better," I accused him.

"Caitlin, with you so far away I was in no mood to leave the house, let alone go to the prom, or even date anyone. Kyle and Marc insisted we all go together so Nicole, feeling sorry for me, agreed to accompany me – that's all."

"You want me to believe that Nicole felt sorry for you? That's why she agreed to go with you? I've seen how see looked at you growing up."

He was silent, staring right at me, shaking his head in discontent. "You still don't get it, do you?" Justin asked, rather frustrated "You know how difficult the last five years were without you. How could I possibly have any type of relationship with another person when my heart was a thousand miles away?" he said, pulling me closer into his arms. "There was never anything between Nicole and me. She's more like a sister than anything else. Nicole was aware of my feelings about you even before I was."

I leaned my forehead against his chest feeling stupid for jumping to my own conclusion – stupid for allowing my petty jealousy to get the best of me. "I'm such an idiot," I said. "I have no business asking you about your personal life. I'm really sorry."

"What personal life?" he asked, drawing my attention to his lips. "Sure I went out with a few girls, but as far as relationships go, my heart belonged to only one," he added, kissing me softly on the lips. "It was you Caitlin – it was always you. You're in my veins – my blood – my heart."

"Yeah – like one of those deadly, incurable viruses." I laughed.

Justin's strong arms lifted me off the floor and held me tight. "I love you. Get that through your thick skull. I always did and I always will, and I want to take you to your prom – if you let me?" He finally said, scanning my expression.

"If you think it's necessary, we'll go."

"It's not necessary." He shook his head at my inability to understand. "It's simply fun. You need to have fun."

"I have about two more months to think about it," I said, not wanting to make promises I couldn't keep.

"Don't do that," Justin said releasing his hold. "Don't think I can't read you. I know you well enough to know why you keep your distance from everyone and everything. You can't hide."

Apparently I wasn't as good at hiding my feelings as I thought. "Well, I'm sorry if I can't get Gabriel's threat out of my head," I suddenly said, raising my voice.

I was tired of keeping it all bottled up.

"I'm sorry that it bothers everyone that I can't see past this. I can't just shrug all this off and pretend it's not happening. The Korbs are my blood – my immediate family. It's their blood that runs through these veins," I said, raising my arms in front of me. "I'm related to the people who are willing to destroy everyone I love and for what – for me? Justin, can you really see me allowing any of that to happen? Allow any one of you to put yourselves in harm's way?"

Justin's mouth tightened into a hard line. "You are nothing like those monsters," he snapped, putting his hands through his hair annoyed at my comments. "How can you even consider them family – they're...," Justin stopped not wanting to continue his sentence and turned his back to me. "Ah...," he growled, "you're so stubborn."

"They're what?" I yelled, wanting him to finish.

Justin turned and stared, not knowing how to continue.

"More secrets, Justin – really?"

"Marcellus has a point we've got no right thinking about the Korbs. We should let the Ellri handle everything," he finally said, heading towards the door. "I really have to go. You need to get your homework done anyway," he said, giving me a quick kiss and simply left.

Staring at the closed door, I wasn't sure what just happened. One minute we were talking about the prom and the next – What was it about the Korbs that was so horrific? Why would Justin respond so strongly to them? Even in my grandmother's letters I didn't notice anything out of the ordinary about them.

I fell back on my bed staring at the ceiling, making mental notes of what little I did figure out about my life.

After all this time they were still keeping secrets from me. This puzzle was getting more complicated by the minute. First, I wasn't who I thought I was. Then, my parents weren't who I thought they were. They didn't live where I thought they lived and if that wasn't enough I still had to figure out what they died of and what the Korbs wanted from me. I thought high school was brutal, solving this on my own, would be impossible.

At that moment it dawned on me. That day on the beach when I slipped into my solace I heard a voice speak to me. *Would the Korbs, themselves, have my answers?* I wondered

Without thinking, I sat up propping myself against the headboard and closed my eyes. I was going to get to the bottom of this if it killed me. At once, I slipped into my solace unforced. My gift was evolving, making it effortless each time.

"Caradon – Caradon Korbs," I said out loud, not knowing what to expect.

In a split second the impenetrable darkness of my solace was immersed in a light blue haze. Then, to my unexpected eyes, the haze lifted only to reveal foreign surroundings. I saw a face as clear as day. The man who I was observing wasn't aware of my presence – not as far as I knew. From what I could tell he was in his fifties with shoulder length white hair and exceptionally pale skin. The honey hued eye color was the only thing that softened his otherwise ghostly appearance. He was dressed rather strange; in a long black robe with red buttons down the middle.

From floor to ceiling, the room was steep in leather bound books. There was hardly room to move around. However, it was the man with the dark and eerie presence that drew all my attention as he stood in front of a ridiculously large antique desk. He was leafing through one volume after another – searching for something he seemed to deem important.

Unable to find whatever he was looking for, he threw the last book he was holding to the floor and walked to a new stack of old books. Just as he was about to pick up a new book, the mysterious looking man suddenly closed his eyes and searched around the room sensing something.

He maneuvered around the great stacks of old books effortlessly, even though both his eyes were closed and turned to the ceiling. *"Caitlin?"* he suddenly said, in a deep voice. *"So, you're curious are you?"* he added smiling. *"Good, girl. Come home, child."*

I instantly opened my eyes forcing myself out of my solace. It was the same voice I heard on the beach. It must have been my uncle, there was no other explanation. I shook my head to banish the ghostly sight of his face.

Just then, my door flew open revealing an angry Uncle Abbot. "What do you think you're doing? You shouldn't be summoning a Varjatus," he said furiously.

"What's a Varjatus?" I asked looking confused.

"Don't you ever do something like that again," he yelled, ignoring my question.

His authoritative voice made my blood curdle. Never having heard Uncle Abbot lose his temper, I felt tears rolling down my eyes, unaware of what I did wrong. In minutes Kyle and Emily were standing by his side; just staring at me. Aunt Leslie came in seconds later, placing herself between me and the rest of the family.

"Abbot, the child doesn't know her own strength. You can't blame her for testing her own limits."

"It's not that, and you know it! She is calling on Varjatus by name," he continued to say in a loud voice. "It's – It's...."

"She's not aware of what all this means, Abbot! Give her a break."

Emily crossed the room and sat next to me on the bed, wiping my tears away. "You'll be okay," she whispered. "Don't worry."

Kyle stood next to his mother with his back facing me.

"Caitlin doesn't know any better. You can't hold her accountable for things she hasn't been told," Kyle said, looking at his father. "Why do the Ellri insist on keeping her in the dark? She has every right to know. She is after all a member of the Circle of Trust. What you're doing to her is cruel."

Leslie grabbed Kyle's hand in order to stop him from saying any more. "We'll decide what we say and don't say to any of you," Aunt Leslie responded, looking to all our faces. "Never question an Ellri no matter who they are. You of all people should know your place, Kyle."

I got to my feet not liking where the conversation was heading. "It's me your angry at. There's no need to yell at Kyle," I said, swallowing hard. "I was curious – curious to see Caradon. He's my uncle for heaven's sake. I wanted to see what the big deal was."

"Get out both of you!" Uncle Abbot barked at Emily and Kyle.

"We're not going anywhere," Kyle said, defying his father's wishes.

Emily and Kyle came and stood on either side of me. Uncle Abbot was fuming at their impudence. Kyle unexpectedly fell to his knees crouched over in agonizing pain. "I might be your father, but I am your Ellri above all," Uncle Abbot roared, staring at Kyle angrily.

Kyle was tearing at his hair, racking his face with his

fingernails, cursing the cruelty of his own father. "Stop! What are you doing to him?" I yelled, in complete disbelief. My blood suddenly burned through my veins igniting my gift – reaching a new level of lethal that I had never experienced before. My gift was surely compensating to meet Uncle Abbot's own powers. "Stop," I warned, not recognizing my own voice "Leave him alone," I screamed.

Uncle Abbot and Aunt Leslie took a step back as did Emily.

"Are you okay?" I asked, completely irritated.

Kyle nodded.

"Look at her," Emily said, stunned. "Look at her hands."

My gaze followed their stunned expressions. From the wrist down, my hands were engulfed in a translucent white light.

"What is it?" I asked still sounding strange. My voice didn't have substance, it sounded like an echo.

"Don't be afraid," Uncle Abbot said, sounding like his old self again. "Your hands are lethally charged, Caitlin. Find some way to defuse your power."

Kyle finally stood and shook off the whole ordeal. I looked at all of them apologetically. "I was just curious to see him. I didn't mean to cause all this," I said, trying to explain.

"It's okay, sis. You did nothing wrong," Kyle said, attempting a smile. My uncle clearly didn't agree. "You don't want to hurt any of us – now do you?" Kyle asked.

"No. You know I don't." I put my palms together and felt the surge of power move from one hand to the other. As soon as I parted my palms a ball of iridescent light was formed around my hands.

"That's so cool!" Kyle exclaimed, looking at me.

Even though I felt calm, my body continued to react erratically. I had no control over my actions. I felt a numbing sensation trailing down my spine to my legs.

"What do I do now?" I asked, scared out of my mind.

Justin suddenly appeared in the doorway, looking a bit apprehensive. "I thought you left," I said, feeling a bit wheezy.

His expression was rigid and unyielding. "She won't be able to hold on much longer, Abbot. You have to do something," he said, sounding overly concerned.

"Child, you must control the energy – ground it, before it grounds you," Abbot said, in a soft spoken hum.

"Easier said than done," I commented, knowing full well I couldn't.

"Abbot! You must put an end to this," Justin yelled, "she's going to collapse!"

My uncle didn't seem to care for Justin's comment, instead he said, "Kyle, are you ready?" And with those words he motioned for Kyle to approach me.

"No!" I screamed. "Are you crazy? I'm going to hurt him." I took a few steps back, crashing into my bed

Kyle continued to move closer, ignoring my plea.

"Kyle, please stop," I begged.

In front of me, dangerously close, Kyle simply smiled. "There's only two ways to do this, sis. Either you hit me with your power – which I'd rather you didn't or you defuse it yourself. It's your call, Caity." He smiled even wider. "I'd prefer if you choose the latter."

That second, my body suddenly went limp. Blackness opened at my feet as I balanced on the edge, consumed with uncertainty, damned with anguish so strong it stripped the air from my lungs. "Caitlin!" Kyle yelled, with a scared expression on his face. The room spun into a grey swirl as my legs buckled under me. With a blood chilling scream I hit the hard-wood floor, collapsed, caught in an ungainly sprawl on the floor. Then, everything was dark and quiet.

"Breathe child. Your body has given up, but that doesn't mean your mind has to." The whisper within the whisper was faint and clear, and more beautiful than any sound I'd ever heard. "Return your power from where it came – command it."

"I know what I have to do," I snapped. "It's just that I can't. I'm too tired."

"No you're not! Only your body is. Now, concentrate and take control, make your power obey. You must pass this test."

"I can't," I repeated.

"Caitlin, you must do as we say." The soft sound filled my mind, replacing the unceasing despair which shredded my soul. "Now close your eyes and make it abide by your rules."

A faint outline of a person approached. It placed its hand on my head and everything suddenly was calm. "You must learn control," It said calmly. Its face was a mask of light, and its eyes were intense and unreadable. The luminescent silhouette whispered one last thing and quickly faded into my darkness. "No more experimenting, young mortal. Summoning a Varjatus is dangerous,"

EIGHTEEN

INNER CIRCLE

I STRETCHED OUT ON the bed wondering how long I was out this time. "How are you feeling?" I heard Justin's sweet voice say from across the room.

"I'd feel much better if you weren't so far away. Why are you sitting all the way there?" I asked, turning on the light. "What time is it?"

"It's only midnight. You haven't been out that long," he said, not budging from his seat.

"Come here," I begged, patting the empty side of the bed.

Justin reluctantly came and stretched next to me, propping his head up with the pillow, staring at the ceiling. For some reason he didn't even motion to touch me.

Ignoring his foul mood, I placed my head on his chest and slipped my hand around his body. "This is more like it," I whimpered, closing my eyes. "One of the Nobe was there again, whispering in my ear."

"Yeah well, you weren't in any shape to handle all that on your own. Abbot had no right pushing you that far – using unsuspecting Kyle as bait."

"Poor, Kyle! He was in so much pain."

"Abbot didn't hurt him that much. His own gift shields him from most powers. Kyle simply felt a discomfort where others would've died under so much pressure."

"The Ellri are devastatingly strong," I said. "The force my uncle used was deadly."

"You surprised us, you know." Justin kissed me on the forehead.

"Surprised you – how?"

"Well, it's not every day one of us goes head to head with an Ellri."

"Oh, please. It was only a test. Uncle Abbot wouldn't have hurt me."

Justin pushed my hair away from my face, looking rather apprehensive. "We knew that, but you didn't. You weren't afraid to defend Kyle – didn't back down one bit," Justin said, sounding more annoyed than proud. "You stood your ground and haven't even ascended yet."

"You make that sound like a bad thing. I thought the whole purpose of these tests is to see how my power reacts under certain circumstances."

"No – not exactly. The tests they put you through are not to prove how your gift reacts, Caitlin. Each test is to see how you react, and how well you control your gift."

I dropped my head against his chest, listening to the even rhythm of his heart beat against my ear. "I guess I failed," I sighed.

"Actually, you did rather well. Usually when the Ellri push to see how far our gift has evolved we tend to pull back, frightened of our own power. You on the other hand, allowed your gift to guide you. You didn't flinch one bit."

I shoved my body a bit higher, only inches away from his

enticing mouth. "I had absolutely no control, Justin. Don't get me wrong, I welcome my gift, but you should know that it truly scares the hell out of me."

"That's a first," he said rather condescending.

"Why do you make it sound like that? You know I have no say in how my gift reacts."

"It's not that, Caitlin," Justin said, pushing himself a little higher on the pillow. "The fact that you believe that you have the weight of the world on your shoulders is what is annoying. You shouldn't be scared of your gift. What you should be scared of is the fact that you are so willing to lose your life to save others. It's commendable – don't get me wrong, but it doesn't need to be that way. You don't take the time to think of other alternatives. You simply jump into the fire without thinking about getting burnt."

I buried my head in the curve of his neck in shame. "You're right. I don't think before I act. I respond purely on impulse."

"Look at me." Justin coaxed my chin up to face him. "If you can control that particular urge – allow yourself time to think of the alternatives, you're power will shift to your needs. It's the only way to dominate the full force. Concentrate on something pleasant, something that makes you feel good."

Looking into his eyes I was surprisingly aware that his mouth was saying one thing, but his mind was elsewhere. Justin sounded concerned, but he looked distracted; something else was bothering him. I kissed him on the neck moving my way up to his mouth, wanting him to feel better. The feel of his warm skin on my lips was maddening.

"Don't," he suddenly said, pinning me on my back.

"What's the matter with you? Why are you like this?"

He sat up, perching himself on the side of the bed with his back facing me. "It's just that you take too many risks, Caitlin."

"I told you – I'll stop!"

He gave me a side glance. Evidently, he was unsure of how sincere my promise was. "You should know that tomorrow after school the Ellri won't be easy on you. They'll push you to the limit."

"You're hiding something, aren't you?" I accused. "You know Marcellus told me about tomorrow. What are you keeping from me, Justin?"

With a stone-cold expression, he turned to face me and said, "Why did you summon Caradon?" Justin suddenly asked.

"I didn't summon anyone. You're all making it sound as if it's witchcraft. I simply wanted to see what all the fuss is about."

"And…?"

"And – he's quite intimidating, unearthly in a sense. You should've seen how he looked."

"The Korbs are…," he stopped again in mid-sentence.

"Would you stop doing that? Stop treating me like a child," I said, kneeling on the bed. "This is my father's side of the family you're talking about. Whatever they are it courses through my veins as well."

Justin's face instantaneously marbleized. "Don't ever say that! You are nothing like those monsters."

"Stop calling them that. I'm a Korbs so was my father. Am I a monster then?"

"You're a temptress, not a monster," he said, leaning down to kiss me, masterfully changing the subject once again.

For a long while we didn't talk – instead Justin kept his gaze glued to the ceiling. However, much later he finally turned on his side to face me and started to say, "I can't imagine how frustrating all this is for you. It must be hard to accept everything."

I allowed his words to hang in the air and gave no answer.

"You have so much to learn about our kind, Caitlin. But, unfortunately we all had to grow into the knowledge."

"What's there to know?" I finally asked, uncertain of what he meant.

Justin intertwined his fingers in mine, looking down at our hands and spoke softly. "You know only the basics – only the stories the Ellri told us when we were small." He lifted my hand to his mouth and kissed it tenderly. "Our gift grows in stages and with each stage we come one step closer to who we really are."

"What do you mean, 'who we really are' – metaphorically speaking?" I asked, raising an eyebrow in suspicion.

"Yes, of course," he said, guardedly. "I know I'm not making any sense, but each circle – each level of ascension reveals something new about us – about our kind."

"Okay, then tell me what's there to know? You've ascended. What have you learned?"

"That's the thing. I can't tell you anything until you ascend. I'm bound by the Circle of Trust. I'm not at liberty to say anything – not that I don't want to. Each stage teaches us – sort of prepares us for the next step of our evolution."

"Ok, so what can you tell me?"

"The only thing I can tell you is that you need to be patient. I know it's something everybody tells you, but you must understand that I've been through it as has Kyle, Marc and the rest of the Ascended. We have all gone through the first stage of enlightenment. Give it time."

"A bit too vague, don't you think? Why does everything have to be so complicated? Why didn't the Ellri just sit us all down when we were younger and explain everything to us? Why wait? Why make us all feel so lost?"

"It's a way to keep us safe."

"Safe? Safe from what?"

"From ourselves, of course," Justin said, looking surprised that I had to ask. "Ask yourself this, Caitlin. If you were told at a very young age that sometime in the future you'd be able to fly – how long do you think it'd take you before you jumped off the balcony to test your own ability?"

"Wait – did you say fly? There are people who can fly?"

"No! No one can fly," he said holding back a laugh. "Stay on the subject, will you? I was only trying to make a point."

"Oh," I said half-witted, giggling at my own stupidity. "Now I get it," I finally said, collecting my scattered brain. "What you're saying is that the Ellri would wait for the gift of flying to manifest before allowing that person to know anything about their ability. That's why I wasn't aware of my own gift."

"Good girl," Justin chuckled, patting me on the head like he would a dog. "It makes no sense to warn somebody about something that doesn't yet exist. With each stage of our life we dig deeper into who we are, learning as we grow. It's exactly the same with our gifts," Justin explained. "The Ellri, themselves, are in the dark about some things. Only the Nobe are truly enlightened. They say that with knowledge comes power."

Justin looked intently into my eyes. He evidently wanted to tell me more, unsure if he should. "You shouldn't use your gift without clearly knowing what its limits are," he continued to warn. "When you summoned your uncle, it was like handing him an open invitation into your psyche." I could tell that Justin was purposely trying to scare me. "The first step is to learn all the facets of your power and then learn how to wield them. Without guidance you put us all in danger. If the Korbs get their claws in you, they can easily control you at will."

I stared at Justin wide eyed. "Why would they want to do something like that?"

"You're obviously special to them – a trophy of sorts. They want nothing more than to gain your trust – to woo you into believing that they are like us."

"Woo me?" I laughed at the sound. "If they aren't like us, then what are they? What makes them so different?"

"I've said too much as is," he said, brushing back his hair with his fingers. "The only thing I can tell you is that our families fall under two distinct categories."

This was completely out of the ball park, and my face surely expressed my surprise as I asked, "Categories – what sort of categories?"

Justin half smiled. "Illumine and Varjatus."

"I can guess what 'Illumine' means but what is 'Varjatus'? My uncle Abbot called Caradon a 'Varjatus'."

"It means something dark, a creature of shadow. I'm not sure of the translation, but it's not good."

"So, all Korbs fall under this 'Varjatus' category?

"Not all the Korbs. It has nothing to do with the bloodline itself. It's more of a personal choice. Take your father for instance. Even though he was the purest of the bloodline, being the first born in a sterile line of first born Varjatus, he chose to be Illumine. It's a choice one makes when one ascends to become Ellri." Seeing how confused I looked, Justin tried to elaborate a bit. "It's like belonging to a certain political party. It has nothing to do with which family you belong to, but where your beliefs lay – different family members can vote for opposing parties. The Illumine are worldly and open to change, whereas the Varjatus are rigid, entirely secretive and devoted to their traditional ways."

"Well," I finally said, "that would explain Caradon's appearance." The recollection of the creepy image caused me to shudder. "He was dressed in a long black robe – medieval like."

"Yeah, that sounds right. The older families tend to keep with tradition. Not all of them. Most of the McDevitt Ellri also dress in traditional attire."

"Kind of spooky if you ask me."

"As far as the Korbs are concerned, it's not their clothes you should be worried about. It's their misguided ways that should keep you alert," Justin said, looking down at his watch, strategically cutting the conversation short. "I have to go, it's two in the morning and you have to get up for school in a few hours."

"Can't you stay?" I pouted.

"I would, but Abbot needs his sleep. He's been trying to read my thoughts for the past two hours." Justin chuckled.

"Wow, I didn't know you can block out an Ellri."

"I can for the most part, but if Abbot insists on knowing what I'm thinking I won't be able to keep him out for long. For the time being he's simply making his presence known – keeping me on my best behavior, if you know what I mean."

Smiling, I subtly slipped my hand under Justin's shirt. With the aim of driving him completely and utterly crazy, I trailed my fingers up his perfectly toned abdomen. He responded instantly to my touch, pulling me closer.

"What do you think you're doing?" he asked excitedly. "Didn't you hear what I said? I have to be on my best behavior."

Seductively, I leaned in and kissed him. "Let's just say I'm doing my best to corrupt you."

"You're shameless," he accused, amusingly. "I really have to go. Abbot's been more than understanding." He quickly kissed me and pulled my hand away as he got to his feet. "I'll pick you up after school."

"No you're not. I'm going over Tyler's, remember?"

"I know. I'm going to be there too. I'll pick you up after school," he repeated before closing the door behind him.

I tucked myself under the covers hugging the pillow Justin used for propping himself up. The cotton fabric was inundated with his faint scent. I breathed in his essence and closed my eyes for sleep to take me.

~~~

I received a few cross looks from my teachers. It wasn't like me not to hand in homework. Not that I really had a chance to do any yesterday.

Tyler and I seemed to be back to normal. The occasional joke, punch on the arm, the usual things best friends share.

"Did you talk to Megan yet?" I asked, looking over the corpse of a fetus pig.

The stench from the formaldehyde was pungent. Advanced biology lab left nothing to the imagination. Tyler let me know that at the start of the month, while I was being home schooled, they started off dissecting a worm then moved up to a frog, but today, as luck would have it, on my second day back, and only minutes after lunch, we were expected to dissect Wilbert. At the beginning of class, Mr. Maxwell was quite democratic about the whole process; allowing the students who didn't want to participate in the lab to hand in a project instead. Tyler and I were in no mood to spend hours on a research project. We were not going to miss out on this opportunity no matter how bad it smelled.

"I didn't get the chance yet. You were right though, she keeps staring at me," Tyler said, holding the scalpel.

I nudged him, giggling. "See, I told you! You didn't think I was lying, did you?"

"No, it's just that – well," he brushed his forehead with his sleeve. "I don't see how she can possibly like me, we're complete opposites."

There was something strange in the way he spoke, wasn't quite sure if he meant any of it. "Well, you know what they say about how opposites attract," I smiled, looking down at our victim. "Besides Tyler, you're awesome, what more can a girl want?"

"I could ask you the same thing," he said, deliberately staring at me

"We're talking about Megan," I whispered, not wanting the rest of the class to hear. "Give me the scalpel!" I ordered, annoyed at his purposeful comment.

"Oh, no you don't, Wilbert is mine – you take notes," Tyler chuckled, shoving me to the side playfully.

Lisa and Gina were standing only a few feet away, at the next lab table, wincing at every incision. Gina shifted her whole body to get a better look at me and Tyler obviously wanting to say something. "We missed you at lunch today," she finally said as soon as Mr. Maxwell was out of hearing distance. "But it's nice to see you two talking again."

"Yeah, Tyler promised to be nice from now on," I answered, shoving him to the side. "He's trying really hard to act human."

"How about we all sit together from now on?" Tyler suddenly offered, smirking in triumph. "It only makes sense, right Caitlin?"

I nodded, but what I really wanted to do was punch him in the face for purposely putting me on the spot.

"Yeah, why not?" he continued to say, "It's our last year here and we've all been friends since grade school."

"That sounds like a plan. We can work out the details for prom," Lisa squealed excitedly, trying to recruit members for prom committee.

"Oh, lets!" Tyler cheered imitating her manner; clapping his hands, making fun of Lisa's enthusiasm.

Lisa looked at him threateningly. "Very funny, Falcone," she grimaced.

"Lunch, I can do – prom, is a whole different matter," I told them.

"Caitlin, the school needs you," Gina exclaimed, sounding more like an army recruit than mere members of the prom committee.

"Yeah, Caitlin, the school needs you," said Tyler knowing full well how annoying he was being. He was pushing my buttons to get a response.

There was no winning this one, so I agreed by saying, "Okay, fine! We'll talk tomorrow at lunch. Mr. Maxwell is staring – get back to work. Maxwell doesn't look too happy with us."

Gina and Lisa instantly returned to their victim, continuing their autopsy. Tyler simply looked at me, smiling.

"I don't know why you're smiling," I said. "I'm not through with you," I threatened, trying to wipe the smog smile off his face. "I'm not sure if I'm even going to prom."

"We're going whether you like it or not," he muttered, pushing me out of the way. "Nurse, the scalpel," he said, opening his hand.

"Let me do it?" I begged, shoving him to the side.

"No, you take notes."

With one hand on piggy, Tyler tried to shove me out of the way. The second he touched my hand, a surge of energy coursed through my body and into his arms.

"What the hell!" I heard Tyler say as he looked down at the fetus. "Damn it, no! Don't touch me."

In horror we looked down at the fetus which was dead no more. Too small to survive it kept moving in spasms.

"Mr. Maxwell!" It was Lisa doing the screaming. "You need to come here like yesterday."

The poor creature was convulsing.

"What the...!" Mr. Maxwell was as shocked as we were. "How did this happen?"

"It's suffering," I heard Gina say. "Somebody needs to put it out of its misery. We can't leave it like this."

"No, that won't be necessary," I said, turning to Tyler. "You can make it better, can't you?"

He shook his head. "It's too small, Caitlin. It's a fetus. What would you have me do?"

Mr. Maxwell ordered the rest of the class to collect there things and go. Reluctantly they all did.

"I don't know how you both did this, and honestly I don't care." He spoke angrily. "You need to fix this, and do it fast."

Tyler looked at me. "I can put it down. That's all I can do, but I can't do it with the Shield of Knowledge blocking my powers. You have to help."

My eyes went wide with disbelief. "I'm not helping you kill this little animal."

"Caitlin it's suffering," Mr. Maxwell said. "You're the only one who can help."

"Are you sure, you can't fix it?"

"It's not sick, Caitlin."

Hesitant at first I finally agreed seeing that the poor animal was fighting for air. "Fine, give me your hand," I finally said.

Tyler placed one hand over the fetus' head and said, "Sorry Wilbert, but this is for the best." And then my best friend closed his eyes. I let my energy pass to Tyler and in seconds the little animal stopped moving, but for some reason I felt strange. It wasn't because I helped Tyler take Wilbert's life, but the fact that doing so gave me an immense gratification. *Is this how Tyler feels?* I wondered. *No wonder his father says taking lives can become addictive.*

"Good," said Mr. Maxwell. "Now collect your things the bell is about to ring."

Heading to our lockers we both didn't speak. I did notice, however, the strange looks we got from some of our classmates.

"We never speak of this again," said Tyler as we walked down the hall.

"I'm sorry. It was my fault. I have no control."

"Not a word, Caitlin," he repeated.

"I'm probably going to be home-schooled again."

"Serves you right," he said leaning into me. Tyler smiled and added, "I can see why my father worries."

I didn't want to admit that I felt what he must have felt, so instead I said, "Can you?"

"I took that pigs life."

I stopped and looked at him. "Yeah, and?"

"Caitlin, it felt good. The energy of its life force was greater than anything I've ever felt. I tasted it on my lips, felt it in my bones."

"Stop that. You're scaring me," I confessed.

"Scaring you? I'm terrified. My dad said it can be addictive. Now I can see why."

I spotted Megan farther up the hall. Wanting to change the morbid subject I nudged Tyler in the ribs. "Well, here's your chance to redeem yourself," I said.

His lazy gaze fell on mine. "Remind me why I have to do this?"

"First of all, you were mean to her and secondly, I'm asking you as a friend!"

"Good enough for me. Here, hold this." he said, handing me his school bag. "Be careful I have half a turkey sandwich in my bag. Don't do anything stupid while I'm gone. We don't want to be chasing a live turkey down the hall."

I smacked him on the arm, "Very funny!"

Tyler headed down the hall towards Megan. Her eyes lit up as soon as he approached. You didn't need to have bionic ears to know that whatever Tyler was saying was to her liking. Megan unexpectedly beamed me a smile and waved in my direction.

What was that all about? I wondered. *He must've told her that the apology was my idea. What an idiot!*

"All done," Tyler said, after a few minutes, taking his school bag from my hands.

"It was worth it, wasn't it?" I asked.

"We'll know soon enough," he answered, putting his arm around my shoulders and led us to our next class.

"You did something stupid, didn't you?"

He smiled and entered the classroom without saying a word.

~~~~

Unlike yesterday, the day was sluggish. Our last classes seemed to drag on forever. I noticed Megan smiling at me several times during History. Cordially, I smiled back not wanting to ruin Tyler's apology. Mr. Myers did reprimand her several times for talking to Kim during his lecture. Megan didn't seem to care; she never looked happier. She must have liked Tyler much more than I originally had thought.

The sound of the last period bell was music to my ears. We collected our things and headed to our lockers.

"I guess I'll see you at home," Tyler said, aware that Justin was going to pick me up.

"Yeah, I'll see you there. Oh, and thanks for being so nice to Megan. You really made her day."

"Don't thank me just yet," Tyler said, closing his locker.

"Tyler, I'm truly sorry for Wilbert. Sorry for putting you in that position."

"See you at home," he said brushing the apology aside, disappearing in the crowd.

As I exited the building, there Justin was, waiting in the school parking lot, leaning against his black Audi. Every time I saw him I breathed a little faster.

Focusing my attention on his warm smile, I hardly noticed Megan calling me. "Caitlin, wait up," I heard her say.

I took a deep breath and turned to face her. This time she was without her accessories. Loraine and Kim probably had detention or maybe it was some kind of hair emergency. It was the only time Megan was without the two girls.

"I'm glad I caught up with you," she started to say, "Thanks for talking to Tyler. I honestly thought you hated me all these years."

Not knowing what she expected me to say, I looked over my shoulder and noticed that Justin was smiling. I shifted my attention back to the She-devil and did my best to hold back my tongue. This was our last year in school together, no sense in dwelling in the past.

"Hate is quite harsh, don't you think? Why would I hate you?" I finally said, swallowing back my contempt.

"Well, let's just say I haven't made your life easy in the past." She smiled weakly.

"Don't worry about it. We're all grown up now, right. No hard feelings, I promise you. The past is the past."

I wasn't sure if I was sincere or not. With everything that was happening in my life, Megan suddenly seemed trivial in a way.

"Oh, good," she sighed, relieved, "Wouldn't want anything to ruin prom night."

"Prom? What does prom have to do with anything?" I asked puzzled.

"Well, since we're going to be all together I thought that we should at least try to be civil towards each other," she said. "Besides, my date is, after all, your best friend."

Dumbfounded, I stood there like an idiot just staring at her. Tyler was completely out of his freaking mind? What was he thinking?

Note to self: Murder former best friend.

"Anyway, let me get back inside. I see Justin is waiting for you." She simply stood there waiting for me to say something, and when I didn't she said, "We'll talk about arrangements later, okay? You seem to be preoccupied." Megan didn't wait for a response, instead she headed back indoors.

Turning to face Justin, I noticed the smirk on his face. "What are you smiling at?" I snapped, not being able to hold back my anger.

"Hey, don't go blaming me for Tyler's actions."

"The guy is an idiot!" I yelled. "Let me get my hands on him – he'll see!"

Justin took me in his arms, amused at my mood. "You did tell him to find a date, didn't you? You can't blame him for following orders."

"Ahhh! You're both insufferable. You're both trying to drive me mad, aren't you? Admit it!"

Justin smiled, giving me a quick kiss. "Caitlin, there's only one way I'd like to drive you mad," he said, kissing me again.

I flushed instantly, turning three shades of red. Justin was trying to coy his way out of the discussion, knowing how uncomfortable I was about the topic of us being, together – together. Once in the car, I was huffing and puffing, livid at Tyler. "Now I'm definitely not going to the prom," I said, looking out the window.

"For a person who wants to be treated like an adult you sure act childish at times," Justin said, looking straight ahead. "Tyler has every right to ask any girl he wants. Why does it bother you so much?"

I turned my back to the window to get a better look at Justin. "It's not that he's asked someone that bothers me, but the fact that – that someone just happens to be the most annoying person on the planet. Megan Gordon? Is he serious? How could he?"

"Give her a chance, Caitlin. You might find out that you both have much in common."

Without meaning to, Justin was infuriating me even more. "Save the after-school special for someone else," I replied. "She's loathsome and unbearable. The girl made my life a living hell growing up. Just ask Emily. She's the only one that knows what I had to endure every day at school."

"Megan simply felt inferior to you. You can't blame her for being jealous. Everybody always liked you. You made friends so easily. She had to work extra hard."

I shook my head in vigorous denial. "That's not how it was Justin. The only people I hung out with were Tyler and Emily."

"My point exactly," Justin said, trying to explain a point I apparently missed while growing up. "Emily just happened to be the most popular girl in her class – the most popular girl in town, for that matter. Oh, and let's not forget your best friend who is also the most popular guy in your class. And if that's not proof enough, Kyle and I used to pick you up after school on many occasions."

"So? Why would all that make Megan jealous?"

Justin smiled and raised my hand to his mouth. "You really don't have a mean bone in your body, do you?" he asked adoringly. "Let's just say that you were only in middle school and hung out with high school students. That alone would be enough to rouse some envy."

"Are you serious? I was such a miss-fit. Megan, on the other hand, fit in perfectly with everyone. She had nothing to be jealous about."

"That's the thing. Everybody liked you without you even trying."

"I was invisible Justin. You must know that. Nobody knew I was alive."

"Oh, trust me," he said pulling up to Tyler's house. "The boys in your class were well aware of your presence – too aware for my liking," he confessed.

We got out of the car and headed to the main entrance. Before ringing the doorbell I turned and looked at Justin. "Now

I know your exaggerating. You're trying to make me feel better. I was a complete mess back then, still am."

Justin just shook his head in disbelief. "Have you ever looked at yourself?" he asked. "I mean, really looked at yourself? How can you not see what other people see?"

"You're biased!" I accused him.

"No he's not," I suddenly heard Tyler's voice say from behind me.

I was so absorbed in our conversation that I hadn't noticed the door open. We didn't even ring the doorbell, but then why would we have to? They all knew we were standing out there.

"You see, even Tyler agrees."

"You're both crazy and blind," I said walking inside. "And you...," I sneered, punching Tyler on the arm, "How could you invite Megan to the prom? Megan of all people?"

I punched him on the arm again – harder.

"Ouch!" he yelled playfully. "Your abusive nature is quite a turn on."

I shoved him to the side. "You're an idiot."

"You told me to apologies to her. How else was I supposed to make it up to her?" Tyler replied. "You're the one who wanted me to be nice to her."

"I said be nice – not invite her to the prom!" Wanting to put an end to our discussion, I turned on my heel and headed towards the kitchen where I heard voices. Both Justin and Tyler were chuckling at my expense. Deep down I was happy they were such good friends, even if it meant being the butt of their joke.

"Oh, great you're here," said Aurelia, setting the kitchen table with Natalie, Tyler's younger sister. "I prepared something light for you guys to eat before we start. Kyle will be here momentarily. He's dropping Sandy off at her house."

"Is Marc here?" I asked remembering that he was going to be a participant.

"He's inside the den with daddy and Emily," said Natalie, folding the napkins in half.

"I didn't know Emily was going to be here too?"

"She's going to be ascending soon as well, so this is a good time as any to kill two birds with one stone," Aurelia responded winking at me.

"Don't you mean three birds?" asked Emily, entering the kitchen.

"Who's the third?" I asked, as always the last to know.

"You, me and Tyler," she said. "Even though you're younger than me, your powers seem to be evolving much faster. It's only a matter of time before you ascend."

"I'm glad you're here," I told Emily smiling. "I've missed you these couple of days."

Aurelia beamed one of her magnificent smiles. "What do you expect of young love? My nephew doesn't let her out of his sight."

"Okay then," I said trying to change the subject, not wanting Emily to feel awkward in front of Marc's aunt. "What can I do to help?" I asked Aurelia, giving Tyler's younger sister a hug.

Natalie giggled. "You're getting so big Natalie," I told her, causing her to smile.

"I'm fifteen, Caity. Only three years younger than you. We're practically the same age," she beamed excitedly.

Aurelia rolled her eyes at Natalie's eagerness to grow up.

"You seem much older than a mere fifteen," I said.

"Don't encourage her," Aurelia said, in her deep Italian accent. "Here, have a seat. You'll need all the rest you can get before we begin."

As soon as I was settled, Aurelia turned to her daughter

once again. "Natalie, go tell daddy to take you and Michelle to your aunt Sabina's."

"Why can't we stay and watch?" Natalie pouted, looking at me.

"I don't have a problem. You guys can stay if you want."

Aurelia took Natalie by the shoulders and led her out of the kitchen. "Do as I say Natalie. You need to learn to be patient," She kissed her daughter on the head. "Now go and tell your father!"

That moment I realized exactly what Justin meant about learning as we grow. Natalie was as much in the dark about everything as I was. But being older I was allowed in on much more. I suddenly felt better knowing that I wasn't being left in the dark on purpose – it was simply the way things were for our kind.

By the time Kyle came we had finished our meal and even cleaned up. The best part of all, not one mention about Wilbert the pig.

"Okay, are you guys ready?" Marcellus asked, standing up. We nodded, visibly unaware of what to expect. "Alright then, let's go!"

He led everybody to the farthest room down the hall.

Tyler's house was my second home, but even though I knew the building inside out, this room was always off limits. It was like any other living space in the house, draped in antique furniture and rich embroidered fabrics in deep wine, green and gold. Two wrought iron pillar candle holders decorated the massive fireplace on the farthest wall. The Persian rugs under our feet masked the century old wooden floor.

"Kyle, Marc…," Marcellus said, heading towards the heavily carved antique desk.

For some reason Marc and Kyle rolled the Persian rug to the

side revealing the rich, walnut color, wooden floor underneath. Unbeknownst to me, Marcellus leaned over the desk and opened one of the drawers. Just imagine my surprise when in seconds, only inches away, a section of the floor slid open, exposing a flight of wooden stairs that descended beneath the building.

"What's this?" I asked, completely taken aback. "I've heard that the manors in Oaks concealed secrets, but not anything this big. I always thought the stories were rumors, told by children with wild imaginations."

"It's where your lessons are going to be held," Marcellus answered winking at me.

Marc took Emily by the hand. They were the first to descend the stairs along with Kyle, followed by Aurelia, Marcellus and Tyler. Justin and I stayed behind. I was still in shock at the passage in the floor.

"Come on," Justin said, "it's nothing to worry about."

"I'm not worried. I'm actually coming to terms with the fact that I don't know anything about Oaks. I wonder how many other things I don't know about."

Justin took my hand and guided me down the wooden stairs. "Let's just say, you haven't seen anything yet," he said, squeezing my hand tenderly.

~~~

The stairs directed us down a long faintly lit passage which led us deeper underground. Dust lay thick beneath my feet. It was quite narrow; to say the least. The tunnel felt like a tomb. The silence wrapped around me like a cocoon shrouding a silkworm.

"Doesn't this remind you of Indigo Caverns, Caitlin?" yelled Emily form further up ahead, cutting through the eerie silence.

"Now that you've mentioned it, it actually does. The only thing missing is a ton of fallen rocks," I said, giggling nervously. I wasn't sure what to expect up ahead. "How far do we have to go?" I asked, trying to get my mind off the weirdness of the whole situation

"About a quarter of a mile," Justin answered, squeezing my hand even tighter.

"A quarter of a mile!" I exclaimed, shocked by the distance the tunnel covered "Why so far?"

"It helps us prepare. The distance gives us time to collect our thoughts – meditate in a way."

"Where does it lead?"

"You'll see." Justin turned and smiled. "The first time I came down here I was scared. You seem to be holding up quite okay."

I knew he was trying to make me feel better. Justin didn't scare that easily.

Not before long, a mammoth hand carved, wooden door towered in front of us. Different sized palm prints were carved deep into the wood.

"This door connects us to the Inner Realm. Behind it is the place where the Ascended meet and practice their gifts," Marcellus said, scanning our faces.

How was it possible that Tyler didn't know that this tunnel existed under his own house?

"Marc, would you do us the honors?" Marcellus told him, taking a few steps back.

"Sure thing," Marc pecked Emily on the cheek and let go of her hand. He stood in front of the door placing his palm on top of one of the indentations. His hand was a perfect match. Within seconds the sound of three clicks echoed through the tunnel. Not a very loud sound, but it might as well have been a thunderclap the way my heart jumped. I held my breath and continued to stare. Apparently, Marc had unlocked the massive door.

"Wow that's so cool. How did you do that?" Tyler jeered in excitement.

"Once you ascend your handprint will automatically be imprinted on the door. It's like a key in many ways," Marc explained. "This here is Kyle's hand and that's Justin's," he went on to point out.

Tyler put his hand up against the door in the aims to leave his own print. "You have to ascend first," his father said, ruffling his hair, "Come on, let's show you guys the inside."

Emily traced her fingers around Marc's hand print, "This is where my hand print belongs," she said, with her palm up against the door, right next to Marc's.

Marc instantly reached out and took her in his arms kissing her in front of everybody. It was the first time I saw him displaying so much affection. Usually he was more withdrawn with his feelings.

"Come on you love birds," Aurelia said, causing Emily to blush. I couldn't be happier for her. Marc was the best thing that could happen to my cousin. Her beaming smile said it all.

Still mesmerized by the massive door, I wasn't ready to

follow the rest inside just yet. "How is this all possible?" I asked, unable to digest any of it. "Whose doing is this?" I added, looking at the intricate door.

Justin held my hand tighter aware of my inability to make sense of anything. "The Nobe have created all this, ages ago."

"I figured as much, but why?" I asked. "Why the mystery and magic?"

"There's no magic about it. It's simply something the Nobe thought of to give the few who ascend a place to call their home, a solace as you call it. All five doors were hand crafted by the Nobe, themselves. They are drenched in power as are the walls that surround us."

I looked at Justin confused "Five doors?"

"You'll see," he answered.

Kyle came to where we were standing. "Why are you both still out here? C'mon Caitlin, you're going to love this," Kyle said, pulling me inside.

Upon crossing the threshold a vast opening sprawled in front of me. It was a place like no other. The walls were carved out of the natural rock that was found at that depth. It was a cave of sorts, only this was man-made. A large gothic chandelier hung from the domed ceiling, imputing some elegance in the rather unearthly surroundings. Priceless rugs from the orient lay on the cold stone floor creating a warm homely feeling. The room itself formed a circle of sorts, with large wooden chairs lining the walls. I noticed two more doors, exactly the same size and shape as the one we entered. They stood on opposite sides of each other.

"Where do those lead?" I asked pointing to them.

"That one...," Justin said, pointing to the one on the left, drawing everyone's attention, "leads to the Cathcarts and the other to my house."

Marcellus stood in the middle of the vast room. "The three of you should know that there are two more doors like these. One is under the McDevitt Castle in Europe and the other under the Korbs' Estate. Once you ascend your hand print will emboss itself on all five doors simultaneously, giving you rightful access to all families. It was a way for the Nobe to keep us united."

Speechless, Emily stared at Kyle. "All these years and you didn't say a thing." She shoved him lightly. "You knew something like this existed under our house and you kept it from me? How dare you. You should've said something. You kept this from me all these years."

"Yes I did," Kyle answered, "as you will keep it a secret from everybody else. If you as much as think about telling someone your hand print will instantly erase itself from the door denying you eternal access."

"Why now? Why are we down here now?" I finally asked.

Aurelia walked around the room, straightening out some of the cushions. "This is the Chamber of Enlightenment. This is where you will each ascend. Those seats," Aurelia said, pointing to the chair-laced wall "will be filled with witnesses to attest to your worthiness."

"And those?" Tyler asked, pointing to the larger, medieval thrones on either side of each door.

"Sometimes the Nobe grace us with their presence, wanting to be present during someone's ascension. They'd sit next to the door that represents their family."

Emily looked as awestruck as I was. "You mean that there's a possibility for the Nobe to show up during one of our ascensions?"

"Maybe, but it's highly unlikely," answered Aurelia.

"Enough already about the Nobe," Marcellus suddenly said,

changing the subject "Nobody comes down here alone. You must be accompanied by an Ellri or someone who has already ascended. Our gifts are quite potent within these walls. There's absolutely no reason to put yourselves in any danger."

I had a feeling there was more to this underground wonder than they let on. I knew not to ask. If they wanted me to know more details they would have told me already.

"So what are we going to do exactly?" Tyler asked, eager to get started.

Aurelia looked to Emily and Tyler. "I'm sorry to have to tell you this. But you're both returning home."

"Why? I want to stay," Emily said whining like a baby.

"You can't be present during someone else's training. Only the members of the Inner Circle are allowed at this stage. Once you ascend you can come and go as you wish."

Marc took Emily's hand and walked her to the door. "Come on Tyler, I'll take you back up. Both of you have great control over your gift – it's Caitlin who needs our help."

I wasn't sure if I should've been happy with his words or mortified that I needed special treatment. Once again I felt like the outcast. I was always the different one.

Tyler hesitantly followed his cousin out the door. With a great big thud the colossal door closed behind them locking with three loud clanks.

My heart was in my mouth, pounding in anticipation.

"Geez Caitlin, don't be nervous. I can hear your heart all the way here," Kyle said smiling.

"Easy for you to say," I muttered. "This is unreal – simply unreal." I repeated allowing my mind the time to file away all this new information.

Beyond The Door

Illustrated for Lines That Bind · Within The Whispers

NINETEEN

TRUE REFLECTION

URELIA AND MARCELLUS each took a seat giving me time to absorb my surroundings. I looked around the edifice wondering how long it took for the Nobe to create such a wonder. It was truly an amazing structure.

"How deep underground are we?" I asked, turning to Marcellus.

He looked at Aurelia and smiled. "Soon you'll learn what you need to know, Caitlin. Just give it time."

And there it was, one more question left unanswered. "Why do I even bother? How difficult would it be to get an answer? I mean, a simple measurement would suffice – three yards, four yards maybe."

Scanning their faces I realized that they were all staring at me. "Is there something wrong?" I asked, stopping my gaze on Justin.

"Do you feel anything?" Justin asked coming to my side.

"No, what am I supposed to feel?"

Justin turned to Ellri questionably.

"What am I supposed to feel?" I repeated.

Kyle took my hand and guided me to the center of the large room. He sat himself down on the lush rug, patting the space in front of him, gesturing for me to do the same. I decided to do as I was told, thinking it was the only way to get some answers. I was taken down there for a reason, might as well get to the bottom of it.

I sat about a foot from Kyle, facing him.

"Caitlin, we won't start your lesson until Marc gets here, but until then you need to do something for me," Kyle said smiling.

"Sure, what?"

"You need to stop thinking so much. This is a place of spiritual awakening. You can't do that if your brain is running a mile a minute. If you want answers you need to stop talking, stop thinking and just pay attention. Allow your mind to be free."

"Okay, how do I go about doing that?"

"You see, that's what I mean, another question," Kyle said, chuckling. "Close your eyes and don't say a word," he added, taking both of my hands in his. "C'mon scary cat, close those beautiful green eyes of yours."

Hesitant at first, I did as I was told.

"Good! Now take a real deep breath and relax." Kyle instructed, shaking my arms loose. "Now think about the room we're in. How big would you say it is?"

"From wall to wall?"

"For heaven's sake, Caitlin, just answer the damn question. How big do you think this room is?"

"I don't know, it's big, about seventy feet wide? I'm not at all good at depth perception."

"Are you sure it's that big? Stretch out your hands to the side," Kyle ordered.

As soon as I did, I felt the cold hard stone against my

fingers. "What the...," I muttered. "How is this possible? The wall can't be this close."

My hands couldn't be lying. I felt the rough, cold surface of the rock under my fingertips. With my eyes closed I let my hands roam each uneven crevice on the rock. The room I was in was massive, but now I seemed to be engulfed in stone.

Where was everyone else? Suddenly I panicked, feeling a bit claustrophobic.

"Caitlin, just relax. Don't forget to breathe," I heard Kyle's soothing voice. "We're all here with you," he added, taking my hands into his again. Everything is not always as it seems. Don't limit yourself; keep an open mind about everything."

"An open mind, I can do," I muttered, "but underground walls moving? Now that's a whole different thing, altogether."

"You can open your eyes," Kyle said, sounding amused for some reason. "You're really something little sis."

"Did I do something wrong?" I asked feeling a bit disoriented. Looking around, I had seen only that the room was large and airy, as big as I had left it. *Could I be any more confused?* I wondered. Kyle stood once more and dusted off his knees, chuckling, straightening out his clothes, he said, "No, I was just surprised you kept your eyes closed. Most of us popped them open as soon as we felt the stone. You don't scare easily. That's good." He sounded proud.

"So what does all this mean?" I asked, scanning their faces from where I was sitting. "This room doesn't even exist, does, it?" I finally asked, vocalizing my suspicions.

Marcellus approached. "What do you mean, Caitlin?"

"You did say the Nobe created all this. I assume they didn't spend years mining the rock."

Marcellus let out a hearty laugh. "You don't seem too surprised or impressed."

"Oh, I'm impressed alright. It's just that I'm in shock, that's all. Give me a couple minutes."

He chucked again. "Now that you're able to see more clearly, I'd like you to look around, Caitlin. How many doors do you see now?"

I slowly counted to myself – three, four and, last but not least, the fifth door.

"You can't be serious!" I gasped. "You said those doors lead to the other families…" I swallowed hard, "to the McDevitts and to the…." A steadily escalating sense of foreboding crashed against me, almost making me gasp with the intensity of it. "You can't expect me to believe that the families across the Atlantic have access to this room through tunnels. That's a little overstretching it, isn't it?"

Could my relatives from across the Atlantic reach me that easily? My mind was screaming out demands for information and warnings with equal confusion, and yet in all the chaos, the second Justin took my face in his hands, every last drop of fear disintegrated.

"The doors are the only things from our material world, everything else, the tunnels included, belong to the Inner Realm. All this…" Justin said, motioning to our surroundings, "simply exists to make us feel more comfortable, in our element. It can be anywhere you wish it to be."

"Think of any place," Aurelia said softly.

For a moment I was too stunned to speak. I finally pulled myself together enough to form a logical thought. "I'm sorry. I just can't think of anything right this minute."

She smiled. "Look," she said.

To startled and surprised to respond with proper words, I remained gaping as the hard stone walls of the inner chamber shifted and conformed, and finally evaporated to reveal lush green meadows with poppies, further than the eye could see.

It was some time later that the silence of the room was suddenly broken by the sound of my own deep breathing. "It's beautiful," I muttered. I was fascinated, as well as terrified, by the unearthly surroundings. "Where are we?"

"Where do you want to be?" she asked, sounding like a psychologist during a doctor-patient consultation. Aurelia paused, and waited for me to understand the significance of what it all meant.

"So, what you're saying is that we can travel anywhere?"

My words incited laughter. They all looked at me rather amused.

"We haven't gone anywhere," Aurelia said. "The Chamber of Enlightenment exists in order for the gifted to find oneness with their gift. Some prefer to meditate in outdoor surroundings. I personally like the original Energy Stone. The scenery changes to conform to our wishes, to our inner needs."

Marc entered the chamber from the farthest door, causing me to momentarily turn and look in his direction. "Energy Stone?" I finally asked, shifting my attention back to what Aurelia was saying.

"Moments ago Justin asked if you felt anything."

"No – nothing," I admitted. "I'm broken, aren't I?"

They stared at me, astonished, attentive and it was easy to tell, very much impressed. They started chuckling again, shaking their heads in disbelief. Watching them, I failed to notice Justin until I felt a touch upon my arm and turned to see him staring at me with love-widened eyes. "You're far from broken," Justin confirmed. "The reason we feel the energy around us is because it's much greater than our gift. Obviously you are much stronger than we had previously thought."

His words hadn't stopped my mind going into overdrive

with the notion of having tapped into something much darker and sinister. I felt tendrils of uncertainty wrap themselves around me.

"You all know this is going to take me some time to absorb all this information. I mean, magic tunnels and invisible chambers. I might even need some prescribed medication."

"Magic? Who said anything about magic, Caitlin? There is nothing magical about this place," Marcellus snapped. There was neither kindness nor humor in his voice. "All this exists in our universe. Just because the non-gifted refuse to believe it, doesn't mean it isn't real. We are more in tune with the elements than they are, that's all."

I stared beseechingly at him. "I'm sorry if I offended anyone. It's just that all this – well – for me it's magical. It's the only way my mind can wrap itself around the notion that something like this actually exists."

I met Marcellus' dark brown eyes boring into mine. "Fair enough," he finally said, taking a seat.

"Caitlin, when you slip into your solace this is where you come, this is the Inner Realm. It is the plane between the physical and non–physical dimensions. There is nothing magical about it. It's a natural part of our existence," Marc explained. "For some reason your power allows you access to this plane without even coming into this chamber."

I was frustrated, pacing the room. "That's a good thing, right?" I finally asked, unsure about anything anymore.

"Of course, I've already told you how special you are," Marcellus remarked, much calmer now.

At that moment I stopped pacing and stood in front of one of the massive doors. This door was not like the rest, it bore a deep grooved symbol of a triangle. I looked down at my wrist and realized to which family this door belonged. Aurelia came to my side and lifted my scared wrist, comparing the symbols. "This door belongs to your family, the Korbs," she said.

"Should I be worried?" I asked looking at her. "Don't they have access to this place?"

"Not when we're here," she said, smoothing my hair behind my ear. "There is absolutely nothing for you to worry about."

For the time being I was satisfied with her reassurance.

"Can we get started already?" Kyle asked impatiently.

Both Aurelia and I turned to face Kyle.

"He's right," said Marc, "we should get started. I'm dying to see what she can do!"

Aurelia took me by the hand and led me back to the middle of the room.

"We need you to slip into that abyss of yours. We need to separate your conscious mind from your body," she said. "All our powers are more potent here on this plane. Unlike us, your gift is even greater when you transcend. The Energy Stone should heighten your ability even more. That's what we need to do today, to see if you can control it."

"But didn't you say this is where I go when I slip into solace?"

"Yes, but the Energy Stone will heighten everything."

"So, all I have to do is slip into solace? Ok, I can do that."

"Good – now go ahead."

"No problem." I sat myself down on the rug and hugged my knees. "Okay, here I go," I said, closing my eyes shut. Instantly, I felt like I always did when I visited my solitude; enveloped in complete darkness.

"Open your eyes, Caitlin," I heard Justin's sweet voice say through the darkness. "You're not alone in here anymore."

My eyes were open, as far as I knew.

"Look at me," he said.

"Justin?" I gasped, peering in the darkness. Then louder, "Justin, what are you doing here?"

I could see all of them as if I were completely conscious.

"Step out," Justin said, stretching his hand for me to take.

The second I stood up I felt the limits of my physical body disappear. I knew that I was having one of those outer body experiences once again. The euphoria was back, stronger than before.

"Wow!" Kyle exclaimed, rather loudly. "Look at you, Caitlin! You're – you're –."

I stared at Justin's stunned face.

"What's wrong? Are you okay?" I asked.

"You're breathtaking," Justin finally said, taking my hand.

"You can actually see me?" I muttered. "The other times you couldn't."

"Of course I can see you. We're both on the same plane now," he said, smiling "You're actually glowing."

I looked at my hands and noticed absolutely nothing different. He was, once again, exaggerating?

"We're not exaggerating, Caitlin," Justin said, answering my thoughts.

I looked around to all their faces. It was obvious that they were able to read my thoughts once again. Justin's expression was full of satisfaction.

"Why are you smiling?" I asked him.

"Shhh, I'm trying to concentrate," he said, grinning even wider. "It would seem you've been thinking quite a lot about us?" he said, beaming that all too perfect smile.

"Like you need any sort of power to guess that one," I teased, smiling at him.

"Come here Caitlin," Aurelia called out.

In a millisecond I was at her side, literally slicing through the distance.

"How does she do that?" Kyle asked, dumbfounded.

"She might be on the same plane as us, but her body doesn't limit her gift as does yours. This is what transcendence is. It allows Caitlin to overcome any natural barriers. You'll get to this stage if and when you ascend to become an Ellri," Marcellus answered.

They were talking about me as if I wasn't even there.

"So are you saying that Caitlin is an Ellri?" Kyle asked, baffled by my abilities.

Aurelia held my hand tight. "By no means are you an Ellri. You simply come from a long line of first-borns. You're the purest of all our bloodlines. Both your parents come from the oldest families, so you see Caitlin, you've inherited remarkable gifts."

A blur of motion caught my eye. It was Marcellus. He smoothly traversed the distance that separated us. "One should not only reconcile the Inner Realm with infinity, but also hold firmly to the concept of the hierarchy we abide by," Marcellus explained, looking intently towards Kyle. "The beauty of our Inner Realm is crowned by the different levels of hierarchy, which ascend into infinite light. Each of you should feel honored to ascend each level to Illumine, to become an Ellri and later Nobe. You will all gather strength and deep knowledge ascending one step at a time." Marcellus came and stood next to me placing his hand on my shoulder. "Much of what is sacred and great will not necessarily appear so outwardly. These dimensions, the Inner Realm assumes true magnitude in the inner consciousness. One may wait for several life times to reach oneness with himself, but we the gifted are born into it," he continued to explain. "It is correct to think that the earthly plane and the Inner Realm coexist – coordinate. The conducting current is one, but you can't always understand the extending significance, that's only possible when you become an Ellri. Only to the consciousness of an Ellri is the understanding of the essential nature of all occurrences accessible."

I shook my head confused. Did Marcellus really expect me to understand one iota of what he just said? I always thought of myself as intelligent, but that was completely over my head.

Justin smiled at me, apparently aware of my confusion. "What Marcellus means is that we are in no way able to absorb a minute grain of the truth. That is why our knowledge and awareness must come in steps," he said, turning his gaze to Kyle. "Therefore we must speak of the hierarchy with deep reverence. Caitlin is powerful, but in no way an Ellri, she still needs to ascend," he added curtly.

"Okay, that's enough of that," Aurelia suddenly said. "Caitlin, come here and look at yourself, see what we see." Unexpectedly, she pulled the crushed velvet material off the wall only to reveal a beveled oblong mirror which was finished in heavily antiqued silver.

The second I laid eyes on my reflection I impulsively took a step back, unintentionally, sending myself clear across the massive room. Without having any real control of my power, I wasn't able to reign in my instinctive reactions.

"Cool!" was all Kyle could say. "How do you move so fast?"

I had too much on my plate to worry about Kyle's fascination. "Is that really me?" I asked, turning to Justin, not wanting to get any closer to the mirror.

He motioned for me to approach. "It's all you, Caitlin," he said, warmly. "Don't be afraid."

Hesitant at first, I moved forward and in one swift move I

found myself, once again, in front of the reflecting glass, studying my own reflection. A ghostly figure stared back at me. How in the world could this possibly be me? I marveled. A white glow radiated off my body creating an ethereal affect. I was neither transparent nor solid. My complexion was flawless like the porcelain dolls that lined my bookshelves. My naturally dull, dark chestnut-brown hair was now vibrant and shiny, silky straight, cascading loosely down my back.

"It's you Caitlin. Don't look so shocked," Justin said, standing next to me.

I looked down at my hands again and realized that Justin was right, it was me.

"Why couldn't I see this before?" I asked puzzled.

Marcellus took a step closer and said, "You simply didn't want to see it."

I looked over my shoulder and allowed my gaze to fall to the middle of the room where my earthly body sat. "How can any of this be happening? How come you're not like this?" I asked, looking around to all their loving faces.

"Who said, we're not," Aurelia answered, winking at me. "Our bodies are but a mere vessel, organs to produce the energy we need to sustain our life force."

I needed another few minutes to soak it all up. I wasn't sure what to think. "Okay, can I return to my body now? This is really freaking me out," I admitted, taking one last look in the mirror.

"We'd like to test the control you have of your powers when you are on this plane," Marc said.

"I can save us all the trouble by telling you that I have absolutely no control. I'm not about to put any of you in danger."

"Well, that's why we're here," Marc responded. "Kyle can

shield us all if needed and I along with Justin can hopefully control you," Mark explained. "Now, how would you like us to start?" he asked, looking at Marcellus.

"Caitlin? When does your gift ignite?" Marcellus asked.

I shrugged my shoulders.

"What usually happens before your wrist starts to throb? What triggers the surge of energy to your hands?"

"Well, when I'm calm and I want to share my energy, I can do with it as I please, but when I'm really, really angry or provoked there's no controlling it."

"Okay then. I guess we have to find a way to provoke you."

Justin devilishly looked at me and smiled. "I can provoke her if you like," he said smirking, causing me to blush all shades of crimson.

"We're sure you can," Kyle added, knowing full well what Justin meant.

Without any warning, Aurelia walked over to where my earthly body sat and grabbed my scarred wrist. Instantaneously, I had an overwhelming surge of energy rush over me. My outer body experience was turning quickly into a nightmare.

My hands were glowing even brighter, aggravated by Aurelia's touch. Never before did I feel such force. It wasn't like other times when I felt it in my veins or bones; this was more compelling. It took over all my senses, submerging me entirely in its thirst to get Aurelia off.

I backed away from Justin, backed away from all of them until the icy cold of the Energy Stone met my back. I stared at Aurelia shaking my head as she watched me, unable to understand why I wanted to snap her in two.

"Why are you responding so negatively to Aurelia?" Marcellus asked, sensing my foreshadowing intentions.

"Please Aurelia, let go," I pleaded, knowing I couldn't hold back much longer.

"Caitlin!" Marcellus yelled, to draw my attention. "She's not a threat. You know this. You must sift through your emotions. Let your gift know how you're feeling; let it know that you're not in any danger. You're not even in your body right now. Take the reins child, and reel in your emotions!"

My need to get her off was toxic. "Marcellus, this isn't the time. I can't control this," I repeated, approaching Aurelia with only one intention in mind.

Justin stepped in front of the Ellri; blocking my path. "Caitlin, remember The Exorcist. What did I tell you on the beach that day? You need to get control of your need to kill."

My mind was in no shape to comprehend what Justin was saying – I wanted to pull her head right off her shoulders.

"Caitlin…," Justin's voice was louder now, "you'll need to get though me if you want to touch Aurelia," he challenged.

Instinctively, I moved back not wanting to harm him.

"You don't know how I'm feeling right now. I want her off," I threatened, in a hollow roar.

"Make me get off," Aurelia challenged me.

Step by careful step, I approached, hardly daring to breathe. A nightmarish sound that drew even closer, riding on a wave of thundering thoughts saturated my mind. The beating of her heart was crisp in my ears as was the melodic sound of her blood cursing through her veins - intoxicatingly luring me in. I put my hands over my ears, tormented by indecision.

"I know what you're trying to do, Aurelia, but I'm not able to contain this. It's simply too much for me."

"Control your emotions," she said, squeezing my wrist even harder.

Chamber Of Enlightenment

Illustrated for Lines That Bind - Within The Whispers

Murderous thoughts flooded in, inundating my boggled mind without any thought to the repercussions of acting on raw instinct. Nothing would keep me from ripping her hand right off. I bolted towards her, and to my shock I instantly found myself slammed onto the cold floor, face down.

"Down, young lady," I heard a slithering whisper say, "Bow down in front of your Ellri or you will know the true nature of rage. Now, down!"

Drenched in anger and distaste I let out an anguishing sound.

"I said, down," It repeated.

A warm glow from the other side of the room immersed the surroundings in a veil of hushed silence. A voice was speaking, too softly for me to make out if it were human or alien, but it slowly edged its way through the horrific thick fog that cloaked my thoughts.

On my knees and in desperation for freedom from my own vices I did what the being asked of me.

"There you go. Swallow back the hatred. Control these dark urges before they control you," I heard the whisper within a whisper say. The soft indistinct sound, like the noise of silk clothing in motion suspended in air riddled every corner of the room. Justin, Kyle and Marc quickly bowed their heads in profound respect.

"Caitlin! Concentrate," Aurelia pronounced.

I glanced in the direction the guys were turned and saw a faint silhouette seated on one of the thrones next to the Korbs' door. The light that radiated from its presence was blinding, preventing any of us from looking at it for too long. I knew it was one of the beings that visited me on several occasions.

"So, you're making public appearances now?" I growled, making no attempt to stand in fear of what my punishment would be. "Show some respect!" barked Marcellus.

"Don't," said the being, waving Marcellus away. "Leave her. It's best she vent her frustration."

"Can somebody please do something? I can't suppress this much longer. Aurelia please, just let my damn hand go!" I pleaded once again, louder and angrier. "Damn you all!"

Justin suddenly took two steps closer to where I was kneeling. Backing a few feet away from him, I stopped and threatened Justin to move. He persisted, pushing me further back until I had my back against the cold, hard wall once again.

Slowly I crept up against the wall, standing on both feet. "Please Justin, don't do this. I'm going to hurt you."

Retreating was not in Justin's mindset, instead, he placed his hands up against the stone wall blocking my escape, trapping me between the rock and his body. The slightest move on my part would trigger an onslaught of dire consequences – ones I was unable to decipher in the state I was in.

"What's it going to be, Caitlin?" he asked, gazing into my eyes.

We stood there at a standstill for what seemed an eternity. Justin was determined not to budge. The surge of power in my body was growing ever so lethal.

"Please, you have to move back," I pleaded.

The most precious thing in my life stood between me and my prey. A nondescript battle ensued within me. My deep seeded need to harm Aurelia had reached unfathomable proportions, but I knew better than to risk Justin's well-being. Aware of how I felt and what I was thinking, Justin simply looked at me and smiled.

"You can do this," he whispered, staring right at me.

He apparently had more faith in me than I had in myself.

I needed to try harder to get control. I owed him that much.

Closing my eyes I concentrated on his breathing, his heartbeat – a mellowing came over me. Keeping as still as possible, not wanting to make any sudden moves. I centered my thoughts on Justin, and then deep in the whirl of my distorted thoughts a sound came out of my soul, "I love you," I whispered.

No sooner had I finished my declaration when, in no time at all, I found myself, once again, confined by the limits of my earthly body and without a second to spare, I pulled my wrist free from Aurelia's hold, attempting to stand up. My legs felt exceptionally weak causing me to fall back down on the floor.

My elation over my small accomplishment was rather difficult to conceal – visibly carved on my face. I just couldn't stop smiling. I wasn't going to let my physical exhaustion thwart my happiness. "I did it! I actually did it," I exhaled knowing that I controlled the beast all by myself.

"Good girl," the whisper said, disappearing as fast as it appeared.

Unlike other times, the radiant being only observed, keeping its distance. The Nobe was apparently keeping close tabs on me, for some reason. At least I learned that my visitor was a member of my father's family, but who?

Trying to shake off the numbness, I turned my gaze to the

other side of the chamber where Justin stood with his back against the stone wall beaming a glorious smile, feeling as proud as I was.

"Don't you ever do that again," I yelled, annoyed at him for putting himself in danger. "You don't know how close I came to hurting you."

"But you didn't, did you?" Justin smiled, lessening the distance between us.

Aurelia gave me a big hug, apologizing for having to be the one who caused such turmoil.

"You don't give Justin enough credit, Caitlin. He's a lot stronger than you think. Your power responded to his gift in the end, not mine," she explained. "You're both on equal grounds as far as power is concerned. Don't let Justin's modesty fool you," she added winking at me.

"That's enough Aurelia. Don't go blowing things out of proportion," Justin told her, bending down to kiss me lightly on the lips. "Caitlin is so much more – she's special."

Aurelia just looked at him trying to figure out why he was down playing his own gift. "You're all special. You complete each other," she said, looking towards Kyle and Marc.

Frustrated, Kyle paced the room and stopped in front of the wooden throne where the being sat only minutes before. "Is it me or are we ignoring the fact that we were in the presence of the Nobe?" Kyle said, still dumbfounded. "Who cares who's stronger? Did you guys feel that energy?"

Marcellus patted Kyle on the shoulder. "We're missing the bigger picture here," he said. "Caitlin got control of her power without any help."

Still sitting on the floor, unable to stand, I looked up at Marcellus shaking my head. "I wouldn't say without any help," I corrected. "I was actually stopped in mid-attack."

Kyle was apparently not listening to one word we were saying. He seemed totally distracted by his thoughts. As far as he was concerned the Nobe was far more interesting than my self-control. I didn't blame him.

"Are you purposely trying to ignore me?" Kyle exclaimed, scanning our faces.

"Yes!" we all said in unison, laughing at our perfect timing.

"Ha, ha, very funny," Kyle said, grimacing. "Why did the Nobe appear? Isn't that a bit strange? They never appeared when I was training."

"To tell you the truth it's not that strange," I told him. "Every time I feel completely out of control, as far as my gift is concerned, they seem to show up when I transcend, guiding me."

Kyle was even more surprised at my revelation. "You mean to tell me that you've seen them on more than one occasion?"

"Yeah, I guess I have."

"I've seen them before as well," Justin added.

Kyle was visibly disappointed. "Why haven't they ever appeared to me? Apart from the one we saw on the Island, this is the second time in my life. What's so special about you guys?"

Marcellus wrapped his arm around Kyle's shoulder for emotional support, and said, "Your gift as well as Marc's is not a threat to your own life. Justin and Caitlin's gift, on the other hand, draws energy from their life force, making it quite dangerous. Until they get full control, they will be closely monitored to keep them safe."

I looked at Justin questionably. He never told me he had trouble controlling his gift.

"What are you thinking, Caitlin?" Justin asked, looking at my puzzled expression.

"I thought you could read my thoughts?"

"Not now we can't. Only when you transcended and only in this chamber," he said, continuing to look suspicious. "So? Are you going to tell me what's swirling in that mind of yours?"

I could have asked him the same thing, but I knew that now wasn't the appropriate time to get into it. "I was simply wondering why you were having so much difficulty controlling your gift."

"Oh," Justin exclaimed. "It's just hard for me sometimes, that's all."

"You're too modest, Justin," Aurelia said, caressing his face lovingly. "Caitlin, Justin's power is evolving as yours is. It takes extra effort to get complete control."

"But you have already ascended, thought your gift would've stabilized by now."

"Can we not talk about my gift," he said, shying away from the conversation. "We're here to help you get control of yours, not mine," he added, hating being put under the spot light.

"Your bond for some reason is causing these fluctuations. The stronger Justin gets the stronger you get and vice versa," Aurelia explained. "Caitlin, until your gift stabilizes, Justin's power is going to be as erratic as yours."

"Oh, great!" I exclaimed looking at Justin. "So I'm doing this to you?"

"Don't be absurd, you're not doing anything. It's just the way things are between us. I'm quite capable of keeping my power in check; it's you I'm worried about."

Aurelia looked at both of us, beaming one of her crooked little smiles. "Neither of you needs to worry," she said, focusing her gaze on Justin. "Soon enough Caitlin will have full control of her gift. You saw how well she did today and it was her first attempt."

Certain that Justin's concern had nothing to do with my gift or my lack of control, I didn't push the issue. Even though he seemed, to be okay with everything on the surface; I knew there was something else, bothering him. After the so called test with uncle Abbot, maybe even before, something changed.

Justin might have been able to block everyone out of his thoughts, but he had no way of keeping me in the dark about his emotions. I could feel his uncertainty and fear as if his feelings were my own. His whole manner was forced, nothing natural about the way he talked or laughed. Why he felt he needed to keep this from me was gnawing on my nerves.

While trying to play cool and collective, he was in fact boiling under the surface. It was frustrating to see him like that. What could I have possibly done to make him feel the way he was? Never being in a relationship before, I wasn't aware of how annoyingly trying it was to keep each other happy.

Back in Stone Hurst most of the girls in my class were, more or less, in some sort of a relationship. Going to an all-girl's boarding school, boys were the main topic of discussion. Over the five years there, I had placed most of my classmates under three categories: The Coquettes, the Needy and the Wall Flowers.

The first group held the reins. They were used to being in control, behaved amorously, without serious intentions. They were the ring leaders in many ways, having boys jump through hoops to get their attention. The poor, unaware males would flock to them like bees to honey. These girls had only three things in mind: hair, makeup and above all shopping. Nothing fazed them. They switched from one relationship to another without a second thought.

The next category belonged to the 'Needy' as I called them. These girls were the kind who'd boast about their boyfriends;

even had their names written all over their notebooks encircled with a heart. Their lockers were filled with pictures of the loving couple. The Needy would brag about how amazing their boyfriends were only to spend innumerous sleepless nights crying over the bastards once the boys tired of their needy nature and eventually broke up with them.

And last, but not least, the Wall flowers, or better yet, the late bloomers. I always believed that the girls in this category had more to offer society. They had better things to do with their time than sit around and fret over boys. Most believed that these girls were simply to plain to attract the opposite sex, but that surely wasn't the case. This particular group was way too intelligent for the common boy to handle. They were independent thinkers with sharp minds, future leaders, I was sure.

I never actually felt that I belonged to any of the categories because that would mean somebody actually took notice. For five years I blended so well into the background that I was virtually invisible. Nobody knew I even existed. If ever asked, I'd rather belong to the third category of girls. Either way, my sheltered life didn't prepare me for any kind of relationship, let alone, one with a guy like Justin.

I simply played it by ear as far as Justin and I were concerned. I wasn't sure if I was acting as I should. Was I trying too hard? Was I not trying enough? Whoever said that girls were more complicated than boys obviously was never in a relationship; not as a teenager anyway. I never wore my emotions on my sleeve, but then, neither did Justin. He was much better at bottling them up than I was.

The physical attraction was there, but there was an underlining factor which he insisted on withholding, making it all the more frustrating.

"Are you okay?" Justin asked.

My expression must have clearly mirrored my confusion. Once again I tried to stand up, but still had trouble supporting my full weight. Justin instantly grabbed me by the waist pulled me up against him. I could feel his warm breath on my brow. I hated myself for losing control of my senses when he was this close, especially now that we weren't alone.

'Needy', I instantly thought. *Shoot me now!*

"Are you in any pain?" he asked again, staring deep into my eyes.

I hated being needy – needy of his touch – needy of his kisses – needy of all of him. I inched away from his hold attempting to stand on my own. "I think I'm fine now," I told him, cracking a smile. Who was I kidding? I couldn't move. It took all my concentration to stand straight.

"Come here," he said, helping me to the nearest chair. Justin quietly sat next to me not uttering a sound.

"Okay then, I guess we can call it a day. You all had enough." Marcellus informed us. "Caitlin, you need to gain your strength before we try this again."

"Again?" I gasped. "You mean I'm going to do this again?"

Marcellus looked at me inquisitively. "Of course! Over and over again until you get complete control. You shouldn't have to be provoked. You need to learn to wield it on command – on and off like a switch. It will take great patience and a lot of practice."

~~~

Justin supported most of my weight, helping me back up the tunnel to the entrance under the manor.

"If this tunnel doesn't actually exist then why make it so long? Half a mile is rather far, isn't it?"

"The length of the tunnel conforms to your mood,"

answered Marc a few steps behind. I turned my head to get a better look at him. "What do you mean it conforms? Why would it do that?"

His kind nature was beaming through, visibly not wanting to leave me in the dark he said, "Since our powers are heightened in the Chamber of Enlightenment we must be in complete control of our emotions," he started to explain. "If, for instance, you are in a foul mood, the tunnel will seem a lot longer than it did today. This is because the long walk to the door will give you time to cool off, give you time to work through your emotions."

"Now, that's cool" I said, turning to Kyle.

Kyle chuckled at my response. "I know isn't it?" he answered. "I once had to walk three miles until I got to the door. It was irritating at first, but knowing that the madder I got the longer the tunnel, I soon got a hold of my emotions."

I started giggling, imaging Kyle walking endlessly, trying to reach the door.

"So tell me…," I turned to Marc, "what's the longest you walked?"

"Not much, a mile – a mile and a half. It's only natural for beginners to walk longer because the anticipation to get through the doors is as bad as being angry. We need to be at peace with ourselves prior to entering the Chamber."

I turned to the divine face next to me and smiled. Justin looked right at me knowing exactly what I was going to ask. Suddenly the guys started laughing raucously.

"What's so funny?" I asked, turning to Aurelia.

She simply shook her head in disbelief. "What do you expect of men? They're all children. No matter the age," she said turning to Marcellus. He was having a hard time holding back the laughter.

"Why are they laughing?" I turned to Justin's serious expression.

"They're idiots!" he yelled, facing his best friends.

"Oh, sure…," said Kyle between the laughter, "you were the one who had to walk for ten miles down the tunnel and we're the idiots."

I looked at Justin amazed "Ten miles? Why so far?"

Aurelia unexpectedly looked at Kyle and Marc sternly, causing them to stop laughing instantly.

There was silence for a few minutes before Aurelia started explaining.

"Caitlin, you need to realize that your absence all those years was quite hard on Justin. He wasn't himself for quite some time," she said.

I remained silent for some time and then asked, changing the subject, "Justin, how come I look like that?"

"We all look like that underneath. Don't let the flesh fool you," Justin said, helping me up the wooden steps that led back in the study. "Your gift allows you to leave the confines of your body taking with it all its energy."

"Is what I saw my spirit – my soul?" I asked, wondering what other explanation there could be to describe the ghostly figure I had seen in my own reflection.

"Absolutely not! The human soul is much more. It's more powerful than anything on this planet; surely nothing we can comprehend,"

Justin seemed to be surprised that I'd even mention such a thing. "What you saw," he continued to say, "what we all saw was energy in its purest form. All living creatures have it."

Once back in the manor, Tyler was at the entrance to see us off. I could tell he was dying to ask me about my experience.

"Well? Was it better than anything I can possibly imagine?"

Marcellus glared at Tyler and said, "Did I not say that we do not discuss things outside the Chamber? What's wrong with you? Rules are rules. Now, say your goodbyes. Caitlin needs to go home and rest."

Too curious to be bothered by Marcellus' warning, Tyler winked at me, hoping that I'd tell him everything at a later date. "See you at school tomorrow, Caitlin," he finally said, "and don't forget to study for Bio. Mr. Maxwell is surely going to quiz us on anatomy."

"Okay, thanks Tyler," I said, giving him a quick peck on the cheek. "Will you pick me up tomorrow for school?"

"Sure, no problem, now go home and rest. You look like crap," he chuckled.

Leave it to my best friend to blurt out the god-awful truth.

Justin was not at all amused. He gave Tyler a menacing look.

"What?" Tyler exclaimed. "You have to admit she's had better days, and don't look at me like that. I can say whatever I want to Caitlin. She looks like a train ran her over."

I started giggling at Tyler's insistence on how bad I looked. It was a nice change from his usual exaggerated compliments.

Justin finally gave up and drove me home, swearing under his breath. Most of the foul adjectives he used were aimed at Tyler. I just sat back amused at his mood. At least now he was venting some of his emotions.

TWENTY

DEFIANCE

S URPRISINGLY, the biology quiz wasn't as difficult as I had expected. It was a well-known fact that Mr. Maxwell had a thing for handing out brutal exams. Thankfully, today he took pity on all of us, probably because everyone was still a bit frightened with little Wilbert's resurrection in yesterday's lab.

Funny, but not one person mentioned the whole ordeal. Even Mr. Maxwell seemed to delete the episode altogether.

Tired as I was yesterday, I hadn't opened a book. This morning, however, I skimmed through my notes and quickly did my homework not wanting to be reprimanded by any of the teachers.

Tyler was in an exceptionally good mood. I knew he was trying to get on my good side in order to get information out of me about what happened yesterday afternoon. I could see it in the way he kept looking at me; it was driving him crazy not knowing what went on in the Chamber of Enlightenment.

"You're going to make me beg, aren't you?" he finally said, on our way to the cafeteria

I gave him a side glance, stopping in front of my locker to drop off my fat Biology text book. I fiddled with my locker unable to open it. "You know I can't tell you anything. So, stop looking at me like a wounded puppy."

"Oh come on! What should I expect? Will it hurt?" he asked.

"You'll just have to wait and see," I answered, sounding exactly the way everybody sounded towards me every time I asked to know something.

I tried the combination on my locker over and over again but nothing, the stupid thing was stuck. I even checked to see that I hadn't accidentally tried to open the wrong locker.

Tyler, the guy that he was, stepped in and banged hard against the door a couple of times, as if hitting the metal would have helped in any way.

"Just forget it," Tyler said. "Let's go to lunch and then we'll try to open it after school."

"We have to open it," I pleaded. "My history paper is inside. I was supposed to hand it in yesterday."

"I'm sure Mr. Myers will understand. Just tell him the truth."

"Absolutely not! You saw how disappointed he looked when I didn't hand it in last time."

Tyler was obviously in a hurry to get to lunch for some reason. "Just open the damn thing," he muttered through his teeth, making sure that no one else heard him.

I looked at him appalled. He wasn't expecting me to use my powers and get kicked out of school again. My project wasn't worth the sacrifice, I was sure.

"Oh come on, you know you want to do it," he whispered. "Nobody will know. The Shield of Knowledge blocks out everybody's power except yours. Nobody will be the wiser. They didn't even reprimand us for piggly-wiggly, what makes you think they'll care about this? Just do it, so we can go."

I looked at him, contemplating my next move. "You better be right," I said, turning to my locker.

I casually turned my head in all directions making sure no one was looking. Most of the students had either returned to class or already headed down to the cafeteria. Shifting my body directly in front of the lock, I simply looked down and concentrated. "Open," I commanded. And wouldn't you know it, instantly the door flung open almost hitting both me and Tyler in the face.

Tyler started chuckling at our close call with the locker. "That would've hurt," he said smiling. "Hurry up, get what you need and let's go!"

With my Bio book on the top shelf and my binder with all my notes and projects in hand, I slammed the locker door shut and followed Tyler to lunch, hoping that the small incident wouldn't be picked up by any of the Ellri. I seriously didn't want to finish my senior year being tutored at home – I'd sooner die. I truly liked being back. I finally started to feel like a normal teenager.

As soon as we sat down next to Lisa and Gina with our trays in hand, Lisa slid a piece a paper across the table.

"What's this?" Tyler asked, picking it up.

"It's a list of things we have to do for the prom," Gina said, taking a bite of her sandwich.

Not wanting anything to do with the upcoming event, I pretended not to hear, concentrating on my lunch.

"We still haven't found a venue. We thought about having the prom in the school gym, but that would be too ordinary."

"How about a hotel outside of town?" asked Tyler, lifting the carton of juice to his mouth.

"We checked already. They're not allowing us anywhere

outside Oaks – not for prom, anyway. We asked – begged twice, already."

"That's ridiculous!" I said, under my breath, continuing to poke my mashed potatoes.

"You can't expect them to let gifted teenagers loose outside of Oaks?" Tyler said looking at me.

"Why not? What can possibly go wrong? Most of us don't even use our gifts in Oaks. What makes them think that we'll use them elsewhere?" I asked, irritated at the Ellri for believing that as soon as we'd leave the compounds of Oaks we'd run around spreading mayhem to the surrounding areas.

"The rules exist to keep us safe not the other way round," Gina said, smiling at me. "If we were to be found out and our gifts revealed, the non-gifted would stop at nothing to use us as guinea pigs. Oaks would become a large laboratory."

I scanned their faces to see their reactions. I couldn't see the logic behind their thinking. It, more or less, sounded like one of those children's tales meant to keep naughty children under control. Nonetheless, it was obvious that I was the only one who didn't agree with such strict measures. I didn't want to go into a debate over this particular subject seeing how strongly they all felt.

"Oh, now I see," I responded, putting an end to the discussion, pretending to agree. "So what other venue choices are there?" I asked.

Lisa looked at Gina and then back to me and Tyler. "What we were thinking was…" Lisa said, girlishly, "that the only place that can accommodate so many people is one of the manors."

Tyler looked at both of the girls completely surprised. "You can't be serious! I don't know about the others, but I can guarantee you that my parents won't allow it in our house," said Tyler. "Caitlin, do you think Abbot will allow the school to hold the prom in their house?"

"Are you serious? Of course not! Why would he, when the school gym is available?"

The girls looked so disappointed. They wanted nothing more than to organize the best prom ever, to make it special for everyone. What they were doing was quite a selfless act. While other students sat back waiting for the date of the event to near; Gina and Lisa were running around trying to create the best atmosphere for everyone. Even though I wasn't entirely convinced that the prom was such a momentous occasion, my heart went out to them.

"I have an idea," I said, knowing I was going to regret even mentioning it. "It's a long shot – but – if you want we can have it at my parent's estate. It's much bigger than any of the other homes and it's not even being used, so we won't be imposing on anyone."

Their eyes beamed with happiness. "Do you mean that? Can we really have the dance at your house? At the Korbs' estate?" Lisa asked smiling, almost ready to cry.

"I don't see why not," I said, happy to see them excited. "I should warn you, the landscaping needs a lot of work and the house hasn't been lived in for so many years."

"We'll fix it up, it'll look brand spanking new," Gina said, overly excited. "Okay, this is so cool. We're going to have the prom at the Korbs' Estate," she said, raising her voice, making sure that everyone in the cafeteria heard.

Everyone's eyes turned to me. I hated being the center of attention once again, but at least this time it was for a good cause. There was a sudden commotion in the cafeteria. Everyone seemed excited to finally get to see the inside of the elusive Korbs mansion.

At that moment it dawned on me that I was the only one who was unaware that the estate ever existed.

"You guys do realize I have to ask my uncle first," I said, putting a damper on their plans.

"Mr. Cathcart won't mind. It's your house anyway. Why would he have a problem?" asked Lisa.

"He is my guardian and above all my uncle," I said. "So don't go posting it around school just yet. Let me get his permission and then do as you like."

"Thank you, Thank you, Thank you," Lisa said, jumping across the table to hug me.

Tyler was just staring at me. I couldn't tell what he was thinking. That second Megan and her two friends stopped at our table.

"What's all the commotion about," asked Loraine, dressed from head to toe in pink. She looked more like a cartoon character than a real human.

"Caitlin offered the Korbs' Estate for our prom," exclaimed Gina. "Can you believe it?"

"That was real nice of you," said Megan smiling.

"There's a lot to be done before we can even consider holding the prom there," I informed her, desperately trying to sound civil.

"We're a town of gifted people, I'm sure if anyone can pull this off, it will be us," Megan said, volunteering her services.

Tyler stood up collecting our trays. "The bell is going to ring in a few minutes. Why don't we all meet in the parking lot and head to the Korbs to see the condition it's in before we make any final decisions?"

Megan stared at him and smiled. "That's a great idea. If anyone can pull this whole thing off it would be the five of us," she said, excluding her two best friends. "We can get the whole senior class to help prepare the grounds, make it a pre-prom event!"

"That's such a cool idea!" Lisa exclaimed. "Thanks Megan, we can use your help."

Loraine and Kim looked at each other devastatingly hurt at their leader's deliberate brush off.

"Loraine, Kim – you guys are coming too, aren't you?" I asked.

If I was going to have to put up with Megan, might as well not feel bad about leaving her accessories out of the picture. Besides, their flare in style could come in handy.

"Yeah, of course we're coming," answered Kim smiling.

"Thanks Caitlin, we'd love to help," added Loraine.

The bell rang sending all the students dashing off to their next class. Megan and her friends headed off leaving the four of us behind.

"After school, in the parking lot," Lisa said, gathering her stuff. "We'll see you guys there."

The girls took off, leaving Tyler and me alone. The cafeteria was practically empty when Tyler turned and said, "You didn't' have to do that you know. The gym is as good a place as any."

Preparing to stand, a vision of Justin waiting in the parking lot slammed into me, like taking a hammer to my skull. The pain was excruciating – causing me to fall right back down.

Instantly, I put my head down on the table with my hands rubbing really hard against my temples, hoping that somehow the pain would subside.

"Are you okay?"

I felt nauseous, unable to speak. My head was on fire and I had no way of extinguishing it. Tyler sat next to me, not knowing how to help. He simply stroked my back, trying to make me feel better. "Are you okay?" he repeated, sounding genuinely worried.

"It hurts – it really hurts," I whimpered.

"Where does it hurt, Caitlin?"

I lifted my head slowly to look at him. "My head feels like it's going to explode. I think I just had my first vision," I whimpered with pain, visibly confused.

Tyler collected our things and put his free arm around my shoulders. "Let's get you outside," he offered, helping me to my feet.

I leaned my head up against his shoulder, keeping my eyes slightly shut to prevent the light from entering. We exited through the back door and sat on the bench next to the door.

"Now let me look at you," he said. "I need you to sit still."

"What are you going to do?"

"Make you feel all better. Now don't move."

"You said healing people makes you weak," I reminded him, wincing from the pain. "Tyler, I'll be fine. Just give me a few minutes," I lied.

The pain was actually intensifying, making it more difficult to concentrate; the nausea was working its way up my throat. Swallowing back the putrid vile was as unbearable as the pain itself.

"Stop talking and let me help. Now be still!" he ordered.

Placing both hands on either side of my head, barely touching me, he closed his eyes and in no time at all the pain was gone, vanished as fast as it appeared.

"How's that?" he asked, looking kind of pale.

"I'm much better than you look," I said, pulling him down on the bench. "Are you okay?"

"I'm fine, just hand me the candy bar I have in my school bag, would you? I desperately need something sweet," he said.

I fumbled through his bag and pulled out a Sneakers bar. Tyler grabbed it out of my hand with force. "I'm sorry Caitlin, but I need the energy," he said tearing open the wrapper and biting into the chocolate. I sat there staring at him gobbling down the whole bar in three big bites.

"Much better," he said, sitting back with his head against the cold brick wall.

"Why did you need to eat?"

With closed eyes he just sat there, not talking for a couple of minutes. I didn't say anything; he obviously needed time to collect himself.

"For some reason sugar helps," he finally spoke, sitting up.

"So are you okay now?"

"Nothing I can't handle. It feels like my blood sugar drops to zero. It doesn't hurt, if that's what you're worried about? I simply feel drained of all energy."

"I know how that feels," I smirked. "So how long will it take you to get back to normal?" I asked. I didn't want him to suffer on my account.

"I'm perfectly fine – honest. You only had an intense migraine."

I smiled at him amused "It's nice to know that a free diagnosis comes with the service?" I said giggling.

"No – that I'll have to charge."

I kissed him on the cheek thanking him.

"You sure know how to repay debts," he said chuckling. "So what was the vision all about?"

"I think Justin is waiting for me in the parking lot."

"We have two more classes, why would he be here so early?"

"I don't know," I said, standing up. "There's only one way to find out if what I saw was an actual vision of the present."

I headed around the front of the school to see for myself.

"I guess we're cutting the last two periods?" Tyler said, two steps behind.

"You can go if you want. I wouldn't want you to get into trouble."

"Are you kidding me? We've never cut class. It's our senior year for heaven's sake, let's live a little!"

"Yeah, right! Hanging out in the school parking lot is living it up."

"It's a start," Tyler muttered.

As soon as we reached the main parking lot in front of the school, we saw Justin only then, pulling up. He didn't bother parking or turning off the engine. Visibly shaken, Justin jumped out of the driver's seat and headed in our direction.

"Did he just get here?" I asked, turning to Tyler puzzled. "Wouldn't that mean that my vision was of the future?"

Lost for words, Tyler shrugged his shoulders in utter disbelief.

Before I even got the chance to say anything, Justin grabbed me by the arms and looked me up and down, checking if everything was intact. "Is everything alright?" he asked worried. "I had a vision of you in extreme pain. You had your head down on the table. What the hell is going on?" he said, raising his voice, turning to Tyler. "I thought you were going to look after her? Why aren't you both inside?"

"She's fine," Tyler explained. "She had a slight headache. Everything is going to be just fine."

"Headache? It couldn't have been that. I felt how much pain she was in, that was no headache," Justin said, releasing his hold. "Are you alright?" he asked again, shifting his gaze back to me.

"I had a vision of you," I admitted, "accompanied by a

massive migraine; nothing Tyler couldn't handle," I said, trying to pass off the incident as something casual. He was rather upset. I didn't think he needed to know every detail. "But you seem to be fine considering you had a vision yourself," I said, looking at him suspiciously.

Justin didn't seem to be suffering as I was. Why didn't he experience the same acute pain as I did? He didn't comment. Justin just looked at me.

"Justin has been having visions for many years. He's inherited the gift from his grandmother," Tyler said.

"Really? What you see are visions? I thought someone else is messing with your head."

Justin was furious at Tyler, but turned to me and said, "They're two different things."

"I didn't know that. What other things don't I know about your gifts," I asked, wondering why he kept me in the dark about his powers.

"He can…"

Tyler was suddenly cut off by Justin's menacing stare. He was obviously being reprimanded for divulging too much. I could tell they were communicating; didn't' need to hear the words to know that Tyler was on the receiving end of what seemed an endless scolding.

"This is ridiculous!" I yelled, drawing Justin's attention away from Tyler "Why are you acting like this? Tyler didn't mean anything by it. He just wants me to know something you, yourself, should've told me, so don't go blaming him!"

Justin simply looked at me; his eyes were devoid of any emotion.

"Why the vision? What does it mean?" I asked.

"I don't know why they happen, they just do," Justin answered reluctantly. "Somehow my mind's reaction to seeing you in pain must've triggered your vision. I'm not sure if that's what it was, it's all too weird. The bond is making everything so complicated, seems to have a life of its own. With each passing day our gifts are blending together in some way," he added. "Come on, I'll take you home."

"I can't go. I told the prom committee that they could use the Korbs residence for the venue. We're all going to meet after school and head out to my parent's house."

He simply stared.

"Do you want to tag along?" I asked, hoping that he would.

"You go do your thing with your friends," he said. "And you – you take care of her," Justin added, turning to Tyler.

Without saying another word he slid back into the black Audi and sped away, leaving Tyler and me all alone. I just stood there not knowing why he was acting so cold. I turned and looked at Tyler who simply raised his shoulders once again.

"What's wrong with him?" I asked, feeling at a complete loss. It didn't take long for tears to well up. Justin was intentionally keeping me at arm's length.

Tyler instantly gave me a hug; pulling me into his embrace. "Don't be such a girl," he said. "I don't know what his problem is. He's been blocking everybody out for quite some time. The Ellri don't even know why he's keeping such a tight lid on everything. Don't worry whatever it is it will surely pass. The guy is crazy about you. He wouldn't do anything to intentionally hurt you."

"And yet he is," I responded backing out of Tyler's hold, wiping my eyes dry. "I feel like I'm walking on a tight rope around him lately."

"Don't go blowing things out of proportion. There's nothing wrong with him, just give him time."

"You might be right," I said, not wanting to continue this conversation with Tyler. I didn't like talking about my relationship with Justin with anyone, especially Tyler – it felt awkward. Whatever was going on, we'd work it out. "So tell me. What were you going to say about Justin's gift?"

Tyler smiled at me, amused at my question. "I wondered how long it'd take you to bring up the topic."

"Well? Out with it," I pressed.

"You see, Justin's gift is evolving quite differently than the rest of ours, excluding yours of course. Don't even ask me what your gift is doing," he said chuckling. "When Justin was small he could only manipulate people's thoughts and read minds, but now he can move objects on command."

"I know all this. What's the thing he doesn't want me to know?" I insisted, annoyed that Tyler was purposely taking his time to get to the point.

"His visions appeared a couple of years ago. They were, more or less, like the one you had earlier. Lately he doesn't only see a flash of an event, but a whole scene in progress sometime in the future. It's a rare gift to hold."

I was stunned

"So you're saying Justin can see the future? I thought that was impossible. I thought that there were simply too many variables for anyone to know what would happen."

"That's what we all thought, but Justin, for some reason, is able to home in on the most probable of all outcomes. He can concentrate on any one person and see into their future," Tyler said, shaking his head. "Scary isn't it?"

That moment it dawned on me – Justin must have seen something disturbing in my future. It was the only explanation to his foul mood. Could he have seen the Nobe's decision? For him to be so distraught, it only meant one thing.

"Tyler, give me your keys!" I ordered, stretching out my hand.

"What about going to the venue?" asked Tyler, searching his pockets.

"Get a ride from the girls. The main gate should still be unlocked, but make sure you close it on your way out."

"Caitlin, where are you going?" he asked, dangling the keys in front of me, refusing to hand them over.

"Give me," I said, opening my palm. Instantaneously, the keys effortlessly broke from Tyler's hold and zipped over to my palm.

"Hey! That's not playing fair!" he protested, on my use of power. "What am I supposed to do?"

"Go to our last period and take good notes," I said, walking away.

Catching up to me Tyler pulled me to a full stop. "Let me come with you," he said. "What am I supposed to tell Mr. Travis?"

"I don't care. You'll find something to say. Tell him I didn't feel well and went home. Now go to class and don't forget to get my books out of my locker," I ordered, unlocking the Porsche Boxster.

"Be careful with my baby," Tyler said, quite apprehensive of my driving his car. "She's nothing like that lemon you drive."

"Don't worry, I'll be gentle, and don't call Old Betty a lemon!" I said, slipping into the driver's seat. "That reminds me, I have to go to the garage and pick that lemon up."

∼∼∼

Driving the sleek, grey Boxster made me realize why everyone in town preferred expensive cars. The leather steering wheel was soft to the touch, nothing like Old Betty's torn hard leather.

No pumping the clutch or turning the key several times for the ignition to start. The ride to Justin's house was really smooth, undeniably the sweetest ride I had in a long time.

Once up Justin's driveway, I saw his Audi parked up front. I was glad to see he was home. Comparing the two cars, I much preferred the smooth lines of the black Audi. I knew I couldn't be objective in the comparison; I was, after all, madly in love with its owner.

I knocked on the door only to have Shannon come to open. "What are you doing out of school this early?" she asked, the second she opened the door.

"Is Justin here? I really need to talk to him."

She stepped to the side and let me enter the foyer. "He's here, but he's kind of busy," she said, heading towards the kitchen. "Are you hungry? I made lasagna."

I wasn't at all hungry. The only thing I wanted was to get to the bottom of his sudden mood swing. If Justin knew my future, I felt I had every right to know what I was in for. How could he keep something like that from me?

"I'll grab a bite later. I really need to talk to him. He hasn't been himself lately and I think I know why."

"He just went down to the Chamber of Enlightenment. He should be back up in no time," she said, arranging a table setting in front of me. "Now, do you want a big piece or a small one?" she asked, pointing to the lasagna.

Shannon was obviously ignoring the problem at hand.

"Shouldn't we wait till everyone eats?" I asked.

"William and I already ate. Justin wasn't hungry, so that only leaves you sweetie. Now is this enough?"

There was no arguing with Shannon. I simply nodded allowing her to serve me a great big piece.

Once finished she sat right across from me and poured a

glass of her special homemade ice-tea. It was my favorite growing up; not too sweet, but perfect for any occasion.

For several moments while I ate my over-indulgent serving of lasagna Shannon and I talked about unimportant things – the weather – the season – school and then out of the blue she said, "You shouldn't have allowed Tyler to use his gift on you."

I swallowed hard, hoping she wouldn't bring up the subject of my locker or of poor Wilbert the pig.

"It's dangerous for both of you. He hasn't ascended yet and your power is quite unstable."

"He was just trying to help."

"It's in Tyler's nature to want to help, but still you both need to think before you act. His gift of healing is as dangerous to him as it is miraculous to others," continued Shannon, serving up another plate of lasagna and set it next to her.

I thought she said she already ate. Who was the other plate for? Just then, the faint tingly sensation was back. *Justin!* I thought.

I straightened myself out, preparing to see him walk through the door. Shannon looked at me and smiled. "Relax sweetie. You're acting like it's the first time you see him."

"It always feels like that," I confessed, blushing.

Shannon beamed a big smile, content in knowing what her son did to me. At that moment Justin walked through the kitchen door looking exhausted. Unexpectedly, he stopped in mid-stride the moment he saw me. He acted as though he didn't even know I was there. Was that even possible?

"This is a surprise," he said, taking a seat.

Shannon instantly poured him a glass of cold water. "You shouldn't exert yourself," she said, kissing him on the head. "You've been down there every day this week. There's no need to push it."

"I'm fine, mom," he said, rolling his eyes at her. He took another sip and turned his attention to me. "I thought you were going to your parent's house with the prom committee?"

"I wanted to talk to you about something first."

Justin didn't even look at me. Instead, he pulled the plate in front of him, concentrating on the contents. "And this something couldn't wait till later?" he asked, digging into the lasagna.

Shannon was staring at me, surprised at her son's indifference.

"No, it couldn't wait," I said, pushing my plate aside. "We need to talk, and why were you so surprised to see me just now? Didn't you feel my presence?"

Justin suddenly stopped eating and turned to look at his mother.

"I'll leave you two alone," Shannon said. "You should know the Ellri are on their way. We'd like to talk to both of you," she said, and walked away.

The tension was intense, magnified by the sheer silence of the room. Justin played around with his food not wanting to be the first to talk.

"I want you to tell me about what you saw in your vision," I finally said.

"I told you, you were with your head down on the table, in pain."

"Not that!

"Then, what?"

"You saw something in my future. What was it?" I asked, surprising him.

Justin sat there completely at a loss for words.

"I have every right to know," I insisted. "We're talking about my future, Justin!"

Without warning, he slammed his hand on the table and stood up, staring down at me. "You see Caitlin, that's where you're wrong. It's not – you're – anything. It's – our – future – ours! You and me, remember?" he yelled, completely beside himself.

"What did you see?" I insisted. I wasn't going to let him sidetrack me. "What did you see?" I yelled, standing up myself, lessening the distance between us.

The second I got closer to Justin, without intending to, my wrist started throbbing, sending a surge of energy to my fingers. "Oh, great – not now," I mumbled, hating how easy my gift misinterpreted my feelings.

"Just sit down and relax," I heard Justin say, softening his tone. "I didn't mean to be so – I'm just really tired, that's all."

"You owe me an explanation. I have a right to know." I repeated.

"Tyler shouldn't have said anything. He had no right."

"Don't go blaming Tyler. He's the only person who's been honest with me." I sat back down, careful not to touch anything.

"He had no right," he repeated, sounding hurt. Justin took a seat across from me and put his head down on the table, completely exhausted; looking at me from the corner of his eye. My mom was right, I think I over did it today.

Instinctively and without thinking, I reached and took his hand. Instantly a surge of energy passed through my hands and into his. Frozen, and scared out of my mind, I pulled back hating myself for being so careless. Just as fast my wrist stopped throbbing and returned to normal without any effort on my part.

"Are you Okay?" I asked, holding my breath not sure what damage I did to him.

"Relax, I'm fine – just a tickle," he said, sitting upright again. He suddenly looked much better.

"How is that even possible? The surge was quite strong," I asked puzzled at why I didn't hurt him; not that I wanted to. "And why in the world are you smiling?"

"Your gift didn't react to my anger. It reacted to my exhaustion. Your touch boosted my energy."

"It's nice to know I could help, I think. Now, about my future."

He stood up, preparing to leave. "I can't...," he started to say only to be rudely interrupted my Marlene.

"You love birds need to come downstairs. We're all waiting for you," she said.

Justin looked as confused as I was. How did she even get here? The Ellri were obviously blocking Justin out.

"Come on – chop, chop," she said, clapping her hands.

"Where are we going?' I asked, getting to my feet.

"The Inner Realm, awaits," she said, making it sound all the more mysterious.

Marlene had a way with words. The way she talked to people was unlike anything I had ever heard. She could say the most offensive – ill-timed phrase and yet get some laughs – nobody would take it to heart. They'd simply laugh it off, it was Marlene after all. Extremely intelligent and worldly, she knew how to handle anyone, mold them like clay to her way of thinking.

Justin and I followed her down the corridor and through the back room. The opening in the floor was already ajar, exactly the same as the one in the Falcone residence.

"Now, before we enter the tunnel, I want you both to relax. I'm in no mood or shape to walk aimlessly until you both get a grip of your emotions. I'm an old lady, take pity."

We both laughed. "We'll do our best," Justin said, taking my hand and lifted it up to his lips. It was the first time in so many days that I felt that his kiss was genuine.

Satisfied, Marlene made her way down the wooden stairs.

Before descending, Justin turned and said, "I'm sorry about before," and kissed me on the lips.

The feeling of Justin's lips on mine was pure pleasure. My heart started beating erratically to his touch, wanting nothing more than to wrap my arms around him and never let him go. Unfortunately, Marlene's deliberate cough ruined the moment.

"Is that how the youth of today relax?" she asked chuckling. We followed her downstairs. "We used to take deep breaths and think about puppies or something as cute." She stopped walking and turned to face us. "Come to think of it guys, I prefer your technique," she said laughing. Seconds later, she turned again and led us down the tunnel. "What I wouldn't give to be your age again," she muttered.

Justin and I followed her down the passage holding hands. To my surprise the massive carved door was only a few yards away.

"Okay, here we are," Marlene said, stopping in front of the towering door. "Would you like to do the honors or shall I?" she asked Justin.

"You're closer," Justin responded, nonchalantly.

Without even touching the door, the sound of the three locks clanking open bounced against the tunnel walls. Instantly the door opened to reveal the rest of the Ellri waiting inside.

"How come you didn't need to put your hands up against your palm print?" I asked Marlene.

Justin squeezed my hand and smiled. "The Ellri have no need for the Chamber of Enlightenment. They can come and go in the Inner Realm as they please, the way you transcend."

"The doors are only for the Ascended," added Marlene.

"I must sound so stupid with all these questions."

"We've all been there, Caity. Ask whatever you like, as many times as you like," Marlene said, stepping in the Chamber.

Aunt Leslie instantly came and gave me a hug. "How's your head?" she asked worried.

"I'm fine, really," I reassured her.

She took me by the hand and led me to the middle of the room. Justin was only a few feet away looking as I was – confused. The Ellri each took a seat leaving me and Justin to stand alone.

"Justin, we need you to show us what you've seen," Nathan said, from where he was sitting. "You had no right keeping this from any of us."

"Absolutely not," said Justin, refusing the Ellri. "You've all said my visions aren't definite."

"They're not!"

"So why do you need to see what I saw? Isn't it enough that I carry it around? Why do you all have to worry? Why does Caitlin?"

Nathan stood from his seat and walked up to Justin.

"You of all people should know that we are family. What burdens you, burdens us all," he said.

"No, never," Justin insisted, raising his voice. "Not with Caitlin here."

"I have every right to be here," I glared at him. "All this is because of me. If I hadn't been born none of you would need to put yourselves in any kind of danger. This is all my doing. I have to see, please," I begged him.

"No! I'm not doing it," he said ignoring my plea. "She doesn't need to see this."

I could tell Nathan was not amused anymore.

"Justin, Caitlin has every right to know as you do."

"I can't! It's not right. No one should know their future. It's just wrong."

Nathan returned to his seat calmer than I had expected. Justin wasn't about to back down. Whatever it was that he saw really scared him.

For many minutes the Ellri stood in deathly silence and then suddenly something shifted. "No!" yelled Justin defiantly, holding his head. "Don't do this! You don't want to force me," he threatened, through clenched teeth.

Suddenly a rush of energy pierced through my spine and down my arms. Responding in need to protect him, my power was, yet again, ready to serve its duty. The raw power of it was even stronger than when I left my body the day before. It was obvious that my gift reacted to all the Ellri combined. They were trying to coerce Justin into obeying. They didn't need to say anything to force his mind into surrender.

Justin was in agony, I could feel it in my blood. Even though I wanted to see what it was he saw, I surely wasn't going to stand by and watch them torture him into submission. Weak from the sheer force of my gift I reached out and grabbed Justin's arm, kneeling at his feet in exhaustion, letting my power drain into his body.

"Caitlin, you need to stop!" I heard Nathan say from across the room.

"You're hurting him," I muttered through the pure and agonizing exhaustion of it all, not recognizing my own voice. It was that hollow sound I heard the day Uncle Abbot was testing me, a ghostly whisper that came from the depths of my soul.

"If you guys plan on taking us both, you need to do better than that," Justin challenged.

In that split second all eighteen Ellri closed their eyes and looked up towards the ceiling. Then the most amazing thing happened. Simultaneously, they all transformed; eighteen radiant beings approached me and Justin. They looked much like I did when I had my outer body experience except there was no way of looking at them. The brightness from the glow was hard on the eyes. They didn't leave any physical body behind as I did. They simply shifted into this new form without batting an eye.

"Let him go!" I heard William's voice vibrate off the stone wall. He didn't sound worried about his son the way I was.

"There must be some other way," I whispered, slowly being drained of all my energy.

"We make the rules, Caitlin – not you!" he snapped.

I was furious.

Nobody should be forced to do something they didn't want to do, no matter the cause. I closed my eyes and instantly crawled into my solace. I felt more alive there than I did in my conscious state. I felt I had more power. I sat up and left the confines of my body. Free from any physical burdens, the throbbing in my wrist was now even deadlier. The Ellri didn't even budge, they just stood there staring at me.

Being in this state, I was able to see them much clearer. Everyone's hair, men and women alike, was long and golden-white. The light that emanated from their ethereal bodies was indescribable; a crystal clear aura surrounded each and every one. It poured around them lucid and clear, like water running over them. If I didn't know any better I'd think they were heavenly creatures, angels even.

I looked behind me and saw my earthly body still holding onto Justin.

"Caitlin, your body is suffering, you must return!" Aunt

Leslie said, sounding more worried than before.

"You all need to stop this," I demanded.

Justin had his eyes closed trying to concentrate on keeping all of them out of his head. It was visible on his face that he was in more pain than he let on. I stepped right in front of him and concentrated on his face. He instantly opened his eyes and a single tear rolled down his face. My heart was about to break. That second I turned to the Ellri angrier than humanly possible, feeling the surge of energy escalating even more.

"Stop," I screamed, in a brassy tone. "Can't you see he's in pain?"

"Return to your body, Caitlin!" Aunt Leslie repeated.

My hands were glowing in response to their defiance. I turned back to Justin and looked at him again "I hope this helps," I whispered and placed my hands on his head, allowing every drop on energy to flow through my body and into his.

In seconds, the Ellri returned to their former selves and stood around me and Justin.

Justin took hold of my ghostly hands. "You need to stop and return to your body," he said. "You can't take any more of this. You're killing yourself."

With much effort I did as he said. Even in that state, I could hardly move. Once back in my body I couldn't seem to open my eyes, everything hurt. My chest felt constricted; preventing me from taking a deep breath. Every single cell in my body was on fire. I could hear myself whizzing – dying for some air.

"What you did was uncalled for," I heard the delicate, soft whisper say.

The warmth from its radiance was welcoming on my cold skin. I knew I wasn't in my solace so that only meant one thing; that the being was in the chamber with the rest of the Ellri.

"Caitlin, you should never be so willing to sacrifice your life.

It's not yours for the taking," another whisper added.

"We'll help you this time, but from now on any foolish act won't go unpunished," said yet another, deeper whisper this time.

How many could there possibly be and why were they all here?

"Don't ever defy the Ellri's wishes. Next time they won't be so lenient. You and Justin need to follow the rules; otherwise you will both pay the price. Something that neither of you are willing to forfeit," said the first soft whisper.

The being with the angelic voice simply caressed my face and disappeared. My breathing returned to normal, but my body was still in no shape to move. Slowly I opened my eyes to see everyone looking over me. From what I could tell I must have collapsed on the floor.

"Where's Justin?" I asked trying to swallow. My throat was like sand paper and it burnt all the way down.

"We took him to his room. He needs as much rest as you do. This nonsense needs to stop, Caitlin," William said "Are you able to stand?"

"I can't even feel my legs. Suits me right for cutting school," I joked.

Only Marlene found it funny.

Uncle Abbot along with William helped me up and led me through one of the wooden doors, but not the one we came through. There was no passage to cross once we were outside the chamber. The steps upstairs were only a few feet away. Both men helped me up one step at a time. At that moment, I realized that I was in Uncle Abbot's study.

"Do you guys need help?" asked Kyle walking in the study.

"Take her to her room," ordered uncle Abbot, "Caitlin needs her rest. Your mother will be up as soon as the meeting finishes," he added. "Your unwillingness to yield will not go unpunished, young lady. You should have listened and obeyed – stubborn, just so stubborn," I heard him say as he left.

I didn't need to be clairvoyant to know what that meeting was going to be about. Kyle swooped me up into his arms and carried me like a rag doll to my room.

"You look as bad as Justin does," he said, fumbling with the covers.

"Is he okay?" I asked through the exhaustion. "He was tired even before this ordeal."

"If I were you, I'd concentrate on getting better and stop worrying about Justin. What you both did was stupid. Justin of all people...," he stopped momentarily and shook his head disapprovingly, "he should know better than to defy the Ellri. I hope his punishment isn't going to be so harsh."

"His punishment? What punishment? Why would they even think of a punishment? Wasn't what they did to him enough?"

"Don't worry your little brain sis, he's a big boy. Whatever they decide he'll have to bare it. All in the name of love," Kyle said, tucking me in.

Instead of heading downstairs he picked out a book from my bookshelf and sat in the armchair across from me.

"What time is it?" I asked, completely unaware of how long this whole ordeal lasted.

"It's only six in the afternoon. By morning you should be back to normal. Now get some sleep," he ordered. "I'll stay until you fall asleep. It's Justin's orders."

Knowing that Justin was still looking after me, even after all he's been through today, was reassuring. "Kyle?"

He slowly raised his eyes from the book. "What is it?"

"Can you tell him that I – well – that I l..."

"He already knows sis. Now go to sleep."

TWENTY-ONE

THE SMALL HOURS

T HE MID-DAY SUN *shone over the surrounding valley, it was by no means Oaks. The sprawling fields stood behind me as I climbed up a narrow winding pathway to the top of the rock. For some reason I was in a hurry to get to the top, defying any danger that might have been lurking on the steep climb.*

The moment I reached the peak, I realized that I was on a large cliff, hundreds of yards above sea level; the eagle's eye view was breathtaking. Below, the currents swirled among the rocky islets where the wind pounded stiffly against the sheer drop. Just then, out of nowhere, a cloud of mist rolled in blanketing the lush green grass as I stood there watching in awe.

Suddenly, I didn't feel alone. Several yards away, leaning dangerously close to the deathly drop, a single silhouette stood against the forlorn backdrop. My breath caught in my chest in fear that the person would jump. Slowly, and without making any sudden moves, I stood there frozen not wanting to frighten him. Within seconds, I knew who the silhouette was — didn't have to look to know, the burning in my blood alerted me to the fact.

"Justin," I whispered.

I panicked as Justin was standing dangerously close to the edge. I took a few steps closer; his head turned to me and stared. Startled by his ghostly pale complexion, I stopped cold, unsure of what was going on. The translucence of his skin accentuated the deep dark circles under his beautiful dark blue eyes. My heart felt like it was going to swell up and burst through my chest.

Without a sound, he shifted his tormented gaze back towards the ocean and continued to stare, dead and lifeless to the world. He didn't seem to be aware of my presence. Then, the shrill sound of my name being called made me circle my head to the source of the voice and noticed Alexander standing a few feet away, reaching out his hand for me to take. Justin remained unscathed by our visitor.

"Step back, Caity," said Alexander suddenly.

He was as I remembered, dressed casually and barefoot. This time his usual calm expression was stern and unyielding. On my left, Justin was standing only inches from the drop, oblivious to Alexander's presence and then there was Alexander on my right, a few feet away, beckoning me to take his hand.

"Turn away Caitlin," Alexander said, raising his voice, pervading my thoughts.

At the time, there was no way of knowing what the big deal was. I wanted to stay there with Justin. He looked so sad, so absorbed in his thoughts. Just as I was about to take a few steps to reach for Justin's hand, the incident abruptly shifted into my most terrifying dream. Out of thin air a dark ghostly figure materialized in front of me causing me to fall back from the shock. The monstrosity didn't seem to notice me, but instead turned his menacing gaze towards Justin.

"Caitlin, look away!" Alexander yelled, sounding even more severe.

That instant the murderous silhouette approached Justin from behind; with one intention in mind. I couldn't believe my eyes. Why was Justin just standing there? Why wasn't he doing something to stop the monster?

"Justin! Behind you!" I screamed, trying to warn him.

"He can't hear you, Caity," said Alexander, only inches away.

"Please Alex – please, do something!" I pleaded, hoping that Alexander would know what to do.

"Apparently your enemies want you to see this," he responded.

"Why? Where are we? What is this all about?" I asked shaken by the vile look on the monstrous face.

In that split second, I saw that Justin turned to face his attacker, but didn't look surprised or angry to see him. Instead he looked indifferent; stretching out his arms to the side, surrendering. "Come and get me," Justin challenged, welcoming his doom.

"No-o-o-o!" I screamed at the top of my lungs, waking with a start.

My palpitations were running amuck, my breathing fierce with anticipation.

"It was only a dream," I kept repeating, over and over again until my breathing returned to normal.

The darkness in my room took the place of the brilliant sun in my dream. Even though I knew it was a dream it did nothing to relax my nerves. I sat up in bed with my head against the headboard, dog-tired thanks to my little escapade a few hours before. I looked at my alarm clock; it was only three in the morning. *I've slept for almost nine hours,* I thought. It explained why my legs and arms felt much better. *But, what did the dream mean?*

Too lazy to move, I fixed my gaze at the side lamp. Hating to sit in complete darkness, I commanded it to switch on.

Sitting there in silence, I let my mind rerun the whole dream. Picking it apart, bit by bit, seeing if I could make sense of any little detail. Just then it dawned on me. "Why didn't I think about it earlier?" I muttered, slipping to the edge of the bed. "Was it at all possible that Justin's vision wasn't of my dark future, but of his own demise? Could he have seen his own death?"

I pulled myself off the bed and went to throw some water on my face to help me snap out of the miserable feeling. Lying in bed wasn't doing me any good. I needed some fresh air and quick. Looking down at my attire I realized that somebody must have helped me out of my clothes last night because I certainly didn't remember putting on my favorite flannel pajamas. After brushing my teeth, I quickly slipped into something casual and brushed my hair back, collecting it in my all too familiar bun; pinning it back with my butterfly hairpin.

The crisp air was exactly what the doctor ordered. I closed the back door and wandered aimlessly around the grounds. The soft, early morning light was invigorating; making my escape all the more welcoming. I headed towards the farthest part of the grounds to where the dividing wall stood. In the past Tyler and I had spent endless hours sitting and laughing on that wall, but now apart from my first night back to Oaks, I hadn't been back to that part of the estate. To my surprise, the feeling of his closeness was back. Apparently, I wasn't the only one who couldn't get any sleep at those small hours.

Justin was perched on the wall looking towards his side of the field, lost in thought. This was the second time, as far as I knew, that he didn't feel my presence; once yesterday in his kitchen and again now.

"What are you doing out here?" I asked taking him off guard. Surprised, he turned to me and smiled a faint smile. "I guess great minds think alike," he said, swinging one leg to my side of the wall.

Justin was visibly exhausted. Unlike mine, his body seemed to need more time to recuperate.

"Come here," he said, patting the stone wall, motioning for me to sit. Without hesitation I sat next to him with my legs dangling off the side. Justin wrapped his strong arms around me holding me tight. "Did you sleep well?" he asked smiling, kissing me on the cheek.

I wanted to ask him about his vision, but seeing how he was I knew it could wait. "I've had better nights. How about you? You still look exhausted."

"I'm fine. I just came up from the Chamber of Enlightenment. That's why I'm a bit off." he admitted.

"Your mom's right, you're over doing it. Why are you pushing yourself so hard? With what you've been through a few hours ago, you should give it a rest."

It was at that precise moment that I had, quite incidentally, answered my own question. Justin's vision was of himself. Why else would he be pushing his gift to the limit to see how far he can go, testing himself, day after day?

"I'm fine, Caitlin," he reassured me, kissing me on the cheek, tightening his hold. "The Ellri did what they had to. Your gift boosted my own power making the whole ordeal bearable."

"Then why weren't you there when I came to? Why did they take you to your room?"

"I'm not sure – said they wanted to be alone with you. So, I went back upstairs. They weren't going to hurt you in any way. Besides, I was half dead anyway."

"The Nobe!" I gasped.

"What about them?"

"That's why they didn't want you there. The Nobe were there. Not just one, either. I heard at least three different whispers."

Justin's expression quickly froze. "I didn't realize you were in that much danger," he said, sounding remorseful. "I shouldn't have let you help me. You could've died and from what you just said about the Nobe being there, you were certainly close to it." Justin pushed his hair back with both hands, aggravated at putting me in harm's way. "I'm so sorry, Caitlin. I was just so angry at them. I didn't think."

"You didn't do anything wrong. It was my choice. I wanted to help. They had absolutely no right to force you against your will."

Justin just smiled at me. He pulled out the hairpin from my bun allowing my hair to cascade down my back. With his long, elegant fingers, he traced the outline of the ornate butterfly hairpin, in deep thought.

"How long have you been wearing this?" he asked, never taking his gaze off the object.

"Oh, I don't know. Aunt Leslie gave it to me right after my mother passed away," I said, wondering what this had to do with our prior conversation. "I've been wearing it ever since."

He started chuckling for some reason. "You know this is an heirloom, don't you?" He placed the butterfly carefully in my palm.

"Of course, I know that. What's so funny about that?"

"Do you have any idea what this is worth?"

I shrugged my shoulders never thinking about its value. "Price wise," I shrugged again, "no matter how little it's worth, to me it's priceless." Knowing that my mother's hairpin was the most precious thing she left me.

Justin shook his head smiling again.

"What is it? What's so funny?" I demanded.

"You are truly amazing," he said. "Do you even know what those stones are?" He pointed to the pretty rocks that adorned the butterfly wings.

"I don't know, some sort of colored glass, I guess. What does that have to do with anything?"

"You see these pretty green ones," he said, pointing to the stones. "These are pristine quality emeralds, and these red ones are rubies and those shiny blue ones are sapphires and these purple ones are top of the line amethyst," he said. "Do you even want to guess what the butterflies head is made of?"

I shrugged my shoulders in ignorance.

"This one here," he said pointing to the big crystal clear rock in the middle.

"No freaking way," I gasped, realizing that I had been wearing the lost treasures of King Tut on my head all those years.

"You guessed right," Justin pointed to the shiny large stone "that's approximately a four carat diamond. Do you want to know how much your hairpin is worth?"

"No thanks!" I said pouting. "Now you've gone and ruined it for me. How am I supposed to ever wear this again?"

"Caitlin, they're only rocks. Their value is really insignificant if you think about it."

"Easy for you to say, you haven't been hauling around the Crown jewels on your head for the last decade or so."

Justin started laughing. "Do you at least want to know who this originally belonged to?" he asked.

My eyes lit up. "Yeah! Who?" I asked, completely intrigued.

"How am I supposed to know?" he finally asked, laughing hysterically. "You really flatter me, believing that I know everything. You really do."

"That's just mean!" I yelled, smacking him on the arm. "You're crazy, you know?"

"Yeah, crazy about you," He held me tighter, still trying to get control of his laughter.

Justin's mood lifted my spirit and wiped away the sinister feeling my dream had left lingering behind. I wanted to talk to him about it, but preferred enjoying that moment with him, without bringing up anything sad.

"I drove Tyler's Porsche," I said, changing the subject.

Justin was playing with my hair. "He actually let you drive it? The guy must really love you," Justin said, feigning a smile.

I ignored his last remark, pretending not to hear the jealousy underlining every syllable. "I literally had to pry the keys from his hand, didn't know guys were so attached to their cars."

"Not all guys," he said, defending his gender.

"To be honest, I think your car is nicer."

"It's only a car Caitlin, but thanks. You can take it anytime you want until yours is ready."

"What do you mean, when mine is ready? I was hoping to drop by the garage later on today."

"It seems Old Betty needs a lot more work than she's worth."

"Oh great," I exclaimed, "I can't afford that. I don't have that much saved up. I knew I should've looked for a part time job the minute I came to Oaks, should've taken the job at The Raven."

"What job at The Raven?"

"About a month ago, Mr. O'Malley came over to visit uncle Abbot. Over their usual card game and beer, he offered me a job at the pub. But uncle Abbot turned down the offer saying I needed to concentrate on more important things."

"Abbot was right. You don't need a job."

"Justin, it'd be nice to have my own money – not to have to ask my aunt and uncle for an allowance."

"Abbot and Leslie don't mind one bit."

"I know they don't mind, Justin. They even offered to give me my own credit card."

His face lit up. "You refused their offer, didn't you?"

"Of course I refused. I don't want to take advantage of their kindness and generosity any more than I already have."

"Why in the world are you even worried about money?" Justin asked, shaking his head in disbelief. "Haven't you heard? You are Caitlin Eileen Korbs, the soul benefactor to Winston and Carolyn Korbs' fortune." Justin was overly exaggerating his voice, purposely making himself sound snotty. "Money, darling, has absolutely no meaning as far as you're concerned."

Amused by his mood, I smiled and said, "Mr. Justinian Bradford, if memory serves me right, you are also the sole heir to the Bradford fortune." I smiled wickedly. "So, that would mean that you don't love me for my money, after all?"

"Your money – no, but I do love everything else about you." He instantly grabbed me and hugged me tighter. I wrestled against his tight grip, giggling. "We need to get you some new wheels. Old Betty needs to be put down."

I didn't like the sound of that. She might have been old, but she was mine. "I'll give her to Kyle," I finally said. "He loves her as much as I do. I'm sure he'll have fun bringing her back to life. But as far as a new car is concerned, I need to think about it, see how much I have saved up in the bank."

He chuckled at my response, thinking it was funny that I denied my families wealth, pretending that it didn't exist.

"Justin, come to think of it what do you think the families do with all that money? Their powers obviously help them make more. It's a pity to invest so much in a place like Oaks."

"Actually, for many generations the families have generated vast amounts of capital for their numerous charities. They help quite a lot of people and don't forget they help and support most of the families here in Oaks. The McDevitts and the Korbs do the same. All five families have an active role in supporting their communities."

"It's good to know our gifts aren't wasted in Oaks."

"You're not happy here, are you?" Justin asked, gazing into my eyes.

"It's not that I'm not happy. It's just that we could be doing so much good in the real world – helping people who are in need."

"We can't intervene with the way of the world. The non-gifted have to find their way – as do we."

Justin was so right, who was I kidding. I couldn't even figure out my own life how was I supposed to help someone else figure out theirs? I looked deep into his eyes and stared.

"What is it?"

I kissed him softly on the lips and said, "Can I ask you something personal?"

"When you ask it like that – anything," he said, kissing me back, triggering yet another giggle.

"Have you ever used your gift to help someone – outside of Oaks, I mean."

"Yeah of course – several times."

His manner was surprisingly casual. "Mind control isn't something the non-gifted can pick up on easily."

Surprised by his honesty I simply stared at him. "Really? Like how? What did you do?"

"Well nothing extraordinary. I helped some of my classmates out of some embarrassing situations – saved some careless people from crossing the street by making them take a few steps back in the nick of time. Of course, they all thought it was their own instinct that saved them, but that's okay, as long as they're safe."

I couldn't stop smiling at him, I was so proud. "You're like my all-time favorite super hero," I said, kissing him again.

"All I'm missing is the cape," he responded, laughing.

"You're like, Superman, all modest on the surface, but underneath – Wow!" I said giggling.

His grin widened, almost animated. "That would make you my Louise Lane," Justin said, tickling me.

"Stop – Stop!" I screamed between the laughter. "I don't like being Louise Lane. She kept getting herself into trouble and expected Superman to save her."

"What's wrong with allowing someone else to do the saving?" he asked, seriously.

Aware that our humorous topic took a dark tangent, I kissed him lightly on the lips. "If you promise to be the one doing the saving, I'll surely wait till the end of time," I said, caressing his beautiful face.

"As if you could ever just sit tight and wait."

I knew Justin's words were full of meaning, this was, I knew, a great opportunity to tell him about my dream, about his own vision. "I might not be able to read your thoughts Caitlin, but that doesn't mean I can't read your expression. Out with it – what's on your mind?"

I swallowed hard not knowing how to start – petrified at how he was going to take it, and then I said, "I'd never put you in a position where you'd have to sacrifice your own life to save mine. You know that don't you?"

Unexpectedly, he swung his leg over the wall and jumped to the ground a few feet in front of me, visibly bothered by my words. "Where did that come from?" he asked annoyed.

Apparently my words hit a nerve.

"I'm just saying that with everything going on. I wouldn't want you to think that I couldn't take care of myself. I'm not stupid to put myself at any risk and from what we both know I'm gifted enough to fend for myself, if I have to. There's no reason to go risking your life for me. We obviously work better as a team," I said, waiting for his reaction.

Justin wasn't buying my song and dance. I could see it in the way he stood there. "How much do you know, Caitlin?" he finally asked.

I sat in complete silence, unsure if I should tell him about my dream. Justin looked mad enough as it was. I didn't want to aggravate him. He had enough probing by the Ellri, didn't need me to do the same.

He placed his hands on the wall on either side of my torso blocking me in. "Are you going to tell me how much you know?" he asked, only inches away from my face.

Even then, awkward as the situation was, the only thing I wanted to do was kiss him. *Needy, Needy, Needy – I hate being this needy.* Trying to concentrate I took a deep breath. "I had this dream;" I started to say, "More like a nightmare, that's the reason I came out here. I needed fresh air."

Justin's posture suddenly changed, he stood up straight and looked down at me. "Not the Shadows again," he said, through clenched teeth, "I thought that bastard said he won't bother you again."

I haven't heard Justin call Gabriel by any other name ever since we left Indigo Island. "No, it wasn't anything like that. It was you, I saw you," I finally admitted. "We were somewhere – far from Oaks standing on some kind of cliff."

"What do you mean 'we'? You were there too?" he asked stunned. His shocked expression was fixed on my every word.

"Me, Alexander, and this ghostly creature popped in for a visit," I explained, sounding as if I suddenly shed several IQ points.

"Alexander? From the island, Alexander?" he asked, intentionally omitting the monster that attacked him.

"Yeah, good old Alex," I said, smiling.

"So what did you see?"

"Oh you know, two alpha males going at it on the edge of a one-thousand foot drop. Nothing I haven't seen before."

"Caitlin, you're way too smart to play it that stupid," he said, raising his eyebrow. "Knock it off!"

"Okay fine, if you want me to be myself...," my voice was annoyingly loud, "you need to tell me everything. My dream had something to do with your vision, didn't it?" I finally gathered the courage and asked.

"You know it did," Justin said, pacing back and forth. "Is that all you saw? You said it was a nightmare, that didn't sound much of a nightmare to me."

His anxiety of what I might have seen was stamped on his beautiful face. I had never seen him look so troubled before.

"Let's just say, I'd rather not think about the ending?" I jumped off the wall and grabbed his arm, causing him to stop pacing. "Why wouldn't you fight for your life? Why would you let that thing get his way?"

Suddenly, I realized that what I saw was merely the ending to a much larger picture. What could have possibly happened beforehand that would cause Justin to want to put an end to his own life? My blood quickly drained from my face. "There's a lot more you're not telling me, isn't there?" I finally asked, looking as worried as he was.

Justin leaned in and gave me a quick peck on the mouth. "Can't I just keep the rest to myself?" he said pleadingly.

"I need to know, Justin. Seeing you like this is torture. I hate that you can't trust me enough to share something like this."

He closed his eyes momentarily knowing I was right. "This has nothing to do with trust. You have to believe me. It's just that nothing is sure. Everything keeps changing. Why worry you about something that might never happen?"

Justin was once again masterfully trying to get out of telling me the whole truth. His fingers brushed back his hair nervously, visibly torn between wanting to tell me and knowing he shouldn't.

I reached out and took his hand. "Whatever the future holds, I'm sure we can handle it. Why do you feel that you have to keep this from me?" I said, holding our intertwined hands against my chest.

He leaned his forehead against mine. "Caitlin, I'm not going to say one word. I know this is hard for you to understand, but some things are better left unknown. Please trust me to know what's good for you – this once." Justin kissed me on the forehead. "Don't bring this up again. I beg you. If and when I feel ready I'll tell you."

"Fine, I won't bring up the subject again, I promise. But...,"
He half smiled. "But...," I repeated, seriously, "You need to do one thing for me."

Exhaling in relief, clearly happy at my comment; Justin nodded. "Anything," he agreed eagerly.

"I want you to try and see things from another perspective," I told him, trying to ease his pain. "Your gift is not accurate. It projects visions that your mind sees as possibilities. Did you ever think that your gift, like mine, can't interpret your emotions correctly? What if your visions are purely based on your fears? What if what you saw is a complete fabrication."

"You might be right," he agreed expediently. I knew he was

convinced that his vision was for real, agreeing only to make me feel better. It was funny really, how we were both trying to ease one another's uncertainty.

"Alexander told me that my Shadows wanted me to see what I saw – that must mean something," I said, hoping to shed some light into his dark thoughts. "My dream as well as your vision was a version of the future – not the actual thing," I told him, caressing his cheek. "No matter how dark it might be, you need to share it with someone. Share it with the Ellri at least. I don't need to know."

Justin's angst expression automatically relaxed – his tired face was, once again, flawless to perfection. "Are you sure?" he asked, apparently touched by my understanding. "They don't need to know."

"Still, you should tell somebody. Get it off your chest."

"I don't deserve you," he said beaming a warm smile.

"I'll say!" I exclaimed giggling, kissing him playfully. "But, I really have to go," I said, reluctantly braking free from his hold. I realized that I had a ton of homework to do before I went to school that morning and Mr. Myers hinted about a quiz in History.

Riled up by my eagerness to leave, Justin swiftly took me in his arms again. "Hold on, where do you think you're going?"

"I have to study. I think we might have a History quiz."

Without any hesitation he closed his eyes and stared up to the sky. "No – no written quiz, but do read up on chapter ten. He'll be drilling you on that. Mr. Myers is mentally preparing questions as we speak."

"Doesn't anybody sleep in this town?"

"Just read chapter ten. Trust me."

"You're my hero!" I exclaimed, kissing him. "Darn! I forgot about Tyler's car. I left it at your house yesterday."

"Don't worry! Tyler picked it up late last night." Justin released his hold. "Now go and get your homework done. I'll pick you up in a few hours," he said, pulling me once again in his strong embrace and kissed me on the lips. "And thanks for understanding," he added.

Reluctantly, I left Justin behind and headed back in the house. Was it even possible to finish all the assignments in so little time?

As usual I was scurrying around last minute to get all by books together, for some reason I couldn't seem to find some of them. "Tyler!" I said, remembering that he was supposed to get them out of my locker. It would appear that he was unable to open my noncompliant locker.

That moment, Emily poked her head in the door beaming her pearly whites "The buzz around town is that you offered to have your senior prom at your house."

Bouncing around on one foot, looking for my other shoe, I nodded in agreement. "I know – it was stupid, you don't have to say it."

"Are you crazy? It's not stupid. It's actually fantastic. That building deserves to see some happiness. So...? Did you even think of a theme for the prom?"

I stopped bouncing around on one foot and looked at her questionably. "Do I look like somebody who cares? I mean really Emily – you are talking to me, right?"

She picked up my sneaker from under the vanity. "You're obviously on the prom committee, aren't you?"

"Yeah, I guess I am. I mean, I think I am. You know, I'm not really sure," I said, looking at her.

I dashed in the bathroom and brushed my hair back in a ponytail, refusing to use my beautiful butterfly hairpin. I had taken it off as soon as I got in the house earlier in fear of dropping it. Now that I knew it was a priceless heirloom I was extra careful in handling it. I decided to place it in the top drawer of my nightstand for safe keeping until I'd hand it over to Aunt Leslie later on.

Like all great ideas, mine came suddenly and completely out of the blue, while finishing off with my hair I said, "Em, why don't you help with our prom? I don't know anyone else who can organize events like you."

She was visibly pleased with my offer. "I've graduated two years ago. Why would I be involved in your prom?"

"Besides your innate ability to get me out of any difficult situation, you can act as a consultant for prom committee," I told her gathering my things. "The Estate needs a lot of work. Who better to revive it to its former glory?"

I could tell I made her day. In a rush as I was, I didn't have time to sit around and discuss prom. The one thing that mattered most in my life was waiting to take me to school. The mere thought of Justin being so close was making my heart skip a beat. "Can we talk about this later, I'm really late and Justin's waiting in the car."

Emily took it upon herself to straighten out my pony tail. "Honestly Caitlin!" she sighed disappointedly. "You need to spend a few extra minutes in front of the mirror. You're not twelve anymore, you know."

I tried to change, even wore all the clothes she'd bought me, but still nothing. I still didn't seem to get it right. Style, I came to realize through the years, is something you're born with. You either have it or you don't, and apparently I didn't.

Emily started fussing with my clothes. "You know, Caitlin, jeans aren't the only thing you have to wear to school."

"They're comfortable," I exclaimed, slapping her hand

away. "I'm late. I have to go. We'll definitely talk after school, okay? You're not returning to campus again are you?"

"Not till Monday I'm not. I have a few term papers to hand in so I kind of gave myself a four day weekend. It'll give us time to catch up," she said positively joyful.

My eyes widened with excitement. I missed her so much these couple of months. What with classes and a full-blown relationship, she hardly had time for herself let alone little old me. "You promise – we'll hang out?" I asked like a little kid.

"That's what I said, isn't it? Now get going; you don't want that fine man waiting for you any longer," she said, shoving me out the door.

"I'm going, I'm going!"

"Keep me posted on prom developments," Emily said, heading for her bedroom.

"Sure thing," I yelled, running down the hall.

Justin was talking with Kyle in the foyer. By the looks of it, it was something interesting. Kyle was moving his hands rather animated describing some incident. The moment I reached the bottom of the step, Justin held out his hand for mine. I took it eagerly, wanting nothing more than to feel his touch.

"Good morning," they both said in one voice, as if they'd practiced it from before.

"Good morning," I responded, scanning both their faces. "Justin, sorry for having you wait. I just had a ton of things to read."

He pulled me closer, kissing the top of my head. "Don't worry you won't be late," he responded. "Kyle, see you in a few," he added, turning to his best friend.

By the looks of things, my cousin and the love of my life had something planned for later.

"We're going to pick up some car parts from the

neighboring town," Justin said. "I hope you don't mind, but I told Kyle that you were willing to give him Old Betty."

I looked at Justin as he was getting in the car. "No, that's fine. I didn't have the heart to get rid of her anyway. Kyle will know what to do."

Justin revved up the engine and headed for Oaks high. "There's a catch," he said, unexpectedly.

I turned to face him, "A catch?"

"Kyle said that he'll restore Old Betty only on one condition."

"I'm afraid to ask," I said, looking slightly apprehensive.

Justin turned his beautiful face and smiled at me. "He insists on keeping her after he's done with the makeover."

"Oh!' I gasped in relief. "Is that all? Of course he can keep her. I don't have enough money to repay him anyway."

"There's one more thing," he said, biting his lip.

"Of course there is? What is it?"

"Well, since Kyle will have Old Betty to drive around in, he won't need his old car. So...," he smiled, anticipating my response. "We were thinking that you switch."

My expression must have said it all. They wanted me to trade a run down, weathered 55' Ford Tbird for a brand-spanking-new BMW Z4 roadster.

"Are you both completely out of your minds?" I gasped. "Do you really think I'm stupid enough to fall for that whole 'let's switch' routine." I looked away shaking my head. "I understand you wanting to get me a new car, but this is too much."

"Don't be so skeptical. Kyle loves his cars, especially old ones. Mr. O'Malley's garage is full of Kyle's collection. He's been restoring old cars for three years now. So you see, Caitlin, Old Betty is quite valuable to him, even though you might not think so." Stunned I looked at Justin. "I didn't know that about Kyle. I mean I knew he was interested in Old Betty. He even took her out for a spin a couple of times, but he never let on that he wanted her. If he said something sooner I'd given her to him; no strings attached."

"Well, there you have it. That's exactly why he never mentioned it. Kyle knows how selfless and giving you are. He'd never put you in a position like that."

Approaching the school parking lot, I saw Tyler leaning against his car, waiting for me as he did on numerous occasions when he wasn't the one driving me to school.

"That boy needs to find himself a girlfriend," Justin mumbled, under his breath.

"Be nice. He's still my best friend," I said, slipping out of the Audi. "Oh, and tell Kyle he can have my car with nothing in return."

Justin was about to protest when I deliberately shut the door behind me.

The window instantly rolled down "Have a nice day," he said, shaking his head smiling. "And we'll talk about this later."

TWENTY-TWO

INVISIBLE

OUR LUNCH TABLE suddenly became too crowded for my liking. Gina and Lisa were more than welcomed, but now, thanks to my idiot best friend, I had to endure Megan and her two sidekicks. We did get some strange stares from the surrounding tables. It wasn't at all common to see students changing sitting arrangements especially towards the end of the year.

Truth be told, it felt nice to finally belong, to feel that I fit in somewhere For some reason my new found surname had brought with it some sort of respect. The Korbs' name was always a topic of conversation; way before I even left Oaks. Kids would sit around and guess how powerful my ancestors were. What strange gifts the long lineage must possess.

Looking back now it was actually funny, all that time that I felt awkward and a misfit I was, unbeknownst to me, one of the Korbs. Had they known my true identity would they still have made fun of my lack in power?

"So, are we going after school?" Lisa asked, looking directly at me.

Oblivious to their conversation, I wasn't sure what she was talking about. "Go where?" I asked.

"Weren't you listening?" she stared, sounding absolutely annoyed. "To the estate to see what condition it's in."

I turned and looked at Tyler. "Oh, I thought you guys went yesterday."

"Tyler said it was postponed for after school today," Gina added smiling.

"Of course, we'll go!" I responded happily. "I hope you guys don't mind, but I asked my cousin Emily to help out with the prom."

I honestly didn't know how they were going to take the news. Lisa and Gina seemed on top of things. Would they be offended? Would they think I was controlling?

"Emily Cathcart wants to help plan our prom?" squealed Lisa enthusiastically.

All five girls looked at each other and squealed in excitement. I didn't know Emily had this reaction on people; didn't know she was so liked. I knew I loved her, but the way the girls reacted was completely over the top.

Tyler looked at me and chuckled. "I guess they like Emily," he smirked, biting into his sandwich.

Megan's eyes were all bright and shiny. "She really said she'll help? I mean she actually agreed?"

"Yeah, I guess she did. She has a knack for organizing and planning events." I smiled at her ridiculous enthusiasm. This was after all Emily we were talking about not some rock star.

Tyler scanned the girl's faces and turned to look at me. "Emily is like – like the coolest, ever. She's to die for," he teased.

Loraine sighed in discontent at his attempt to be funny. "Emily is just the kind of sister we'd all like to have," she pronounced, explaining their enthusiasm. "She's like, cool to hang out with. The best dressed in town, dating Marc. Who is like – gorgeous!" Her voice continued to escalate with every word, reaching a remarkable shriek. "And if that's not enough," she continued to say excitedly, "her brother is," Yet another shriek, "Kyle!"

"Isn't he hot?" exclaimed Kim, looking around the table.

"Most definitely a ten," agreed Gina excitedly.

I almost chocked on my last bite at the sound of their description of Kyle. I did everything to hold back the laughter. Tyler, on the other hand, wasn't so discreet. He started cracking up, completely out of control, inciting my own laughter. We looked at each other and continued to laugh even harder. These were my cousins she was describing, the people I grew up with.

"You guys shouldn't laugh," said Kim, looking at Tyler and me seriously. "On our yearly list of 'Too Hot to Trot' Kyle's name is like, second on the list for the past three years. Isn't that right Megan?"

Megan looked at Kim in distaste. "I've seen better," Megan assured, turning to Tyler.

We all followed her gaze. Instead of feeling awkward about Megan's flirting, Tyler simply smiled at her; content and absorbing all her attention. It was obvious that she thought Tyler should be on the top of their list.

My curiosity got the best of me. "What number is Tyler?" I asked, kicking him under the table. I was curious to know where my best friend stood among the males in Oaks.

Tyler kicked back.

I grimaced and stuck out my tongue. "Kim? Is he at least on the list?" I asked, holding back a laugh.

Tyler looked at me menacingly.

"Hold on a sec.," Kim said, pulling a Hello Kitty notebook

out of her oversized Prada and flipped through the pages. "Ah, here he is. He's fifth. You're fifth Tyler."

"Great to know," he mumbled, and returned to eating his lunch.

The notebook, apart for the animated cover was quite official looking.

"Wait, did you say fifth?" Tyler suddenly exclaimed. "Only fifth?" He sounded disappointed. "You girls obviously need to rethink your criteria. Who's before me?"

Kim looked over her notebook again. "Lovely Robert is forth," she exclaimed delightedly.

"Who's lovely Robert?" I asked.

Tyler shook his head. "They're talking about Rob, Rob Bradford, Lucille's son."

"Oh!" I exclaimed. "He's only forth? The guy's gorgeous."

Tyler looked at me angrily. "He's twenty- eight years old!"

"And an absolute hunk," said Gina giggling.

The girls had good taste, I must give them that. Justin's older cousin was handsome. Looks did run in the family, I had to admit. Robert's rugged good looks and dark brown hair only brought out the deep sapphire in his eyes. Gina was right – he was gorgeous.

"You need to make two different lists, one for each age group," remarked Tyler disapprovingly, taking the list way too seriously. "Dare I ask who's first on your ridiculous list?"

All five girls looked at each other and in unison screamed "Justin Bradford," causing my heart to skip a beat. *Did they actually say Justin Bradford?* I couldn't stop smiling. I was so proud of him as if he won some sort of award. Justin's was the only name on my personal list, but it was good to know that my classmates felt he deserved first place on theirs. I felt that I should say something, thank them for seeing in him what I admired all along. The girls had impeccable taste, though there whole list idea was ridiculous.

"Oh, that's just great," sneered Tyler contemptuously, looking at me in disbelief. "You put them up to this, didn't you?" he asked me, clearly annoyed.

I whacked him on the arm annoyed at his presumption. "You know I didn't. Now grow up!"

Megan was awfully quite, she kept staring in our direction. "Tyler, the guys who hold the top four places are older than you. The girls know them longer. Next year I'm sure you'll be at the top of the list," she finally said, all sweet and flirty like.

Tyler smiled again at her remark. Was I seeing things or was there something going on between the two of them? Prom or no prom, if Tyler and Megan started going out that would be the end of him. I'd have to kill him to put the poor guy out of his impending misery.

All kidding aside, it wasn't my place to interfere with his personal life. He deserved to be with someone that made him happy, even if that someone was Megan Gordon. I just had to learn to contain my instincts to strike while I was around her. How hard could that be?

"Are we all meeting in the parking lot after school?" Megan asked, returning to the main topic.

Tyler just looked at her. "Yeah, of course, in the front lot."

I noticed the rest of the table staring back and forth at them. Obviously, I wasn't the only one who noticed the sparks flying.

"Megan? Do you need a ride to the Korbs?" he asked, ignoring the rest of us.

Ecstatic at his offer, Megan couldn't hide her happiness. The girl was hardly able to breathe, let alone answer. She took a deep breath and looked at her two friends and then back to Tyler. "Yeah, sure. Kim can take my car," she eagerly accepted.

I pretended not to listen, concentrating on finishing my lunch. I didn't want Tyler to notice how stupid I thought the whole thing was. I thought that if he was happy than I would be happy too. Yeah right, who was I kidding? I hated the girl, always did and always will. Some things just can't change overnight.

"I hope you don't mind," Tyler smiled softly. "Justin's picking you up, anyway."

"No, that's fine, why would I mind?" I said, taking my frustration out on my innocent grapefruit. With a side glance I noticed him staring at me. "What are you looking at?" I asked, irritated.

"Nothing! We'll talk later," he said, collecting his tray.

Just then the bell rang. Everyone slowly gathered their belongings and headed off to their class. I wasn't in any hurry to leave. I had gym next period and I was planning on cutting. Being in no mood to change into my gym suit I remained seated and finished my grapefruit.

The cafeteria was now empty except for three or four others who were probably contemplating cutting their next period as well.

"Let's go! Come on!" Tyler urged, pulling on my school bag.

I glared at him to let go. "I'm not going! You go or you'll be late."

Instead of leaving he sat back down, this time across from me. "Since when do you make it a habit of cutting class?"

"This is the first time I'm cutting."

"Yesterday, you cut too!"

"Yesterday was different. Now go! I don't need a babysitter."

"If you're cutting, I'm cutting," he declared.

I pushed my tray to the side and just looked at him. "Why?

That's all I need to know, Tyler. Just, explain to me, why?"

He shrugged his shoulders and smiled. "Gym won't be fun without you," he answered.

"Not that, you moron," I pronounced, infuriated that he had no idea what I was talking about.

"Then what?"

"Why? Why out of all the girls in Oaks does it have to be Megan? Are you doing it to spite me?"

Tyler chuckled. "She's much nicer than she seems, give her a chance Caitlin. You never know, you might find that you have a lot more in common than you think."

First Justin and now Tyler; this was some sort of conspiracy to get me to like Megan. What else could it be? How could they believe that Megan and I had anything in common? If it weren't for her crush on Tyler she wouldn't have given me the time of day. Why couldn't they see the distaste she had every time she looked at me? Guys were clueless when it came to girls. They had no idea of how sadistic some females could be; no matter if they wore pink and lace.

I looked at him questionably. "So you really like her?"

"Geez, I don't know. It's not like I can fall in and out of love overnight," he said, bringing up the topic of his feelings towards me intentionally; making be blush.

I rolled my eyes at him, "Fine! Date Freddy Krueger for all I care, but don't come crying to me if she turns out to be exactly how I picture her."

"You mean you won't be there to hold my hand if I need a shoulder to cry on?"

"Hold your hand? No! But help you bang your head against the wall, now that, I can help you with."

His laugh echoed through the empty cafeteria. Causing the cleaning crew to turn and stare; waiting for us to leave.

Tyler and I headed outside through the back entrance and sat in our usual place – the bench by the door. We sat there in silence for quite some time. I didn't want to bring up the subject of Megan again. I didn't think it was right.

I turned my body sideways to face him. He had his head up against the wall, eyes closed. "How do you know that Justin will pick me up after school? I thought you were taking me home."

"He told me this morning when he dropped you off." Tyler leaned over his school bag, looking for something. "Here it is," he said, pulling out a bar of chocolate. "You want some?" Tyler asked offering me a piece

"No thanks," I responded, waving it away. "How come you couldn't open my locker yesterday after school? It opened easily this morning." I said, watching him devour the contents in the wrapper.

"Ms. Morris at the front desk got somebody to fix it. It took the guy only a few minutes."

"So you're going to make me be nice to Megan, aren't you?"

"You're already nice to her," he said, concentrating his eyes on my face. "You've always been too nice," He pushed some loose strands of hair behind my ear.

"Shouldn't you guys be in class?"

As soon as I heard his voice my whole body reacted to the smooth sensual tone. Tyler instantly pulled his hand away and straightened his posture.

"Justin, what are you doing here?" I asked, jumping to my feet thrilled to see him.

"He's been reading my thoughts ever since we came out here. You're not playing fair, you know," Tyler said, tossing the paper wrap into the trash can.

"And you're not being honest," Justin retorted, raising his

eyebrow, challenging Tyler to divulge some kind of secret.

"Did I miss something? Honest about what?" I asked Tyler.

"It's nothing that concerns you Caitlin," he exclaimed. "And you – you shouldn't pry into other people's business," said Tyler standing up. "I'll leave you guys alone. Don't forget that we're meeting in the parking lot after school." He grabbed his bag and walked away angry.

"We'll meet you at the estate," Justin called behind him, causing Tyler to stop. He purposely wrapped his arms around my waist and pulled me against his body. Tyler's eyes dropped to where Justin was holding me. "We might be late, so why don't you take the girls out to eat before you head out to the house?"

Tyler was visibly upset. "Okay, whatever. Just let me know when you'll be heading there. We'll, see you later then." Without another word, he made his way back into the building.

I pulled free of Justin's hold, hating how he used me to get to Tyler. "What was that for?" I asked, thinking that Justin would never stoop that low.

"What are you talking about?"

"You know exactly what!" I accused him. "Don't ever use me to make a point. Ever!"

He pulled me back into his arms. "You're mine," he said adoringly. "Tyler simply has to get used to it."

"I'm not...," I was about to defend the fact that I didn't belong to anyone – that I was no man's possession when he laughed breathlessly as his urgent kiss interrupted my protest. I didn't mind one bit. My arms tightened around his neck bringing him much closer, turning his innocent kiss into one full of passion.

"Much better," he said between kisses.

"So what are you doing here?" I finally asked, not letting go of my hold. He kissed me again, picking me up off the ground.

"I missed you. Isn't that enough?"

His good mood was up-lifting. Our talk earlier this morning must have helped, I hoped. "You know you can get in trouble for being here," I informed him, as if he needed me to remind him of the school rules.

"Well then," he said, returning my feet to the ground. "Let's get out of here!"

Justin grabbed my bag and took my hand in his. "Wait!" I said, pulling him to a full stop, "I was only going to cut gym, I have two more classes."

"Come on, you're a straight A student, you deserve some fun," Justin said, giving me a quick peck on the lips. "Besides, I already notified the front office."

My eyes widened in excitement. "No you didn't, did you?"

"Of course, I did. Actually, your aunt notified them, I simply went in to confirm it. "

Excited, I literally threw myself on him, hugging him with all my strength. "I love you! I love you! I love you!" I yelled, at the top of my lungs not caring if the whole school could hear.

Justin was happy with my response. "Maybe I should help you cut more often," he said chuckling at my childish reaction. "Come on, let's go."

I was so happy about skipping class that it took me a couple of minutes to realize that Justin wasn't taking me home, instead he was driving in the opposite direction. "Where are we heading?" I asked.

Justin turned on the radio and turned up the volume. "I'm taking you to see something special. It's on the outskirts of Oaks."

"Sounds perfect – anywhere with you will be just fine." I rested my head against the headrest, enjoying the music.

He hardly spoke for the duration of our ride, knowing I needed some rest from the previous night. It didn't take long to reach our destination, a mere twenty minutes. Not that I knew where our destination was. Justin had stopped on a dirt road parallel to the main road, leading in and out of town.

"Why did we stop here?" I asked clearly confused. "Is there something wrong with the car?"

He got out and came round to the passenger's side helping me out. "There's nothing wrong with the car. I told you I want to show you something."

I looked around and saw absolutely nothing worth seeing, aside from the large stone columns on either side of the road that suspended the huge wooden 'Welcome to Oaks' sign.

"Okay, you got me, what am I looking for?" I asked puzzled.

Justin took my hand and approached the towering stone columns.

"Remember when I told you that with age comes knowledge?" he asked stopping in mid-stride. "That – with each stage we learn something more?"

I looked at him in horror, "I'm not going to like this, am I?" He smiled. "I really shouldn't cut class."

Justin laughed and asked again, "Do you remember?"

"How can I forget? It was right before I found out about the Chamber of Enlightenment."

"Okay, well, let's just say this is one of those times again where you'll need to be really open minded about what I'm about to tell you," he said, looking at me, making sure that I was paying full attention to what he was about to say. "The Ellri feel that it's time for you to find out. For some reason they think I'm the right person to tell you."

I instinctively breathed in deep, "Okay, shoot!" I said ready to hear just about anything.

"What I'm going to tell you is one of those secrets you take to your grave and never repeat to another soul unless instructed to do so by an Ellri. Do you understand?"

I looked annoyed, wanting to know what the mystery was all about. "What am I an idiot? Of course I understand," I blurted out.

"Apart from the Ascended and the Ellri from the five blood lines that bind us, nobody in town or anywhere in the world, for that matter, know what I'm about to tell you"

"Okay, Okay – I got it. It's a 'big' secret. Now out with it!"

Justin was procrastinating, not wanting to get to the point. Whatever he wanted to say was apparently quite significant, otherwise he wouldn't have talked in circles.

"Okay...," he said, taking a big breath, "Oaks doesn't exist!" he blurted out.

I knew I heard right, but my mind refused to process the information. Thunderstruck, I stared expressionless at Justin. He must have meant something else. "Caitlin, did you hear me?" he asked, trying to snap me out of my haze.

"I heard you just fine. I'm not sure if I understood correctly," I responded "Did you say that Oaks doesn't exist?"

"Well yeah, sort of."

He looked as baffled as I was. "What does that mean? Does it exist or not?"

Justin ran his fingers through his tousled hair as he did only when he was really frustrated or angry. I wasn't sure what he felt now. "To us, the gifted, of course Oaks exists, but to the non-gifted it doesn't. Apart from the main road that runs through the heart of Oaks nothing to them exists. They can't see anything but vast fields on either side of the main road."

I was speechless. I couldn't form a question. Not that I didn't have one; a million to be exact, but I was too stunned to speak.

Justin took my hand and led me to the large column that held up the sign.

"This is made of the same rock that the Chamber of Enlightenment is made of, the same Energy Stone. These two pillars...," he said, pointing to the one across the road, "were erected by the Nobe when the community was first formed. This is a gate into Oaks where only the welcomed can see its true form. This sign is invisible to anyone else."

After a few minutes of gazing up at the towering column I finally found the words I needed to form a complete and coherent question. "So why can we see it and not the non-gifted?" I asked, still looking up at the massive column.

"The Energy Stone is able to read us. It senses who does or doesn't belong in Oaks," Justin said, looking up. "The members of the blood lines, of course, are in tune with the gate."

"In tune?"

"What I mean is that at birth we are imprinted to its memory, allowing us access to all communities around the world – like the hand prints on the doors of the Chamber. The rest of the gifted, the non-family members unfortunately, don't have that privilege. They have to be invited by an Ellri. That's why Ava and other Ellri go out into the world looking for gifted individuals that do not belong to the blood lines. If it weren't for the Ellri the rest of the gifted wouldn't know anything about our secret communities."

That surely explained Ava's extensive travels. She had mentioned looking for gifted people around the world, but left out the entire truth.

"So what do ordinary people see? I mean as far as Oaks is concerned – what do they know?"

"As I said before, they see nothing apart from a long stretch of country road."

"You do realize that this will take me forever to absorb."

"I know. I still can't believe it and I've known about it for three years," Justin said, smiling. "You want to see something amazing?"

"More amazing than what you've just told me?"

Justin nodded his head in excitement. "Here, put your hand against the stone," he said, only inches away from the base of the colossal column.

Hesitant at first I did as he said. The most miraculous thing happened the second I touched it. The whole thing simply disappeared right before my eyes as did everything that tied Oaks to the outside world – street signs – the mile post across the road changed instantaneously even the landscape flattened out in parts. I turned in amazement and just stared at Justin.

"Where did it go?" I asked, moving my hands back and forth where the column once stood.

"It didn't go anywhere. This is how the outsiders see this area, no sign welcoming them to Oaks – no Oaks whatsoever."

"Okay, how do we get the Pillars back?" I asked anxiously, not wanting to break anything.

Justin chuckled. "Just ask it to appear."

I looked at him baffled. "Please appear?" I said, hardly audible.

Wouldn't you know it; there they were again, like two giants holding up the hand carved wooden sign.

I turned to Justin smiling. "Now you know I have a ton of questions to ask."

"I'm sure you do," he responded. "But first let's get back in the car. I don't want you to freeze to death."

Once in the Audi I sat completely facing him unsure how to start.

"You know you can't share this knowledge with anyone not

Emily or Tyler. I don't know if they know or who else knows. It will be hard at first, but you'll get used to it, I did."

"I got it! Tell no-one," I said, still trying to figure out what question to start with. "How can you stand all these secrets? It's infuriating keeping track of everything.

Justin caressed my face. "It gets easier as you get older. For me it just started getting easier because I can share some of my secrets with you. Once you ascend I'll have nothing to hide. You'll know everything I do."

"And that will happen when?"

Justin smiled and kissed me ever so lightly on the lips. "Now that, I'd like to know as well," he said laughingly.

"So wait...," I shook my head, trying to wrap the idea around my mind, "when the non-gifted drive through Oaks they can't see us either?"

"They only see a stretch of road in front of them, nothing more. They are just as aware of us as we are of them when in Oaks."

"How strange? I've never actually noticed. I mean now that you mention it I've never seen someone who doesn't belong. But then, I don't know everyone in town. I can't believe I've never noticed." I was rambling. "I never thought about it before. How strange not to notice?"

Justin squeezed my hand. "You had no way of knowing. None of us knew. None of us ever questioned it."

I shook my head vigorously, closing my eyes, trying to take it all in. I was shaking my head way too often those past few months. It was only a question of time when the darn thing would simply roll off my shoulders.

"Yeah, I see your point," I said, staring out into nothingness, responding to Justin's simple explanation. I was making a mental note of all the things I found out since my return.

"Are you sure you're okay?" he asked concerned.

"I'm trying to put some order to my thoughts. It helps if I mentally list things. Make sure I haven't missed something."

Justin generously gave me his full attention. "How can I help?"

"Okay let me see what I know so far about our kind," I said, counting the information on my fingers. "First, we are both members of families that span back thousands of years."

"Check," he said, smiling.

I pulled a face.

"Sorry, I'll shut up now. Go on," he said, motioning for me to continue.

Before I went on, I gave him a quick kiss, and again another one just because he was being so cute. "Second," I continued to count, "our kind doesn't measure age by the years that we live, but by the maturity of our powers, which makes me an infant," I added smiling. He pursed his lips tight, fighting the urge to talk. "Am I right so far?"

Amused he just bobbed his head in agreement.

"Okay where was I? Ah yes, the Nobe. They are immortals with insurmountable powers that can literally move mountains. Then we have the non-existent tunnels under the earth that lead us into the non-existent chamber. And as if that's not enough for one person to take in, we have Oaks, which apparently doesn't exist either."

Justin simply smiled at me. "I see you've been paying attention. You did however forget the Rites of passage, our ghostly auras and of course the dark sinister demon," he added laughingly. "Now you know why we need to learn in stages. It's all too much to take in as children."

"About that sinister demon, monster thing…,"

He pulled a face and motioned that his lips are zipped shut.

"Okay, yeah I get it," I finally said smiling, "I do see what you mean. It's too much to take in now."

At that moment I realized that even though I was learning more and more things, I was still in the dark about the things that meant most; my parents. "You don't happen to know any secrets about my parents, do you?" I asked fishing for information.

Justin lifted my chin up to his face and smiled. "That would be a secret I wouldn't be able to keep from you. I want to know as much as you do, but as all other things, we'll just have to wait." He leaned in and kissed me.

His lips were velvety smooth. His hand pulled me in closer intensifying his kiss. I returned his affection with the same eagerness causing my wrist to throb. I loved him more and more each day. There was nothing on earth as sweet and lovable as him.

My gift wasn't willing to allow me to enjoy such pleasures. I pulled back slowly, unwilling to let him go entirely. Both of us sat back in our seats with our heads pushed against the headrests.

"This is murder," Justin sighed, expressing my feelings exactly. "We can't enjoy the simplest things. I mean the Isle of Indigo was murder, with you looking the way you did. I can't seem to get the image of you out of my mind."

"Imagine if I wore the black lacy thing Emily got me. That would sure have been the last for both of us."

His brow lifted in excitement. "Just don't get rid of it. I need to know there is some hope left for us both." He closed his eyes. "Ascend already, will you?"

I blushed as I said, "This is all my fault," I admitted, "I can't seem to get control of my gift. Your touch seems to spiral my insides out of control."

"It's good to know you feel the same as I do." He kissed me again. This time it was more of a friendly peck than a kiss. "We should be heading back," Justin said, revving up the engine.

"Yes, back to the non-existent town," I mumbled.

"It exists, Caitlin. It's just invisible to the non-gifted. There's a difference."

"I'm glad you see a difference," I said, trying to digest the fact that Oaks was far from anything normal. "I've told you, I need some time with all this."

"You take all the time you need," said Justin putting the car in motion, "now about your car."

"I was wondering how long it'd take you to bring that up," I said, giving him a side glance. "You're quite stubborn," I muttered.

"It takes one to know one," he answered amused. "Kyle insists on a trade, wouldn't have it any other way."

I honestly couldn't accept Kyle's state of the art, new BMW roadster. First it was way too expensive for it to be any kind of fair trade and secondly I thought it was over the top. The only way they'd all back off was for me to buy my own car, something sensible. I'd have to borrow money from my aunt and uncle, but I was certain they'd be more than happy to give it to me. Uncle Abbot was, after all, pestering me about a new car from the second he set eyes on Old Betty, fearing I'd get in an accident or something.

"I won't need Kyle's car, I've decided to buy my own," I finally said, turning to look in his reaction.

Justin glanced at me from the corner of his eye. "When? When are you going to do that exactly?" he asked suspiciously, knowing all too well that I'd say anything to get out of accepting Kyle's trade.

"Tonight! I'm going to ask Uncle Abbot for a loan."

"You don't have to ask anyone for a loan. You have your own money. Hell, you probably have your own bank," he said, bothered by the fact that I refused my family's wealth. "You know what? I'm getting you a damn car and that's that."

Now I was the one who was irritated. "Just because our families have money doesn't mean everything should come so easily for us. It's more rewarding to work for something, to gain it because we deserve it."

"Oh, please! Don't kid yourself."

"I'm not kidding myself. I mean every word."

"You're such a hypocrite," he exclaimed, driving much slower than usual. "You can safely say things like that knowing you have an abundance of wealth. I'd like to see you say that if you really had to work for your keep, to come home night after night exhausted from a long day's work knowing that the money you slaved over wouldn't be enough to pay a portion of the bills piled up in the corner."

Justin was aggravated by my persistence to refuse help.

I sat back quietly.

His words were a much needed slap across the face. He had a point. Who was I kidding? The only money I ever saved up was from my own allowance, nothing I had ever worked for apart from the pocket change I got with some part time jobs at Stone Hurst. I was denying my wealth in fear of becoming a materialistic, self-centered, spoilt brat – instead, I became worse, a self-righteous snob.

I judged others for accepting who they were all along.

Feeling ashamed of who I had become, I melted into the car seat, hoping I would disappear. I refused to look at him. I simply stared out the passenger side window looking at the surrounding area, wondering where I went wrong and how unfair I was to judge everyone.

Justin reached out and took my hand. "Caitlin, it's not wrong to indulge yourself now and then. We're blessed with the things we have, our gifts most of all. Why pretend to be something that we're not? Money has absolutely no meaning to our kind. I can foresee tomorrow's lottery number, horse race, stock market prices. What makes you think that the price of a car has any real meaning?" he said, turning his face towards me. "It's these perks that we allow ourselves, that keep us sane. Being restricted in a town for one's life is not exactly easy. Sometimes a new car can make things seem so much brighter."

He did have a point. Normal everyday things didn't apply to our kind. Asking for permission to leave Oaks, every time we wanted to do something, was belittling. It made most of us feel inadequate. Personally, I still didn't get the whole restriction theory, but if those were the rules who was I to break them. It helped that my aunt never denied me anything. If I wanted to go somewhere outside Oaks she would allow it. Of course, I had to take someone older along, Emily or Justin were always eager to accompany me.

"I'm awful!" I muttered looking outside. "All these years I truly believed that everybody around me was shallow and for some unexplained reason I was the only one who saw things from the right perspective." I shook my head detesting myself. "How stupid was I? I'm the snob – not them. I'm the one who keeps everyone at a distance."

Justin pulled the car to the side of the road only yards away from the secluded road to my parent's house. "Okay, now you've gone just a bit overboard. Most of the kids in Oaks are shallow, they are materialistic. You weren't wrong about any of that," he said, shifting his weight to face me. "You analyze things. You think about people's feelings, putting their needs and wants way before your own."

"Still, it's wrong to judge."

"It's worse to pretend to be something that you're not," he said lifting my hand to his wonderful lips. "That's what I love about you. You don't have this insane notion that you have to fit in, that you need to be like everyone else. I love the fact that you prefer to read a good book than talk nonsense or that you question everything and accept criticism without getting angry. It's what makes you so amazing."

"I need to try harder to fit in," I said, looking up into his dark pools of blue.

"You'll do no such thing," he spat out. "If I even see you walking around toting a designer bag and gold looped earrings, I swear I'll kill you myself," he said laughing. "You're perfect the way you are. You don't need to change for anybody. The only thing you need to do is to accept help now and then, let people in. You're not leaving here anytime soon so why not make the best of it?"

Suddenly tears sprang to my eyes in the realization that Justin loved me, no matter how screwed up I was.

He wiped my tears with his hand. "Oh, come on. You know it kills me to see you like this. Fine, you win, no car," he finally said surrendering.

I smiled at him for giving in so easily. "It's not that. It's just that I love you so much that it actually hurts," I confessed gazing into his eyes.

Justin just stared at me speechless. He wasn't expecting anything so sincere. "Then marry me," he said, looking quite serious.

My brain automatically shut down, refusing to accept any more shocking news. "No!" I answered. "What are you talking about? Our kind doesn't get married. We've been through this," I pronounced, in one long breath.

"Who cares what our kind does. Let's do what the rest of the world does. I want to see you walking down the aisle wearing the wedding gown you cut out of the magazine so long ago," he said, obviously putting a lot of thought into this.

"Are you intentionally trying to send me to the loony bin?" I asked. "Just minutes ago you tell me I live in an invisible town and now, in the middle of nowhere you ask me to marry you? Are you on something? We're not getting married!"

Justin started laughing with all his heart. "You're going to say yes eventually, you know that don't you?"

"Can I get through high school first?" I said blushing.

"So, you'd accept my proposal after you graduate?"

"I didn't say that. I'm only eighteen – an infant, remember?"

Justin turned in his seat and put the car in motion, amused by my awkwardness. "You sure don't kiss like any infant I know," he muttered, laughing again, making me smile.

LINES THAT BIND

PART THREE

COMING

2015

ANNA LAZARIDIS

LIGHT & DARKNESS